# LOVING LANCELOT

Lancelot plunged into the water and surfaced beside Gwen. He ran his fingers lightly over her shoulders. "The water makes your skin feel silky."

She trailed her fingers across his chest, loving the feel of his smooth, tight muscles. He gave her throat a series of small kisses until he finally lifted her in his arms.

As they emerged from the water, Lancelot brought her down on the embankment. The grass was springy beneath her back and smelled of clover. The sun warmed her wet skin. She spread her hair to dry and stretched her arms over her head.

Lancelot caught them there, crossing her wrists and holding them easily with one hand. Very lightly, his fingertips touching her skin, he traced a path on the tender underside of her arms. Gwenhwyfar closed her eyes blissfully. She shivered in delight and tried to bring her hands to him, but he held them in place.

She opened her eyes to find him watching her. "Let me hold you, Lance."

"Not yet." He began kissing her neck.

"Let me kiss you then!"

Obligingly, Lancelot brought his mouth to hers, kissing first her top lip, then her bottom one; then he drew back, kissing her chin and her throat. "Lie still, Gwen." His voice was soft as he ran his tongue over her belly. "I want to explore all of you . . ."

# Camelot's Destiny

## CYNTHIA BREEDING

ZEBRA BOOKS
KENSINGTON PUBLISHING CORP.
www.kensingtonbooks.com

ZEBRA BOOKS are published by

Kensington Publishing Corp.
850 Third Avenue
New York, NY 10022

All Kensington titles, imprints, and distributed lines are available at special quantity discounts for bulk purchases for sales promotion, premiums, fund-raising, educational, or institutional use.

Special book excerpts or customized printings can also be created to fit specific needs. For details, write or phone the office of the Kensington Special Sales Manager: Attn. Special Sales Department. Kensington Publishing Corp., 850 Third Avenue, New York, NY 10022. Phone 1-800-221-2647.

First printing: August 2006
10  9  8  7  6  5  4  3  2  1

Printed in the United States of America

*This book is dedicated to my departed husband,*
*Larry,*
*who always understood when the "writing frenzy" was upon me.*
*May you forever walk in the Light.*

*And*

*To Lancelot:*
*He knows who he is.*

# Acknowledgments

Although *Camelot's Destiny* is a work of fiction, it would have been impossible to lend any air of authenticity to the historic period without the facts I gleaned from the following nonfictional works.

I have not met any of these writers, but I owe each of them a heartfelt "thank you" for lending me insight into life in post-Roman Britain in the sixth century, as well as into the many varied theories of the existence of the Holy Grail.

| | |
|---|---|
| Barber, Chris; Pykitt, David: | *Journey to Avalon* |
| Baigent, Michael; Leigh, Richard; Lincoln, Henry: | *Holy Blood, Holy Grail* |
| Barber, Richard: | *King Arthur: Hero and Legend* |
| Berresford Ellis, Peter: | *The Druids* |
| Castleden, Rodney: | *King Arthur: The Truth Behind the Legend* |
| Dunning, R.W.: | *Arthur: The King in the West* |
| Gardner, Laurence: | *Bloodline of the Holy Grail* |
| Goodrich, Norma Lorre: | *King Arthur; Guinevere* |
| Karr, Phyllis Ann: | *The Arthurian Companion* |
| Markale, Jean: | *King of the Celts* |
| Snyder, Christopher: | *King Arthur* |
| Strobie, Denise: | *Exploring King Arthur's Britain* |
| Turner, P.F.J.: | *The Real King Arthur: Volumes 1 & 2* |
| Wood, Michael: | *In Search of England* |

# Prologue

# Glastonbury, AD 490

Tendrils of morning fog swirled upward from the Lake along the footpath where young Gwenhwyfar made her way down the slippery slope. The damp air was quite cool for spring in the Summer Country, but she didn't mind. She swung her arms, playing with the vapor's shifting patterns and shapes.

The dark-haired boy bumped into her as he emerged from the mists, causing her to lose her footing and slide down the wet bank toward the marsh water. His arm caught and steadied her.

"Where did you come from?" she asked shakily, her green eyes wide with fright.

He hesitated. "It doesn't matter, really. I don't see many children around here. You probably should go back." Stepping to the side, he maneuvered the wooden sword he'd been carrying, lunging and thrusting at an imaginary opponent.

"I'm six years old!" She tossed her auburn curls. "Da doesn't treat me like a child; I can handle a sword, too!"

*The boy stopped abruptly. "Show me." He grinned lopsidedly and turned the sword, extending the grip to her . . .*

"Fate has begun to turn the Wheel." The whisper on the wind receded as the faerie light shimmered translucently beside Myrddin's ear and then was gone. The arch-druid stood quickly, upsetting his chair and drawing astonished silence from the monks and kings gathered to debate a resurgence of the Pelagian Theory. Even as he hurried to the abbey door, he knew he would be too late.

Hampered by his hooded monk's robe, Myrddin finally reached them. His golden eyes darted quickly at the boy; then the hawklike gaze shot to the girl.

"Children shouldn't be playing this close to the water's edge; it's deeper than it looks." Myrddin inclined his head toward the girl. "I think it would be better if you joined your father at the abbey."

Gwenhwyfar lifted her chin. "First I am going to show that boy how to use a sword."

The boy's smoke-colored eyes became darker. With despair, Myrddin saw a look of admiration sweep over the ten-year-old's face.

The druid stretched to his full height. When he spoke, his voice was softly rolling thunder. "Go. Now." He lifted his hand and knew Gwenhwyfar felt the nudge, even though he had not touched her. Wide-eyed, she dropped the sword and ran.

Myrddin raised his hand and the mists enveloped them.

# Chapter 1

# The Once and Future Queen

"I will NOT marry Arthur!" Gwenhwyfar suddenly lost her appetite for the still-warm bannocks and freshly churned butter. She pushed away from the table in the private dining quarters of the Romano-Briton villa and stomped across the blue mosaic tile, her boots clattering, to the window overlooking the bailey. She pressed her head against the sill. Her father didn't know about the tall, dark-haired fantasy man who had visited her in her dreams for years. That man was definitely not Arthur.

Outside, her father's people went about their early-morning tasks, scurrying across the dusty courtyard. The dairymaids lugged warm pails of milk to the kitchens; the field workers toiled beyond the gates; the potterer had his kiln humming. Their lives were structured, routine, and secure. They knew Cameliard would provide for them.

Leodegrance sighed and leaned back in his oaken chair. "Daughter, the messenger said that Bedwyr and Arthur would be stopping to discuss a permanent alliance to protect the land north of Eboracum. The last time Bedwyr visited, he said Arthur was thinking of settling down. What else could it be?"

Gwenhwyfar snorted. She turned away from the window and saw her father wince. "Let him marry Elaine then," she said more gently. "Ever since she has lived with us, she's prattled on about how much she wants to be married. Pelles's lands would offer Arthur even more protection from Pictish barbarians."

"Carbonek is a wasteland," her father replied, "hardly anything the Picts would want. For certes, Pelles is in no condition to command a fortification, with that leg that won't heal." He shook his head. "No, Arthur is more concerned about the Saxon raids from the Northern Sea. Cameliard is a good northern location for the command. Besides," he added, "your cousin is only fourteen."

"And I am only sixteen!" Gwenhwyfar said with a hint of desperation. "Arthur's thirty and has been married before! I don't care if he does have the title Dux Bellorum—duke of battles—all that means to me is he leads men into war."

Leodegrance interrupted, "And if he didn't lead men to war? What then? The Saxons would overrun us. Uther Pendragon was our king and he acknowledged Arthur as his son before he died."

She shrugged. "I have no intentions of getting married, now or ever. You raised me to take care of our lands, our people. I have duties here. Someone must command the overseers to make sure the laborers are treated fairly, the storerooms kept stocked, and the hypocausts maintained. My brother has been Arthur's man for the last seven years. Bedwyr will be with him until he dies. Who will take care of you? You were ill last year."

"I never expected you to give up your life for Cameliard," her father answered. "Arthur is highly respected; this is a wonderful opportunity. If your mother were alive, she'd agree."

Gwenhwyfar turned back to the window. She'd never known her mother, Guenhumara. Her father used to say her mother preferred to take part in men's discussions rather than spin and weave. Somehow she felt her mother would have approved of her learning to ride and use a sword. Celtic women like her mother had once been warriors and quite capable of ruling. Gwenhwyfar was only half Roman. She lifted her chin.

"My place is here, Da."

Leodegrance stood. "You're too stubborn, child, but I am proud of you."

She moved quickly to hug him. "That's all that matters, Da, that you be proud of me."


Gwenhwyfar pushed a bronze-colored strand of wayward hair from her damp forehead. The afternoon was as hot and humid as high summer, although it was only May. "A storm will probably be brewing before sunset," she crooned to her mare as she brushed the silken sorrel coat. Cali answered her with a flickering of her ears and a gentle nicker. The wolfhound, Glena, never far from Gwenhwyfar, agreed with a whine.

She felt the rumbling vibration of the earth just before she heard the pounding of hooves on the cobbled road to the villa. With a final, quick pat on the mare's neck, she tossed the brush down and rubbed her grimy hands on her breeches. She hurried outside and up the nearest rampart.

A dust cloud surrounded a small group of men. From her vantage point, she recognized her brother's horse as well as the dragon banner. Arthur! "By the Christos!" she said aloud, and quickly made the sign of the cross. She wasn't supposed to curse. "They aren't expected for several more days!" Nothing was prepared and her da would be upset that she smelled like a horse and was dressed in pants.

The horses slowed to a trot as they approached the gate and the guard waved them through. Gwenhwyfar scrambled

down from her post. She had no time to cross the courtyard
to the main house. *They're going to have to accept me the
way I am.* She straightened her shoulders and walked to the
center of the bailey.

As Bedwyr and Arthur rode forward, Gwenhwyfar stared.
Never had she seen a more beautiful horse than the dappled
grey stallion Arthur was riding. The animal was compact, its
neck and tail arched gracefully, and the delicate, dish-faced
head was set with intelligent, liquid brown eyes that warily
watched her approach. The small ears flicked back and forth.
"You beauty!" she breathed, reaching up.

"Careful, Gwenhwyfar!" Bedwyr dismounted and pulled
her away. "Valiant is not some lady's palfrey!"

"I think," she retorted, "that I can recognize a palfrey
when I see one!"

"I'm glad to see you haven't changed, little sister. Still as
sassy as ever." His green eyes twinkled as he bent over to
give her a quick kiss and then wrinkled his nose. "You don't
exactly smell like a lady, either." He ducked, missing the
hand that flew over his head.

Gwenhwyfar glared at him. He had always been a merci-
less tease.

Above them, Arthur cleared his throat. Gwenhwyfar's
hand flew to her mouth. *What must he think?* Embarrassed,
she looked up at the man who was still sitting astride that
magnificent horse.

Arthur was a broad-shouldered man who sat easily in his
saddle. Penetrating grey eyes slowly surveyed her, beginning
with the top of her head and ending at her boots. Gwenhwyfar
blushed and hated herself for doing so. *Sweet Mary, but I must
be a sight!* She wore her brother's old trews with an oversized
linen shirt of her father's. Her boots were caked with dirt,
most of her unruly hair had escaped from its braid, and both
her face and her hands were smudged from working in the
stable. Then she almost laughed out loud. *He won't be thinking of marrying me like this!*

"Forgive me, Lord Arthur," she said with as much dignity as she could muster. "I bid you a belated welcome to our home."

Arthur swung down. "There's nothing to forgive, my lady." She saw a flicker of mirth in those discerning eyes. *So, he's laughing at me!* She frowned.

Arthur held up a hand in mock defense. "I meant no offense! I am glad to see you, Gwenhwyfar. It seems you've grown up." He grinned and ran a hand through his sun-bleached brown hair.

Before she could reply, she heard her father call out a greeting as he and Elaine came hurrying across the yard. As usual, Elaine was the perfect picture of a lady. Her auburn braid was neatly done and wound around her head. Her light blue dress matched her cornflower eyes. As they approached, Gwenhwyfar caught the sweet scent of roses.

With a not-too-fond glance at Gwenhwyfar's attire, Leodegrance greeted Arthur. "I must apologize for our bad manners; why has no one taken your horses?" He motioned to the stableboys who waited by the paddock, gaping.

They quickly came forward to gather the reins; Valiant tossed his head, stamped, and jogged sideways beside the hapless boy who was trying to lead him. Arthur moved to help, but Gwenhwyfar stepped ahead of him.

"Allow me, my lord." She took the reins from the stableboy. She and the stallion studied each other for a moment. Arthur paused. Unexpectedly, Valiant nuzzled her shoulder. She laughed, rubbed his forelock, and started to lead him away, turning to give Bedwyr a triumphant look.

But it was Arthur who met her gaze and grinned.


In the distance, thunder rumbled as Arthur set aside his red slipware plate for the almoner, who would give the leftovers to the poor. They were all seated in the main dining room that overlooked the atrium. He turned to Elaine as he savored the clarity of the burgundy in its crystal goblet. "My compliments. The meal was excellent, especially on such short notice."

Elaine smiled prettily, glancing up at Arthur through her eyelashes. Gwenhwyfar noticed she had changed into a dark blue gown for this evening and her hair hung loosely from her shoulders, catching the firelight when she moved her head, which she did quite often. *Go ahead and flirt, Elaine. Please.*

"Thank you, my lord," Elaine said. " I enjoy putting such meals together. I like knowing a man is satisfied."

Arthur's eyebrow lifted and behind him, someone coughed.

Gwenhwyfar changed the subject before Elaine made a complete fool of herself. She had already accepted the compliment for Cook's hard labor. "Lord Arthur, would you tell me where you got that wonderful horse of yours?"

"Palomides needs to tell that story." He motioned to one of his men, a golden-skinned Saracen. "He is my horsemaster. The only other man who handles horses as well is the Lancer."

"The Lancer?" Elaine interrupted. "What a strange name. Who is he?"

Bedwyr replied, "Just the best horseman I ever saw and fearless in fighting. He came to us about six years ago; he got his name because he handles a lance better than any of us."

"You'd like him, Miss," Gryflet, one of Arthur's captains, said. "Most ladies do."

The lieutenant, Ulfin, laughed. "It's the fey blood in him, we always say. He was born of some pagan rite; women can't seem to resist him."

"Queen Elan didn't want a reminder of Ban's bastard is why we got him," young Agravaine said with a sneer.

Arthur silenced his nephew with a look. "He saved my life at Castellum Guinnion. I was chasing Colgrin and I never saw the Saxon who stepped out of the trees. The Lancer took the blow that was meant for me. He took another wound a few weeks ago at Badon. Now he's at Cadwy's fort, recovering." Arthur looked pensive. "At least the Saxons retreated after we killed their commanders, Colgrin and Baldulf. Anyway," Arthur added, "the Lancer has my geis—my oath to protect him as long as I live." He roused himself and turned to Palomides. "But we haven't answered the lady's question."

The Saracen's hair shimmered blue as azurite in the glow from the lamps as he nodded. "The horse is from my people's land, beyond Byzantium," he replied in his softly accented voice. "In Mecca, the city of my birth, these horses have been bred for many years. They have great strength and endurance and are very sure-footed in the loose sand. They can outdistance the wind on a flat, hard road."

Gwenhwyfar was fascinated. "Are they all as compact and beautiful as Valiant? Most of our warhorses are heavy."

Palomides smiled. "Valiant is a very special stallion, one of the best. I was lucky to have gotten him when he was a foal, but yes, all of our horses have the same conformation."

"Do you have more of these horses here?" *How I would love to own one!*

Arthur answered, "We've been able to obtain several mares and another stallion, but we need more. I would like all my light cavalry to ride these horses."

She pictured this. "Such a force would surely stop the Saxons! The barbarians fight on foot; there is no need for heavy armor. And," she added, "light infantry could move so much faster!"

Arthur turned to Bedwyr. "Mayhap I should enlist your sister for my war council!"

Gwenhwyfar bristled. "You don't consider a woman's opinion important?"

"I do." Arthur sounded amused. "I've just never known a woman who wanted to discuss horses or warfare before." Several of his men laughed.

Gwenhwyfar started to retort, but caught her father frowning at her. Reluctantly, she clamped her mouth closed. *Did Arthur think women were good for only one thing?* Then she remembered Bedwyr had once said Arthur had his father's reputation for wenching. *Just one more reason for not marrying this irritating man.*

Palomides took a sip of wine and continued, "The horses, my lady, are considered by the sheiks to be more valuable than many of their wives."

Elaine gasped. "Your men have more than one wife? But that's heathen. Our Lord Christos does not approve of such things!"

Leodegrance raised his hand to silence Elaine. "I beg pardon for her outburst, Palomides. Elaine has not yet learned tolerance of other beliefs." He fixed Elaine with a stern look. "However, since my house follows Pelagius, who is declared a heretic by most of Holy Church, she should have a little more insight."

Palomides turned to Elaine. "Most of my homeland is poor. Families consider it an honor to have their daughters married to a wealthy man. I assure you, all the wives hold a position of respect."

Elaine looked unconvinced and Gwenhwyfar looked sideways at her father. "Christians don't force their women to marry at all. The choice is the woman's."

Arthur repressed a smile. "Have you chosen such a brave man, Gwenhwyfar?"

For a moment she was nonplussed. Slowly, she lifted her chin; green eyes met grey. A moment of static current flew between them that had nothing to do with the storm that was approaching. "I have no intentions of getting married. My desire is to stay here and rule Cameliard one day."

Arthur grinned again.

Gwenhwyfar felt her temper rising. *I will not be thought weak.* "Do you not think a woman capable?"

"I think you would be capable of anything, my lady," he answered easily.

She frowned. *He's making fun of me.* Leodegrance coughed loudly.

Bedwyr intervened, "What is wrong with you, Gwenhwyfar? For certes, you'll marry. Da and I won't always be here to protect you."

"I don't need a man to protect me! I have been taught how to fight!"

"That," Arthur said drily, "I can believe."

More laughter followed that remark. Embarrassed and furious, Gwenhwyfar stood. "Should I ever decide to marry, Arthur Pendragon, you'd be the last man I would choose!"

Silence followed. Arthur shrugged, a smile playing about his mouth, but his eyes were serious. He fingered his wineglass absently.

"We'll see," he said.

The crashing boom of thunder drowned his words as the storm broke and unleashed its fury of hail and pelting rain.

Gwenhwyfar turned and fled the room.


Gwenhwyfar groaned and rolled over as the sunlight hit her face the next morning. She simply could not get up and face her father. She had totally shamed him and her brother by breaching the codes of both Celtic and Roman hospitality.

She'd also made a complete fool of herself, allowing herself to be baited about getting married. *But he kept goading me!* She groaned again and pulled the covers over her head.

Elaine entered her room, followed by her old nurse, Brisen. "Uncle wants to see you, Gwenhwyfar."

Brisen stalked over to the bed and pulled the covers off. "On your feet, girl, and be quick. I've never seen his lordship so angry. You'll be lucky if he doesn't tan your hide, you will." She poured some cold water in the basin and handed the washcloth to Gwenhwyfar before turning and pulling a dress from the wardrobe. "Here, put this on."

Gwenhwyfar started to protest, then closed her mouth. This was not the time to argue with Brisen or to remind her of her place. Not that it would be effective. When Elaine's mother, who was Guenhumara's twin, had died five years ago, Brisen had arrived with Elaine. In a matter of weeks, Brisen was ordering the other servants about.

"Is Arthur waiting, too?" Gwenhwyfar asked meekly. She suddenly felt more apprehensive about facing Arthur than she did her father. She had insulted him, but she definitely did not feel like apologizing. He was arrogant.

"Arthur and his men rode out at dawn this morning to join the rest of his army, so that's one problem you won't have to face. Your father and Bedwyr talked long into the night with him. I expect you'll be hearing about it soon."


Leodegrance was sitting alone at the long oak table when she got to the doorway of the dining hall. The normally appealing aroma of freshly baked oatcakes did nothing to settle her stomach. She searched his face for clues and found none.

"Sit down," he said, without looking up from his meat pasty. He took another bite and chewed it thoroughly before he looked at her.

"Da," she began.

"Silence!" His voice wasn't loud, but the sound was like the steel edge of a blade striking metal. "I believe you have done enough talking. Do you have any idea of what happened after you so gracefully left the room?"

She looked down. She hated having her da angry with her, but she deserved it.

"You embarrassed Arthur in front of his men. You know the code of honor the Cymbry follow. They're his hand-picked men, sworn until death. A man would be killed for talking like that to a warlord, let alone a man who will be high king."

Gwenhwyfar looked up, startled. "High king? What are you talking about, Da? Petty kings like yourself would never allow someone . . . why would they swear allegiance?" *Uther had created almost as many enemies as he had allies.*

"Because," Leodegrance said grimly, "the Saxons are invading from the North Sea, the ones that Vortigern allowed to settle in the east are moving westward, and the Picts are always a threat, to say nothing of the Scotti from Eire. The only way we Britons can survive is to provide a united front. For that, we need one chief, one king. A high king. That was the reason Arthur wanted assurance of a permanent fortification here. I gave it to him, but it has its price. "

Gwenhwyfar felt slightly relieved. "So, Arthur will maintain part of his army here? Oh, Da, I can make amends. I can even stand watch." She would make her da proud of her again. She would even apologize to Arthur.

Leodegrance's face softened and a small look of sadness replaced the anger.

"Arthur wants to marry you."

"What?" Gwenhwyfar jumped to her feet. "But you just said . . ."

"Sit down, daughter, and be quiet."

Confused, and feeling like the wind had been knocked out of her, she sank down.

"We were right. Arthur is seeking a bride because he will have need of heirs once he becomes king. Your behavior challenged him," Leodegrance continued. "He said you were the most spirited woman he has ever met."

"Does he think he can break me, like a horse? Is that it?" Her stomach was churning and a chill swept through her.

"No, no." Her father shook his head. "I don't think he meant that. He didn't seem angry. He said he thought life with you would be, um, interesting."

"Da, I can't do it. I don't want to be a queen. Please. Don't make me leave home." Her eyes were brimming, and she prided herself on not crying.

He picked up her hand. "This is an honor. I do not believe Arthur will mistreat you. He would not have the allegiance of the petty kings if we didn't trust his judgment."

Gwenhwyfar gulped for air. Her hopes and dreams were shattering about her and there was no one to turn to.

"Anyway," he continued briskly, "Arthur will be sending someone to escort you south to Cadwy's fort, which he is using." His voice softened. "When Cadwy's wife was alive, she called the place Camelot after the war god, Camulos. Said it fitted her husband. And Cadwy's spared no expense for her comfort."

"I like our villa." She tossed her head. "Besides, if Arthur wants me to leave here, he can escort me himself."

"He is riding farther north to Lothian to check on his widowed sister, Margawse. When he returns, the wedding and coronation will take place within a day of each other, while all the lords are gathered for the corn festival of Lugnasad. He wants you there waiting." He rose. "At least you will have a chance to work with those desert horses you so admire. As your dowry, I am purchasing a hundred of them for him."

Gwenhwyfar sat at the table for a long time after her father left. She stared, unseeing, and did not feel the wet nose or hear the anxious whine of the wolfhound who had come to her.

She thought about the man who came to her in night visions. Even though the dream kept his face hazy, she knew how he made her feel. Safe. Protected. And lately . . . well, just last night he'd wrapped his arms around her and kissed her gently, causing her body to tingle and quiver in unusual places. She blushed, recalling the sensation of her breasts pressed against his chest. It had seemed so real. She doubted that Arthur could make her feel like *that*. Not that she even wanted him to try.

She gritted her teeth. *Arthur didn't even ask me; he just assumed . . . and then he sends some servant to get me. How can I be a wife to that conceited man? And heirs?* She shuddered at the thought. *There must be a way to prevent this marriage from taking place.*

# Chapter 2

# Wheel of Fate

Her father appeared at the door of her bedroom on the first floor. "Riders." He looked from Gwenhwyfar to Elaine and Brisen. "I think they're Arthur's men."

Gwenhwyfar sank down on the chaise beside the bed after her father left. For all her bravado, she was shaking. For more than three weeks, she had dreaded the day the escort would arrive. She had refused to eat until Brisen threatened to force-feed her. She had prayed that Arthur would change his mind and even begged her father to make the horses a peace offering instead of a dowry. She had thought of running away, but there was no place to go. She had even given her father the silent treatment, which hurt her more than it did him. In frustration, her father had finally reminded her that the matter was out of his hands. A high king had the right to forfeit land ownership. There was nothing he or she could do.

Gwenhwyfar threw the gowns Elaine had brought on the

bed. "I don't want to take these!" She looked longingly at her breeches and shirts.

Brisen picked up a green silk and began folding it neatly. "You won't be wearing those men's clothes at court, Miss. Luckily, your mother had some fine things and you're about her size. Others can be made for you once we're settled."

"I'll wear my trews! How else am I going to ride?" she asked apprehensively.

Brisen shook her head. "I'm going to get the trunk."

When they were alone, Elaine asked, "Do you think Arthur's going to allow the high queen to dress like a man?"

Gwenhwyfar stared at her. High queen. Of Britain. She hadn't thought that far. *Surely, Arthur wouldn't be so cruel as to not let me ride!* Already, she planned on helping Palomides train the new horses. He and the Lancer person.

She could hear the heavy boots of the men entering the Great Hall. Soldiers coming to take her from her home, from everything familiar to some godforsaken fort. She would be forced to marry, forced to wear gowns, forced to . . . She couldn't even finish the thought. She flung a pair of boots across the room, hitting the wall with a resounding thud.

Elaine looked worried. "Gwenhwyfar, women get married and have children. It's our duty. Arthur is a strong, good-looking man. And he'll be king; think of the power he'll have! I wish he had chosen me instead!"

Gwenhwyfar nearly screamed. Elaine had never understood her. "I wish he had, too! You're coming with me; if you think that cocky man is so good-looking, why don't you just take my place?" She sat up and shouted, "I don't want to get married!"

Brisen rushed back into the room, her face stricken, and slapped her. Stunned, Gwenhwyfar quieted.

"Arthur's men are just across the hall, " Brisen hissed. "You will not humiliate your father nor discredit your brother. Clean your face. Wear this." She pulled a yellow linen gown

from the heap. "It's your duty to make your father's guests
feel welcome."

Gwenhwyfar glared at the nurse. For a moment, she was
tempted to slap back; then, her shoulders slumped. No one
understood her anxiety or knew how scared she was. She
wished she had someone to talk to. She took a deep breath.
Brisen was right. As the lady of the villa, she had hostess duties. She would have to make her father proud of her and not
show her fear again.


Lancer was about to check on his horse when he heard
feminine footsteps and turned from the door. The girl who
had entered the room was pretty enough, but she didn't look
like the fireball he had been warned to expect. She didn't
look like a girl who had been shouting when he came in.

She cast her eyes down and a small smile played on her
lips as she tilted her head slightly and brushed her lashes
against her cheeks before looking up at him again. She was
flirting, he realized, and forced himself to smile.

She walked toward him, extending her hand, which he
dutifully bent over. When he looked up, he stopped breathing.

Another girl stood in the doorway dressed in a simple
yellow gown that brought out the burnished strands of red
and gold in her long hair. Cool green eyes above high cheekbones surveyed the men in the Great Hall. Her face was immobile. When her gaze reached him, her eyes widened
slightly as if in recognition, and then she turned away.

He breathed again. *What just happened? For certes, she is
the most striking-looking woman . . . but something else. . . .*

Lancer watched her walk slowly to where her father and
the other men were standing. Introductions were made, and
she did everything correctly. A polite smile and the proper
gestures, but he could feel her misery from across the room.

His reverie was broken by the girl who still stood beside him. "I'm Elaine," she said in a soft, light voice, "Gwenhwyfar's cousin. I will be making the trip with her. I hope we can count on being well cared for?" She looked at him with wide eyes.

"For certes," he replied courteously. "Arthur would have my head if I let anything happen to his bride."

Elaine looked annoyed.

Lancer did not notice. "Why don't you introduce me to your cousin?"


Gwenhwyfar watched Elaine approach with the stranger. She thought he wasn't many years older than she was. Nearly six feet, lean but muscular, his thigh muscles rippled with each step. *A horseman.* The face was angular, with a slightly crooked nose; a full, sensuous mouth; and a firm chin. Strands of his dark hair fell over his forehead; momentarily, she wanted to brush them back for him. His eyes were deep set, neither brown nor grey, but somewhere in between. *Elaine wants him.* She had the sudden urge to pinch her cousin.

Gaheris, one of the escort, slapped him jovially on the shoulder. "As usual, you've not lost time in attracting a beauty!" He looked Elaine over approvingly and she giggled coquettishly.

Gwenhwyfar grew even more annoyed. "Elaine, would you see to Cook, please? And have Rufus bring the good wine."

Lancer looked directly at Gwenhwyfar. "I'm Galahad, but the men call me Lancer." His voice was pleasantly mellow. "I will be your escort. I have pledged to see you safely to Cadwy's."

She held his gaze. His eyes were unfathomable; she felt herself getting lost in them. *Who is this man?*

"Arthur said you and Palomides were his horse trainers?"

If he was surprised by the bluntness of her question, he didn't show it.

"I've worked with horses all my life."

"Do you have word when the new horses are to arrive?"

Lancer looked puzzled. "No, my lady. New horses?"

"My dowry," she said drily, "is to be one hundred of those wonderful horses from Mecca." Apparently, he didn't know what a hard bargain Arthur drove.

His eyebrows lifted in surprise.

"I'm going to help you train those horses, Lancer, whether Arthur agrees or not," Gwenhwyfar announced firmly. *These men might as well know I don't intend to spend my time embroidering!*

Sudden silence filled the room. Then Lancer grinned slowly, a lopsided smile with one corner of his mouth quirking up, making his eyes crinkle at the corners so they looked even darker, more like the color of dense smoke. Gwenhwyfar felt as though she were basking in the warm sunshine that suddenly breaks through the clouds after a cold, dismal rain. She smiled back, the first genuine smile she had produced in days.

The silence was broken when Elaine arrived back with the wine and the men turned their attention to her.

Lancer, though, did not take his eyes off Gwenhwyfar as he raised his cup to salute her.


The horses were saddled and wagons loaded with provisions and personal items when Gwenhwyfar strode into the bailey the next morning, wearing her usual outfit of a linen shirt, men's breeches, and leather boots.

"Where's Cali?" she asked, looking over the horses.

Leodegrance cleared his throat. "Brisen and Elaine are riding in litters. As the future queen, you should do the same."

"I have never in my life ever ridden in a litter," she said in an outraged voice. "I'm not about to start now." She looked at them in disgust. *Claustrophobic things.* At least they would slow the trip down and she wouldn't have to face the people at Cadwy's.

Arthur's men busied themselves checking harnesses and cinches. Leodegrance began to reply when Lancer came out of the stable, leading Cali and his own stallion, a sleek black that was of the same bloodline as Arthur's grey.

He handed Cali's reins to Gwenhwyfar. "I thought you might prefer riding."

*He knew.* She gave him a grateful look. He stood by the mare's shoulder, talking quietly to her, turning her head toward him while he tapped the left leg. Slowly, she knelt.

Gwenhwyfar stared. "How did you get Cali to do that?"

"She's a smart horse; I practiced with her a little." He smiled at her, his eyes warm. "In battle, if we're unseated with our armor on, we're able to get mounted again. Try it."

Gwenhwyfar slid into the saddle quickly and the mare lifted her. "You'll teach me to do that?"

His smile widened. "My pleasure."

Leodegrance stepped up to the saddle. "Arthur will be good to you. Have faith in him. I will see you at the crowning."

*Nearly two months away.* Gwenhwyfar looked away from her father. Tears were threatening and her lip trembled. *I will not show fear.* She stared straight ahead as the party began to move forward, not daring to look back because she didn't trust herself. Never had she felt so small and all alone.

They were barely past the gate when the black appeared alongside. Lancer didn't say anything, just kept the stallion's pace adjusted to her mare's. She was grateful for the silence as well as the company. Several miles farther down the road, when the tears had been successfully held back and she felt she had a measure of self-control, she finally spoke. "Tell me about Arthur."

He glanced over. "What would you like to know?"

"Everything! Arthur was here for an evening. I stupidly insulted him. To save his pride, my father agreed to purchase those horses and call it a dowry," she said simply. "I am just part of the package. Arthur has no love of me."

He was silent a minute. "Arthur would not marry you, my lady, to salvage his pride. He is not a vengeful man. Even in battle, he spares Saxons their lives for their fidelity."

She felt doubtful. "Mayhap not for an ordinary insult, but I . . . I . . . told him he would be the last person I would marry!"

Lancer laughed. "My lady, you may be the only woman in Britain who's told him that!"

"Call me Gwenhwyfar, please." She continued miserably, "I challenged him. Now he wants to break me, tame me, make me a docile, obedient creature." She lifted her chin. "Well, I won't be broken!"

Lancer shook his head sympathetically. "Arthur respects spirit. With his men, he demands obedience, because all of our lives depend on it. Punishment can be harsh, but I've never seen him deliberately degrade or humiliate anyone, not even when he claims victory, my la . . . Gwenhwyfar."

She watched him closely. "You really care about him, don't you? As a person."

"It's hard to describe Arthur," he answered. "He believes, thinks, and lives to unite Britain and maintain prosperity and peace." He looked thoughtful. "I can't imagine not fighting by Arthur's side."

Gwenhwyfar was silent for a while after that, thinking.

They rode along, companionably, until he was called to the front of the procession to decide where to make camp.


The first night, when a member of her escort, Garient, came to take care of Cali, Gwenhwyfar surprised him because she had already groomed and hobbled her horse and was spreading her bedroll.

"My lady, we are preparing a tent for you. Allow me to walk you there."

"No need," Gwenhwyfar answered. "I like sleeping outdoors unless it's raining. Glena will keep me warm."

Garient tried to persuade her, but she was adamant. She would not put these men to any extra trouble.

The next morning Lancer convinced her to sleep in a tent because, he teasingly said, he didn't want her getting abducted in the middle of the night. She found it hard to resist his smile, but she insisted on pitching and striking the tent herself.

After the first day, when Elaine got no special attention, she began to whine. The litter was jostled too much, they did not stop often enough, and she wanted different food. The men maintained a stoic silence. Gwenhwyfar tried to interest her in a game of chess, but she petulantly refused. Lancer offered to play, and to Gwenhwyfar's delight, they were evenly matched.

With the litters, it took them well over a fortnight to travel from Cameliard to Cadwy's fort in the south. The first five days of the journey had taken them from the rolling hills and moors ablaze with purple heather through dense forests heavy with the scent of pine and onto the old Roman Fosse Way at Lindum. From there the travel became easier.

Gwenhwyfar and Lancer spent most of each day riding side by side while he talked of life at the fort. She learned of the battles which had gained Arthur his reputation as warlord: the battle near the weald in the southeastern tip of Britain where the Saxon bretwalda, Aelle, pledged friendship; the battles in the north at the River Glen and Dubglas when Arthur was given his own command; and especially the battle at the Humber and the Wash where the crafty Saxons had split into two forces to meet on the west coast and effectively divide Britain in two. Arthur had foreseen the maneuver and established a base at Lindum. That battle had decided the petty kings on unity.

As they rode through the lush, fertile green of the Summer Country's gently rolling hills, Gwenhwyfar asked Lancer of his home. "You are a prince of Benoic?"

He nodded. "King Ban's son. I have a younger brother, Ector. My mother is Lady of the Black Lake, in the heart of Brocéliande, and sister to Vivian, your Lady of the Isle."

"You are pagan, then?" She kept her tone light.

He turned to look at her. "Yes. Does that bother you, Gwenhwyfar?"

"I guess not. It's just that I've been raised Christian. We've been taught that pagans are dangerous. . . ."

Lancer grinned. "Do I seem dangerous?"

"No!" Gwenhwyfar said hastily. "In fact, you remind me . . ." She bit her lip. She couldn't very well blurt out that he reminded her of her fantasy man. He'd think she was daft. "I mean, I feel as though I've known you forever," she finished weakly.

"Mayhap we have known each other before, in another lifetime."

She was startled. "The priests say we live only once; that is why we must do what's right, so we won't burn in hell."

"I don't know your concept of hell," he answered softly, "but doesn't it make more sense to have many lifetimes to learn the lessons of life? How can we experience everything in a few decades?"

"I don't know." Gwenhwyfar grew more thoughtful. "Is Arthur pagan, too?" She knew so little about the man.

"No. Well, maybe," he shrugged. "Ector, his foster father, is Christian, but the arch-druid, Myrddin, mentored him. Arthur sees no wrong in the worship of the Goddess or the Christos. Or Woden, for that matter."

Gwenhwyfar looked at him, puzzled.

"The Saxons' god."

"Arthur allows that?" she asked in surprise.

"He's a tolerant man."

She was quiet for several minutes, the steady clopping of

the horses' hooves the only sound. "Is he tolerant enough to let you be my friend?" she finally asked. "I would like a friend at the fort."

Lancer smiled. "I will always be your friend; he cannot deny me that."

She breathed a sigh of relief. "Then I won't be so scared."

A strange, inscrutable expression settled on his face as they rode on.

A day's ride from the fort, with the sun's rays already slanting, Gwenhwyfar asked the question she had held back. "Arthur said you saved his life. Will you tell me about it?"

Lancer looked down at his reins. "We had invaded Anglia. The Saxons were retreating when Arthur spotted Colgrin. Arthur was concentrating on capturing him. I saw the Saxon step out of the trees, war ax raised. I threw my lance and deflected it." He shrugged. "What I didn't see was the second man. Luckily, I was still bent over my horse. His ax nicked my shoulder and didn't remove my head."

Gwenhwyfar sidled Cali over and put her hand on his bare forearm, warm from the sun. She felt his arm tense. "You were almost killed! No wonder Arthur said you have his geis. It is not a thing lightly given, the oath of fidelity. You earned it."

Lancer shifted uncomfortably in his saddle. "Arthur is like a brother to me; I'm sworn to protect him, also."

Gwenhwyfar lifted her hand and considered this, head tilted to one side. She hoped Arthur had enough sense to appreciate Lancer. "Do you suppose I will ever be as loyal to Arthur as you are?"

He turned toward her. "Arthur will earn your respect and your trust, just as you've earned mine."

She smiled. "I don't know that I could have finished this journey without you. I like you, Lance, a lot." Inadvertently she had shortened his name and it had rolled off her tongue as one word. Lancealot. Then she laughed. "I like the sound of that." She tried it again, faster. "Lancelot. Could my special name for you be Lancelot? When I use it, I will remember these days." Her green eyes grew serious now. "Would you mind?"

He gave her his lopsided grin. "I'd like that."

"And you could call me Gwen," she said. "No one ever does. It would be our secret code of friendship."

"Yes. Friendship," he answered as he looked at her with an enigmatic expression.

A feeling of joy washed over her and suddenly the day seemed intensely beautiful. Lancelot would be her friend. Mayhap living at Cadwy's wouldn't be so bad, after all.

# Chapter 3

# The Seeker

Nimue loved this daily ritual. She faced west and raised her arms in supplication. Her long flaxen hair fell to her waist as she threw her head back and raised her voice to join the other priestesses as they chanted, saluting the day's end. Their song lifted and carried across the stillness of the Lake and drifted upward to where Vivian, the Lady of the Lake, stood with the arch-druid Myrddin near the House of Maidens. That he was here, on the Holy Isle of Avallach, meant there was need for a priestess. Nimue wondered why.

The priestesses finished and filed singly up the path toward the Tor. Nimue stopped not far from the Lady's quarters and watched as the last tangerine ray of the sun rippled and floated on the surface of the water before it disappeared and the water returned to pearl grey. Soon the protective fog bank that always surrounded Avallach would roll in.

The stillness that had settled over the Isle allowed Myrddin's conversation with the Lady to drift toward Nimue.

"The Goddess lives, Vivian. Our numbers may be few, but

we druids haven't been entirely vanquished. Even the Christians acknowledge the greatness of the Mother; they just call her by a different name. This new religion instills fear and guilt and people are confused." He paused. "That is exactly the reason Arthur must embrace both the new ways and the old. Britain must be united. He will have a Christian Mass for the coronation to satisfy the Romans' converts and perform the Great Rite for the land and our people."

"We must unite the king and the land as in the old days," Vivian agreed as she and Myrddin turned and walked away.

Nimue shivered, although the air was warm.

The moon was dark that night, filling Nimue with fore boding. She ate little of her supper. Her uneasiness increased as the novice, Etain, approached. "The Lady Vivian wishes to speak with you when you have finished."

She was surprised to see Myrddin in the Lady's chambers, even though one of the druid caves lay deep beneath them. His troublesome faerie, invisible to most humans, hovered at his shoulder. The faerie tossed her long brown hair back and winked at Nimue, unnerving her still more.

"Please sit," the Lady gestured. Her raven, normally on her shoulder, flew to its perch, where it squawked at the faerie. Nimue hardly noticed, nervous as she was.

Nimue focused on the tapestry of the white hart that hung on the wall behind the Lady. As a messenger of the Otherworld, it heralded major changes when seen. Tonight the silver threads seemed to glow with a preternatural light, accentuating the rich, velvety green background.

"The kings of Britain have been counseling." Myrddin began to pace. "And they have agreed to unite, choosing Arthur to be high king!"

Nimue nodded. She had met Arthur when he was younger; even then, he'd been vibrant. "So be you and Arthur blessed. A united Britain will stop the barbarians."

"Unity is just the beginning, Nimue! Arthur will establish justice. Fairness will rule. Tolerance. The Goddess will flourish, once again," he stopped, his face aglow.

The vision took form in Nimue's head as well. She supposed Myrddin was sending it, but nevertheless, the prospect was exciting. The Old Religion would prevail! The people would send their daughters to be accepted by the Lady. The House of Maidens would again be full.

"Nimue," the Lady said gently, "you have a part to play in this destiny."

The uneasiness settled on her once again, but she held her tongue and nodded.

Myrddin spoke. "Presently the kings have agreed to support each other, but the time will soon come when differences will arise. Beliefs in the Old Ways will be challenged by the new religion. Arthur must have the support of all men."

Nimue looked from him to the Lady and back again. "What is my part?"

"In times past, if the land were not fertile, the king would be sacrificed and another chosen to take his place," Myrddin said. "We no longer sacrifice our kings, but the people want proof that the Great Mother accepts the king, for She truly blesses the land and makes it prosper. The Great Rite must be performed."

Vivian leaned forward in her great armchair. "For Arthur to keep the support of the pagans, once he holds Mass in the Christian church, he must unite with the Goddess as well. She chooses her vessel, through whom She will act. The ritual itself is sufficient, but if a child results from the act, the land will be truly blessed."

"I am the . . . vessel?" Nimue's voice was barely audible. When Vivian nodded, she inhaled sharply. "Lady, when I came to Avallach, I was a child, an initiate. Now I am priestess." Unconsciously, she touched the blue crescent moon tattoo on her forehead. "I thought to remain virgin always. My special gift is the Sight; will I not weaken or lose my power if I give my womanhood to a man?"

"The coupling will be symbolic of the Great Mother accepting Her son. The sharing of male and female energy will be a perfect balance for what is to come for Britain," Vivian answered. "The Sight is a gift from the Goddess. It is She who determines whether it strengthens or weakens."

Nimue bent her head. "I have pledged myself to Her. So be it blessed."

The filmy skirts of the faerie fluttered as she shimmered in the air beside Nimue. "Don't look so stricken. This could be fun . . ." Her giggle sounded as light as a small, silver bell.

"Come back here." In irritation, Myrddin waved his hand and the faerie skimmed back to him.

"Well, it could," she pouted, her slanted green eyes narrowing.

He ignored her. "Nimue, Arthur is going to need your help in the future, as well."

She looked up. "In what way? Kingship is a worldly thing of men and war. I dwell on the inner plane."

Vivian replied, "To understand the spirit, you must understand the physical: as above, so below. Myrddin is troubled by partial visions he's had; he needs your Sight."

Nimue was distressed. "Surely, I can practice the Sight from here, from the Reflecting Pool. It is a sacred spot!"

The Lady turned to Myrddin. "Tell her of these visions."

"I see fragments . . . a stag brought down . . . Morgana, Arthur's sister . . . she has a dark aura about her, but I don't know why . . ." he stopped, for Nimue suddenly stiffened and her clear aquamarine eyes glazed.

Her forehead furrowed as the trance took her. "Two women ride to Arthur. One is small and has black hair. The other has copper-colored hair . . . something evil lies between them." Her eyes refocused.

Myrddin hesitated, then shrugged. "I know not who the second one is, but the dark one is Morgana, and she bears watching. She has stirred up many a hornet's nest in Uriens's kingdom. She craves power. Once she finds out Arthur is to be high king . . . well, if she rides to Arthur, I need you to be physically present at court."

"At court?" she echoed. "My life is here! Am I not to be trained to take your position one day, Lady?"

Vivian smiled gently. "To be the Lady requires an understanding of how the world operates. The ambitions of men and the control of power must be understood, or our work will simply spin us in circles, for naught. You must go with Myrddin; learn everything you can from him."

Nimue was thoroughly miserable. "This is the will of the Goddess?"

"Yes, child."

"Then I must obey," she whispered. "When must I go?"

Myrddin replied, "The day after Lugnasad is the sacred day of marrying the king to the land, still several weeks away, but if Morgana is on her way to Arthur, we have not time to dawdle."

Nimue caught her breath and looked at the Lady. With a barely perceivable nod, she was excused. She stumbled out the door, tears blinding her vision.

The crisp, sour tang of green apples drifted in the still night air. Nimue carried her ritual box as she slowly walked down the Processional Way to the Sacred Pool. Overhead, millions of wavering jewels glittered against the black velvet sky. Nimue wondered if the stars really were souls, waiting to return to earth, as the Lady had once said. *This might be my last night to walk this path.* Her bare feet felt their way over the smooth, familiar flagstones that led down the hill. At the base, a large rock served as an altar. She knelt and took a pinch of incense from her box. Revering the earth, she placed the powder in the indentation on the top of the rock. She struck the flint and thanked the fire that sprang forth. Fanning the small flame with her hand, she sanctified the air. The incense curled upward in a spiral of blue smoke. Satisfied, she sat down by the reflecting pool, which tonight mirrored the ebony of the sky.

Carefully she scooped water from the pool, anointed the thirteen points of contact on her body, returned the unused water to the pool, and made the sign of blessing. She assumed the ritual position, closed her eyes, and journeyed inward.

"Please, Mother of All, do not forsake your servant. Help me to understand why I must leave Avallach."

There was silence save for the whispering of the wind-singers in the trees, but the sprites brought no message. She tried again. "Please, I wish only to serve You. Can I not do that here on Avallach? Why must I leave?"

Slowly the image of a stag appeared in her mind, beautifully antlered and standing regally. Behind him a dark cat sprang from the shadows; the stag leaped but did not shake the creature. He shook his head and looked directly at Nimue. She wanted to help but was locked into her trance. Both animals shape-shifted, the stag becoming a man, save for the rack of antlers still on his head. The small beast changed into a woman with long black hair and pale skin. They began to dance, whirling faster and faster until they were lying intertwined on the ground, his manhood thrust deep inside her.

The image faded away and another form rose. A child with black hair and grey eyes grew before Nimue into adulthood. He bellowed a challenge to the forest and the king stag reemerged, pawing the ground. The challenger shape-shifted and the two stags circled each other warily before the younger one charged. Dust and dirt from flying, kicking hooves obscured her view. When it was over, the older one lay on the ground, apparently lifeless.

Nimue returned to reality abruptly. She sat still, clearing her head, then slowly started up the hill. She knew she had experienced Myrddin's vision. She must prevent that fight from occurring. If she could.

She stopped suddenly and turned, knowing what she would see. The white hart was drinking at the pool. He raised his head to look at her and then gracefully leaped into the shadows.


"He did what?" Nimue cringed inwardly for Gryflet as Myrddin's hawk-colored eyes bore through the young soldier. They had ridden to Cadwy's that morning and been surprised to find Arthur's mother, Ygraine, at the fort. Now the air about the arch-druid was fairly crackling as Myrddin paced before the dais at the far end of the Great Hall. The faerie sprite floated to the sideboard and gave him a baleful look. Nimue felt an affinity for her this morning.

"Since we were riding to Lothian, Arthur thought that would be a good time to confirm Leodegrance's alliance with him." Gryflet hesitated, swallowed, and then went on. "Arthur met Gwenhwyfar. She is pretty, my lord, but what a temper, and they were talking and then suddenly they were arguing. . . ."

Myrddin pulled at his tawny hair. "Would you get to the point, man, or do I need to pull this speech from you?"

Gryflet paled and involuntarily stepped back. "Gwenhwyfar told him he was the last person she would marry," he blurted.

Myrddin stopped and stared.

"So, now he is. Marrying her, I mean," Gryflet finished.

"By Mithras!" Myrddin resumed his pacing, a slight smell of sulfur following him. "The one campaign I didn't ride on . . . Where is Arthur now?" he demanded.

"He sent me back to get the preparations started and he rode on to visit his sister. Since King Pellinore killed her husband, Lot, Arthur wanted to make sure Margawse was in no need."

Myrddin made a strangled sound. "You don't know Margawse, do you, Gryflet? That woman could hold off the Saxons by herself, if she didn't bed them first! Didn't Pellinore send his son, Lamorak, to take care of things?"

Gryflet nodded. "Yes, but Arthur thought he'd invite her to the wedding himself. That's why Ygraine is here; we have less than two moons."

Myrddin took a deep breath and Nimue suddenly heard his thought. *So soon! There isn't much time. I must stop this.* She wondered why.

"Where is this Gwenhwyfar?" Myrddin asked. "Is Arthur bringing her back?"

"Oh, no, my lord." Gryflet replied, "I was to send an escort to fetch her."

Nimue was suddenly enveloped with the dread cold that flowed from Myrddin. She had a glimpse of a young dark-haired boy and an auburn-headed girl sharing a wooden sword and of a monk running toward them. The image faded.

Myrddin's voice was deadly quiet. "Whom did you send, Gryflet?"

Gryflet looked surprised. "Why, the Lancer. He's been fuming that he was healed and missing the action in the north. He said bringing Arthur's bride home was the least he could do."

The smoldering fire in the hearth suddenly leaped into full flame.

"Leave me!" Myrddin roared.

Gryflet lost no time in complying, but Nimue left more slowly, the faerie twittering anxiously behind her. Something about this upcoming marriage was not right. But what?

# Chapter 4

# Forbidden Paths

Morgana slipped from the fur coverings on the bed. She glanced at the elderly, snoring man who was her husband, Uriens of Rheged. He would sleep soundly: a little henbane in the last glass of wine had taken care of that problem. Accolon would be waiting. A warmth spread through her lower belly at the thought.

She gathered a robe about her and silently padded down the hall and into the courtyard. The early summer night was warm, and waning moonlight barely illuminated the way to the stables; she glanced quickly around before she entered the hay-scented granary. Before her eyes had time to adjust to the darkness, strong hands encircled her waist, tumbling her down. Roughly she was turned over and her robe pulled off, her large breasts exposed.

Accolon groaned as his mouth covered one nipple. His hand squeezed the other breast brusquely, making Morgana's moan match his. She wrapped her legs around his buttocks and he thrust violently inside her as their open mouths tasted each other.

"Harder, Accolon, harder! Make me hurt!" Morgana arched her back to receive more of him, raking her nails down the straining muscles of his back. His frenzy increased until he was lifting her off the floor and pounding her back on the stack of hay.

She writhed under him, feeling his weight and the rigidness of his body, and she matched her climax to his, her scream stifled by his hand. She gave his finger a hard bite.

"Ouch! What was that for?" Accolon rolled over and sucked the blood on his hurt finger.

"Because I felt like it." In the dim light, her pale, sweaty skin glistened and she leaned over him, her long ebony hair brushing against his chest. She nibbled at his lip. "Didn't you like it?" She slid her hands down his thighs, enjoying the sensation of his young, hard body.

He stayed her hands. "I ran into Medraut on my way here. He is awake very late for a seven-year-old."

"Medraut has strange habits."

"He had the nerve to ask me where I was going!"

Morgana tousled Accolon's long dark hair. "Did you tell him, my sweet?"

Accolon looked amused and then he shook his head. "What was he doing out, Morgana? I wouldn't mind helping you with him; I know Uriens doesn't take much interest."

"That's because he isn't his son." Morgana stopped. She hadn't meant to say that. The time to reveal Medraut's identity was not yet. *I will take more care in the future.*

She tried to pull Accolon over for a kiss. He did not budge and she straightened, annoyed. "Something is really troubling you!"

Reluctantly, he replied, "Morgana, this situation . . . do you think I want to keep on meeting like this, sneaking around like you were some tavern wench? Taking you in the stable?"

"I could always increase the dosage I give Uriens!"

"No!" He sounded shocked. "I don't like the fact that you're drugging Uriens, as it is. He is a fair king to his people. And one of Arthur's strongest allies."

"Don't worry. I'm not planning to kill him. I know what I'm doing. It's not his fault Uther Pendragon wanted to get rid of the rightful heirs to Kernow." Morgana sulked. "Lot got Margawse, and eventually, Uther married me off to Uriens." She stood and put on her robe, brushing the hay from it. "I've got to go."

Accolon stood, too. "I think we should stop meeting for a while."

"Oh? Really?" Morgana's voice was sultry as she spread her robe and pressed her breasts against his chest. Slowly, she slid her body down the length of him until she was on her knees in front of him. She took him in her mouth, her hands working expertly. Accolon closed his eyes and groaned. As he stiffened, Morgana suddenly pinched hard. He yelped in pain and stepped back, pulsating with a need for release. She stood and moved quickly to the door.

"Do you really think you can stop seeing me?" She turned and vanished into the shadows.

Morgana was sitting in the courtyard the next morning, watching Medraut practice with his wooden sword, when the rider passed through the gate.

She shaded her eyes against the morning sun. The rider wore Arthur's livery of red and gold. "What message do you bring?" she asked, approaching.

The man handed her a scroll as Uriens came out. Morgana quickly scanned the Latin writing, her eyes widening in surprise and then narrowing in consternation.

"Your new king is gaining a high queen as well," she said, handing the script to her husband.

Uriens beamed. "Arthur is getting married? He's been widowed long enough! Who's the lucky woman?"

Morgana shot him a sideways look. "Or the unlucky woman, mayhap. I doubt that Arthur will keep only one bed warm for long."

Arthur's rider sat straight in the saddle, staring intently at something across the yard. Uriens cleared his throat hastily and looked back at the paper. "Yes. Well. This is wonderful news!" He gestured to the rider. "Come down, man! Join me while I break my fast and hear the details about this match."

Morgana stared after the men, thinking. *I hadn't planned on Arthur getting married. Not after Leonora. Still . . .*

"You're not happy, Mother."

She resisted the impulse to jump. How did that boy always manage to appear without being heard? She turned to him. His grey eyes were studying her. "Nonsense. I was just thinking of all that needs to be done before your father and I leave. Your new uncle, Arthur, is going to get married as well as become high king." She smiled suddenly. "Medraut, do you know what that means? You're his nephew." *And his son.* "You could possibly take his place one day!"

Medraut frowned. "Won't he have children?"

"You ask too many questions. Don't worry about it." She stroked his black hair. "Right now, you need to practice with that sword, so you will be fit to be a king. Go on." Diverted, Medraut ran off.

Morgana slowly walked down the path that led to the walled garden and went to the hidden area behind the grapevine trellis where she grew her special herbs. She sank down into the cool grass, her fingers playing with the shaggy liontail-shaped leaves of motherwort, and drifted back in time.

*At fourteen, she had been sent by Uther to Amesbury Abbey because she was too inquisitive at home and too young to be married.*

*Convent life definitely did not suit her, although she gained* a reputation as a healer, for she had a natural disposition for herb lore. The Sisters didn't know she practiced a darker art as well, learned from an old forest hag in Tintagel.

Men fascinated her. She had watched the village smith working without his shirt on, those huge, heavily muscled biceps and shoulders swinging the hammer and striking the anvil. She thought of those arms holding her; her body tingled and her breathing quickened. She had the same reaction when she saw the tall Celtic horse trader who came through or the youthful, lithe cooper who sold his wares.

She had endured ten years at the abbey; then, eight years ago, on Beltane, she met Arthur.

Uther's lusty men had returned to nearby Ambresbyrig. Tonight, she would satisfy this constant ache she had between her legs.

Morgana left quietly while the Sisters were at Compline. The needfires were dying and the hillsides becoming quiet. In the village, most of Uther's men were still drinking and boisterous.

She pulled the hood of the black robe more closely about her face and stayed in the shadows of a copse of beech trees. Clumps of bracken and hawthorn formed a natural hedge behind a curve in the road about halfway between the village and the fort, creating a secluded place. From here, she could watch and wait.

She let several groups of drunken men stagger by. Near midnight she saw the lone man walking toward her. In the slanted moonlight, he appeared to be about her age, tall, with broad shoulders. As he came closer, she could see his face; a good-looking man with chiseled features and a square jaw. She stepped into the road.

*The man stopped abruptly. He stared blearily at her, rubbed his eyes, and looked again. "Who . . . Who are you?"*

*"Follow me," she whispered as she backed away to the thicket.*

*Like a man in a trance, he did. She removed her cloak, spread it on the ground, and held out a hand.*

*He quickly pulled off his clothes. Naked, he approached her. She looked at his massive shoulders, the narrow hips and tight muscles of his thighs, the hardened, flat belly. She stopped at the protruding appendage. Fascinated, she reached out to touch him.*

*He pulled her down, pushing her smock over her face, pinioning her arms among the folds. Pushing her breasts together, he ran his tongue from the tip of one to the other, kneading their fullness with his hands. Morgana groaned in pure ecstasy.*

*Lustily, he spread her legs and rammed himself home. She wasn't prepared for the white-hot, searing pain that shot upward, tearing her apart. The pain continued slashing through her as the man pumped himself into her, withdrawing, and thrusting again. She screamed. A hand clamped over her mouth while he plunged even harder, one more time.*

*Then it was over. The man rolled away. Morgana didn't move; she felt the wetness running down her thighs and smelled blood.*

*When he spoke, he sounded surprised. "You were a virgin." She didn't answer.*

*Suddenly, boots were heard coming up the road. Several men, still laughing and obviously drunk, shouted, "Arthur! Arthur! Where are you?"*

*The man with Morgana pulled his clothes on quickly. He whispered to her. "My men. I didn't mean to hurt you. I was expecting . . . you wanted . . ." He shook his head. "You must stay still until I can get them moving." Softly, he brushed her lips with his, and then he was gone.*

*She never did hear what excuse he gave his men for his whereabouts. Her thoughts were a jumble of pleasure and pain and the sensualness of that kiss. His men had called him Arthur; she would find him again.*

Morgana broke out of the past with a start. How long had she been sitting here? The sun was definitely higher in the sky.

Her thoughts turned to the future. Now that Arthur was to become high king, Medraut was the rightful heir. The fact that he was conceived through incest didn't bother her. Didn't the ancient Egyptians rule as siblings and consorts? She deserved to be called the king's consort. That could happen whether Gwenhwyfar were queen or not, but she would have to prevent this girl from getting pregnant, at least until Medraut could be established as Arthur's son, and she wasn't ready to do that yet. *The moon will be dark tonight; I can begin the enchantment for the girl's barrenness. I know what herbs to use, but I will have to be at Cadwy's to make sure they are taken.*

She found Uriens a short time later. "I have a wonderful idea," she said as she put her arms around his neck and nibbled his ear. "Gwenhwyfar is going to be my sister by marriage. She's young. She might appreciate having an older woman to confide in. I could help her, tell her how wonderful marriage is, how well I am treated, and how you protect and take care of me." She smiled sweetly. "If I arrive early, I would have time to know her and mayhap I could stay after the wedding to help her adjust. It's convenient that my own land is not far from Cadwy's."

Uriens caressed her cheek. "I love you most, Morgana, when you're being kind. What a noble thing for you to do!"

"You're kind for allowing it." *Fool.* She pressed her lips against his and teased him with her tongue, thinking she would have to arrange for Accolon to accompany her as escort.

# Chapter 5

# The Arrival

Gwenhwyfar's party rounded a bend and broke through the forest line. Cadwy's fort came into view and she felt her face pale. From the road, the Roman structure looked like a small city nestled at the summit several hundred feet upward. The earthworks on the steep slopes consisted of four lines of bank-and-ditch defense; a deadly palisade of wooden stakes protruded from the first bank. A thick stone curtain-wall encircled the massive plateau and a huge double-ended gatehouse sat at the end of the wide cobblestone road they rode on. She could see the guard on the battlement gesturing to someone below.

She hadn't expected this. *Cameliard's villa is so small; I could easily run it. How can I ever be a ruler here?* Her hands trembled on the reins. Cali flicked her ears back and forth.

Lancelot stopped his horse beside hers. "Cadwy's fort can seem pretty intimidating: it was a major stronghold for the Legions," he said sympathetically. "It houses one thousand soldiers plus servants, but Cai, Arthur's brother, is an efficient seneschal. He basically oversees the whole fort."

The wagons, litters, and escort slowly moved forward to the now-open gatehouse, where men were already gathering, lining the cobbled road. She threw a desperate look at Lancelot. "I can't do this."

Momentarily his eyes turned darker; then he laid his hand over hers. "I'll be here."

The warmth of his touch steadied her. *Thank God for Lancelot.* She took a ragged breath. "Ride beside me?"

Gwenhwyfar stopped her horse a few feet behind the litters. A regal-looking woman stood on the steps, obviously waiting to greet them.

"Queen Ygraine of Tintagel," Lancelot whispered. "Arthur's mother."

Gwenhwyfar watched as Elaine lifted the flap of the litter and accepted the hand of the soldier who helped her out. Even though they had spent days on dusty roads, she somehow managed to look fresh and rested. Her hair was neatly coiled, her crimson gown relatively unwrinkled. She dropped a small curtsy and smiled at Ygraine.

Gwenhwyfar could tell Ygraine approved of Elaine from her expression.

"Welcome, child." The queen's voice was quite clear. "After you've had a hot bath, we'll have time to talk." She turned to lead the way inside. The men in the escort shuffled their feet, odd smiles on their faces.

"What ails you?" Ygraine asked. "Surely, you have other things to do than gape at Arthur's bride?"

Garient answered. "I can assure you I do, my lady. I've missed Enid and my new babe." He motioned. "You have not met Arthur's bride."

Gwenhwyfar knew how she must look: a girl with wild flyaway hair sitting astride a horse, dressed in men's clothing. She tried to wipe some of the road dust from her smudged face. She could feel the disbelief of Arthur's mother, and it didn't help when a red-haired man appeared on the steps.

"Is that her?" he asked bluntly.

"I think so, Cai," Ygraine said weakly.

Cai grinned. "This is going to be interesting."

Gwenhwyfar clenched a fist and tried desperately to act as though she hadn't heard. *His mother doesn't like me and his brother insults me. Elaine can have Arthur. I'm going back home.* She turned desperately to Lancelot. "I can't. . . ."

"Yes, you can." Lancelot reached over and touched her arm. "Let me introduce you."

She wanted nothing more than to hold on to him, but people were watching and she forced herself to smile. He nodded slightly and they moved their horses forward.

Ygraine recovered enough to be gracious and took Gwenhwyfar to the bathhouse after the introductions had been made. To Gwenhwyfar's delight, the old Roman hypocausts still worked and the baths had been maintained. She took her time progressing from the tepidarium to the heat of the caldarium and the final chill of the frigidarium. Anything she could do to delay going back to those people.

She was shown her room upstairs when she'd returned. Cai, mayhap in an effort to make up for his remark, had promised more rich tapestries and thick rugs, but she had assured him the room was fine. A garderobe was situated at the end of the hall and a door linked her room to Arthur's quarters. She had not ventured to open it.

Later, she explored the Great Hall. On the ground floor, the main entrance led to an eating area that could easily seat two hundred people. The high table ran parallel to the back wall while the lower trestle tables were perpendicular to it. Pennants and banners of the warlords pledged to Arthur

hung on the walls, their brilliant colors softening the harsh-
ness of the grey stone walls. A large hearth was built into the
side of the west wall, and the dais that would hold the throne
chair was at the east side. A hallway ran between the dining
area and the rooms behind it. The hallway doors opened to
the outside at either end. The western one led to a walled
herbal garden, the pungent fragrances competing with the
savory flavors of the nearby kitchens. An old but usable
Roman chariot stood propped against one of the walls.

She walked back the length of the hall and opened a door
at the far end. She stepped inside and gasped. The room
housed a great circular table with high-backed chairs. This
must be the Round Table that Lancelot had told her about.
The one Myrddin had brought, somehow, from across the
sea. Its purpose for being round was that each man invited to
sit at it would have an equal voice, and decisions would be
made by consensus. Lancelot had told her how Arthur had
said it would help bring unity. She walked around it now, admiring the highly polished oak. The chairs had the names of
Arthur's Cymbry engraved on them. She stopped when she
got to Lancelot's, situated to the right of Arthur's. Her fingers traced the carving of the letters. Forlornly, she wondered where he was. There would be no chess game and
conversation tonight. She sighed and closed the door.

She wandered to the dining hall and was relieved to find it
still empty before supper. She walked to a window and
watched the people going about their business. *Just like
Cameliard. I wonder what Da is doing.* A sudden longing
filled her.

The afternoon had been tiring. Ygraine had been gracious
enough, but distant. Gwenhwyfar remembered the look of
approval she had given Elaine.

Elaine, of course, was pleased with the attention; she
would have no trouble being a part of this household.
Gwenhwyfar sighed. *If only Arthur had chosen Elaine!*

"You must be Gwenhwyfar."

She spun around. At the back entrance stood a petite woman with long, raven black hair. Her eyes were nearly as dark as her hair and slanted slightly upward, accented by fragile cheekbones. She wore a silken gown of dark red wine, which contrasted with the porcelain color of her skin. The soft material outlined the curve of her body perfectly.

"I'm Morgana, Arthur's sister." Her voice was seductively soft as she came forward and embraced Gwenhwyfar. She smelled of some musky spice that Gwenhwyfar couldn't place. "I am looking forward to having you here!" Morgana stepped back and tilted her head. "You're pretty, too. Arthur chose well."

Gwenhwyfar smiled gratefully. *Someone from Arthur's family who accepts me!* "Thank you," she replied, "but I didn't know Arthur had two sisters; I knew only of Margawse, Lot's widow."

"Margawse is my older sister, the mother of several of Arthur's men." She gave a little giggle. "She's much older than I am; I have only a small son, much too young for all of this." She waved a hand at the courtyard.

"Do you live here?" Gwenhwyfar asked.

"No, my dear. I'm married to Uriens, king of Rheged. However, I do have some land nearby, left to me by my father, Gorlois." She paused. "I was thinking that I might spend some time there. I don't know Arthur well, since we were told of his true parentage only several months ago. Now I've found that I have a new sister too!" Morgana looked wistful. "We could be a family."

Gwenhwyfar nodded quickly. "Yes, I'd like that. I don't know Arthur well, either." As soon as she spoke, she blushed. "What I mean is . . ."

Morgana gave a light, silvery laugh. "I understand. Arthur can be somewhat forceful. You're young, and about to become the high queen, and probably a mother as well. It's a lot of responsibility for you."

"A mother?" Gwenhwyfar blanched, reaching for the windowsill with one hand.

"For certes." Morgana looked concerned. "The king will want an heir as quickly as possible." She smiled again. "Does the thought of bearing a child frighten you, Gwenhwyfar?"

She swallowed hard and whispered, "Yes." *She liked children, but women died in childbirth.*

Morgana patted Gwenhwyfar's arm. "I've borne a child and had an easy time of it because I used a potion that made the begetting easy and the delivery painless. I will share it with you, if you'd like. That's what sisters are for."


"I see you two have met." Ygraine entered the hall and gave an almost imperceptible nod of approval at Gwenhwyfar's simple green linen gown and somewhat more tidy hair. "If you will take your places here beside me, I believe the others are on their way."

The large room filled quickly and Elaine joined them at the raised table.

"When Arthur is here, he chooses men to sit at this table as well," Ygraine explained, "but tonight, we can enjoy our woman talk without listening to stories of battle and feats."

Gwenhwyfar would much rather have talked of battles and horses than women's chores, but she held her tongue. She did not want to offend Ygraine and she didn't know how Morgana felt about such things, either. Morgana sat on the other side of Ygraine and appeared to be more interested in the attention of a blue-eyed young man with long dark hair who sat at one of the lower tables.

Garient brought his wife, Enid, to the high table and introduced her. She was a short, rather plump woman with a big smile. Gwenhwyfar liked her immediately. Unfortunately, Ygraine did not invite them to sit.

She listened marginally to Elaine and Ygraine chatter, responding appropriately as needed, while she watched the

jester, Dagonet, bounce among the trestles. There were so
many people! Servants bearing heavy platters of succulent
roasted boar and tender mutton wove in and out of the
crowd. The clatter of pewter plates and loud conversation
was overwhelming. She felt very small sitting at the raised
table. At Cameliard, she and her father ate in the small private dining quarters, except when they were entertaining.
Even then, the atrium with its fountain lent a quiet atmos-
phere to the meal.

Her gaze was drawn to the door a second before Lancelot
entered. He had shaved and his dark hair glistened. He walked
directly to the high table and stopped in front of Gwenhwyfar.

"I thought you'd want to know that I've given Cali an
extra large stall, and Glena has a special spot there as well."

"Thank you, Lancelot!" She smiled delightedly at him,
wishing he could sit beside her. *I've already heard enough
about spinning and weaving and embroidery work that must
be done.* But Ygraine did not invite him, so he grinned back
and bowed before he went to find a seat.

"You called him Lancelot?" Ygraine inquired. "I believe
the men call him Lancer."

"That's just my name for him."

Ygraine's attention was diverted. She gave a quick frown
of disapproval. Gwenhwyfar followed her gaze.

The woman who stood just inside the hall was ethereal.
She was petite, and her straight white dress was overlaid
with a plain soft blue tunic. Her hair was the color of high
moonrise and her eyes the blue green of the sea on a cloudless day.

The man beside her was equally awesome. He was only
of medium height, lean and wiry, but he radiated power. As
Gwenhwyfar watched, he swatted at the air over his shoulder
and a spectrum of light seemed to gather. She blinked and
studied him. Unlike the soldiers, he wore a dark blue robe.
His tawny hair fell to his shoulders, but his eyes held
Gwenhwyfar spellbound. They were the same color as his

hair, and with his hooked nose, he gave the appearance of a hawk or an eagle. *Somehow, those eyes are familiar.*

"Who are they?" she whispered to Ygraine.

With a note of contempt in her voice, Ygraine replied, "The man is the arch-druid, Myrddin, Arthur's advisor. The woman is Nimue, a priestess from the Isle of Avallach. Pagans. I do not approve of either of them, for I am a devout Christian. They are here for the kingmaking."

Morgana sat straighter and leaned forward. "Are they going to perform the Great Rite, then?"

Gwenhwyfar asked, "What is the . . ."

"Don't speak of such things at a Christian table!" Clearly, Ygraine was upset. "Arthur's crowning will be held with a Mass in Holy Church."

Gwenhwyfar frowned. *I'll ask Morgana later.*

When she looked back, Myrddin and Nimue were seated at a small table in the corner and both were looking at her. She suddenly felt very warm. Disconcerted, she tried to pay attention to the conversation that Elaine and Ygraine had begun again. She pushed the quail in pomegranate sauce aside. What little appetite she'd had was suddenly gone.

Several minutes later, she chanced another glance in their direction. The table was empty, and Gwenhwyfar breathed a sigh of relief and gave herself over to listening to Ryden, the bard, sing the Tale of Badon.


Arthur and his men rode in the next afternoon. If the fort had been busy before, now it bustled. Amid the cloud of dust raised by churning hooves, grooms ran to collect the horses; soldiers who had remained at the fort were greeting, slapping, and exchanging stories with those returning. The serving girls came into the courtyard, some shyly, others more boldly, until all were hustled back inside by Cook. The men laughed in anticipation.

From the steps of the Great Hall, where she waited with

Ygraine and Morgana, Gwenhwyfar watched Arthur. He was taller than most men and was surrounded by a crowd, all of whom seemed to want to talk to him at the same time. Gwenhwyfar saw Lancelot break through and be greeted with a bear hug. She saw them exchange words and Arthur glanced quickly in her direction. Then he was lost in the swirl of people again.

A short time later, the crowd began to disperse and Arthur moved off toward the mews. She watched the druid and the beautiful priestess approach him. Myrddin gestured to Nimue. A look of delight crossed Arthur's face as he knelt in front of her, took both of her hands, and kissed them. He bent his head; she laid her hand on top of it.

Morgana's eyes flashed. She turned to Gwenhwyfar. "He's going to perform the Great Rite!" she whispered out of Ygraine's hearing. "That was the ritual blessing and acceptance you just saw."

"Just what is this rite, anyway?" she muttered. Did he have to look so ecstatic?

Morgana smiled, a look of excitement on her face. "It is the pagan way of accepting a new king. He is 'married' to the land through uniting with a priestess of the Goddess. If She accepts him, the land will be fertile and prosper. The ritual is ancient and not much used since the Romans brought their Christos to Britain."

"When does this happen?"

Morgana slanted a look at her. "The night of the crowning, outdoors. Part of the ritual is formal and part is private." Her eyes gleamed as she turned to go.

Gwenhwyfar didn't notice. She was flooded with mixed feelings. *Nimue is beautiful. Why would Arthur want me?* Then she shrugged. *I don't want to marry Arthur anyway, so it won't matter what he does. I don't understand why this is supposed to have some religious meaning to them.* Mayhap she could ask Lancelot.

Arthur approached her. "I'm glad you came, Gwenhwyfar."

She met his gaze and lifted her chin slightly. "I was not aware that I had a choice."

He was silent, his level grey eyes studying her. "Do you want a choice?"

Confusion overcame her again. *Is he offering me a choice? Would he actually accept the humiliation if I turned him down?* Ironically, if he would, then maybe he was everything Lancelot claimed him to be.

"I should have asked. Forgive me." Arthur bowed slightly, but his eyes were steady, watching her face. "Will you marry me, Gwenhwyfar?"

She fought the impulse to say no. More than anything, she wanted to be back at Cameliard, safe from this huge place that moved so fast. How could she be a ruler here? Cameliard was so small and so familiar. Then she thought of the shame she would bring to her father and Bedwyr. *Da will not be proud of me if I go home.* And this man would have the power to seize her father's lands.

She took a shaky breath and straightened her shoulders. "I will not back down from an agreement, my lord. I know there is no love between us, but I will do my duty."

Arthur frowned. "Duty is not what I have in mind." He touched her face lightly and she froze. He dropped his hand. "As high queen, you will have responsibilities, but I will give you as much freedom as I can. What we do, when we are alone, is a learned pleasure. You will see."

She shuddered involuntarily and he suddenly grinned and leaned toward her. "I haven't had any complaints from women, Gwenhwyfar. I think you'll like what bedding brings." He offered her his arm. "Shall we go in?"

# Chapter 6

# Camelot Is Born

From her place in the makeshift seating near the practice field, Gwenhwyfar watched Lancelot's smooth ease with his horse. She waved to him as he cantered past, and he grinned. For the past week, petty kings had been arriving at Cadwy's fort for the crowning in three days' time. Arthur arranged for his men's practices to be in game form; each afternoon men boasted, wagered, and bested each other in swordplay, lance-throwing, archery, and horsemanship. She wished she could take part in the contests, for her father had taught her well, but Arthur had just laughed and told her no man would compete against a woman.

Arthur seemed to be everywhere at once; she had never met anyone with so much energy and force. He never stopped working. She had hardly spoken to him these past days.

Still, Gwenhwyfar admitted to herself, all the proceedings kept her from thinking too much about the wedding in two days' time. This afternoon was entertaining because

Margawse's three sons accompanied her while waiting for their mother to arrive.

"Gareth was barely walking the last time I saw him," Gwalchmai commented to his younger brothers. "Do you suppose she'll bring him?"

Gaheris squinted into the sun. He was twenty-four and had been away from home as long as Gwalchmai. "That was five years ago, brother. He must be nearly seven by now. Still a little young to travel this far."

"More likely, she'll bring Lamorak with her!" Agravaine sneered. At eighteen, he had recently joined his brothers.

"What would be wrong with that?" Gaheris asked.

"Nothing, if you don't mind that our father's killer sent his son up there to seduce our mother!" Agravaine's face turned red.

"His death was an accident. Pellinore never meant to kill him! Lamorak is helping our mother, not seducing her," Gaheris said heatedly.

Gwalchmai intervened, "Why that old man was even in the battle, I'll never know. He should have stayed home looking for that strange beast he says lives in his forest. But Gaheris is right, Agravaine, Lamorak is our friend. If the rumors are true . . ."

Agravaine interrupted, "I rode there with Arthur, remember? I saw the way Lamorak looked at her, like a stallion scenting a brood mare."

Gwalchmai held up his hand. "Enough, brother! Do I have to remind you that we have Arthur's bride present? I'm sure she would rather not listen to this!" He turned to her. "Forgive us, Lady."

Gwenhwyfar shook her head, thinking how different these three brothers were. They looked nothing alike. At twenty-eight, Gwalchmai was massive, nearly as tall as Arthur, fair-headed, and gallant with the ladies. She had heard that some time ago he had killed a woman, but she found that hard to believe. Agravaine was short, wiry, and swarthy. Even at his young age, his attitude was cynical. Gaheris had brown hair, a medium build, and a quiet air of authority. He and Lancelot were friends. The brothers argued constantly. She sometimes wondered if they all had the same father.

"Were your mother and Morgana close?" she asked, changing the subject.

Gwalchmai shook his head. "Our mother is nearly fifteen years older than Morgana. Uther married her off to Lot when Morgana was but two. He sent Morgana to the convent when she was fourteen."

She was surprised. "Why would he do that?"

"Because Uther Pendragon didn't want any reminders of Gorlois or what he had done to our grandmother!" Agravaine said angrily.

Gwalchmai glared at him and he subsided, muttering to himself. Gwalchmai continued, "According to our grandmother, our aunt was a strange child. When she started practicing enchantments, Ygraine feared for her soul, and Uther sent her to the abbey near his fort, Ambresbyrig."

"How do you know all this?" Gaheris asked him.

"Because, brothers, I listen to our grandmother's stories and I ask questions, unlike you two muddlebrains." With that, Agravaine punched him and Gaheris intercepted and all three of them rolled off the bench onto the ground.

Gwenhwyfar moved away, thinking about Morgana. She certainly was an enigma.


From her seat at the high table, Gwenhwyfar looked over the crowd seated at the trestles. Dagonet was in rare form, but she couldn't enjoy his antics tonight. The night before the wedding, the men were rowdy in anticipation of the next day's event, followed by the huge feast that would last all day. The cooks had been preparing tantalizing sauces and sweet puddings for several days. Bread had been baked for the common trenchers, and tomorrow the spicy scent of meat pasties would fill the air, as well as the succulent scents of roasting boar and venison. Hundreds of barrels of ale and wineskins were stored. Aelle sent several skins of mead. Gwenhwyfar liked the honey-flavored warmth, and Arthur promptly put it away to be enjoyed "later," he said.

She looked at him now, seated next to her. Her impression of him had changed somewhat. She still thought him arrogant, but she also saw what power he had among the men and how they followed his authority. Then, too, when she told him she wanted to help train the horses, he had agreed instantly. "Palomides and Lancelot will like that. You've made quite an impression on both of them," he'd said.

Lancelot. The name had stuck; nearly everyone was using it. He had left Camelot suddenly after that last practice she had watched and she wondered why.

Even Morgana was not available. Aside from the early morning when she brought Gwenhwyfar the drink that would make conceiving a child easier, she had been hard to find. Gwenhwyfar observed her leaving with the young blue-eyed man, Accolon, through the postern gate one day and wondered where she had obtained a key.

In the midst of all the gaiety, Gwenhwyfar felt quite alone. Even her father, who had arrived this morning, was involved with men at Bedwyr's table. She had met so many people like Lancelot's brother, Ector, and his cousins, Bors and Lionel and . . . suddenly, she became aware of being watched.

The man had a sinister look. His grey hair was flattened and hung in strings about his face. His eyes were pale and bulged slightly. The thick lips under his beard gave him a soft, pudgy look.

"Arthur, who is that?"

He followed her look. "Ah, that would be Maelgwyn," he said. "He's harmless enough. He's Gorlois's son from his first marriage, before my mother. His lands are on the other side of the Isle."

She noticed that neither Myrddin nor Nimue was present this evening. Gwenhwyfar wondered what thoughts were going through the priestess's mind this night. She broached the subject of the Rite once with Arthur, but he had told her not to concern herself. She wondered if he was trying to shield her or if brusqueness was just his way.

Myrddin also confused her. Sometimes he mumbled over his shoulder, apparently to thin air; once, she thought she heard faint distant laughter, but he was alone. She would find him watching her, on occasion, with those penetrating, odd-colored eyes. When she tried to converse with him, he answered shortly and excused himself on some errand. The day after Arthur returned, he and Myrddin had an argument. Angry voices could be heard, but not clearly. She heard her name mentioned. When Myrddin had left, she went to Arthur, but he had put his finger to her lips and then quickly kissed her on her cheek and walked away.

It was the only kiss he had given her.


Gwenhwyfar woke early on her wedding day and sat up in bed, listening to the sad call of a dove outside her window. The bailey was coming to life, the scullery maids cleaning utensils, others bringing fresh eggs from the henhouse, and the stableboys grooming the horses for today. Some of the soldiers left garrison duty; others came on. Regular, everyday events like at home, in Cameliard. At least her father was here. She thought back to the conversation they had had yesterday.


*"Are you feeling better about this marriage, Daughter?" Leodegrance asked when they were alone in Arthur's private living quarters upstairs.*

*"I've agreed to it, Da. I'll do my duty."*

*"Does he not treat you well?" Her father's voice was full of concern.*

She shrugged. *"Well enough. We haven't spent much time together. There are always people around, wanting something."*

*"Have you made friends here?"*

*"Oh, yes. Arthur's sister, Morgana, has been good to me. We visit every morning."* She stopped, embarrassed to tell her father about the potion for fertility. *"And then there's Lancelot."*

*"The dark-haired one who escorted you here?"*

*"Yes."* Gwenhwyfar smiled. *"We spend a lot of time talking, working the horses, playing chess in the evenings . . ."*

Leodegrance frowned. *"And where is Arthur?"*

She stopped smiling. *"Arthur is always busy, Da. Lancelot has time for me. We're friends."*

*"Be careful, Gwenhwyfar. Remember, it's the high king you'll be marrying."*


The high king. She wished she could stay in bed and postpone the day. If she didn't have Lancelot's friendship, she didn't think she could abide living here. She was still apprehensive about marrying Arthur. She had seen the physical demands he made of his men. What would he expect of her? Could she be a strong queen? Or a mother?

*I'm still free; I think I'll go for a ride.* Gwenhwyfar dressed quickly, pulled the hooded cape over, and slipped out to the stables. She rubbed Glena's ears and put the bridle on Cali, climbing on her bare back as the mare knelt. They walked sedately past the gate guard and past the rows of tents that had sprung up on the slopes the last week.

She let Cali have her head once they were past the people. The wind blew her hood back and she leaned low over the mare's neck, the coarse mane hair whipping her face. Glena bounded ahead, enjoying the fresh scents of night animals.

Finally she pulled to a stop. They were several miles from

the fort, and the forest had thinned to copses of trees and thickets. A short distance from the road, at the rise of a small hill, she saw the standing stones.

Sliding off Cali, she dropped the reins and climbed the hill. It was a small circle of twelve menhirs, not quite as tall as she was. They had a bluish tint in the early morning sun. Outside the circle, between the stones, small fires had been laid but were not lit. She laid a hand on the rough texture of the stone and felt a charge of energy.

"Unless you have been prepared, it would be best to stop." The voice was soft but carried authority. Gwenhwyfar whirled in surprise.

Nimue stood beside the copse of hazel trees at the bottom of the hill. "This place has much power. The dragon lines on which the circle was built are beyond time. If you are not ready, the power can harm you. I would not wish to see our queen harmed."

Gwenhwyfar considered. It was uncanny how strong the pull was . . . and the desire to go inside. *Mayhap another time.* She stepped back.

"Is this where you will bring Arthur tomorrow night?" she asked.

Nimue's eyes were blue as the stones this morning. "What is done here tomorrow is the will of the Goddess. It will not affect you."

"That's what Arthur said!"

Nimue smiled and a pale light seemed to surround her. "Then heed him, Gwenhwyfar, and be not troubled." She called to Cali softly. "Take the queen home, noble one."

Cali raised her head, ears twitching, and trotted over to Gwenhwyfar. Astonished at the mare, she swung herself up and turned back to the road. When she reached it, she looked back to find Nimue still watching her, the white light brighter. *The sun must be reflecting off the stones.*

As the fort came into view, she saw several riders canter

out and separate in different directions. She recognized Lancelot's black, Pryderi, coming toward her. He was back! Curious, she trotted Cali to meet him.

He pulled to a stop beside her. A mixture of relief and indignation filled his face. "Thank the gods, you're safe, Gwen!" He continued, "Where have you been? Arthur has been turning the place upside down looking for you!"

"I've been out riding. Why does it matter to Arthur?"

Lancelot's eyes turned smoky, his expression inscrutable. He seemed to be searching for the right words. Finally, he simply said, "Most brides don't leave the morning of their wedding day."

Suddenly, Gwenhwyfar understood. *Arthur thought I had changed my mind! That I was running away.* What kind of embarrassment and humiliation had she already caused him? Once more, she had insulted his pride.

"Oh, Lancelot," she cried, "what have I done? How angry is he?"

"Arthur takes care not to show his anger," he answered.

"I would not run away once I've given my word." *I'm no coward.*

He started to reach out to her and then abruptly backed his horse away. "We'd better go."

"Do you believe me, Lancelot?" *You must!*

Conflicting emotions crossed his face and a muscle twitched in his cheek. "I just hope you've made the right decision."

*Ah, Lancelot. What choice do I have?* But she didn't voice the thought and silently followed him back.


"I just went for a ride, Da!" Gwenhwyfar pleaded on the steps of the hall where Lancelot had left her. "Bedwyr, did you think I would run away?"

Morgana spoke before Bedwyr could reply. "We have a wedding to prepare for, and unless you want her smelling like a horse, I would suggest you let me take her. Arthur can settle this later."

The men nodded and Morgana led Gwenhwyfar through the hall.

"Thank you, Morgana! You really are a sister to me!" she said as they made their way up the stairs.

Elaine joined them as Morgana managed to subdue Gwenhwyfar's unruly hair and added touches of herbal extract color to her face. Last she brought out a small vial and carefully put one drop in each eye. "Belladonna," she explained. "Your eyes will be more alluring."

Elaine clapped her hands. "You work magic, Morgana!"

Morgana smiled at her, but her eyes were serious as though she were contemplating another use for Elaine. Gwenhwyfar thought that Elaine had certainly become friendly with Morgana these past weeks.

Elaine brought her dress. Gwenhwyfar slipped the white samite dress carefully over her head. Its silver and gold threads shimmered. She smoothed the material hesitantly, then took a deep breath and straightened her shoulders.

"How do I look?" she asked.

Morgana held up the polished tin for Gwenhwyfar.

A queen looked back.

Arthur fidgeted with his scabbard. He tugged on his white woolen tunic, studying the silver border of embroidery along its edges. He whistled and glanced at the ceiling. Bedwyr, Cai, and Lancelot stood watching him silently.

They were in the priest's little daub and wattle hut, next to the church in the village square. The bells for Nones had chimed some time before. Gwenhwyfar was late.

Finally, Lancelot broke the silence. "She'll be here."

Arthur nodded. He was surprised to realize how much he

wanted Gwenhwyfar. His first marriage to Leonora had been
a forced one due to a careless pregnancy and an enraged
warlord father whom Uther had wanted appeased. She had
been sickly throughout her time and when the babe came
early, they both died. He had long ago suppressed his urge
for Nimue, the one woman he couldn't have, and decided he
would remain single. Marriage shackled a man. Then came
the vote for high kingship and he realized he would need a
wife. Myrddin had made a list of possibilities based on po-
litical alliances, but he had despaired at the thought of
spending his life with any of them, even if he decided to
continue wenching on the side. Gwenhwyfar had not been
on Myrddin's list, but her father was a powerful ally and
Arthur had been amazed that Gwenhwyfar understood the
things he liked to talk about: battles, horses, and the need for
unity. He enjoyed needling her; he liked women with fire in
their souls. Wild-haired, stubborn, quick-tempered: certes,
never boring! This morning, he'd found that she, her horse,
and her dog had all been missing.

The noise outside stopped suddenly, and a shout went up.
The carriage and its escort were arriving. Relieved, Arthur
grinned and all four men hurried outside. Arthur took his
place by the doorway of the church.

Gwalchmai dismounted and went to open the carriage
door. A hush fell over the square as the woman in white
stepped down.

Gwenhwyfar had been transformed. Her coppery hair
was piled in curls on top of her head. Her green eyes were
exceptionally dark, the pupils dilated. A faint touch of green
on the eyelid enhanced their color. Her cheeks and lips were
pink. She trembled slightly and the samite reflected the sun's
gold and silver rays.

Arthur was spellbound. She appeared to be blushing. *In
anticipation, I hope.* He remembered how she had tensed at
his touch that first day. *Well, I can change that tonight.* He

felt a familiar sensation begin in his loins. He bit the inside of his cheek, hard. *Later.*

Leodegrance approached him, escorting Gwenhwyfar.

"Arthur, I give you my only daughter, Gwenhwyfar. Give me your oath that you will treat her well, protect her, and honor her."

Arthur looked into her eyes, the color of a forest's twilight. He took her hand and said simply, "I will honor and protect you for as long as I live, Gwenhwyfar. I give you my oath as a man and as the future king." He tucked her hand inside his arm and turned to walk into the church.

As they passed Lancelot, he made a choking sound. Arthur paused, but Lancelot stared straight ahead. *He certainly has been acting strangely the past few days.* "Are you coming, Lancelot?" Arthur asked.

Lancelot took a deep breath, glanced once at Gwenhwyfar, and then nodded to Arthur. "After you."


Inside the church, the air was cool and sweet with the smell of incense. Bishop Dubricius motioned the congregation to be seated and began his marriage sermon by quoting Ephesians: "Wives, submit yourselves unto your husbands as unto the Lord." As Gwenhwyfar listened to what he was saying about women being the weaker vessel, she felt her temper begin to rise. She saw a muscle twitch in Arthur's cheek and could have sworn he was trying to repress a smile. *If he thinks I'm going to be subservient . . .* The bishop was speaking to her. The vows. Arthur had just finished.

"Do you, Gwenhwyfar of Cameliard, take Arthur Pendragon to be your lawful wedded husband . . . forsaking all others, until death do you part?"

*Forsaking all others.* She wanted nothing more than to look back at Lancelot, but she didn't dare. He had said he hoped she'd made the right decision. Was this what he meant?

*If only you were standing here beside me, Lancelot, I'd have no qualms in saying yes.* But Lancelot had not indicated anything more intimate than friendship. He treated her with the utmost respect. Yet, being with him, she felt utterly content doing even the most mundane tasks. With Arthur, she was always on edge.

"Gwenhwyfar?" The bishop interrupted her thoughts and she saw Arthur's face, his mouth set, his gaze steady. He lifted an eyebrow.

*I can't back out. I must make my da proud.* She took a deep breath and willed her voice not to tremble. "I do."

Sunlight broke across Arthur's face as he grinned boyishly and slipped the gold band on her finger. He drew her to him for a thorough kiss which left her somewhat dizzy and more than a little embarrassed.

*Until death do us part. I have made my vow; now I must honor it.*

Many of the barrels and flasks quickly emptied as the feast began. The laverer brought the fingerbowls of scented sage and rosemary water to the high table as the servants hurried to and fro, carrying huge platters of sizzling meat and steaming gravies. The bard strummed his harp while the jugglers and acrobats moved gracefully through the crowds.

Gwenhwyfar was listening to King Pellinore, Elaine's uncle. She found him interesting. He talked about chasing a strange beast in the forests near his land. He had not really seen the entire animal, just a hide here, or a leg there, once a part of a head with huge horns. As his cup got refilled, the story changed somewhat.

Agravaine staggered up to the table. "Pellinore, I demand retribution!" he shouted. "You killed my father!" The huge room suddenly became still. "You sent your son to seduce my mother!"

Arthur leaped over the table and put Agravaine in a stranglehold that bent his head down to his thighs and then forced him to the floor on his knees.

"Let me have him," Gwalchmai said as he and Gaheris rushed over.

"No." Arthur continued to hold Agravaine in the same position. He looked over the crowd. "Return to what you were doing." It was a command, not a request.

Gwenhwyfar was amazed when the noise and activity resumed. Arthur looked at Pellinore. "Your choice. What would you have done to him?"

Pellinore reached a gnarled hand across the table. "I'm sorry, boy. I never meant to kill your father. I mistook him for the enemy."

"Don't apologize, Pellinore." Margawse was standing in front of Arthur, Lamorak beside her. "I'll handle this." Her brown eyes were piercing; her flaming hair, much redder than Cai's, fairly crackled.

Slowly Arthur released his hold on Agravaine, and Margawse grabbed his hair and threw his head back. She slapped his face, first on one cheek, then on the other.

"Do you want more?" she asked. He whimpered.

She leaned low and grabbed his chin with her other hand. "Since you are so concerned about my welfare," she said, "I will tell you that I choose my own bed partners, not the other way around. Do you understand?"

He tried to nod. She shook his head. "Answer me." She raised her hand to cuff him, but Lamorak caught it. She looked sharply at him for a moment and then stepped back, releasing Agravaine to his brothers, who promptly dragged him out of the hall. Gwenhwyfar breathed a sigh of relief.

Pellinore shook his head and looked at his son, Lamorak. "I thought I was doing the right thing by sending you. I guess that's why your mother sent your younger brother away to be raised by Dyonas of the forest. She doesn't want the last of her sons getting involved with war and bloodshed."

Lamorak reached across the table to pat his father's arm. "You have done the right thing, Father. Put it from your mind."

Arthur agreed, "Let's put this to rest. Who will toast my new bride and me?"

A round of toasts ensued. Finally, Cadwy called for silence. He was an elderly man, but his back was as straight as any young soldier. Beneath a full head of grey hair, his blue eyes still held a zest for life. He stood in front of Arthur and Gwenhwyfar as he addressed the crowd.

"I have fought with many of you," he began, "and I was Uther's captain." Heads nodded around the room. "When I met young Arthur, I had no idea he was Uther's son. Uther did not treat him with any special favor." Again, the older heads nodded. "In fact, Uther gave him the job of procurator, a position no one envies!" Laughter filled the room. "Arthur earned his way, first as squire to me, then as my right hand." The men responded with shouting and stamping.

"I've never had children," Cadwy said, turning to face Arthur. "You have been like a son to me. For your wedding gift, I am giving ownership of this fort to you."

A roar of approval made even the high table shake.

Cadwy quickly turned to Gwenhwyfar. "My dear, this fort has simply been known as Cadwy's. What would you have it called?"

Gwenhwyfar blushed with pleasure. "You honor me, Lord Cadwy." She hesitated, thinking. "My father told me that your late wife called this place Camelot because she thought Camulos, the war god with the invincible sword, befitted you." She glanced at Arthur. "I think if Arthur is to keep the barbarians away, we should revive the name. For him, and to honor your wife."

A brief look of melancholy passed over Cadwy's face. Then he smiled at Gwenhwyfar and turned to Arthur. "Your wife is as thoughtful and charming as she is beautiful.

You've chosen well." He raised his cup. "To a united Britain and the destiny of Camelot!"

Gwenhwyfar returned to her seat while Arthur accepted congratulations from his men. Morgana joined her, carrying two wine goblets. She gave one to Gwenhwyfar.

"Drink this, Gwenhwyfar. It will calm your nerves." She took a sip from her own glass. "Soon, Arthur will want you to go with him."

Gwenhwyfar started. With Agravaine's outburst and then the news from Cadwy, she had almost forgotten what still remained for the night. She picked up the heavy crystal and took a big swallow. The taste was slightly bitter.

Morgana smiled and patted her hand. "This is your wedding night, Gwenhwyfar. You should enjoy Arthur. He will certainly take his pleasure of you. The wine will help you relax and will ease the pain."

"The pain, Morgana. How bad will it be?" She was apprehensive now, for Morgana had told her on several occasions that the first time would hurt and there would be blood.

Morgana smiled again. "Drink, Gwenhwyfar; it won't be so bad."

Dutifully, if doubtfully, Gwenhwyfar drained the cup. She watched as Bedwyr challenged Lancelot to arm wrestling and soon men surrounded them, shouting encouragement and taking wagers, for they were well matched.

Arthur returned to the high table. He covered Gwenhwyfar's smooth hand with his own callused one. Leaning toward her, he whispered, "I had those two arrange that so no one will notice our leaving. Are you ready?"

*No! I want to stay here, where it's safe.* But she nodded and stood and immediately toppled against him.

"Are you all right?" he asked, steadying her. "Did you have too much wine?"

She shook her head. "No, just two cups this whole night." She leaned on Arthur as he supported her up the stairs.

Arthur barred the door to his quarters. Gwenhwyfar looked around the room, but objects were swaying in front of her. She felt dizzy. She sat down on the edge of the bed gingerly. Arthur smiled and came to her. He raised her hand to his lips, then released it and ran his fingers up her arm, caressing her neck. She tilted her head slightly and closed her eyes. The room stopped spinning.

He loosened her hair and let the curls tumble, then traced her eyebrows with his thumbs, following the curve of her high cheekbones. His touch felt light and gentle. He slid his hands to her shoulders and leaned forward to kiss her slowly. She stirred slightly and parted her lips at the pressure of his tongue. She felt very mellow; mayhap this wasn't going to be so bad.

He stopped suddenly and shook her. "Wake up, Gwenhwyfar. Open your eyes. Look at me!"

She opened them slowly. "Wha . . . ?" she asked groggily.

"Poison, Gwenhwyfar. I tasted the bitterness on your tongue." He pulled her to her feet and started walking her around the room.

She protested. "I don't . . . want . . . to dance."

"Neither do I," he said grimly, "but I've got to keep you moving until whatever you took leaves your system. You ate or drank something that was drugged."

Gwenhwyfar lost track of the number of times they circled the room. Her head was whirling and she wanted to lie down, but Arthur kept her moving.

Hours later, Gwenhwyfar finally returned to herself. She sat at the small oak table, still in her white dress, sipping the water Arthur had given her from a flask. Her mouth felt like parchment. Arthur sat on the edge of the bed with his head in his hands.

"I can't believe that someone would deliberately wish me ill," she said weakly.

"I think it was meant for me, Gwen. Maybe not all the kings want a high king, after all. Anyone could have done it; we were surrounded by people." He held out his hand and Gwenhwyfar moved to sit next to him. "Are you feeling well enough . . . ?"

Gwenhwyfar looked at the floor. This was what she had been dreading. At least Morgana had prepared her. "Yes," she said in a small voice.

Arthur tilted her chin with his hand. "It must be done. The bloody sheets must be offered as proof of your virginity in the morning."

She stared at him. "Will there be lots of pain?"

"Pain?" He looked puzzled; then he grinned. "Not if I do this right. Let me introduce you to one of life's greatest pleasures."

He eased her back onto the soft bed and began a series of slow, easy kisses. Gwenhwyfar hesitated and gradually her body responded, yielding to the caress of his hand and the soft pressure of his lips. The kisses became more demanding and she felt a tingle begin in her stomach, spreading throughout her body. She met his demand, their tongues finding and tasting each other. Deftly, he unfastened her dress, sliding it down past her breasts. As he teased the nipples with his mouth, Gwenhwyfar gasped; the sensation was exquisite. She'd had no idea something could feel this good. She pulled on his shirt and he shrugged out of it as her hands explored as much of him as she could reach. Suddenly, she liked the feel of his hardened back muscles, his strong arms and broad chest.

Arthur pushed her dress farther down and traced a circle on her stomach with his tongue and she moaned. He guided her hands to undo his trews and when she saw him, she inhaled sharply, not sure, but then his fingers created a delightful diversion between her thighs until she whimpered in joyful agony.

The first thrust was gentle and Gwenhwyfar clung to him.

He eased himself into her, keeping the rhythm slow until she found herself matching him. Then, as the tension mounted, Arthur's body went rigid. Something warm flooded her and she felt herself spasm, a thoroughly new and delightful sensation. The feeling expanded and rolled through her, causing her body to quiver. Then she lay still and content.

Arthur raised himself on an elbow. He leaned over and kissed her lightly.

"Any complaints?" he asked.

She grinned up at him foolishly. *I can't believe I dreaded this!* She didn't answer, but merely trailed her fingers down his belly.

"Oh, no, you don't!" he laughed and turned her over, pressing himself up against her backside and wrapping his arms around her. "I've got to get some sleep."

As they drifted into slumber, Gwenhwyfar thought, *What was Morgana talking about? There had been no pain.*

# Chapter 7

# The Kingmaking

When Gwenhwyfar awoke the next morning, sunlight was streaming in the bedroom window and she was alone. Disappointed, she sat up.

"If I had known what being married is like," she mused aloud as she washed and donned a kirtle and slipped a tunic over, "I wouldn't have balked so." She smiled to herself, remembering Arthur's touch.

Then she sobered, remembering the drugging. Who would want to do that to her? To Arthur? They would have to be careful while all the guests were here, she thought as she went down to the dining hall.

The only person sitting at one of the long trestles was Elaine. She was not looking very happy, but Gwenhwyfar felt too good to care.

"Good morning, cousin!" She hugged her. "I must have slept later than I thought. What time is it? Where is everyone?" She buttered a soft bannock from the sideboard and went to sit next to Elaine.

"The men are grooming their horses and preparing their armor. If you're looking for Arthur, Myrddin came for him early." Elaine eyed her cousin appraisingly.

"Myrddin? Why would he come for Arthur? Arthur should be getting ready for his crowning," she said.

Elaine gave her a dour look. "No doubt, he is."

*Certes. The religious Mass and the pagan rite. Nimue.* Gwenhwyfar felt a pang of jealousy stab her. After last night, she did not want to share Arthur with anybody, especially the beautiful priestess who could talk to her horse. What other magic might she do?

"So, cousin, I take it that marriage is agreeable?"

"Very much so, Elaine," she answered with a smile. "I'm going to help you find someone! Have any of our guests caught your eye?" She took a bite of bread.

"Not a guest, no." She paused. "But there is someone I would marry."

"Oh? Whom?" Gwenhwyfar asked, chewing.

"Lancelot."

Gwenhwyfar choked. Coughing, she reached for Elaine's milk, which she drained. She swallowed several times. "Has Lancelot asked you?" she finally managed.

"Not yet," Elaine tilted her head and looked at Gwenhwyfar. "He's been smitten with you ever since we rode from Cameliard. But now you're married to the high king! Lancelot can't have you and you can't have him." She shrugged. "It's only a matter of time."

Gwenhwyfar stared at her. When, in the few short weeks they had been at Camelot, had her cousin become so bitter? *I don't want Lancelot marrying Elaine . . . but she's right: I'm Arthur's wife. I swore my oath.*

She tried to sound calm. "Lancelot and I are friends. I see no harm in continuing to remain so."

Elaine snorted. "We'll see how much Arthur approves of that in the future!"

Gwenhwyfar stood up. "I believe he will, Elaine. And,"

she added as she turned to go, "I believe Lancelot will have a wife of his choosing, not yours!"

She met Morgana on her way out. Morgana gave her a sly smile and Gwenhwyfar wondered how much she had heard.

The church bells chimed at Sext. Gwenhwyfar shivered in anticipation even though the August sun warmed the cobbles of the village square. Arthur's polished hauberk glistened. Beneath it, he wore a finely woven crimson tunic embroidered with gold. His trews were of the softest doeskin, as were his boots. Ygraine adjusted the golden mantle over Arthur's shoulder so the red dragon on the back would fall properly. She stepped back and nodded.

"You're ready."

Arthur drew a deep breath and looked from his mother to Gwenhwyfar. "I only hope I can fulfill these vows that I'm about to take. I must be able to unite Britain and establish peace." He turned to face his Cymbry.

They were impressive with their red mantles over their left shoulders, and their swords held hilt-to-the-chin at attention. Both sides of the walkway across the village square to the church were filled. Lancelot's father, Ban, and his brother, Ector, had come from Benoic. The petty kings, who had agreed to his high kingship, lined the paths as well: Cador of Kelliwic, Marc of Kernow, Cato of Dumnonia, Agricola of Glevum, Pellinore, and Leodegrance. Their torques gleamed and their armor flashed in the sunshine.

As Arthur passed through his columns of Cymbry, men started clapping and stomping until, by the time he reached the church door, the earth was rumbling. Lancelot set the great dragon standard to the right of the church door while Bedwyr set Arthur's personal bear standard to the left. Gwenhwyfar's heart swelled with pride. She wished she'd had a chance to talk to Arthur today.

Bishop Dubricius welcomed him. He made the sign of

the cross and led Arthur to the altar. Mass was celebrated, and Arthur knelt to take his vows. A stillness settled.

The bishop intoned, "Arthur Pendragon, son of Uther and Ygraine, the stewardship of Britain is about to be placed in your keeping. We will hear your pledge."

"By all that is holy, I vow this day my life, my honor, and the strength of my sword to unite this land and keep it free, and to establish justice for all. I do so pledge."

Arthur bent his head to receive the Church's blessing. The candles from the altar lit his face, erasing the hardened lines of the warrior and giving him the appearance of an earnest youth.

From her place in the first pew, Gwenhwyfar saw the radiance of Arthur's face. She felt a deep stirring of loyalty to his goal, his belief. *Justice will be my goal as well. We will unite the people and bring peace to the land.*

The bishop raised Arthur and placed the gold torque around his neck. As one, the kings and Cymbry rose and gave the Roman salute. Arthur turned and held out his hand to Gwenhwyfar. Surprised and pleased, she stood and went to him. He placed her hand on his arm and they proceeded down the aisle.

As they stepped into the sunlit square, the crowd broke into applause and stomping once more.

The bishop came out and held his hand for silence. When the crowd quieted, he announced, "A high king is crowned this day and blessed by the Holy Church. This king will bring unity and justice to all people. It is his pledge." He paused. "I give to you: King Arthur Pendragon and his queen, Gwenhwyfar."

The crowd roared. Gwenhwyfar sought her father. When she saw his face, she knew she had made him proud.

On Avallach, Nimue was being prepared. She had been fasting since sunset the day before, but the lightheadedness had not yet settled on her.

As dawn broke, Nimue stood in the Temple of the Sun on the summit of the Tor. She felt the strengthening of the sun's warmth on her bare skin as she lifted her arms and chanted, "I salute the East, from which our birth forms and leadership is borne on airy wings. May the king who comes to me tonight be a true leader."

"I salute the South," she said as she turned, "for the fires of enlightenment and clarity. May the king receive both of these gifts."

She faced west. "I salute the West, the waters of the Beyond to which all souls go for rest. May the king prevail."

"I salute the North, the plain of our Earth and our abundance. May your fertility be proved this night."

She turned from the north and faced the east again and lowered her arms. "The circle has been closed, Lady."

Vivian nodded. One of the priestesses produced a bundle carefully wrapped in sun-bleached linen. She shook out the dark blue robe that only the Lady of the Lake was allowed to wear. She held it for Nimue.

Nimue looked from it to Vivian. "Surely, Lady, I cannot wear . . ."

"Tonight you will be Her representative. This day I am only another priestess."

Nimue's fingers stroked the delicately spun wool; the ancient symbols embroidered in silver threads reflected the golden sunlight. She pulled it close, enjoying its softness.

As they made their way back to the sanctuary, Vivian summoned Nimue to her chambers. As she entered, Nimue looked at the tapestry where the white hart gazed at her solemnly. Her life certainly had changed since the last time she had been here.

On the table stood an old wooden crate. Nimue had never seen it before. Vivian beckoned her. Her eyes widened as she noted the craftsmanship that had gone into the carving. Images of gods and goddesses long ago worshipped, along with many sacred symbols that she recognized, were worked into the wood. A small gold lock secured the box.

"What is this?" she asked.

Vivian produced a small silver key. Carefully she opened the box and lifted out the object rolled in fine silk.

The sword rested inside an oiled leather scabbard of burgundy color that was engraved with the same symbols as the box. Nimue ran her hand lightly over the scabbard. It was smooth and soft to her touch, and she could feel the still-potent ancient powers. Much ritual had gone into the labor of this scabbard.

"Yes," Vivian said, reading her thoughts. "The scabbard is sacred. Its power to protect is still very strong. The last man to wear it was Magnus Maximus."

"Macsen Wledig?" Nimue used the Briton name. "This is his sword?"

"He wore this sword; he used it. It belongs to the Goddess," Vivian said. "The story goes beyond that of Magnus. In the time before the druids, a great star fell from the sky. This sword was fashioned from that metal. Its original name was Caladvwlch; Magnus renamed it Excalibur."

Nimue hesitantly reached for the sword. Energy radiated from it. She closed her hand on the hilt and pulled gently. Excalibur sang as she lifted it. The blade's metal reflected her image back to her. The edges were honed to a sharpness that matched those of the surgeons' knives. The guard was overlaid in gold and from the pommel, a large rare ruby flashed like firelight.

Excalibur felt good in her hand. She didn't know much about weapons, but she knew this one must be perfectly balanced, for she had no trouble gliding it through the air. Reverently, she replaced the sword.

Vivian spoke. "It is Arthur's until his final battle. Then it returns to the Lady. Take the sword, Nimue, and sit with it this day. Learn its stories. Share your thoughts. Add your energy to what is already there. Your power will help protect

Arthur as well, for once he marries the land, there will always be a connection through you." The Lady smiled. "Now go and be alone until we come for you."


Shortly before sunset Myrddin came for Arthur.

Arthur led Valiant to where Gwenhwyfar stood near the hall's entrance. He cupped her chin in his hand and gave her a quick kiss. She could tell his mind was elsewhere; tentatively, she wrapped her arms around his neck.

He squeezed her shoulder, then disengaged himself and mounted. "You know I must go, Gwenhwyfar."

*How can you be so detached, Arthur? After last night? And you seem almost eager to be gone.* Aloud, she asked, "How many of the men ride with you?"

He glanced down at her. "Myrddin and I ride alone. The men and women who keep the Old Ways will follow soon."

Myrddin appeared beside Arthur astride his white mule. "It's time, Arthur. The moon will be rising soon, and you still have preparations."

Arthur nodded and nudged Valiant to a walk.

With a nod to Gwenhwyfar, Myrddin urged his mule to a trot.

She stared after them. *He will do with Nimue what he did with me.* She tried to repress the thought, but it stuck in her mind. *And I will be alone.*


When Nimue and the other priestesses arrived at the stone circle, dusk had fallen and the delicious aroma of fresh bread wafted up the hill, for Lugnasad was the celebration of the summer harvest. The slope was alight with needfires. Climbing down from the wagon, the priestesses took their positions by each fire bundle.

Nimue caught sight of Myrddin standing outside of the

circle, arguing with his faerie. Strands of the conversation floated to her.

"But I want to go in," the faerie pouted. "*He* will be there. I haven't seen . . ."

"I forbid it. This is Arthur's night."

"*She* won't know I'm there," the faerie wheedled, tweaking Myrddin's ear.

He swatted at her. "No. I would ask for your oath, but faeries place no faith in oaths."

She looked hurt. "If he calls for me . . ."

"He won't," Myrddin said snappishly. "Now be silent or I will send you away."

Nimue smiled and approached, carrying the wrapped sword and scabbard.

Myrddin straightened when he saw it, his argument apparently forgotten. "Caladvwlch is to be his, then," he said softly.

She nodded. "I will present it to him at the close." She looked out at the people. "I had not thought there would be so many."

Myrddin answered softly, "Many follow the Old Ways, although some may agree to be Christian. The people believe in the Great Rite, Nimue. Uther didn't perform it, but Ambrosius did, and it was during his reign that Hengist was brought down."

Vivian nodded. "Ambrosius was twice blessed by the Goddess, I remember." She turned to Nimue. "The moon rises; I have already placed the cups on the altar. Remember that what happens this night is the Goddess's will."

Nimue took a deep breath and entered the circle. Behind her, the priestesses lit the fires, set the newly made corn dolls in front of them, and began the ritual chanting that would continue throughout the night.

Nimue approached the cromlech and placed her bundle on the ground beside it. She stepped up on the altar stone and raised her arms in salutation to the moon. The large moonstone embedded on the silver headband, called a niam-lann, glowed on her forehead. She inhaled deeply. The effects of fasting were making the trance state easy. She chanted the sacred sounds to call forth the earth and sky energy. Nimue lowered her hands on the exhalation, then nodded to Vivian outside the circle.

Arthur stepped inside. He wore a mantle of deerskins, his chest and legs bare. Only a leather loincloth covered him. His headpiece was a magnificent rack of antlers.

Nimue saw the golden white aura radiate from him. She sent her own to meet his. Arthur's eyes widened, but he did not move.

Nimue said softly, "Welcome, Lord Cernunnos. I will call the Goddess. Approach and kneel."

Nimue let the robe slip from her as she picked up the chalice. Sky clad, she allowed the moonlight to wash over her as she went deeper into her trance. A moonbeam shimmered in the liquid. A child's face appeared, looking back at her. She blinked rapidly and looked again, but only the moon's reflection shone in the now-still water.

"Blessed Mother of us all, we begin as maidens; we finish as crones. This night, as Your pale light covers me, I ask that Your life energy fill me as well, that what we do here tonight will bring prosperity to this land. Come to me, Mother, that I may marry this king to the land. I draw You to me and I am one with You." She set the chalice down and picked up a smaller gold vessel.

"Join me, Cernunnos."

Arthur stood and removed his mantle, spreading it over her robe on the altar. Stepping up, he faced her.

She handed him the cup. "Drink the fruit of the kingdom from the Sun's cup."

Without taking his eyes from her face, he drained the wine. When he finished, she continued, "I am woman; I am the land. You are the Horned One who will plant the seed of prosperity this night." Nimue removed the antlers, letting them fall softly to the ground. "May the blending of our life forces please the Earth." She pulled the string of the loin-cloth to release him.

He lifted her easily as he nudged open her lips with a kiss, his tongue exploring her mouth. He knelt to lay her on the soft skins. He ran his fingers lightly across her stomach and she shivered when he nibbled her neck and traced his way down to her breasts. His tongue teased the nipple; she moaned when he began to suckle. When he kissed her again, her body responded.

Turning her away from him, Arthur slipped an arm and thigh under her for protection from the hard stone. With one hand, he continued to play with a breast; with the other, he held her firmly pressed against him as he slowly began to enter her. Nimue gave a sharp gasp and he stopped. "I don't want to hurt you."

She willed herself to relax and he began probing again, even more gently this time. Each push was a little harder, until he filled her. She wiggled, getting the feel of him, and he began the rhythmic thrusting. He moved his hand lower to massage the special woman-spot and her body shuddered. He plunged deeply, spending himself.

Nimue had not intended to enjoy this. Even with her self-induced trance, she was aware of the maleness of him, of his strength and force. She did not like the first kiss, but the nape of her neck and the tips of her breasts betrayed her. He had a gentleness she had not expected. She nearly froze at the first sharp pain, but Arthur waited for her, respected her. Suddenly, the pain disappeared, replaced with a vibration that hummed throughout her whole body.

Arthur kissed the top of her head. They lay still, locked in position, for some time, watching the moon's passage over them. In the ether above them, a rack of antlers hovered above the face of Cernunnos. Outside the circle, the faerie's emerald eyes glittered.

Finally, Arthur stirred, releasing Nimue. Sitting up, she

turned to look at him. His grey eyes were nearly slate in the pale light. The moonlight caught the sunstreaks in his hair and softened the hard angles of his face. He traced her cheek lightly.

She started to tingle. *What is wrong with me? This is not what the Goddess intended. I am a priestess, in control of my emotions.*

Arthur raised an eyebrow. "One of us is going to have to say something eventually."

Embarrassed, she reached for her robe, wrapping it around her as she stood. She mumbled, "I . . . didn't expect to react like that."

Arthur threw back his head and laughed. "I didn't expect you to, either, but I'm glad you did." He took her shoulders and turned her to face him, becoming quite serious. "I thank the Goddess for allowing me this Rite, Nimue. I shall never forget, either what it means, or you." His gaze lingered on her face; then he kissed her once and let her go. "I don't seem to have much clothing here," he finished, picking up the loincloth.

Nimue remembered the sword then. "I have something you can wear, Arthur."

He looked at her quizzically as she produced the package.

She laid it on the altar and unwrapped it. In the cool moonlight and warm firelight, Excalibur gleamed with an Otherworldly glow. The large ruby in its pommel splayed fire.

Arthur reached out his hand and touched the hilt. Excalibur thrummed. Grasping the hilt, he slid the sword from the scabbard. It emitted a soft whistling. He slashed with it, feinted, turned. It was a part of him, light and perfectly balanced.

"Where did you get this?"

She smiled. "It is the Lady's. The sword accepts only the man who can lead his people justly. Magnus Maximus was the last person to wear it. He called it Excalibur."

Reverently, Arthur moved the blade to reflect the light. Nimue handed him the scabbard.

"Treat this scabbard equally well, Arthur. The magical runes were encrusted before the time of the druids. When you wear it in battle, you will have protection from wounds and blood loss."

He caressed the pliable leather. As his fingers continued to brush it, Nimue knew he was feeling the short tingling impulses. He looked at Nimue wonderingly.

She nodded. "What you feel is the magic, Arthur. I spent the day with it and received learning. The scabbard now has my energy, as well."

Arthur knelt, holding the sword by its blade, the hilt lifted toward her. "I swear, by all that is holy, Nimue, that I will add honor to this sword. Its strength will aid me in establishing justice for this land. This night has produced its own magic."

After Arthur left, Gwenhwyfar went to the stables. Being with her horse and her dog would help. *Other than at the Mass, Arthur hardly acknowledged me today.* As she was brushing the mare, she listened to the men saddling up to follow Arthur. *I am probably the only one who won't know what actually takes place!*

Twilight was fading into night when she heard one more man walk in and toward the tack room. *A late one leaving,* she guessed as she slipped out of Cali's stall.

Lancelot was waiting for her, leaning against the wall.

Her heart gave a little leap. "Why aren't you with the others, Lancelot?"

He looked away, then shrugged. "I thought you could use a friend tonight."

*He understood!* No one else did. Elaine was still angry with her, and Morgana and Accolon had gone to the ritual. Bedwyr had told her to dismiss the whole thing. She smiled and held out her hand. "Well, friend, shall we walk and talk?"

He grinned and tucked her hand inside his arm. They

nearly bumped into Elaine as they crossed the bailey. She stared at them for a minute, then stomped away.

"What ails her?" Lancelot asked.

"Oh, we had a disagreement this morning," Gwenhwyfar answered. "It's not important. Let's go up to the battlements; I like the view from there."

They climbed the ladder and rested their arms on the merlon ledge. "Has there been any word from Palomides on bringing the horses over?" Gwenhwyfar asked.

"A messenger arrived several days ago; Palomides is having trouble purchasing so many. He has about thirty horses right now and is thinking of bringing them."

"I hope they arrive soon!"

"We could use them for the next campaign," Lancelot agreed and then asked, "Has Arthur said anything to you about a man named Cerdic?"

"No, who is he?" she asked.

Lancelot grimaced. "An upstart grandson of Vortigern, which is bad enough, but his grandmother was a Saxon. He's a mercenary that Uther paid to protect the southern shore, but I don't trust him."

"He is not loyal to Arthur?"

"Cerdic sent word of a rebel uprising near Llongborth. Arthur will need to go to him soon, but the man bears watching himself."

She was silent. *So Arthur will be leaving me already.* "How far away is this place?"

"A hard day's ride from here, although there is a good Roman road. You can see a part of it from here." He pointed southward.

Slightly to the east, she noticed a soft orange glow spreading. "What's that?"

He hesitated.

"What is it, Lancelot?" she repeated.

"Fires of Bel. It's where Arthur is," he finally said.

She looked out again, shocked. "There are so many! I

thought this ritual, this rite, whatever they call it, was supposed to be a sacred, quiet thing!"

"The rite is sacred. I was conceived through the same ritual," he said quietly.

Her eyes widened at the implication. "Is a child expected to be the result?"

"Sometimes." He looked miserable. "We shouldn't have come up here. I wanted to help you think of something else tonight."

She tucked her hand back inside his arm. "The fault is mine, Lancelot. I can't seem to control my emotions today. You know I didn't want to marry Arthur. Now, I can't stand to think of him with that beautiful priestess."

Lancelot smiled crookedly. "Being bedded sometimes affects a woman that way."

Gwenhwyfar blushed, glad that it was dark. She said, without stopping to think, "My argument with Elaine this morning was because she wants to marry you."

"Wait! What are you saying? Why would I want to marry Elaine?" He covered her hand with his. "Surely, you know that's not true! I want . . ." He stopped abruptly.

Gwenhwyfar looked up at him. He stared at her.

Their lips met gently, a soft, easy caress.

*So natural, as if I'd known him all my life.* With a start, Gwenhwyfar jerked back, a hand to her mouth.

Lancelot's face was a mixture of emotions. "Forgive me, Gwen. I will make sure this doesn't happen again."

She shook her head. "There is nothing to forgive. But you are right; this cannot happen again." She turned and started down from the battlement. Lancelot followed, but she stopped him. "No, don't come with me. I need to be alone."

Lancelot nodded and sank down against the wall. "I have some thinking to do, as well."

Gwenhwyfar was trembling by the time she reached the Great Hall. *What I really wanted, Lancelot, was not to stop at all. But I can never let you know.*

# Chapter 8

# Exposed!

The small stone building at the back of the fort had once been a shrine to Minerva, but when Ygraine arrived, she had it cleaned and rededicated as a Christian chapel. They were finishing the morning prayers at Terce when Arthur returned.

*He looks different, somehow,* Gwenhwyfar thought jealously. *More energetic, happier.* She followed him to the bailey.

He was surrounded by many of his men, although they left an empty circle around him. She could hear exclamations of surprise and awe. He was swinging a sword, and not an ordinary one. It flashed white silver in the sunlight.

She moved nearer and he saw her then. "Come, Gwenhwyfar! See what the Lady has given me!" He put his left arm around her, the right hand still brandishing the sword. "Maximus himself used it. Its name is Excalibur."

"It's beautiful," she said admiringly, but with more than a twinge of envy that Nimue had given him so fine a gift. "May I try it?"

"Don't tell me that you know how to handle a sword!" Arthur looked amused. "This one is too heavy for you."

*Does he think me too weak?* Irritated, she shot back, "I know how to handle a sword as well as any man."

The men guffawed and one or two grinned openly. Bedwyr sighed. Arthur still sounded amused. "Show me, then." He turned the sword around and extended the grip.

A startled expression crossed Lancelot's face and Gwenhwyfar frowned slightly. Somehow, she felt she had had this exchange of words at another time. She reached out for Excalibur. The sword had a lightness she hadn't expected. Its grip fit her smaller hand perfectly, just as it had fit Arthur's much larger one a moment ago. She stepped forward with her left foot, made a rising cut from the right, and moved forward again with an immediate second right cut. She lunged and thrust, feinted, and delivered two imaginary blows, one from either side. She advanced in a gliding motion as the soldiers widened the circle and then retreated smoothly. She flipped the sword and offered it to Arthur.

The men were silent.

Arthur looked at her with something close to awe as he took Excalibur and placed it in the scabbard. "Well done, Gwenhwyfar," he said, and the men broke into applause. He pulled her to him and gave her a long kiss, which brought good-natured laughter and louder applause from the group around them.

Embarrassed, she tried to push away from him, but he just held her tighter, deepening the kiss. *He is treating me like some tavern wench.*

She was in high temper when he finally released her. "Remind me to hide the weapons tonight," he whispered under the noise and grinned.

She glared at him and opened her mouth to retort, but over his shoulder she caught a glimpse of Lancelot's face. His eyes were the color of peat; his mouth was set in a straight line. He stared straight ahead, his face ashen.

"You needn't concern yourself about tonight, my lord," she hissed back and turned, forcing herself to walk regally away from the laughter that still followed her. She stopped at the herbal garden, the tears of humiliation spilling over. No one would take her seriously as a queen if Arthur were going to treat her like a common camp follower.

*Why can't you understand I want to be an equal partner?*

"Are you sure you want to do this?" Arthur asked Lancelot a short time later. They were in the map niche next to the council room that housed the Round Table. "I can send someone else."

Lancelot shook his head. He had thought about this as he sat on the battlement until near dawn. He was dangerously attracted to Gwenhwyfar. In the past, neither he nor Arthur had thought anything of sharing a woman, but this was different. He wanted Gwen, body and soul, yet he owed his loyalty to Arthur. What he had just witnessed made it impossible to stay. "Palomides said he had thirty mares and colts ready to bring back; if he brings them, he will waste valuable time in purchasing others. You know those horses have hot bloodlines and a lot of spirit. They'll be hard to handle."

Jokingly, Arthur said, "Mayhap I should send Gwenhwyfar with you since she can handle anything, it seems."

Lancelot inhaled sharply and then realized Arthur was jesting. He forced himself to smile. "If I have your permission, I would like to leave immediately. I can catch the next ship at Portus Adurni."

Arthur considered and then nodded. "Yes, I would like to have them before the winter storms set in and the sea becomes impassable. And, if the rumors that Cerdic reports are true, we may have to defend both Clausentum and Llongborth soon. Take Margawse's brood with you: mayhap you and Gwalchmai can convince Agravaine to let Lot's accident rest. Tell Cerdic I will come soon." He grinned at Lancelot.

"Since I'm married now, I intend to spend some time getting to know my wife. If our wedding night is any indication, she'll be a quick learner."

Lancelot did not trust himself to speak. Her kiss still burned on his lips.

"Go then, my friend, and come home safely. I think Gwenhwyfar is still in the garden, fuming, if you want to let her know the horses will be coming."

Lancelot took the long route to the stables, directly away from the herbal garden.

"We need to talk about how things will be managed while I'm gone," Arthur told Gwenhwyfar, several nights later after they had finished supper. They were sitting in Arthur's upstairs quarters, enjoying a cup of cider for which the region was famous.

"My mother is good with handling servants; she'll be willing to help," Arthur said after they had discussed some of the daily operations. "But I think it's time Morgana moves to her own place."

"Oh, no, Arthur! Morgana has been like a sister to me. We talk every morning, and she's helped me get adjusted here. Why should she go?"

Arthur didn't answer immediately. Something about Morgana was vaguely disturbing. He knew Accolon was besotted with her and he understood why. Morgana exuded lust with everything she did, from the way she moved and talked to the close-fitting clothes she wore. A woman who used men. And for all her sultriness, there was something . . . He didn't think she was a good influence on Gwenhwyfar. "I'm surprised that Uriens didn't take her back with him to Rheged."

"Oh, she asked him if she could stay," Gwenhwyfar replied. "She told him she wanted to help me adjust to life here and to . . ." she stopped, turning pink.

"To what?" Arthur asked.

". . . to here, to this place . . ."

"How would she know, Gwenhwyfar? She only arrived a few days before you did, and six months ago she had no idea she was my sister! To what?" he asked again. He folded his arms and waited.

She looked down at her hands. "To marriage," she whispered. "I was so scared . . . of the pain . . . of you. . . ."

Arthur stared at her. He moved around the table and lifted her from the chair.

"What nonsense has she been filling your head with?" he demanded, as the uneasy feeling that Morgana really was cold and calculating returned.

Gwenhwyfar looked back at him, wide-eyed. "I guess it was silly of me, but she told me there would be pain, lots of it when . . . and I thought . . ." she stopped again, looking down.

He tilted her chin with one hand and held it. "You thought what, Gwenhwyfar?"

"I insulted you in front of your men. I thought you were making me marry you so you could break me, like a green horse!" she blurted. "Your men would know you tamed yet another filly and your pride would be saved!"

He felt the anger building. *How could she have misunderstood these past nights of wanton sex?* He didn't want to tame her; by the gods, he wanted her wild. He turned and paced, raking his fingers through his hair. Finally, he came back to where she still stood.

"And what," he asked evenly, "do you think now?"

She bent her head and whispered, "I don't think that's true anymore."

He reached out and took her face in both his hands. "Have I hurt you?"

"No," she said softly.

"Was there pain for you on our wedding night?"

"No." Tears began welling in her eyes. "But let Morgana stay; I need a friend."

He stood for a minute, thinking. Gwenhwyfar was becoming emotional and he didn't handle emotions well. He'd never been fond of bedding virgins; they required delicate handling, then expected oaths of undying love, but Gwenhwyfar was his wife.

He put his arms around her, awkwardly rocking her like a child. She clung to him and let the tears come. He hated the tears even more. *In the few months we were together, Leonora often cried. . . .*

*I will send for Nimue. She's calm and detached. She'll know what to do.*

Several weeks passed before the men were ready to ride to Cerdic. The day before they left, Myrddin brought Nimue to Camelot. Gwenhwyfar watched them ride in, none too pleased. Arthur had been adamant, though; Morgana could stay only if Nimue were here. *He seems to trust her completely. I wish he'd put that trust in me.*

He came and stood beside her on the steps as Myrddin slid off his mule and helped Nimue down. The druid eyed Gwenhwyfar curiously. As always, she felt uncomfortable under his gaze, but at least he didn't seem hostile as they approached. In fact, he seemed to be having another argument with himself, turning as though to speak to someone who wasn't there. Annoying little habit. She turned away.

"Welcome to our home, Nimue," Gwenhwyfar said, somewhat stiffly.

Nimue studied her face and Gwenhwyfar felt a warm current pass through her. *What kind of powers does this priestess have?* "Why don't I show you the room you'll be using? Dinner will be ready soon and you might want to rest before then."

"Yes, rest would be good for me." Nimue hesitated and looked at Arthur. "I carry proof that the marriage to the land has been accepted," she said quietly.

Arthur blanched.

Gwenhwyfar looked from one to the other, puzzled for a moment. Nimue had such compassion on her face. *What was wrong? Proof? Accepted?*

Then she understood. A child. Nimue was going to have Arthur's child. She heard a great roaring in her ears and the air turned grey; she slumped onto Arthur, barely hearing the words that came from nowhere.

"I told you this was the wrong way to let her know," the faerie said angrily as she tweaked Myrddin's ear and flitted away before he could swat.

Gwenhwyfar felt Nimue's cool hand on her forehead and then nothing.


Arthur had been gone over a week when Nimue approached Gwenhwyfar in the flower garden where she was digging up the dead plants.

"Gwenhwyfar, we need to talk."

"About what, Nimue? Arthur's heir? I'm sure he will support you." She knew she was being snappish, but she didn't care.

Nimue sat down on a bench near the rosebushes. "The child I carry will be a child of Avallach. I have no need of Arthur's support, nor do I want it. She was conceived during the Great Rite; she belongs to the Goddess."

"I don't understand all your talk about your Goddess," Gwenhwyfar said sharply, shaking dirt from her fingers. "Arthur will need an heir; you are already producing one."

Nimue stroked a rose petal, carefully avoiding its thorns. "Samhain approaches, the beginning of a new year. This child is a sign of prosperity for the land and the people. I will pray to the Goddess that you be delivered of a child, as well, so the Christians can see their queen is also fertile."

"I don't need your help, Nimue," Gwenhwyfar answered irritably. "Morgana's already helping me!"

Nimue looked puzzled. "In what way is she helping you?"

"Every morning since I have been here, she has prepared a special drink for me to strengthen my ability to conceive and bear a child." Gwenhwyfar gathered her tools.

Nimue's hand dropped from the rose. "What is in this drink, Gwenhwyfar?"

"Just some herbs that Morgana says strengthen me."

"What does it taste like? Is it bitter?"

Gwenhwyfar suddenly remembered the bitter wine she had drunk on her wedding night. Morgana had brought it to her. She had forgotten to tell Arthur about it. She began to fidget a little.

"No, not bitter . . . but not good, either," she amended.

"Do you know where she gets them?"

"Well, yes, in the herbal garden. She spends lots of time there," Gwenhwyfar replied with growing uneasiness. "Do you want me to show you?"

Nimue nodded and they made their way to the other side of the hall. Gwenhwyfar gestured to the neat arrangement of various herbal beds. "Take your time and look around."

Nimue moved slowly until she came to a freshly planted patch nearly hidden along the far wall behind the large butterburrs. She reached down and pointed. "Henbane, nightshade, foxglove, waldmeister, motherwort, feverfew."

She straightened and suddenly, to Gwenhwyfar's eyes, she seemed to grow tall. A whitish sort of light surrounded her. She began to chant in a language Gwenhwyfar didn't understand.

She turned to Gwenhwyfar, her voice full of sympathy. "These plants are all poisonous. Some can kill; others will prevent you from conceiving or will cast out any child that is conceived." She added softly, "Morgana is not your friend."

Gwenhwyfar stared at her in horror and then wrapped her arms around herself as her body racked with sobs. "Why?" she screamed, "Why?"

"I don't know," Nimue murmured as she pulled Gwenhwyfar to her and held her. "But I think Myrddin and I need to find out."

Gwenhwyfar finally succumbed to Nimue's ministrations, but it was too late to confront Morgana. She'd fled during the night.

Gwenhwyfar did not go down to break her fast the next morning. Nimue brought some warm oatcakes and cheese to her room, but she wouldn't eat. "I just want to be alone," she mumbled. *I've been such a fool.*

She was still in bed the second morning when Arthur and his men arrived home. From the nearby window she saw Nimue run to him in the bailey.

Gwenhwyfar heard his boots pound on the stairs, but she didn't look away from the wall as he burst into the room; she just hugged herself more tightly.

He knelt and pried one of her arms loose and held her hand. "I will find Morgana, Gwenhwyfar," he said. "This will not go unpunished."

"That won't fix me, Arthur," she said, still facing the wall. *I trusted her.*

"We have years to make a baby. Now that you won't be drinking that horrible stuff, you'll be able."

She said tonelessly, "Did Nimue not tell you that the damage might be permanent? Or the child deformed?"

Arthur recoiled. "Nimue said the damage *might* be permanent? We won't know until we try, Gwenhwyfar."

She turned then to look at him. "And if the child is deformed? Do you want to take that chance?" *To bring a monster into this world as Arthur's heir would make even the Christians superstitious.*

He paused. "I don't know." He stood and began pacing, raking his hair with his fingers. Then he stopped. "I think I know where the answer might be found."

"Where?"

"Avallach."

"The pagan Isle?" she asked in doubt, "Nimue is from there, and if she doesn't know . . ."

"The Lady of the Lake would," Arthur replied. "Promise me you'll think about it." He pulled the covers back. "Get dressed and come downstairs. I'd like some company for breaking my fast." He gave her a quick kiss and left.

She stared at the door. *Couldn't you have at least held me, Arthur?*

Bedwyr was waiting by the dais with Accolon when Arthur came down. "He says he doesn't know where she's gone. Cai has already left to check her lands."

Arthur sank into the huge throne chair and leaned back to think. *Now I know why I didn't trust Morgana. Bel's Fires! This is bad timing. The uprising that Cerdic warned about needs to be squelched, and soon.* He sighed. "Accolon, I'm sending you back to Rheged. Bedwyr and Gryflet will escort you." Arthur turned to Bedwyr. "Once there, you will tell Uriens everything that has taken place while Morgana and Accolon have been my guests. Everything."

Arthur turned back to Accolon. "You will deny nothing and accept what your king metes as punishment."

"I've done nothing wrong!" he protested.

Arthur raised an eyebrow. "Uriens might think differently. What man would accept his wife turning into an adulteress?" He rose from the chair in disgust and went to find Nimue.

She was on her knees selecting vegetable greens from the sunny southern garden. Her back was to him, her silver hair tied behind her and gleaming almost white in the sun. Her small hands worked the leaves gently loose from the plants.

Settling himself on the workbench, Arthur watched her

for several minutes. He wasn't sure where to begin. Settling differences between men he could handle. Women's problems were another matter.

"I've removed the poisonous plants," Nimue said without turning around.

He started. He had almost forgotten that she was a priestess. She looked like a child, playing in the dirt. A beautiful child-woman, yet so much in control of herself.

"Gwenhwyfar tells me the damage may be permanent?" he finally asked.

She sat back on her haunches and looked at him. "It is possible."

He inhaled sharply. "And if she does bear a child, it could be monstrous?"

Nimue got up then, brushed the debris from her hands, and joined him on the bench. Her face was serious, the aquamarine eyes sympathetic. "One of the herbs, the waldmeister, can cause defects. I do not know the formula that Morgana used."

"I will find out," Arthur said grimly, "if I have to kill her in the process."

Nimue touched his arm. "You're the high king, Arthur. Don't abuse the power."

He growled in frustration. She was right; he would have to deal with Morgana fairly. He had sworn justice for all; he must not let his emotions interfere. He became aware of the warmth of her touch spreading through his arm. He covered her hand with his own and leaned back.

"Could Gwenhwyfar be healed on Avallach?" he asked.

She considered. "Mayhap. The Goddess accepts all, even the followers of the Christos. The Lady would know."

"Would you take her?" he asked.

"She must come willingly. If she does, I will take her," she answered.

Arthur smiled and stood. "I knew I could count on you, Nimue."

* * *

Gwenhwyfar held tightly to the sides of the coracle as Nimue poled it out of the shallow waters at the edge of the Lake the next day. The fog hung in heavy shrouds of dismal dampness and she could see nothing.

"Why is the mist so dense?" she asked.

Nimue looked down at her. "Myrddin calls it the Dragon's Breath. It protects Avallach from the outside world." She smiled. "Do not be afraid, Gwenhwyfar. Women are always welcome on the Isle of the Goddess."

Gwenhwyfar nodded but didn't release her hold. *How did Arthur talk me into this? I'm a Christian.*

"All gods are one; the names may change," Nimue said quietly as though she read her thoughts. "The mother of your Christos is honored by your faith, is she not?"

Gwenhwyfar was considering this when the little boat broke free into blue skies and sunshine. A tall woman in dark blue was waiting on the shoreline; behind her stood eight women in white robes. A translucent shimmer radiated from Nimue, and the boat picked up speed until it bumped on the sands.

Several of the white-clad ladies helped Gwenhwyfar to shore. Nimue knelt before the Lady. "I have brought her to be healed, Lady Vivian."

Vivian turned to Gwenhwyfar. "You are welcome here, although I sense your doubt. The moon will be full on Samhain. Stay with us until then and we will see what the Goddess wills for you. Now come; the maidens have prepared a room."


The late afternoon sun warmed Gwenhwyfar's back as she sat in the apple orchard. In the two weeks she had been on the Isle, the orchard had become her favorite place. The apples had been harvested and there were no blossoms on the trees at this time of year, but she fancied she detected the faint smell of the sweet flowers. *This place is so peaceful.*

She listened to a curlew calling its mate in ascending notes, its song sounding like its name. She watched the gurgling brook bounce over the rust-colored rocks nearby, making its way down the slope toward the holy chalice of red water. Farther below lay the calm surface of the Lake.

She had met Meg, the healer, the night she had arrived. The old woman had used the Orb of Fire, the Caller of Dreams, she called it. The next morning she had proclaimed the poison's effects shouldn't be permanent, although the crone had cautioned her not to try for a baby too soon.

Now Nimue approached. "At moonrise, Gwenhwyfar, we will visit the sacred pool and see what message the Mother sends. Come with me, so you may be prepared."

Sometime later, Gwenhwyfar sat nervously on the edge of the bed, waiting for Nimue. The room smelled of spicy incense and fresh rushes. The maidens had drawn a bath for her, into which they sprinkled several drops of frankincense oil and then gave her a robe of green.

She listened while the priestesses chanted their salute to the end of the day. Their voices were melodious, rising slowly as a summer zephyr, wafting in the air and fading away. This was the religion Lancelot's mother practiced as well. Her thoughts drifted to Lancelot. She missed him, but she knew why he had gone. She could still recall that brief moment of utter contentment that his kiss had brought. *Why do I remember that one small kiss when Arthur has made love to me every night that he's been home?*

As the moon began to rise, Nimue appeared at the door. She was dressed in the traditional white robe this evening, as were the others. The Lady herself was with them, wearing the deep blue of the high priestess. The intricately designed silver niam-lanns on their foreheads reflected the pale light. The Lady's was ringed with softly glowing moonstones.

They proceeded in silence down the Processional Way. When they reached the bottom, the Lady lit the incense on the small stone altar. The same rich Eastern fragrance as the bath swirled upward in a tiny spiral of smoke. Gwenhwyfar shifted uncomfortably. *Christians aren't supposed to participate in the Old Ways, but I want desperately to know if I will bear a child someday!*

Nimue motioned for Gwenhwyfar to stand next to a pool of dark, still water. The Lady raised her arms to call the elements.

"Lleu Llaw, king of wind; Bel, king of fire; Llyr, king of water; Cernunnos, king of forest: I invoke you. Join the Goddess this night to bring perfect balance to this life." She lowered her arms.

Nimue placed a plain silver niam-lann on Gwenhwyfar's head. "This will unite your energy with ours," she said, and then pointed down. "Watch."

The moon now reflected in the pool of water. Joining their hands, the priestesses sealed the circle, closed their eyes, and began a soft, slow cadence. Nimue sank to the ground by the water. She slowed her breathing to induce the trance and began to scry.

The water remained still. No image formed. Gwenhwyfar clenched her hands together. *Mayhap this is my fault. God is punishing me for still thinking about Lancelot's kiss. I should be thinking only about Arthur.*

Nimue closed her eyes for several minutes and Gwenhwyfar sensed she was deeper into her trance. At last, Nimue looked into the pool.

The water shimmered. Slowly, a child's face appeared. The boy had black hair and grey eyes. Arthur's eyes.

Gwenhwyfar stared, her eyes wide and her mouth slightly open. She broke into a huge smile. *An heir. My son. Morgana, you didn't win.*

# Chapter 9

# The Champion

"They'll be back," Maelgwyn said, seated across the table from Morgana at his holding, a fortnight after she had fled. "What do I do when they come?"

Frustrated because she had had to leave Accolon behind, she snapped, "You didn't have to spend a week in the forests, hiding like an animal while the Cymbry ransacked my lands! Can you not think of some way to protect me? Is this place not defensible?"

Maelgwyn turned pale. "Stand against Arthur? You must be mad!"

She gave him a disgusted look. "So, now you're loyal to Arthur?"

He snorted. "Uther killed our father; I've no love of his bastard. Although," he snickered, "I'd be willing to love that wife of his!" Then he added, "She would make a good hostage, wouldn't she?"

Morgana was thinking of ways to contact Accolon and almost didn't hear him. "What?" she asked. "A hostage?"

"A hostage," Maelgwyn repeated, "for your safe passage home to Rheged. We capture Gwenhwyfar, and Arthur doesn't get her back until he pledges his oath that you will be unharmed and given safe passage home."

"A splendid idea, but how do you propose to capture her?" she asked.

Maelgwyn looked hurt. "Lancelot and your nephews are gone. Didn't you say Arthur will probably have to defend Llongborth? He isn't expecting danger here; he'll leave but a few men to guard the place. There must be some way to gain entrance."

Morgana thought quickly. Having Gwenhwyfar as a hostage would ensure her safety. Arthur would never believe that she hadn't meant to kill the girl with those drinks. She had a key to the postern gate, thanks to a not-so-quick tryst one night with a well-endowed, young guard posted there.

She looked at Maelgwyn with something close to respect. "We would need to post scouts and be ready at a moment's notice. Once inside, you'll have to be quick, though. One person to gag her, two to tie her and carry her out. They'll need to be strong. She'll fight."

Maelgwyn ran his tongue over his thick lips. "A fighter, eh? I always like those."

Morgana eyed him contemptuously. "Maybe I should lead the men, since your mind is obviously elsewhere." *I'll have to make sure Gwenhwyfar is kept safe, for Arthur will show no mercy if Maelgwyn actually follows through on his fantasies*. Well, she would worry about that later. Right now, she had arrangements to make.

Lancelot had planned a grand entrance for the horses he brought back. They were approaching Camelot, the dust rolling up the hill preceding them. The horses were magnificent, galloping with their necks arched, heads tucked, tails high. Riders on both sides held them to the road. Lancelot saw Arthur spin Valiant around from where he had his men practicing maneuvers in the field. The herd slowed as they approached the gate. The men in the field broke ranks to lead them to the prepared enclosure.

Lancelot rode over to Arthur. "Did you see them run? Weren't they impressive?"

"They are, indeed," he answered, grinning widely, still watching them move about. "You did well, Lancelot."

"Palomides drove the bargains. I just brought them home," he answered. "Where's Gwenhwyfar? She's got to see them!"

Arthur sobered. "Let's go inside, Lancelot. I have much to tell you."

Lancelot's face darkened as Arthur told him the story. *By Mithras, why had no one known? Ah, Gwen.* "Where's Morgana now?"

Arthur shook his head. "We don't know. Cai searched her place and Maelgwyn's as soon as we came back. We have a guard posted on her land. She hasn't been seen."

"Let me find her, Arthur."

"You would kill her, Lancelot."

"For certes, she deserves it." He paused, then continued, "But I won't torture her. Death will be swift."

"Better you than me then, for my way would not be so quick." Arthur held up a hand. "But neither of us will have the pleasure. Bedwyr and Gryflet returned from delivering Accolon; Uriens has asked that I show mercy and send Morgana to him."

"You don't have to grant that, though."

Arthur sighed. "Do you remember what I pledged when I took my vows, Lance? Justice. For everyone. Even her."

"I did not take your vows, Arthur," Lancelot persisted. "Let me avenge Gwenhwyfar for you."

Arthur clamped a hand on his shoulder. "Thank you, my friend, but you swore your allegiance to me. Neither one of us can harm her."

"And Gwenhwyfar? Do you think the Lady can really heal her?" Lancelot asked.

"I pray to all the gods that she does, Lance, for I miss her company at night."

A muscle twitched in Lancelot's jaw. He deliberately pushed the thought of Arthur in bed with her from his mind. "How long will she be gone?"

"Not much longer, I think. Nimue will bring her back when she's ready." He hesitated, then went on, "I won't be here, though. The insurrection in Llongborth needs to be quelled before those wayward captains, Maegla and Bieda, can land any more men in their ships. We are preparing to march tomorrow."

Lancelot replied, "I can be ready. I'll assign the horses to someone."

Arthur stopped him. "So far, there are fewer than a hundred men involved in this. I have enough troops. Besides," he added as they went back into the bailey, "Morgana has not been found. I want Gwenhwyfar protected when she returns. I trust you to do it, Lancelot."

Lancelot turned away. Not a night had gone by that he hadn't thought about Gwenhwyfar. *Great Mother, let me not betray Arthur's trust.*

A red sky dominated the dawn the next morning. Lancelot glanced at Arthur. "There will be a storm by this afternoon. Why don't you wait another day?"

Armor rattled and clinked as the cohort mounted. Uther had trained under Roman generals; Arthur's army followed many of the Roman ways. The infantry was divided into three maniples of foot soldiers. Each line followed several feet behind the other. Two alae of one hundred seventy cavalry flanked either side of the infantry, a third in the rear. As Captains, Bedwyr, Gwalchmai, and Garient were everywhere.

"I would hope these men could take getting wet!" Arthur frowned. "I want to quell this uprising and return as soon as I can. We must find Morgana."

Lancelot nodded. "You're leaving Agravaine and Gaheris

behind?" he asked when he noticed the two of them standing across the yard.

"Until Agravaine grows up and stops blaming Pellinore for Lot, I can't depend on him, not even as a squire. I'm leaving Gaheris to keep an eye on him."

"I know. We had the same problem with him while we were getting the horses," Lancelot said and looked at his ala that Garient would lead. "Let me go talk to my men before you leave."

A short time later, Lancelot watched nearly a thousand men moved down the road in a well-disciplined procedure, but he failed to see the lone rider who headed toward Maelgwyn's lands.

The sun had set, but the moon was well up, lighting the way for Gwenhwyfar's party, when they arrived back at Camelot. Gwenhwyfar handed Cali's reins to the groom as she dismounted. "I'll take time to brush you tomorrow, girl. I want to talk to Arthur."

She and Nimue walked to the hall where Enid met them inside the doorway.

"Where's Arthur?" Gwenhwyfar beamed. "I have good news!"

Enid hugged her. "I am so happy for you, Lady. But you've missed Arthur; he and Garient left with the whole cohort this morning."

Gwenhwyfar's shoulders drooped.

"You can give me the good news," Lancelot said from across the room.

She whirled at the sound of his voice. He was leaning against the back wall, his arms crossed in front of him. The sleeves of his white linen shirt were rolled back, contrasting with the tan of his forearms and face. Dark strands of hair fell over his forehead. He gave her his lopsided smile. Happiness seared through her.

"Lancelot! What are you doing back?"

He straightened and walked to her. "Are you not glad to see me, then?"

"No, that isn't . . . Yes . . . I mean . . . I wasn't expecting you. We didn't think you'd be back before spring," she managed to stammer and then saw the laughter in his eyes. "Stop teasing me, Lancelot. You know I'm glad to see you!" Without thinking, she threw her arms around his neck and hugged him.

He lifted her, spun her around, and set her back down.

She laughed, a little breathless. "I want to hear about your trip! Did you bring the horses? What was Mecca like? How is Palomides?"

"Whoa! One question at a time!" He grinned and took her hand and they moved toward the hearth, both of them talking at once.

They were still sitting and talking, hours later, when they heard the noise: it sounded like a small scratching at the back hallway door. Lancelot rose quietly, went to the front door, and pulled his sword from its scabbard. He glanced outside; the bailey was quiet, the guard on duty at the gate.

He heard the footsteps and raced into the back hallway to surprise three men and a boy, all wearing hoods. Gwenhwyfar ran in behind him.

"There she is!" one of the men yelled as he and another turned to run around to the front entrance.

The first man dropped the gag and drew his own sword. The narrow confines of the hallway limited the swordplay, but he deflected the point as Lancelot lunged. The man swung his sword back and Lancelot dropped suddenly, managing to grab the hilt and pull the man off balance. He toppled forward as Lancelot delivered a blow to his head.

The boy held a dagger, but not expertly. A flick of the

sword tip dislodged it. Lancelot hit the youth squarely in the face with his fist; the boy slumped to the ground.

Behind him, he could hear scuffling, grunting, and cursing. He picked up the second sword and ran back into the hall.

One of the men was holding Gwenhwyfar's arms while the other was attempting to catch her legs. They had pulled their hoods off and he recognized them as Maelgwyn's mercenaries, the Saxons called Eric and Gustav. Eric caught one of Gwenhwyfar's legs and she used the leverage of placing her foot against his shoulder to kick him in the face with her other boot. The man howled and let go. Gwenhwyfar let her weight sag and Gustav lost his grip temporarily. Before he could grab her again, she curled herself into a ball and rolled away. She sprang up as Lancelot slid the second sword toward her.

Lancelot edged closer to Gwenhwyfar, thrusting at his opponent, forcing him backward. Gwenhwyfar's assailant advanced and she parried laterally, retreating until she was standing back to back with Lancelot. Lancelot spun, delivering a blow that cut open Eric's shoulder, making his sword arm useless.

Men came running from their barracks; the first two who reached the front door tackled Gustav and brought him down.

Nimue appeared in the back doorway, Ygraine and Elaine staring wide-eyed behind her. Gwenhwyfar leaned against Lancelot, her head on his shoulder, eyes closed, but still holding her sword. He propped her up with one arm and motioned with the other to one of the men.

"Two more are in the back. Maelgwyn's men."

"One of them is Morgana," Nimue said.

Gwenhwyfar opened her eyes and straightened. "Morgana?" she asked incredulously. "Here? Why?" She took a step, but Lancelot held her back.

"Is she dead?" he asked grimly. "By Mithras, I didn't know . . ."

Nimue shook her head. "No, but she's going to need attention. They all will. I had better get started. Bring them to the infirmary," she told the men. "Enid is already there, readying the supplies." She turned to Ygraine and Elaine. "I can use your help."

As they were carrying Morgana out, Gwenhwyfar stopped them. Morgana was still unconscious, the left side of her face already a mass of black and blue bruises. Her eye was swollen completely shut, her nose probably broken. She moaned slightly as the men left with her.

Lancelot gave orders to the remaining men. "I want all of them under guard. I don't know why they did this. There may be more out there. Gaheris, I want double guards on the battlements now. Tell the archers that at first light, they take their positions in the earthworks. I want the remaining cavalry ready to ride at dawn. Then bring me the captain of the guard. I want to know how this was allowed to happen."

The men scattered.

Gwenhwyfar sank down on one of the trestle benches, shaking.

Lancelot sat down beside her. "You did well tonight, Gwen."

She looked up at him, her green eyes huge and dark. "You saved my life, Lancelot! Arthur will be grateful to you."

He grimaced. "Arthur may be very angry with me. First, because I let this happen and secondly, because I nearly killed Morgana and I swore I wouldn't."

She looked puzzled. He explained.

"Arthur told me what she did to you, Gwen. I asked to avenge you. I'd have killed her. Arthur reminded me that I was pledged to him and his goal of justice."

"I would hope that tonight would change that opinion of his!" she said indignantly. "I was the target of this, but I don't know why." She started trembling again and turned to him. "Lancelot, why?"

He placed a finger across her lips. "I don't know why, Gwen, but tomorrow, I will find out." His hand dropped to her shoulder and his eyes grew darker as he looked into hers. "I swear to you, I won't let her hurt you again."

She looked back trustingly. As if mesmerized, he slowly brought her closer to him. She slipped her arms around his neck.

His first kiss was soft, a mere brushing. Then, a series of gentle explorations, a slow pressure exerting itself. Gwenhwyfar embraced the kisses, inviting more. Lightly, he placed kisses across her forehead, cheeks, and the tip of her nose before returning to her mouth. He caught her lower lip, teasing her with his tongue.

She parted her lips and he immersed himself in her, lips and tongue demanding as he explored her mouth. She pressed her breasts against him and sought still more closeness.

Reluctantly, he pulled back and opened his eyes. He brought her arms down, holding her hands, feeling miserable.

"We can't do this, Gwen."

For a moment, raw hunger blazed in her eyes and he knew he didn't have enough willpower to stop himself if she kissed him again. Then she bent her head. "You're right. I am married to Arthur. Forgive me."

"I'm the one who should apologize. You are overwrought; I took advantage of the situation."

A look of pure longing crossed her face as she took her hands away. "Let's just call this a reaction to tonight's events. It won't happen again." She stood up. "I'd better go help Nimue."

"I'll walk with you; I need to find Gaheris and the captain of the guard."

They found Agravaine outside the door. "What are you doing here?" Lancelot asked, but Agravaine just smirked and walked away.

By the time Arthur returned two weeks later, Morgana was able to talk, although she refused to. Lancelot kept her and Maelgwyn under constant guard. The two men he had let go with a flogging; they were just soldiers following orders.

Lancelot stood beside Gwenhwyfar now as Arthur rode through the gate. He slumped in his saddle as he led Garient's riderless horse. Myrddin walked alongside, leading his mule. They moved quickly out to him.

Enid shrieked when she saw her husband in the litter, and fell to the ground beside him.

"He lives, Enid," Arthur said, "but barely." He turned to Nimue with despair. "Lady, can you heal him?"

"Are you wounded also, Arthur?" she asked as she went to Garient.

"No, just weary. This is my fault." He removed his gauntlets. "I was with Cerdic when it happened." Arthur reached for Gwenhwyfar and put his arm around her. "A skirmish after we had already captured Maegla and Bieda. This was the last group of holdouts. Garient had laughed and told me he would handle it." He gave a depressed shrug. "I was eager to learn if Cerdic had word of Morgana traveling in the direction of the Saxons."

"I can use your help," Nimue said to Gwenhwyfar. Arthur kissed her quickly and released her. Nimue gave Lancelot a long look as she and Myrddin followed the men who carried Garient to the infirmary.

"What was that for?" Arthur asked, turning toward the hall.

"Morgana is here," Lancelot answered.

"What?" Arthur stopped in his tracks. "I would not have

thought her brave enough, or foolish enough, for that. Was she wanting Accolon that badly?"

"No. Gwenhwyfar."

Arthur's eyes turned to slate. "Where is Morgana?"

"She's in a cell in the gaol, under guard. Maelgwyn, too," Lancelot explained as Arthur changed direction. "They had some scheme to abduct Gwenhwyfar and hold her as hostage to ensure Morgana's safe passage to Rheged." When he reached the door, Lancelot stopped him. "Her face is not in good shape. I hit her."

"I see," Arthur said in a flat voice. "After you swore to me you wouldn't harm her?"

"They were wearing hoods. I thought she was a boy."

For a minute, Arthur studied him. He threw back his head and laughed. "Lancelot, you are probably the only man in Britain who would mistake Morgana for a male."

He opened the door and the two guards on duty stood up. "Leave us."

Lancelot brought Maelgwyn out first. He was visibly shaking, his face white.

"Tell me," Arthur said in a voice like slow-rolling surf on a summer day. "What were you thinking?"

Maelgwyn gulped. "It was Morgana's idea. She was afraid you'd kill her. If we could hold the queen as hostage, she thought you'd have to let her go." He cringed as if to avoid a blow.

Arthur was silent.

Maelgwyn cleared his throat, "She would truly have been a guest in my home, lord, and been treated well. I would have given her anything."

Arthur's eyes darkened. "Hmmm," he said and put his hands behind him. He slowly walked around Maelgwyn and approached him from behind.

"What would you have given her, Maelgwyn?" Arthur asked, almost pleasantly.

Watching him, Lancelot doubted that Maelgwyn recognized the danger in that tone.

Maelgwyn jumped. "Anything, my lord, I swear." Sweat appeared on his brow.

Well, maybe he did sense the danger, Lancelot thought. It was one of Arthur's most devious ploys.

"And you wouldn't have touched her, wouldn't have wanted her, wouldn't have taken her?" Arthur continued in a conversational tone, inches away from Maelgwyn's ear.

"Oh, no, my lord! I would not."

With the speed of a striking adder, Arthur twisted Maelgwyn's right arm behind him. "Do you think I believe you?" he asked politely and pressed the arm higher.

Maelgwyn whimpered.

"I'm waiting for the truth," Arthur said and adjusted the arm again, this time raising the man to his toes.

Groaning, Maelgwyn whispered, "No, I do not want her."

*Fool,* Lancelot thought, *it's not wise to lie to Arthur.*

Arthur lowered the arm somewhat and Maelgwyn took a deep breath. Then, Arthur clamped a hand on his left shoulder and brought him to his knees. He held him in position. "Do you know what I think, Maelgwyn?" he asked, still deadly pleasant. "I think you do want her. I watched you drooling over her at our wedding supper." He tightened his grip until Maelgwyn cried out. "I think that you would have raped her, again and again."

Maelgwyn screamed as Arthur dislocated his shoulder and he slumped to the floor, unconscious.

Arthur straightened. "Bring me Morgana, Lance."

Lancelot unlocked the next cell. Morgana stood with her back against the far wall, looking frightened. *You should be.* He gestured and she hesitated, then lifted her head and walked out ahead of him.

He knew Arthur would not be prepared for the sight of her. The bruises had turned to yellows, greens, and browns and covered half her face. Her eye was still nearly closed, and her nose somewhat swollen.

But Arthur merely moved a chair forward. "Sit down, Morgana."

She looked down at Maelgwyn on the floor and then at Arthur. She remained standing. "Do what you need to do and have done."

Arthur raised an eyebrow, but motioned again. "Sit."

Lancelot towered over her. "I would not tempt the high king."

Slowly, she sat. With her good eye, she looked up at them defiantly.

Arthur began pacing, then stopped in front of her. "Did you want to kill her?"

She looked at him steadily. "Not that you will believe me, but no, I did not."

He raked his fingers through his hair. "What was in the drinks?"

"Something to keep her from getting with child," she answered, "similar to the leaves your soldiers give the wenches to chew so there will be no brats. I use it myself."

Arthur stared at her. "But why would you give it to her?"

"When she first arrived, she was scared." She shrugged. "She didn't want to marry you. I thought this would, at least, keep her from having your child."

He winced. "You lied, because she thought the drink would help her conceive."

"I lied," she said smoothly, "because Gwenhwyfar is seventeen. What harm for her to enjoy a year or two of married life before the child comes along?"

*She's lying. And she's good at it. Arthur can always break a person down.*

Arthur changed tactics. "Tell me about this planned abduction."

"For my part, I wanted safe passage." She glanced down

at Maelgwyn, still unconscious. "He could scarcely keep his trews from bursting at the thought of her."

Arthur clenched his fists and began pacing again. Finally, he said, "Against my better judgment, I am sending you home to Uriens. He knows what you've done and has requested my mercy." Arthur smiled humorlessly. "Because he is loyal to me, I granted it. Accolon was escorted back by Bedwyr, so Uriens knows of your infidelity, as well. You will have to answer to him for both counts."

He stopped and turned her head so the bruises were facing him. He tightened his grip and Lancelot saw her tense. For a moment, he thought Arthur would strike her.

Arthur let her go. "Perhaps justice has been served, after all," he said. "I was tempted to bruise the other side, but Lancelot did enough."

*And I will do more if she ever tries to hurt Gwen again. Justice or no justice.*

Gwenhwyfar came into Arthur's room as he was washing for supper. She looked at him curiously. "What happened with Maelgwyn?"

Arthur pulled on a clean tunic. "Nothing more than he deserved, Gwenhwyfar, but do not ever be alone with that man." Then he changed the subject. "The news from Avallach was good?" he asked. When she smiled, he put his arms around her and kissed her. "Mayhap supper can wait."

She returned his kiss, but pushed away from him. "The Lady told me not to try to get a child too soon," she said. "The effects need time to wear off."

Arthur groaned. "How long?"

"Several moons, at least," she answered. *Since Lancelot's kisses, I'm confused.*

He growled at that, then sighed and pulled her close once more. "I can show you other ways to take our pleasure," he said as his hands slid down her back.

She stepped away. "People are waiting for us." *I feel so guilty.*
As they left the room, he whispered, "Later, then."

Gwenhwyfar forced herself to smile. *How can I want two men? God, help me.*

At the evening meal, Gwenhwyfar asked about Garient. Nimue exchanged a look with Myrddin before she answered. "Tonight will tell, I think."

"I'll visit him after the meal," Arthur said. He turned to Gwenhwyfar. "Tell me what happened here; I still haven't decided what else Maelgwyn deserves."

Gwenhwyfar felt Myrddin's hawk eyes trained on her as she recounted the details, and how Lancelot had fended off the intruders. "He saved my life, Arthur."

Myrddin frowned suddenly and swatted at his ear.

Lancelot added, "If it had not been for Gwenhwyfar's skill with a sword, I might not have had such success."

Arthur grinned. "My wife never stops surprising me." He hesitated. "Still, she could not have defended herself against three or four. If I had not left you here . . ." He turned to Gwen. "You need someone to protect you when I'm gone. I don't want to take any more chances like this one."

Myrddin interrupted, this time with his hand clamped on his shoulder as if to hold his shirt in place. "Perhaps a group of guards assigned to her, Arthur?"

Arthur nodded. "But she needs a person who will defend her, who will champion her when needed. I should have thought of this before."

"Your best fighting men are needed in the field, Arthur. Gwenhwyfar has shown she is capable of defending herself, especially if she has her own guard." Myrddin's voice was edgy as he leaned forward. The faerie floated in front of him disapprovingly.

"I can spare a fighting man, Myrddin, especially if he will protect my wife."

"Bedwyr, then. He is her brother."

Arthur looked at him oddly; then he turned to Lancelot. "You saved my life once, Lancelot, and I gave you my geis of protection. Now I find you have saved Gwenhwyfar's. Will you give her your geis? Will you be her champion?"

Gwenhwyfar stared at Arthur, stricken. He had no idea of how much willpower it would take for them.

"Willingly," he answered Arthur, but his dark eyes were on Gwenhwyfar. "If she will accept it."

She looked at him now, wondering if he had suddenly gone daft. *Arthur trusts us both too much. Can we hold that trust?*

"Lancelot's needed in the field," Myrddin exploded. "You just said yourself, Arthur, he's saved your life!"

Irritated, Gwenhwyfar glared at Myrddin. He glared back. She turned to Lancelot. "I accept your geis."

Lancelot stood and bent over her hand. "May the earth break beneath me, the sea submerge me, and the sky fall on me if I ever revoke this oath." He looked at Arthur. "I will protect her always."

# Chapter 10

# Changes

The next morning Gwenhwyfar stood with Arthur on the hall steps and watched the armed escort leave with Morgana for Rheged.

Lancelot joined them. "I wish you'd let me go, Arthur. I would have explained the bruises to Uriens."

Arthur shook his head. "I need you here. Marc has sent word of rumors that Comoran plans to pirate off Ictis Insula."

Gwenhwyfar frowned. Marcus protected the southwestern port of Marazion in Dumnonia where the Kernowian tin was traded for goods from Armorica and Gaul. "I didn't know the Scotti were moving that far south."

"The Scotti grow restless, I think," Arthur answered. "Young Hueil tries to rile those in Dalraida. I've sent Hoel north to Alclud to watch him. I think we may have trouble from both directions."

"Arthur! Lancelot! Come quickly!" Ygraine called, running from the infirmary. "It's Garient."

They were too late. Myrddin shook his head as Nimue

pulled a sheet over the still figure on the bed. Gwenhwyfar went to put an arm around the weeping Enid.

Nimue straightened, holding a hand to her back. Arthur lifted the sheet. "What went wrong? I thought you had gotten him past the worst," he demanded angrily.

"The infection had already set in by the time you got him here. He lost too much blood," she said tiredly. "There was nothing else I could do."

Arthur cursed, spun on his heel, and stalked off. Minutes later, they could hear Valiant thundering out the gate.

Gwenhwyfar looked at Lancelot and then at Myrddin. "Isn't one of you going to ride after him?" she asked.

"He needs to be alone," Lancelot answered. "It's how he handles death."

Enid raised her head at that and stepped away from Gwenhwyfar. "And I, also, would like to be alone with my husband," she said.

As they left, Enid began keening, a chillingly dismal sound that swept Camelot like a dark cloud bank preceding a winter storm.

Arthur returned shortly before supper that evening. Gwenhwyfar wondered where he had gone. He talked to no one and the meal was a quiet one. As soon as they finished eating, Arthur took Gwenhwyfar's arm and lifted her out of her seat.

"I need you, Wife," he said and led her up the stairs.

Once inside his room, he kissed her roughly, his mouth hard as his hands kneaded her buttocks, pulling her against him. He pushed her onto the bed and started to undo her shirt when she caught his hand and struggled to sit up. He brought his knee over her and held her firmly in place.

"We've got to wait." Didn't he remember what she had told him? "Get off me."

He grabbed both her hands and shifted his weight so he was nearly astride her.

She tried to free her hands and felt her temper rising. "Are you going to force yourself on me?"

He recoiled and stared at her, then rolled over to lie beside her. "Forgive me. I have not been myself. I didn't expect Garient to die and I just wanted . . . to be assured . . . to find some comfort . . ." His voice trailed off.

Gwenhwyfar raised herself on her elbow to look at Arthur. He had his eyes closed; his jaw was clenched and his face showed the hardened lines of the warlord he was. She sometimes forgot that side of him; he led his men into battle and some of them didn't return. He had to live with that every day. Today, he had lost a good friend.

She stroked his forehead. He opened his eyes, his grey gaze steady.

"I'm sorry, too," she said. "I forget what it must be like for you. But," she added, sitting up, "we can't indulge ourselves; you know that. The priestess said to wait several moons to be safe."

Arthur sighed. "Does that mean I am not to touch you at all, Gwenhwyfar?"

"It would be best," she said gently. "Once we start, it is hard to stop."

Arthur stood. "Hard, yes. Impossible, no." He lightly traced her cheekbone with his finger. "Trust me."

Gwenhwyfar trembled at his touch. A part of her wanted very much to trust him. "I can't take the chance of having a deformed child, Arthur. If you love me, you will indulge me in this."

His eyes darkened momentarily. "As you wish, then." He went to the door. "Let me know when my touch is again wanted." He walked down the hall.

She winced but did not call him back. *Arthur, why can't you understand?*

* * *

Arthur went to the kitchens and poured himself a cup of wine. He carried the skin back with him and sat down by the well-tended fire in the hearth in one of the big, comfortable chairs Gwenhwyfar had brought from Cameliard. He downed half the cup and closed his eyes, listening to the crackle of the spitting flames. *By Mithras, it hurt to lose a good man needlessly.*

"Mayhap a sip of that would help my back," a female voice said.

Arthur jumped, nearly spilling the rest.

Nimue sat in the far chair, curled in a ball. She was so small that he hadn't seen the top of her head when he sat down.

He got up immediately and brought the cup to her. She took two sips and handed it back to him. "I'll get you a goblet," Arthur said, but she stopped him.

"I can't have very much," she said. "Drink is not healthy for the child."

Arthur pulled one of the footstools over and sat beside her. He set the wine cup down, took both of her hands in his, and looked deeply into her eyes. "Will having my child be overly burdensome to you, Nimue?"

She smiled at him. "Not overly so, Arthur. Certainly not yet, since I haven't grown huge." Then she added, "She is a child of the Goddess and will be welcome at Avallach. I am not unhappy with this."

"Might it not be a boy, Nimue? A son I could call heir?"

"This child will be female. I saw her face in the chalice at the kingmaking."

"I will support you and the child in any way I can. I'm sorry for getting angry with you earlier today. I just . . ."

She withdrew her hands and placed a finger across his lips. "I understand," she said softly. "A life was taken today; you could do nothing to save it."

*Exactly. And I needed my wife.* "I tried to explain to Gwenhwyfar how I felt, but . . ." Again, Nimue hushed him.

"You want to assure yourself that life continues, Arthur. It is natural when life is taken away unexpectedly." She took his hand and placed it on her slightly rounded stomach. "If you are patient, you will feel the child move, and you will know that life continues."

There was a slight flutter of movement. Arthur pulled his hand away as if burned. Nimue laughed. Slowly, Arthur broke into a big grin and touched her belly again.

*A daughter, my child! Something that is pure and inno-cent. A girl wouldn't have to wage battle or kill. I can protect her.* Reluctantly, he withdrew his hand.

"Thank you, Nimue"—he leaned over and kissed the top of her head—"I think I will be able to sleep now." He left her sitting there, stroking the child within.


Several weeks after the funeral, Gwenhwyfar lunged a two-year-old colt in the paddock and suddenly, she sensed Lancelot's presence. She drew the horse toward her.

"He's come a good way," Lancelot said.

She turned, one arm over the colt's neck, and smiled at Lancelot. "He's the most skittish, but he's also my favorite. I've named him Safere, after Palomides's fearless warrior brother."

Lancelot walked over. "He'll be ready for the saddle soon, I think," he said as he ran his hand along the smooth muscles of the animal's shoulder and down his foreleg.

"I'm ready, too," Gwenhwyfar laughed. "This one will be a challenge!"

Lancelot straightened and looked at her skeptically. "Do you really think Arthur is going to let you get on a horse that has not been broken?"

She swiped an imaginary fly off the horse's satiny flank.

Arthur had not come to her room since that night. "I don't think he'll notice."

He gave her a sideways look and then continued to examine the horse.

"Arthur and I had a . . . disagreement," she said finally, not looking at Lancelot. "Now he spends his time with Nimue, admiring her growing belly."

Lancelot put a hand on her shoulder. "Do you want his child so badly, Gwen?"

"Yes! No! I mean . . ." she paused. "It's just that Nimue looks so content, Arthur wants an heir, and this is all my fault. I've driven him to spend his evenings with her. I'm such a fool." She looked down at her boots.

Lancelot tilted her chin and forced her to look at him. "Whatever you've done, Arthur loves you."

"Why do I always fight with him, Lance?" she asked. "Why can't I be happy with him, as I am with you?" She stopped abruptly, her eyes widening, for Lancelot looked as if the colt had just kicked him.

"Lancelot!"

With a strangled sound, he turned away from her gaze. Elaine was standing on the other side of the fence, smiling. The smile did not quite reach her eyes.

"What is it?" he asked shortly.

"Arthur called a council and sent me to find you," she answered, dimpling. "I'll walk back with you while Gwenhwyfar tends to that animal."

With a last look at Gwenhwyfar, he turned and followed Elaine back to the hall.


As the winter solstice approached, Ygraine readied Camelot to celebrate the Christos Mass. She told Arthur that after the celebration she would be returning to the abbey where she had retired.

Arthur knew, too, that Nimue ached for the warmth of

Avallach's own festival that heralded the rebirth of the sun. She had approached him two evenings before the solstice. They had developed a habit of meeting in front of the hearth after supper to share a cup of wine. The child growing within her fascinated him. Nothing in his male world had prepared him. After the first night he felt the babe move, she had let him rest a hand on her belly.

"It is a gift of the Goddess that you appreciate this child and feel the tenderness that you do," she had told him last night. "It cancels some of the blood that must be shed when you do battle. The humanness in you will make you a great king."

Gwenhwyfar had walked in on that situation. She had said some nasty things to both of them, but Arthur had not removed his hand. Instead, he'd let anger get the upper hand and told her that she could be in the same position if she'd let him near her. At that, she had stomped off, angry with him again. He wished things could be as easy with Gwenhwyfar as they were with Nimue.

Now Nimue settled down beside him in front of the fire. She placed her small hand over his. "Arthur," she said gently, "I need to return to Avallach."

"What?" He roused himself, for he had been dozing. "Winter is on us; travel would be too hard on you."

She smiled. "I still have several months and we have little snow between here and the Isle. The festival of the holly king supplanting the oak king will soon take place. I should be there. Besides, Gwenhwyfar is upset over our situation, and that should not be."

"Don't feel sorry for Gwenhwyfar," he said sharply. "She refuses my touch." *And I'm not taking the chance of being rebuffed again. She needs to come to me.*

Nimue looked distressed. "Still, Arthur? Meg told her to wait only a moon or two. You must find a way. She is your wife."

He laughed, but it sounded like a bark. "All we seem to do is argue."

"All the more reason I need to leave. I've become too comforting to you."

"But I want to be with you when the child is born!"

"Oh, no, Arthur. That cannot be," she said softly. "This child must be born on Avallach. Men are rarely invited to the Isle and certainly not in the birthing glade." She stroked his head gently and then pushed herself away. "I will leave tomorrow morning."

"I forget that you are a priestess of the Goddess, Nimue. So be it." Absently, he placed his hand on her belly and leaned back to doze again.


After Ygraine and Nimue left, the rest of the winter season passed quietly. Arthur had Lancelot work several colts until they were accustomed to the saddle. He adamantly refused to allow Gwenhwyfar to be the first person on any of the horses. She had been angry with him until Lancelot nearly became unseated when Safere reared and twisted to complete a full spin in the air. He'd had the good sense to say nothing to her about it.

In late March, Palomides arrived home with the other seventy horses. His golden skin was bronzed darker by the sun, and his white teeth flashed in a big grin as he slipped down from his horse. He exchanged greetings with Arthur and Lancelot, then dropped to one knee in front of Gwenhwyfar, took her hand, and kissed it. "I have brought your horses, my queen. I hope you approve of them."

"Oh, get up, Palomides!" Gwenhwyfar laughed. "It's so good to see you! Tonight, you will sit beside me at supper. I want to hear about everything!"

"My pleasure, my lady." His black eyes sparkled.

*I wonder where I'll be sitting tonight,* thought Arthur. *Lancelot always sits to her left.*

"Now," she said, taking Palomides's arm and extending

her other hand to Lancelot, "let me see those horses!" She looked at Arthur. "Are you coming?"

He shook his head. "You go on ahead." He watched her for several minutes, between the two men, before he turned away.

A fortnight later, a training schedule had been established and the breeding of the mares begun. Arthur was conducting one of those training drills when a rider from Dumnonia approached the gate at a flat-out run on a nearly exhausted horse.

The rider was Marc's nephew, Tristan. "The Scotti?" Arthur asked as he came to greet him.

Tristan nodded and gratefully accepted the water cup that Elaine brought out. "Yes, Marc saw one ship only; he thinks the others wait past the horizon."

Arthur dispatched riders to summon the warlords from Isca, Lindinis, and Kelliwic. He made plans to gather the men from Isca and Lindinis on his way to Kernow where he would meet Cador and Marc. Comoran must be stopped at Ictis Insula or these warlords' lands would be vulnerable. As an afterthought, he sent a rider to Maelgwyn as well. Since Palomides had returned and could see to the horses, Lancelot would be riding with them. Gwenhwyfar would be safer if Arthur knew where Maelgwyn was.

Arthur's Cymbry met at the Round Table to discuss strategy. Gwenhwyfar was excited that he had invited her to attend; it was one of the few times she had been in this room since he rarely included her in his meetings. She sat to one side with a disapproving Myrddin. At least he wasn't batting at his ear today.

When all were seated, a chair remained vacant. She squinted

a little to read the name. *What man would be brave enough not to attend Arthur's council?* "Perilous," she read and turned to Myrddin. "A strange name. Whom does that chair belong to?"

He did not respond for so long that she thought he was ignoring her. Finally, he turned, his golden eyes gleaming. "It's reserved for one who will not shed blood."

"A soldier who will not kill?" Gwenhwyfar smiled.

Myrddin's gaze became distant, and when he spoke his voice had a hollow ring, as though he were far away. "He will be a different type of soldier—a keeper of a holy relic that will offer peace to Britain's people."

"But that is Arthur's goal!" Gwenhwyfar was confused.

The druid nodded and so did the faerie before she flitted over to the Round Table to hover over Arthur. "No more questions now. Listen and learn how Arthur leads."

What she noticed immediately was that Arthur had an uncanny ability to assign each of his captains and lieutenants areas of their own strengths. He treated each opinion as equal and she saw the looks of pride in the men when a suggestion was taken. He was in his element when he was planning with his men. She wished they would take the time to sit and talk like this, but the only time she had his undivided attention was in bed, for that relationship had resumed when Nimue left. She gave a little sigh. *It would be nice to be treated as an equal. I am the queen.*

Arthur's cohort had been gone a month and the late April sun felt pleasant as Gwenhwyfar put Safere through his paces in the paddock. She had asked Palomides to observe.

She stopped in front of him. "I want to take him out and really feel him run."

Palomides shook his head. "Arthur doesn't even want you riding that horse, Gwenhwyfar. And," he added as she started to protest, "I don't trust the colt yet, either. A young horse, at extended gallop, will be difficult to control."

"But I can . . ." she began when the gate guard shouted the arrival of Arthur's cohort returning. A moment later, the horses' drumming cadence could be heard.

She slid off Safere and ran to the gate. She was trying to smooth her hair back in some semblance of a braid when Elaine joined her, neatly dressed and smelling of roses, as usual. *We must make a strange sight.* She squinted against the sun.

Arthur rode at the head of the line, Lancelot beside him. *They make a handsome pair,* Gwenhwyfar thought, *Arthur with his sun-bleached hair and Lancelot's so dark.* Behind them, the standard-bearer was furling the red dragon. Arthur said something to Lancelot and turned his horse around, cantering to the back. She noticed neither Bedwyr nor Gwalchmai was there. They should have been behind Arthur. One hand went to her mouth.

"Elaine, where are Bedwyr and Gwalchmai? Do you see them?"

Elaine had been watching Lancelot, but she turned now. "They may be at the end of the line," she offered. "Just wait . . ." but Gwenhwyfar was running down the road.

Lancelot pulled Pryderi to the side and dismounted. She ran into his arms. "Where are they, Lance? Bedwyr and Gwalchmai?"

He swept her hair back with one hand. "They stayed behind to help Marc get his men back into fighting condition. Arthur had a nasty problem with one of them." He leaned back from her and looked down. "I'm sorry for the fear it caused you, but this is a nice welcome home." He grinned.

Embarrassed, realizing what she must look like to the men who were passing, she stepped back and studied her boot. *But how good it had felt to be in his arms!*

"Are you blushing, Gwen?" he laughed. "I've never seen you do that!"

"Don't tease, Lancelot!" she sputtered, knowing she was getting pinker.

Valiant skidded to a stop as Arthur returned and threw himself off the horse. "What's wrong?" he asked. "Why are you out here in the dust?"

"She couldn't find Bedwyr and Gwalchmai," Lancelot said.

Arthur looked puzzled. "I guess I could have sent a messenger; I didn't think of it. You know I'd let you know if something went wrong."

She shook her head. "I'm fine, now. I just want my men home, safe. All of you." She glanced at Lancelot and then back to Arthur.

Arthur put his arm around her waist as they turned and proceeded up to the gate. Elaine was still waiting and lost no time in linking her arm to Lancelot's. She smiled at him, her dimples showing. "I'm glad you're back, Lancelot."

Gwenhwyfar narrowed her eyes, but there was little she could do. Lancelot's gaze locked with hers before Arthur tugged at her arm and led the way back to the hall.

# Chapter 11

# The Rescue

Beltane. The needfire had been lit, and from the battlements hundreds of smaller fires could be seen flickering, dotting the hillsides. On the northern horizon, the unusual lights of pale green, pink, and blue swayed to their silent music.

Arthur and Gwenhwyfar stood watching them, his arms wrapped around her waist. "A pretty sight, isn't it?" he asked.

She rested her arms on top of his. For once, they were alone and Arthur was relaxed. For once, he and Gwenhwyfar seemed attuned to one another.

"Hmmm," she answered, "they are unusually bright tonight. Doesn't Myrddin usually have a prediction to make when the lights play?"

He nibbled her ear. "Myrddin isn't here," he whispered.

She looked surprised. He shrugged.

"Since we've been back, I haven't been able to spend much time with you."

"I think you may be feeling the effects of Beltane," she answered with a smile.

"Mayhap. The moontide is strong on such nights." He looked at the sky's changing colors. "Nimue says this is the night Belinus reunites with the Earth Mother, and sons become lovers. All women are the Goddess."

Gwenhwyfar stiffened. "Nimue. Is she leading the rites tonight? Should you be with her again?"

"Are you jealous?" Arthur was amused.

"Don't I have a right to be?" Gwenhwyfar asked with a slight quiver to her voice.

*Careful. She's getting emotional again.* "You don't need to worry, Gwenhwyfar. Nimue is too near her time . . ." Too late, he realized his error. Gwenhwyfar stepped away from him.

"Is that the only reason you aren't with her?"

He recognized the building anger in her voice and reached for her. "Forget Nimue. Let's make our own magic tonight."

She jerked her arm away. "I will not participate in anything pagan."

Arthur watched as she climbed down the ladder and stalked across the bailey. *No use going after her now.* He turned back to the sky. *Why must we always argue?* Nimue would have understood.

Myrddin arrived the next morning as several of them were breaking their fast. He was wearing his white robe, which he did only for druid rituals. The hood was thrown back and his long tawny hair made his golden eyes seem even more piercing. He walked directly to Arthur.

"Has she . . . ?" Arthur began.

Myrddin nodded. "You have a daughter, born on Beltane night. Nimue named her Argante. The lights danced for her last night."

Gwenhwyfar made a strangling sound and went totally still.

Arthur jumped up from the table, a boyish grin covering his face. "I'll saddle Valiant and be ready in minutes."

Myrddin reached out and stopped him. "You will not be allowed on the Isle."

His eyes turned to flint as he stared at Myrddin. "I will not be denied my daughter, if it takes Excalibur to get through."

"Excalibur belongs to the Lady, Arthur. Remember that," Myrddin said sharply, then relented. "Listen to me first."

"What?" he asked impatiently. *I am the king; I have a right to my daughter.*

"Rituals are held for nine days when a child, especially a girl child, is born on the Isle. One ritual a day. Women only. Even I could not have access to those secrets," Myrddin said. "On the tenth day, Nimue will bring the child to the people and she will bless the land and its king."

"We will have a great feast then," Arthur declared, "with games and entertainment." He turned to Gwenhwyfar, feeling totally happy. "I have a daughter! Gwenhwyfar, I know you'll love her, too, just wait . . ."

Gwenhwyfar turned pale. Lancelot took a look at her face and gestured to the others to leave, but Elaine stayed, staring at Gwenhwyfar, her mouth slightly open.

Lancelot pulled her up by her arm, none too gently. "We leave, now." He propelled her to the door, shutting it behind them.

Arthur knelt in front of Gwenhwyfar and placed his hands on her shoulders. "Gwenhwyfar, I know once you see her . . . Nimue would want you . . ." he stopped, dropping his hands, and leaned back on his haunches. Gwenhwyfar would not look at him. *Now what is wrong? Can't she see how glad I am?*

He tried a different approach. "You knew this would happen. You knew she was with child. I don't understand. Do you not want me to be happy?"

She did look at him then, her eyes like flames of emerald fire in icy marble. She slapped him as hard as she could. He lost his balance and fell back. Without a word, she walked from the room.

Arthur lay where he had fallen, his hand on his stinging cheek. "Why did she do that?"

Myrddin's faerie stifled a giggle, but the druid just shook his head and held out a hand. "Arthur, my boy," he asked, "what did Uther teach you about women, anyway?"


Lancelot found Gwenhwyfar, later that morning, sitting on her favorite bench in a secluded corner of the herbal garden. As always, she sensed his presence, but she continued to stare at the wall, not moving. He sat down next to her and waited.

After some minutes she said, "I slapped him, Lance. Hard." Her voice was flat.

"I know," he answered. "I've seen the bruise."

She turned to him, her eyes widening. "How angry is he?"

He shrugged. "It's hard to say if he is. He's not talking, and Myrddin, for some reason, seems to think he deserved it."

Her eyes grew even wider. "Myrddin? He dislikes me. Why would he . . . ?" She grew quiet again. "What am I going to do, Lancelot? I can't handle this."

He put his arm around her and she leaned against him, her head on his shoulder. "If I could fix this for you, I would. I can't take you away because you are the queen."

"A queen who must accept another woman's child," she said bitterly.

He laid his head atop hers. "Yes," he whispered, "at least for now. I'll help you get through it."

She buried her face and let the tears come. He stroked her

back until she calmed down, the sobs turning to sniffles. Eventually she sat up.

"I must look terrible."

"You're beautiful, Gwen. Always." He brushed away the tear streaks and kissed her gently. She returned his kiss, her mouth hungry.

He deepened the kiss; then he pulled back. "I think we had better stop." He took a ragged breath. "You know what might make you feel better, Gwen? You've wanted to take Safere out and run him. Why don't we do it?"

She sighed and nodded. *Too bad if Arthur doesn't want me riding the colt.*

"I think, though," Lancelot said, as they started walking toward the stable, "Palomides had better come, too. I don't trust myself to be alone with you."

She stopped and looked directly at him. "Maybe I don't care. Maybe I want . . ."

"Hush, Gwen, you're hurting. We can't do what both of us know is wrong. I will not cause you more pain." He shook his head. "Let's just concentrate on running that horse."

They rode through the gate a short time later. Gwenhwyfar purposely ignored Arthur, who was standing in the doorway, watching them leave. She glanced over at Lancelot and caught him looking at her. He grinned lopsidedly. For the first time, she wondered how wrong it would really be for them to come together, after all.


The next nine days went by swiftly. Riders went out to invite Arthur's allies to the Blessing of the Land, as he called it, and to the games the following day. As the guests arrived and set up tents, the cooks scurried to accommodate them and prepare for the feast day. Hunting parties went out daily, and Arthur organized competition practices.

Gwenhwyfar took little part in any of it. At supper that

first night, she had seen the purple bruise on Arthur's left cheek and formally apologized. He had formally accepted but made no effort to include her in his conversation with Myrddin. She returned to her own room that night. Arthur let her be.

One of the late-arriving guests was Maelgwyn. He brought the two Saxons with him, much to her dismay. However, since Arthur was determined to accept all guests for this occasion, she couldn't do anything except avoid them as much as possible. They had both made public apologies.

She went riding daily. Cali had been bred to Valiant and was at pasture waiting to foal, so Gwenhwyfar worked with the colt. Lancelot rode with her, always careful that someone else accompanied them as well.

The night before Nimue was due to arrive, Arthur finally included Gwenhwyfar in the plans for the next day. He asked her to join him and Myrddin in the council room.

"The people will gather at the circle of stones. The ceremony will be held at Sext, while the sun is at its peak. Nimue thought it best to go directly there, rather than coming here first." He looked at Gwenhwyfar directly. "We will ride together to meet her."

"I have no wish to take part in your pagan activities," she retorted, "and I don't plan to go anywhere." She looked away.

Arthur continued as though she hadn't spoken. "After she has presented my . . . the child . . . to the people, I will accept the blessing and then acknowledge you as my queen. You will react graciously."

She glared at him. "I will not!"

"You will."

She raised her arm, but he caught her hand and brought it down on the table, hard. She tried to pull away, but he simply tightened his hold. "Not again, Wife"—he looked at her levelly—"I might forget my good manners."

She fumed and looked away.

"As I was saying," he said in the pleasant, conversational tone that was so deceptive, "you will accept the acknowledgment and the ceremony will be over. Then we return here and you will be a proper hostess to our guests."

"May I have my hand back?"

"For certes," he answered politely and released it.

She eyed him dubiously and rubbed her wrist. "Arthur, why do you want to humiliate me? I am your wife, but I have not produced a child and I may not be able to. Yet one night with your pagan priestess with her loose ways . . ."

A storm brewed in his eyes. "I will not have you insult Nimue, Gwenhwyfar. Not now, not ever." His voice was dangerously soft.

She recognized the danger and changed tactics. "How will it look for your wife to stand there, accepting a child by another woman? That does not seem queenly to me."

"It is exactly what a queen would do." Myrddin spoke for the first time and Gwenhwyfar jumped. "A queen does not allow the people to see her upset." He stopped as if listening to something, then nodded to himself and continued, "A queen recognizes that the people are accepting this child as proof that the land will be fertile and they will prosper. A queen understands this has little to do with personal desire."

"Ha!" she interrupted, "I have no doubt he desires her; you were not here to see them together every night, his hand on her belly."

Arthur raised an eyebrow. "If I were you, Gwenhwyfar," he said quietly, "I would be careful whom I accuse of having desires."

She stared at him, feeling her face pale. "I have not done . . ."

He leaned forward, placing his hand across her mouth. His grey eyes searched hers. "No lies, no confessions, Gwenhwyfar." He sighed and leaned back. "Let it be."

* * *

Arthur waited near the front door the next morning, tapping his foot. He sent Brisen to make sure Gwenhwyfar was not only getting ready, but wearing a dress. She was late.

He had started pacing when he heard her footsteps and looked up. And blinked. Gwenhwyfar was wearing a silk gown of emerald green that deepened her malachite eyes and enhanced the auburn of her hair. The gown clung softly to her and swayed gently when she moved, enhancing the outline of her hips. Somehow, she had managed to get her hair to stay in curls on top of her head, and she was wearing the face coloring she had worn on their wedding day. He frowned at the amount of breast showing above the low neckline. Gwenhwyfar looked both regal and ready to be ravished.

"Don't you have a gown that is less revealing? Where did you get it?"

"Morgana had it made for me in those first days." She gave him a sidelong glance, her eyes catlike from the cosmetics she had applied. "Do you not like my appearance?" she asked innocently.

It was a loaded question and he knew it. "I very much like your appearance, but I would like for you to save it for me, not the entire countryside."

"Well," she answered demurely, "I could change into my shirt and trews and ride my own horse to this ceremony. But I thought you wanted me to act like a queen?"

He gave up. They didn't have time to argue the matter and Gwenhwyfar was spoiling for a spat. He offered her his arm and they proceeded outside.

Lancelot brought the old Roman chariot around and held the reins of the gelding pulling it. When he saw Gwenhwyfar, he turned his attention to adjusting the harness.

Arthur walked to him and tugged at the reins he was clenching tightly in one fist. "You might as well enjoy the sight of her, Lance; every other man is going to," he whispered grimly and then turned back to Gwenhwyfar. He forced himself to smile as he helped her into the chariot.

They arrived at the stone circle a few minutes before Sext, Arthur driving the chariot and Gwenhwyfar standing beside him, holding her head high.

Arthur saw the corner of Myrddin's mouth twitch as he approached them and tried to avoid his gaze, concentrating instead on some sort of shimmer in the air beside Myrddin. He wondered what caused it.

"She looks beguiling, doesn't she?" the faerie giggled in Myrddin's ear. "I can dress like that if you like . . ."

Myrddin swatted at the air and then bowed toward Gwenhwyfar. "You look ready to control your destiny today, my lady. I hope it meets your expectations."

Gwenhwyfar stood with Lancelot near the circle, observing. The Lady had stationed Arthur beside an outside stone. He looked straight ahead as a single file of white-robed priestesses walked from the copse of hazel trees and formed a double column. Nimue followed them, wearing a robe of light blue and carrying the child. She proceeded through the column and stopped in front of Arthur. Silence fell over the crowd.

Nimue smiled and held the baby out to him.

His look of wonder changed to terror. "I'll drop her; she's too small . . ."

She turned her back slightly to the crowd and placed the baby in his arms, bringing them up around the child. "She won't break," Gwenhwyfar heard Nimue reply. "You must hold her up in acknowledgment to the people."

Arthur inhaled sharply and looked at the baby's face. She cooed and smiled at him, and he broke into a huge grin. He turned, facing the people, and held the child out.

Gwenhwyfar could see the change of emotions sweep over Arthur's face. Suddenly she felt totally worthless. *How can I compete with that? I'm dressed all wrong . . . I'm a fool.*

"Arthur is getting ready to call you, Gwen." Lancelot laid a hand on her shoulder.

She panicked. "I can't go over there! I'll look horrible beside her!"

"You are the queen, Gwenhwyfar. Show the people that. Hold your head high. I'll be waiting right here." His hand caressed her back lightly.

Gwenhwyfar straightened her shoulders and lifted her chin. Slowly, she walked to them. Nimue had taken the baby again, and Arthur took Gwenhwyfar's right hand and brought her slightly in front of him, putting his other arm around her waist. He raised their right arms together. The crowd cheered.

As he lowered their arms, he whispered, "Just one more thing, and we can leave."

She froze. Nimue handed the baby to her. She tried to turn away, but Arthur was behind her, one hand on either of her arms, locking her in place and forcing her to accept the child.

Carefully, Nimue placed the baby in her rigid embrace. She sent a worried look to Arthur, and he closed Gwenhwyfar's arms around the bundle, tightening his hold. The baby was secure and Nimue stepped back.

The crowd cheered again and Arthur whispered in her ear, "Smile and look like you mean it, Gwenhwyfar."

At that moment the baby wiggled and instinctively, Gwenhwyfar grasped her. She looked down to see those grey eyes—Arthur's eyes—studying her. The baby flailed a fist and grabbed onto Gwenhwyfar's finger. Conflicting emotions stung her. Slowly, she smiled and looked up.

The crowd reached a frenzied pitch as Nimue took the child back and Arthur turned Gwenhwyfar in his arms and kissed her soundly.

"Thank you," he whispered against her mouth. "Thank you."

* * *

Gwenhwyfar dressed in her usual shirt and trews the next morning. She had seen Maelgwyn and his men leering at her yesterday, even though they had looked quickly away. Today she was back to normal.

She grew bored. Everyone had something to do. Cai was in charge of the food preparations, Lancelot was practicing with some of his men for the games later this afternoon, Palomides had gone to get the horses ready, and Arthur was in the map room with Uriens discussing the problems in the north with a rebel named Hueil. She would have liked to take part in that discussion, but Arthur had told her not to worry about it. She watched the field practice for a while and then wandered to the paddock. Safere nickered and trotted over to her.

She stroked his soft muzzle. "You wouldn't throw me if I were to ride you alone today, would you, boy?" she asked. He pawed the ground.

She made up her mind. Quickly she saddled him and mounted. No one would notice if she rode for a few miles. She'd be back well before the games began. Eric and Gustav came around the corner and stopped, watching her. She ignored them and was readying an excuse for the gate guard but noticed there wasn't one this morning. Unusual, but there were plenty of people around. Safere trotted out the gate and down the road.

The horse behaved beautifully. Gwenhwyfar held him to a slow canter, not risking the full gallop. He wasn't even winded when she stopped by the stone circle. She had never been inside it. Today she felt reckless.

She dismounted, dropped the reins over his head, and left Safere to graze on the grass by the hazel trees. She hesitated when she got to the spot where they had stood yesterday. It felt different, but maybe it was her imagination. She stepped between the blue menhirs.

Inside the circle, she felt peaceful. A small flock of meadowlarks soared through, their yellow breasts brilliant, their buzzlike air song sweet. Somewhere over the small hill, she could hear the sound of the tumbling water of the river. She went to the altar stone and touched it tentatively, then drew her hand back quickly. A spark had come from the stone.

She heard horses approaching. Idly, she wondered if she had been seen and someone was coming to escort her home. She stepped out of the circle as the two riders rounded the curve by the copse.

They were Maelgwyn's men, the two Saxons. Quickly she stepped back behind one of the stones.

They stopped and dismounted. A moment later she heard the sound of a whip and Safere's scream, then his hooves pounding away at a flat run.

"Gwenhwyfar!" one of them called out. "Where are you?"

She crouched behind the stone.

"She's here someplace," Eric said. "Probably up there."

Gustav held him back. "Those places have old magic in them. Let's look around first." They moved off.

Gwenhwyfar fought the panic welling up inside her. She had to get to the horses. The Saxons had stopped just over the hill, arguing about how far up the stream to look or whether they should separate.

Finally, after some minutes, they started to move again. She slipped away from her stone and quietly approached the horses. One of them whinnied and she froze, halfway between safety and escape. She heard one of the men returning.

She ran to the horses, which made them edgy, and was trying to get her foot in the stirrup when Eric saw her. She got mounted just as he grabbed for the reins.

The horse had been trained for battle and was not the Saxon's personal mount. It responded to her kick and reared up, striking out with its hooves as it was taught. Eric backed away, but Gustav joined him, coming around on the other side. The horse kicked out with its back legs. Gwenhwyfar took the extra length of rein and started swatting at the men.

*If only I had a sword!* Thankfully, she noted neither of them was armed, either.

The horse did his best to respond to her commands. Finally, Gustav grabbed the rein close to the bit and pulled the animal's head down. Eric reached for Gwenhwyfar and she kicked him.

"You'll pay for that one, little queen," he jeered and lunged for her again. She clung to the saddle, her legs gripping the frightened horse.

Eric struggled to dislodge her while Gustav held the horse still. Finally he dragged her off and threw her to the ground. Panting, he stood still for a moment.

Gwenhwyfar leaped to her feet and ran; Gustav sprinted after her, eventually able to grab one arm. She turned and punched him as hard as she could in the stomach and then brought her knee up to his groin. He groaned in pain and sank down.

She struggled loose and ran again, but Eric was mounted and caught up with her easily. He half lifted and dragged her back to the copse, dangling from the horse.

Gustav sat, moaning. "I guess it will be your turn, first, brother. I'll try to hold her for you."

Gwenhwyfar kept moving, thrashing her arms and legs. She managed to kick Gustav again and he went down. Eric had a hard time pinning her but finally, he managed to throw himself over her. Gustav crawled to them and pulled her arms painfully over her head.

She spit in Eric's face and he slapped her, hard, before he ripped her shirt open and greedily helped himself.


Lancelot was astride Pryderi when he saw Safere galloping up the road, riderless. He shouted to Palomides to catch the colt. Pryderi reached out for his full stride before they cleared the gate.

*She must have been thrown . . . she probably went out alone.* He knew she didn't want to spend time in the hall with Nimue. He had planned to stay with her this morning, but she had insisted he work with the men.

Lancelot heard her scream as he drew near the hazel copse. He came around the curve and saw two men galloping off. He started to give chase, but then he saw Gwen.

She lay crumpled in a heap, her shirt in shreds around her, her arms covering her face. He pulled off his own shirt as he ran to her. "It's Lance, Gwen. You're safe now," he said as he dropped beside her.

She reached out blindly, pulling herself up against him, clinging to him, shaking. He saw that her face was bruised. He ran his hand along the soft, warm skin of her back and felt something sticky. She was bleeding.

"What have they done, Gwenhwyfar? How badly are you hurt?"

She only buried her face deeper into his neck. Finally, her muffled voice came to him faintly. "I feel so dirty, Lancelot, so unclean."

He held her tighter, stroking her hair. "You're safe, Gwen. I will find them."

He started to wrap his shirt around her when she sat up and he gasped. Her left breast was already bruising badly near the teeth marks. Her right breast had long, bloody scratches across it.

"I will kill them, Gwen. Slowly. I give you my oath."

She closed her eyes. "Just make me feel clean again and not used. Please." She took one of his hands and pressed it to her breast.

For a minute he didn't grasp her meaning. *Does she want me to . . . by the gods, her breasts are beautiful . . .* Very gently, he cupped the bruised one and bent, taking the nipple of the other in his mouth, suckling carefully. She groaned and gripped him tightly. He nuzzled her neck and softly parted her swollen lips with his tongue, tasting the saltiness of her tears. The kiss lingered and grew. He knew he should stop; this was developing into unbridled passion and Gwenhwyfar was not his. But she felt so vulnerable in his arms, so soft. *Ah, Gwen, why did you marry Arthur?* With tremendous effort he tore himself away from her embrace.

She sighed and opened her eyes. "Maelgwyn's men. The Saxons . . . they followed me."

Guilt flooded him. *I let them go that night.* "They will be dealt with and Maelgwyn, too, if he is any part of this," Lancelot said grimly. "But first, I need to get you home." He helped her into his shirt and fastened it. "Can you walk?"

She nodded. "You came before they could get my trews off."

When she stood, however, she wobbled. He whistled for Pryderi and lifted her into the saddle, mounting behind her. She settled against him and he set the horse into a comfortable, rocking-chair canter.

As they reached the main road, they met Arthur, Uriens, and Palomides.

Lancelot brought Pryderi alongside Valiant. "Maelgwyn's Saxons," he said quickly, "tried to rape her. They rode toward his place."

Arthur leaned over and touched the side of Gwenhwyfar's bruised face. His mouth set in a hard line. "How badly are you hurt, Gwen? Did they . . ."

She shook her head. "Lancelot got there in time."

He gave Lancelot a grateful look and nodded. "Take her home, Lance. I'll get the details later. I'm going to ride after them. And have Maelgwyn waiting when I get back. If he's any part of this, he's a dead man." He spun Valiant around and was gone, Palomides and Uriens thundering after him.

\* \* \*

Lancelot was waiting when Arthur returned home shortly before sunset. "Did you find them?"

"No. They're gone," Arthur said tiredly as they walked inside. "How's Gwenhwyfar?"

"Sleeping. Nimue prepared a draught."

"Good." Arthur accepted the wineskin from the servant and motioned Lancelot to follow him to the map room. He closed the door. "Have you questioned Maelgwyn?"

Lancelot nodded. "He swears he knows nothing." He shrugged. "I'm inclined to believe him; he made a stinking mess in his pants. He did say they had worked for Cerdic before they came to him."

Arthur asked, "Where would you go if you were those two?"

Lancelot thought. "Possibly back to Cerdic, depending on why they left. Not Aelle; he would not harbor them. Aesc would be the best choice. He is the farthest distant and no friend of ours."

Arthur nodded. "I will go . . ."

Lancelot stopped him. "Let me go, Arthur. I gave Gwenhwyfar my oath that I'd kill them. I failed once when I let those two go the first time; let me make amends."

"I am her husband, Lance."

"You are a king first. That's why she has a champion."

Arthur sighed and his shoulders slumped as he sat down by the table. "You're right. Duty comes first. Uriens was explaining the state of affairs in the north when Palomides came in."

"It's not good, then?"

"Hueil is restless. He spends his time with the Scotti. I think he is gathering forces from across the Hibernian Sea. Hoel is assisting Prince Dubnovalus in Alclud, which will protect the west, but I'm also worried about the North Sea. We need fortifications on the eastern side, as well."

Arthur poured both of them some wine. He leaned back

in his chair and propped his feet on the table. "How is she, Lancelot? Tell me what happened."

When he finished, Arthur sat for some minutes. Finally, he said, "I'm glad you were there, Lancelot. How do I thank you?"

Lancelot hesitated, the guilt nearly overwhelming. "Let me find them, Arthur. And, after I do, grant me a leave."

Arthur looked surprised. "Why?"

He studied the ceiling, then took a deep breath and looked directly at Arthur. "Because I care about Gwen. Too much."

Arthur's boots landed with a thud as he sat up. "I know you care about her; you always have." He grinned suddenly. "I think, Lance, what you need is a woman. How long has it been?"

He shrugged, "A while." *Not since I met Gwenhwyfar.*

"Hmmm. When you came to us, seven years ago, you quickly gained a reputation. What was it? 'You work hard and you play easy,' I think." Arthur continued, "You had more women following you than I did, and I wasn't exactly cooling my heels most nights."

Lancelot shrugged. It was true and he would always be grateful to the courtesans his mother had selected to teach him the difference between satisfying himself and pleasuring a woman. *Now, there is only one that I care to be with, and she's not mine to have.* He sighed. "I've lost my taste for wenching."

"A wife then. It's time you married. Elaine, mayhap?"

Lancelot started. "No! I want no commitments." He added emphatically, "I'm not interested in Elaine."

Arthur studied him. "So," he said at last, "you love Gwenhwyfar."

He met Arthur's look. "Yes." *At least, now Arthur knows. I won't have to lie.*

Arthur took a deep breath. "We've shared women before, but not this time, Lance. She's my wife."

Lancelot nodded. "And that's why I must leave."

They were both silent, lost in their own thoughts. A short while later, Arthur put his cup down. "If you went back to Benoic, you would be a king one day in equal status to me."

"My brother, Ector, will hold the regency. Unless . . . are you sending me back?"

"No," Arthur said emphatically. "I need you here." He sighed. "I will send you to those eastern fortifications I was talking about earlier. A fort, north of the Hadrian's Wall, has been empty since Hoel took it from Marianus and moved him to Gwynedd. Take Gaheris and a company of men with you and prepare it for defense. The name is Din Guayrdi."

"Joyous Garde?" Lancelot smiled mirthlessly. "You will let me champion Gwen, though, and find the Saxons?"

Arthur stood. "You gave her your oath, didn't you? She will expect you to keep it." He left and Lancelot heard him walk slowly up the stairs to Gwenhwyfar.

He stayed in the chair and broodingly finished the wine.

Nimue and Argante returned to Avallach shortly after the ceremony. Arthur set up a schedule of monthly visits that would least affect Gwenhwyfar, meeting Nimue and his daughter near the circle of stones where they would spend the day. He had a small cottage built near the stream there and kept it stocked.

Less than a moon after Lancelot left, a messenger arrived from Aelle, bearing a container with a sealed jar and a letter. Lancelot had caught up with the two men passing through the weald, trying to reach Aesc's lands. "Lancelot hoped," the letter said, "that the contents of the jar would bring peace to the queen."

Arthur removed the jar from its carefully wrapped container and laughed as he handed it to Gwenhwyfar.

She stared. Four testicles floated in liquid, the flesh still preserved on them. She made a strangled sound and the jar started to slip from her nerveless fingers, but Arthur caught it.

"These men will never rape again, Gwenhwyfar," he said, still bemused. "I couldn't have done a better job of avenging you myself. Are you not pleased?"

She looked shocked. "I'm glad it's over, yes, but I don't want to see that horrible jar again."

Arthur replaced it in the container. "I think I will make a present of it to Maelgwyn," he said, "so that he will remember the lesson. Will that suit you, Gwen?"

Slowly, she nodded. "Why did Lancelot not bring it himself?"

He hesitated, expecting an explosion when he told her he was sending Lancelot to Joyous Garde, but she said nothing, just searched his face, then turned and walked away.

# Chapter 12

# The Young Prince

The north remained quiet that year; Hueil spent time in Hibernia, and Hoel and Dubnovalus kept patrols on the western coast. Lancelot sent regular reports on the fortifications in the east. In the south the Saxons were peaceful.

Arthur took this time to establish protocol for his system of justice. He worked from dawn until well into the night, sometimes forgetting to eat. He reverted back to the Roman concept of *civitas,* the city-state condition of the lands each petty king held. He ordered a census of all the people in each civitas and called a council to determine the fairness of taxation. The Christian priests and their cellare, the provision-keepers, were not happy that they were to be taxed as well, but Arthur was determined that all people who lived in Britain would share the burdens.

In the spring before battles were engaged, Arthur heard petitions. He also hosted the games for men who wanted to challenge each other's prowess.

He knew Gwenhwyfar looked for Lancelot at the games

that first year, but he did not attend. She didn't mention Lancelot much and he wasn't sure if that was good or bad. Sometimes he felt like he'd never understand her. Women were too complicated; planning a war campaign was much easier.

In late summer of that year, Hueil made his move. He crossed the western sea with one hundred and fifty Scotti, collected another one hundred from Domangart's north-western isles, and laid siege to Alclud.

Arthur approached the upcoming battle with as much energy as he had his justice system. He sent riders to Lancelot, Leodegrance, and Uriens's son, Owain, to prepare their troops. Leodegrance would join Lancelot and advance from the east, while Arthur's men would meet with Owain's and approach from the south.

"We should be home before the snow flies. Cai and Gwalchmai should be able to handle any problems here." They were in the map room; Gwenhwyfar sat on the cot while Arthur collected what he needed to take the next day.

"You will see Lancelot, though?" Gwenhwyfar asked hesitantly.

Arthur looked at her sharply. *So she still thinks of him.* "Yes," he answered. "Is there a message you'd like me to deliver?"

"Just that I hope he is well, and will stay safe." Arthur raised an eyebrow. Standing, she quickly added, "And you, too. I would want you to come home to me, whole and sound."

He set down his maps and stepped closer, tilting her chin and forcing her to look directly into his eyes. "Would you really miss me if I didn't come home, Gwenhwyfar?" *Lord, there are times when I don't think she'd care at all.* Since he'd sent Lancelot off, Gwenhwyfar had become remote and detached.

"Of course I would! What kind of a question is that?" She tried to pull away.

"It's a fair question. This year, our times together have been few, and I have instigated them." His eyes bore into hers.

"You've been busy, Arthur. You haven't had time for me," she answered.

He released her. "I have time now, Gwenhwyfar. If you want me, go and bolt the door."

He watched as she walked to the door and hesitated. He took a deep breath and prepared himself for the worst. Then she threw the bolt.

Happiness surged through him. He pulled her to him and the two of them tumbled onto the cot. The repressed urges of each kindled as long-dried wood in a forest might at the first spark of the flint. When they finished, Arthur propped himself up on his elbow and searched her face.

"What?" Gwenhwyfar asked, her fingers tracing a pattern on his chest.

"Nothing." He leaned over to kiss her quickly before sitting up and reaching for his clothes. *How can I ask her if she had been thinking of me or Lancelot?*

The siege lasted longer than Arthur had anticipated. The troops were in position, effectively sandwiching Hueil's army between themselves and the fort, when Fergus Mor sent reinforcements from the north, opening a way for Hueil to escape. Early snow was already falling in the region. They would have to pursue Hueil in the spring.

Arthur sent most of his troops home, keeping only a turma of thirty cavalry with him as he followed Owain back to Rheged.

Uriens was pale and gaunt, and Arthur wondered if Morgana had anything to do with it. He decided to question Owain and found him working in the map room.

Owain shook his head when Arthur told him his suspicions. "I would have agreed with you a year ago, but since you sent her back, she has done nothing but dote on my father. Mayhap she's come to her senses. Or"—he shrugged, grinning—"it's because Accolon got horse-whipped before he was sent away and no other man will dare to go near her, not even Bertilak, her previous lover."

Arthur grinned, too. "So, justice prevails!"

"I don't like her, Arthur, but I can't say she's mistreated my father this past year. When she isn't with him, she spends her time with Medraut."

"That's her son?" Arthur asked. "Where is he? I've never met my nephew."

Owain gave him a strange look before he answered. "He's visiting Margawse. Her youngest son, Gareth, is about the same age. They met two or three years ago."

Coming into the room, Morgana heard the last bit of conversation. "He's nearly eleven and quite the swordsman for his age." She hesitated and then said softly, "Arthur, can we put the past behind us? I am your sister and I would like to make amends."

He looked at her warily. All of his warrior senses were on alert. She sounded sincere, but he felt like a mouse in the presence of a cat. "That would be up to Gwenhwyfar."

"For certes," she demurred. "But I would love to present Medraut to you and her. Would you ask her?"

He hesitated, thinking there was something more. "I'll ask," he finally said.

After leaving Rheged, Arthur and his men rode north over the high moors into the graduating green canyons that led down to the coastal plain of Joyous Garde. Arthur had not inspected the place and wanted to see what improvements Lancelot had made.

The holding was situated on a hill, near the bend of the Coquet River with a good view of the surrounding valley, and was fortified with earthworks and a stone palisade. The buildings inside the enclosure were of wood and stone, solidly built. On the northern side, the stables had been redone to accommodate a hundred horses.

On the southeastern side, affording a glimpse of the sea, lay the gardens which gave the place its name. Laid out in precise triangles, they formed a wheel, a line of rocks creating spokes between each bed. At its hub, benches surrounded a central fountain. The gardens had been well tended, even though they were now prepared for winter.

The austerity of the hall came as a shock to Arthur. There were the usual trestles and high table, but no tapestries adorned the walls to shut out the cold. The guest quarters, as well as Lancelot's own, were equally barren. *Why is the man living like a monk?* Clean, serviceable, but with few creature comforts.

Arthur turned to Lancelot. "Why didn't you tell me you needed furnishings? I'll have Gwenhwyfar send some things."

"There is no need," Lancelot answered. "I have the fires lit at night for warmth; the men have rotating leave to visit the village for their pleasures."

Arthur looked at him sideways, but decided not to ask. "Who tends the gardens? Gwenhwyfar would love them."

"That's been my pastime," Lancelot answered. "I've found I like grubbing."

Arthur nodded. "Nimue always says getting her hands dirty helps her maintain her link to the land. Mayhap it's the fey blood in you."

Lancelot's eyes became unreadable. "There is something to be said for making things grow, rather than destroying them."

Arthur raised an eyebrow. "Are you turning philosophical on me, Lance?"

He shrugged. "I've had a lot of time to think."

"Well," Arthur said, "I'll keep you busy this next week. I want to see how well your soldiers perform."

Lancelot arranged daily competitions for Arthur to observe and a week later, as his turma was preparing to leave, Arthur leaned down from the saddle.

"Things are in good order. Why don't you train Gaheris to

take command and return to Camelot when that's done? Gwen . . . both of us have missed you."

Lancelot met his gaze silently. Then finally he spoke. "I'll come when I can."

Arthur returned to Camelot shortly before Yule and within days, a messenger came with the news that Uriens had died. Arthur disappeared for several days and when he returned, he canceled all celebrations for the Winter Solstice. All he told Gwenhwyfar was that he'd lost a good friend.

Gradually the winter passed. Nimue and Myrddin arrived shortly before Arthur heard petitions the day before the spring games.

Toward late afternoon a messenger arrived with a note for Arthur. His face darkened as he read and passed it to Gwenhwyfar.

Morgana had returned, at least temporarily, to her own lands adjacent to Maelgwyn's. Accolon had joined her as her seneschal. She would appreciate Arthur's allowing him to participate in the games on the next day.

"It's your decision, Gwenhwyfar," Arthur said.

"She certainly didn't lose any time in finding Accolon again," Gwenhwyfar remarked. "But this is Petition Day; you are obligated to grant the request if you can."

He thought, then nodded. "I suppose you're right, even though my better judgment says otherwise."

And so, Morgana and Accolon were invited to the games.

The day of the tournament dawned with clear skies and a slight breeze. The field had been staked out, the benches set and awnings raised. Brightly colored standards fluttered along the sidelines, complementing the spring colors of the ladies' gowns.

The archers competed first, followed by the swordsmen.

Accolon won the hand-to-hand combat challenge; next came the lance-throwing.

"If Lancelot were here, there would be no question of that outcome," Arthur said.

Gwenhwyfar nodded. He had been sent an invitation and she had hoped he would come, but he had not. Two years had passed since she had seen him. *How can you stay away, Lancelot? Do you not miss me? Has someone taken your heart?*

Early afternoon brought shows of horsemanship as individuals put their animals through the gaits and battle maneuvers. The last event for the day was the joust. It required full armor and helmets. The men could choose the traditional long lance or the shorter, less wieldy one that Lancelot preferred. The only rule was that the lances had to be of equal length in each event as the men tried to unseat one another. Arthur planned to ride in this event, in disguise, and slipped off to change clothes.

Gwalchmai went first, unseating his brother Agravaine. Gryflet challenged him next and was unhorsed. Bedwyr was one of the last to ride against him, and they made three passes before Gwalchmai fell from his horse.

Arthur rode onto the field. He was dressed in simple armor, carrying the long lance. Bedwyr accepted the challenge and exchanged his short one. They set their horses at each other once, twice. Bedwyr nearly unseated him on the third pass, but he regained his balance. On the fourth pass Arthur's lance caught Bedwyr and he landed with a thud, but rolled to a standing position. The crowd cheered. Arthur was about to remove his helmet when the crowd suddenly grew silent. He turned around.

A large sorrel destrier stood at the end of the field, its rider wearing bronze armor that blended with the horse's coat. His visor was already in place. He held up his lance.

Arthur raised his in response and wheeled his horse to the end of the list.

The other rider did the same. As the horses began the first run, Gwenhwyfar gasped. She knew of only one man who rode a horse as though he were an extension of it. From her bench she could see the graceful, fluid balance he had and the direction the horse was taking from his thighs. *Lancelot!* Pure bliss swept through her. *I can't wait to see you . . . to talk . . . to touch you! My love.*

Her heart beat faster as she watched each of them strike a blow that was heard across the field. The audience held its collective breath; neither rider was unseated.

The second run was silent save for the horses' hooves beating the ground. Again, two strong blows and the riders passed.

On the third pass, Arthur missed his mark, bouncing off the other's lance.

The fourth time, Arthur caught the rider on the shoulder, pushing him back in the saddle. Somehow, he managed to stay astride.

When Lancelot wheeled his mount for the fifth run, Gwenhwyfar saw blood seeping down his arm. She stood up and screamed, "He's wounded. Stop this!"

Both of them paused to look at her. Arthur shouted, "Shall we call it a tie? I have no objections."

Lancelot bowed slightly to Gwenhwyfar and then raised his lance again to challenge. She sank down on the bench. *What was wrong with him? With both of them?*

As they rode toward each other, the challenger swayed. The horses were closing. As the last possible moment, Arthur veered his horse off the path and threw his lance on the ground, conceding the victory.

Gwenhwyfar sank back in relief. *Thank God, Arthur had done the sensible thing.* Now she would get Lancelot's wound taken care of. In just minutes, she would be with him again. She stood and then sat down again, dumbfounded.

Lancelot was riding away at a full gallop.

*     *     *

At the feast everyone talked about the mysterious challenger. Next to Gwenhwyfar, Elaine chattered away about how thrilling the joust had been.

At the high table, Gwenhwyfar ignored most of the talk. Her eyes kept searching the room for late arrivals, hoping that Lancelot would be among them. *Lance, how could you be so close and not stay?* The gifts that had been brought were opened and they were nearly finished. He had not shown.

On the other side of Arthur, Nimue and Myrddin were in discussion. Gwenhwyfar wondered how Nimue could concentrate with that annoying habit Myrddin had of swatting the thin air. Even as she watched, he did it again; surprisingly, Nimue smiled and seemed to nod at the emptiness beside him.

The main doors opened and Accolon entered. Arthur and Gwenhwyfar glanced over to him at the same time. He bowed slightly and gestured to someone behind him. Morgana appeared; at her side stood a tall, black-haired boy.

Nimue and Myrddin stopped their conversation, his hand in midair. Nimue clutched Arthur's arm. "The child we have been searching for," she murmured.

Gwenhwyfar thought she saw a streak of light flash toward the trio, but it faded as the boy turned to stare at them. A smile played on his lips as he looked at Nimue; then his gaze traveled to Gwenhwyfar; his expression changed to one of awe and infatuation.

"The gods help us," Myrddin whispered. "I had no idea she had created this." The faerie twittered anxiously beside him.

Arthur looked at them quizzically. "What ails you?" he asked, loosening Nimue's talon grip on his arm. "That must be my nephew. When I visited Uriens last year, Morgana asked to present him."

Morgana pushed her son forward and they stopped at the table in front of Arthur. The room had quieted.

"This is my nephew, Medraut?" Arthur asked her.

"You could say that," she answered. "You might also call him your son."

Gwenhwyfar gasped. *The eyes . . . the night at the Sacred Pool . . . the heir. Not my son. Morgana's.*

"Hello, Father," Medraut said politely.

Arthur's face set. "What is the meaning of this, Morgana? Some sort of jest?"

"No jest, Arthur," she said quietly and clearly. "He is your son, conceived on Beltane, twelve years ago. Don't you remember?"

Arthur's brow furrowed. Then he blanched. "No, it can't be," he whispered.


*He had been a captain for Uther. They had invaded Compretovium the week before and had successfully held the Saxons back. His men were returning to Ambresbyrig on Beltane . . .*

*"Come on, Arthur," Cai said from a corner of the tavern. "She's willing to take all seven of us."*

*Arthur finished his tankard and set it down. He shook his head, a bit drunkenly. "Seven's too many for any woman, even on Beltane."*

*He left them there and started slowly up the road toward camp, thinking that this was one Beltane he would be getting an early night's sleep.*

*Suddenly, without sound, a black hooded figure appeared from the bushes. He stopped, ready to draw his sword, when he heard the female voice.*

*"Follow me," she said.*

*He stepped through the bracken. He saw she was small, but her face was lost in the darkness. Her breasts were large under a flimsy gown.*

*This was an invitation he didn't want to pass up. She seemed eager for him and he took her quickly, nearly in frenzy. He hadn't realized she was a virgin until she screamed from pain.*

*She didn't speak to him when he finished. He heard his men coming up the road and quickly dressed, telling her to stay still until he could get them away . . .*

*He hadn't even asked her name.*

Now he stared at her in horror. "It can't be," he whispered again. "You're my sister."

Morgana smiled tightly. "I heard your men call your name and then I realized that you were Uther's protégé. I had no more idea we were related than you did. But if you have any doubts, look at him. Look at his eyes."

Arthur forced himself to look at the boy. The black hair was Morgana's, but otherwise, the features were his: the square jaw, the straight nose, the direct look in those grey eyes. They were Uther's eyes as well. *Dear God, what have I done?*

"What is it you want, Morgana?" His voice was cold.

She smiled again. "I want you to acknowledge him and raise him as your son. He is the rightful heir to the throne, both through you and through me, for my father was king of Tintagel. And I," she glanced at Gwenhwyfar, "will be the king's consort."

At that, Gwenhwyfar began to laugh. Higher and higher, her pitch rose. Arthur watched as her body was racked with sobs. She couldn't quit. He turned to Nimue.

Nimue placed a cool hand on her forehead and the hysteria subsided momentarily. Arthur put his arms around Gwenhwyfar and she sagged limply against his chest.

Medraut stared at him, a jealous, lovestruck expression on his face. Arthur ignored him as he pushed by and carried Gwenhwyfar toward the stairs.

Once upstairs, Arthur laid Gwenhwyfar carefully on the bed. Nimue fixed a draught for her while he paced, raking his hair with his fingers.

Myrddin walked over to the window. "We have some serious decisions to make."

Arthur looked at him. "What decisions? I will exile them."

"If you do that, it gives her all the time she needs to make him your enemy," Myrddin answered. "He will come back to fight you."

"You don't expect me to acknowledge him, do you?" Arthur asked incredulously.

"Not only acknowledge him. Raise him." The faerie twittered anxiously in Myrddin's ear and he looked annoyed when he repeated, "Yes. Raise him."

"What?" Arthur's voice was hard. "Have you taken leave of your senses, Myrddin? You want me to harbor Morgana and that . . . that . . ."

"Son," Nimue said gently, putting her hand on his arm. "He is your son as much as Argante is your daughter."

Arthur began pacing again. By Mithras, the repercussion of a few moments of physical pleasure, carelessly taken! "I can't do that to Gwenhwyfar."

"She accepted Argante, Arthur. Mayhap she will accept Medraut as well."

"Why should I raise him? He is nothing to me."

"I'm not suggesting you harbor Morgana," Myrddin interposed. "Medraut must be separated from her if we are to have a chance to save him."

Arthur looked miserably from Myrddin to Nimue and then at Gwenhwyfar, sleeping now. How he was going to tell Gwenhwyfar, he didn't know. *She will want nothing to do with me now, for certes, knowing I have committed incest. She'll never forgive me.*

Incest. The full impact of what he had done exploded within him. He sat down and put his head in his hands. Nimue reached out for him. For the first time in his adult life, he felt numbness in his groin at the touch of a woman.

# Chapter 13

# The Lily Maid

Lancelot winced as he extinguished his campfire. His shoulder wound was festering. He had been a damn fool for riding in that tournament with a long lance instead of his own; he had had no idea he would be riding against Arthur. The blow from the lance had pierced the borrowed armor, which had cut him.

But he'd gotten a chance to see Gwenhwyfar. When she stood and shouted for Arthur to stop, he wanted nothing more than to go to her. To crush her against him and breathe in the lavender scent of her hair, to touch her skin, to kiss her . . . she was more beautiful than ever. He knew he had to get away.

He had agonized over returning to Camelot after Arthur's visit to Joyous Garde last year. Lancelot did not trust himself anymore. He owed Arthur his loyalty. He was honor-bound to him. He didn't think he was strong enough to see Gwen, to be close to her, and not betray all three of them.

So he had trained Gaheris to command and decided he would leave, perhaps live among Aelle's people, away from Arthur's world and somewhere he wouldn't be found. Aelle himself had asked Lancelot to stay after he had killed the two Saxon mercenaries. When the tournament invitation came, though, he had to see Gwenhwyfar one more time.

Lancelot had been on the road two days, heading east. On this third morning, he painfully saddled the sorrel and mounted, leaving his armor behind. As he rode, the pain in his shoulder blended with the jogging of the trot . . . pound, pulse . . . pound, pulse . . . until it filled his head and the light grew dim on the road . . . *have I wandered into the forest?* . . . and dimmer. He never felt himself slide from the saddle.

Elen of Astolat finished breaking her fast and smiled at her father, Bernard.

"What will you do this morning?" he asked.

"It's such a pretty day. I thought my ladies and I might ride to the lily pond and bring some flowers home." They were her favorite flower; people always told her they matched the whiteness of her skin.

He smiled indulgently at her. "Don't wander too far. Take old Erec with you as an escort."

She frowned and tossed her long blond hair over her shoulder. She didn't need an escort. She was fifteen, almost a woman, but her father kept her so protected. She had begged him to let her visit Camelot when her brothers went last year for the tournament, but he'd told her she needed to wait. She'd never find a husband if she had to stay at Astolat, but she knew better than to argue, so she merely said, "As you wish, Father."

As they set out, a cool easterly breeze embraced them, contrasting with the welcoming warmth of the sun. Puffs of cotton filled the sky, making it a perfect day for a ride. The cook had given them meat pasties and cheese for their mid-day meal.

"I know," Elen said to her ladies, "let's ride across the chalk downs to the forest first! We can pick the flowers later."

Erec gestured furiously with his hands, for he could not speak. "No! It's too far!"

Elen laughed and shook her head. She knew he really wasn't angry.

They rode for nearly two hours before they reached the dappled shade of the green enclosure. They followed a narrow trail until they reached a small clearing.

"We'll stop here for lunch," Elen announced. Erec looked relieved.

As they prepared to dismount, a horse neighed down the road. They listened for hoofbeats but heard none. The horse whinnied again, this time louder.

"It could be hurt." Elen was always taking in strays. She wheeled her horse and cantered down the path. The others followed more slowly. She rounded a turn and saw the huge destrier standing near something on the ground. She slid off for a better look, talking softly to the large horse. He flicked his ears at her but remained calm.

As she approached, she could see the heap was a man. He wore riding boots, leather pants, and a white shirt, but had no armor or cuirass, which was strange since he had a warhorse. Only a bronze helmet hung off the side of the saddle. *Is he alive or dead?* She knelt down beside him and slowly turned him over. The man groaned.

The right shoulder of his shirt was torn and soaked in blood. Carefully she slid the shirt back. The wound had dirt in it and was badly infected. Brushing his dark hair back, she put her hand on his forehead; he was running a high fever.

She called to let the others know where she was and sat back, looking at him. His face was streaked with road dust and had a three days' growth of stubble, but he was still a handsome man and strongly built. She wondered what color his eyes were.

Erec gestured wildly when he saw him. "Who is he?"

"I don't know, but we have to get him home before he dies," she said. She reached for the destrier's reins and rubbed his shoulder and left leg absently. She nearly fell as the big horse went down on his left foreleg. She stared at it for a minute and then said, "Quickly, while the horse is down, let's get him on."

Erec half lifted, half dragged him the few feet. The man moaned again. They used the reins to tie his arms around the horse's neck. The wound started seeping blood.

The ride back to Astolat was slow, for Elen was scared to jostle him at more than a walk. The sun slanted long shadows by the time they rode into the bailey; her father and brothers were forming a search party.

All three rushed over at the sight of the man tied on the horse. "He's hurt badly," Elen said as she slid from her horse. "Be careful bringing him inside." She turned to her oldest brother. "Tirre, will you ride to get the healer from the village?"

They had a barber/leecher, but her blue eyes were tearful and she knew her brother would not deny her. He ran to his horse.

Her father and other brother, Lavaine, carried the stranger to the guest quarters. Riderich, the barber, soon followed, carrying his pail of leeches.

"Take those away," she said. "He's lost enough blood already."

The barber looked at Bernard, who nodded. With a sigh, the man set the pail down. He went over and pulled the shirt away to have a look.

"The wound is several days old," he said, "and has not been looked at. Could be he's running from someone."

Elen stamped her foot. "That's not important right now. Can you help him?"

"If you would let me leech him . . ."

"No!"

"I can clean it, if you'll boil some water." Elen nodded to a servant, who quickly left.

He looked at the wound again. "There's no arrow point, and it doesn't look like a slice from a blade. Ragged edges. Strange." He looked at Bernard, "Do you suppose that horse is his? I didn't see any armor on it."

"I don't know," Bernard said, "but he looks like a soldier."

"It's a good thing he's out," Riderich said as the servant returned with the water and a clean cloth. He took the cloth and started wiping the dirt off. The man's eyelids fluttered and his face contorted with pain.

"You're too rough!" Elen cried. "He must have felt that!" She grabbed the cloth from him. "I'll do it." Very, very gently, she began to dab at the edges of the wound, squeezing water over and allowing it to run off. By the time she finished, Tirre had returned with the healing woman.

The old woman hissed at the sight of the leech bucket and hustled the men out of the room. The healer removed the rest of the man's shirt, looking for other injuries. She examined the wound and made a worried sound.

"Will he be all right?" Elen asked.

"The infection is deep." She rummaged in her supply bag and started pulling assorted herbs and twigs from it. She handed the birch and oak bark to the waiting servant. "Steep these quickly." She sprinkled liquid from a small vial on the wound and made a poultice of willow and elm powder, to which she added the infusion that was brought back. She stuffed the wound and bound the shoulder with a strip of cloth.

The healer rolled several more small bundles. "That dressing will need to be changed twice a day to seep the infection out." She went through her bag again and brought out a small jar. "This salve will soften the skin around the wound. You can apply it when you change the dressing."

Elen looked at the man on the bed. Somehow he seemed a lot larger now, lying half-naked on the bed. Suddenly her aplomb left her and she felt like a child again.

"I don't know if I can," she said, backing away. "I've never . . . touched . . . a man before."

The old woman hid her smile. "Did you not clean his wound?" Elen nodded. "He's not in any condition to do you harm, child. Would you rather have that leecher working on him?"

Startled, Elen looked at her. "I won't let Riderich anywhere near him if I have to spend day and night in this room."

She sat down in a chair next to the bed, staring at the man, not noticing when the healer left.

*Lancelot was swimming in a pool of black water. It must be night, for all was dark. He struggled to see. He could feel something pushing his shoulder down, trying to get him underwater. He had to be able to see, to defend himself. He reached for something to hold on to . . .*

Elen had just finished changing the first dressing the next morning. She was scared to apply too much pressure, but the healer had said the wound must be stuffed. She was binding the cloth when he struck out with his good arm. Terrified, she jumped back.

He drifted in and out of consciousness for two more days. She kept a watchful eye on his good arm when she changed the dressings and applied the fever-reducing poultices of marigold and sorrel, but he slept peacefully through them.

The fever finally broke on the third day and when she came into the room, he was awake. She stopped.

"I'm Elen. I have to change your dressing." She made no move toward him.

He looked down at his bandaged shoulder and then back at her. "From there?" he asked, smiling.

His voice was pleasantly soft. She came a little closer. He had the most unusual color of eyes. Like peat smoke. "No, it's just that . . . you tried to hit me once."

The smile left his face. "I'm sorry. I must have been out of my mind."

Elen nodded shyly. "You were, but you scared me."

"I can see that." He grinned lopsidedly. "Well, I don't hit women, and I promise not to bite."

She liked his smile. It made his eyes all warm. With a little more confidence, she came to his side. He leaned back. She worked delicately, avoiding looking at his face. When she finished, she said, "I'll get you something to break your fast."

He caught her hand and kissed it lightly. "Thank you, Elen."

She felt unable to move; then she began to tremble.

He dropped his hand. "I really am hungry."

She nodded dumbly and stumbled to the door. *He kissed my hand!* She giggled. *No one ever did that before!*


Bernard came in while he was eating. Lancelot started to put the tray aside, but Bernard gestured for him to keep eating as he pulled up a chair. He explained to Lancelot where he was and how he had come to be there.

Lancelot answered, "My name is Galahad, come lately from north of the Wall. I was injured at the tournament at Camelot."

"Are you one of Arthur's men, then?" Bernard asked.

Lancelot hesitated. "I support the king. Am I so far into Saxon territory that you do not?"

Bernard shook his head quickly. "We are loyal, but we live too near the Saxons to be bold. My sons would like nothing better than to go to Camelot, and my daughter has some silly notion that she wants to marry one of Arthur's men—the Cymbry, I think he calls them."

"I've heard of them."

"Yes, well," Bernard said, "Elen's only fifteen, much too young to be entertaining such thoughts. A good girl, though, thoughtful and kind, and always a soft spot for the sick and feeble."

*If her reaction this morning had been because I am sick and feeble, I will be much relieved.* "She's taken good care of me. I am grateful to you both for your hospitality, but I should be on my way. If someone would bring me my clothes . . ."

Bernard waved his hand. "Nonsense. The healer said at least a week's rest and then it would be slow recovery. My sons always want news of Arthur's court. They could use a little practice in swordplay as well, once your strength comes back." Elen knocked on the door and entered. "Stay with us for a while. We don't get many visitors this way; we're too close to the border."

"That would be too much of an imposition," Lancelot said. "I should . . ."

"No, it wouldn't," Elen exclaimed and then blushed, looking down. "I mean, it would be fun to have a guest."

Her father patted her shoulder soothingly and turned to Lancelot. "My daughter has her heart set on being the lady of the house. You would be doing her a disfavor if you left so soon."

She smiled at Lancelot adoringly, her blue eyes shining. He knew that look. With a small, inaudible sigh, he acquiesced. *I hope I'm not doing her more of a disfavor by staying.*

When Elen came in the evening to change the bandage, Lancelot felt like a new man. The barber had come in to shave him and the chamberlain had brought warm water and soap and a shirt.

She appeared more confident than she had this morning.

"How are you feeling, my lord?" she asked, handing him a cup of barley tea and setting her supplies on the table. She reached to undo his shirt.

Quickly he pulled the ties for her and pushed the shirt back. "Much better, thanks. I would like to be up and about tomorrow."

"Well, we'll see," she said, sounding like a universal mother. She carefully removed the dressing and looked at the wound. "The redness is less, I think."

He bent to look and their heads bumped. "Sorry," he said, sitting back quickly.

She picked up the jar of salve and lightly began massaging the ointment around the wound. *Her fingers really are magic.* He sighed.

She looked at him. "Am I hurting you?"

"No," he said in surprise, "it feels good. You have a very nice touch, like butterflies lighting."

She gave him a huge smile, looking pleased. When she finished with the bandage, he reached to pull his shirt up the same time she did. His hand covered hers briefly before he dropped it. Smiling again, she tied his shirt.

"There," she said, stepping back a little. "I suppose I should be going." She lingered for a moment.

"Thank you, Elen." Lancelot feigned tiredness. "I'll see you in the morning."

Lancelot stared at the door after she had gone. That she was vulnerable, Bernard had told him, but he wondered if the father had any idea of how fanciful she was. He must be careful not to encourage her. He felt as though there were shifting sands all around him.


Once Lancelot was able to walk about, he quickly regained his strength. His sword arm was weak, so he began morning practice with either Tirre or Lavaine. Within two months, he was working with both of them.

Elen asked him to walk with her after supper. He could think of no polite way to refuse, but he insisted that one or two of her ladies accompany them.

As the summer days lengthened, the walk became a daily habit. Sometimes Elen would talk about trivial things and, when she was serious, about her hopes. She was naïve and idealistic in her desires.

"Isn't it wonderful that King Arthur won't have to fight any more battles?" she asked one night.

Lancelot glanced down at her. "What makes you think we won't have war?"

She looked up at him innocently. "Well, all of the kings agreed to make him high king, so they wouldn't fight among themselves. The Saxons are afraid of them."

Lancelot stopped at that. "Don't ever believe the Saxons are afraid, Elen," he said. "They just bide their time."

"Well, anyway," she said when they resumed walking, "everything must just be perfect at Camelot. King Arthur is well liked and has loyal men; Queen Gwenhwyfar is beautiful. She has a champion. I envy her."

Fresh pain tore through Lancelot. *Gwenhwyfar.* Her face, the green eyes framed by her wild hair, flitted through his mind. For weeks he had managed to keep her in the back of his mind. *Arthur.* The only way he could be loyal to Arthur was to stay away. He missed fighting beside Arthur; even more, he longed to be close to Gwenhwyfar.

"What is it, Galahad?" Elen asked. "Are you ill? You look so strange."

She slowly came back into focus. He shook his head. "Don't envy the queen," he said softly, "for queens have responsibilities. She must put duty first. Be happy here."

Elen shook her head. "I'd rather be married to a good-looking king and have a handsome champion." She giggled. "I heard the champion can make a woman swoon!"

Lancelot cocked at eyebrow at that. "Have you seen him?"

She giggled again. "No, or I would surely have swooned myself!"

"Hmmm. I doubt that you would, nor any other lady. More likely," he said, "that men would fall at the queen's feet."

"I wonder if it's true," she said, still on her track, "that the queen really prefers him to her king."

He stopped. "Where did you hear that?"

She put her hand through his arm and tugged at him. "Oh, we have coopers and tinkers and others selling their wares, and they bring the court gossip with them."

He was so lost in thought that he absentmindedly put his hand over hers as they continued to walk.

Later he tossed and turned nearly all night.



While he was recovering from his fall, Lancelot studied Astolat. It was a small holding, situated near a river that would eventually flow into the Cam, and was surrounded by a high wooden barricade with narrow battlements. Bernard maintained a semblance of a military unit, perhaps sixty men and thirty horses.

"You're at peace now with your Saxon neighbors, but Aesc still rumbles to the east. How prepared are your men to actually fight?" Lancelot asked one day.

Bernard gave it some thought. "We're closer to Aelle than Aesc," he finally said. "I have always felt comfortable with that. My men can defend us against the occasional raiding party."

"Would you like them to be stronger?" Lancelot asked. "In case Arthur should need to call on you?"

Bernard studied Lancelot. "You mean, Roman-style training?"

Lancelot nodded. "To an extent. Most of your horses are cavalry worthy, and the men might need tighter discipline, but I think you could have a good unit here. If your sons were in charge, they might not be so eager to leave and seek Camelot."

Lancelot knew Bernard liked the idea of keeping his sons close. That winter, Lancelot taught Lavaine, who was the stronger of the two brothers, how to manage and discipline the men. He spent hours talking strategy with both brothers.

Yet Lancelot was uneasy. He found Bernard observing him whenever he could. He hoped there wouldn't be too many questions because he hated lying, but he was determined that no one from Camelot would find him. It was the only way he could remain loyal to Arthur.

Elen took to watching Galahad ride on the practice field. He and the horse worked as smoothly as water flowing around rocks. She watched his arm muscles ripple when he threw the lance and fantasized about having his arms around her and how his kiss would feel. Her dreams stopped there, for she wasn't sure what happened next.

One evening at supper, hoping to get Galahad to talk about himself, she asked, "Would you tell us about the tournament, the one in which you got hurt?"

Lancelot looked up from his trencher. "What would you like to know?"

"Everything!" Elen giggled. "Are the men all dressed in armor and the ladies in their finest gowns? Do the winners get a kiss from the queen?"

"Elen!" Tirre laughed. "Must everything be romantic for you? We told you what the games were like last year when we came back. Armor is worn only for the joust; everything else is leather cuirass."

Lancelot smiled at Elen. "The ladies usually do dress in their finest, and many of them give favors to their man to wear." He paused and his eyes grew dark for an instant. "The king would not appreciate his queen granting kisses."

"Could we have a tournament here?" Elen asked, excited. "With just our men?"

Bernard looked at his daughter approvingly. "An excellent idea, and rewarding for the men. What say you, Galahad?"

"It would take a lot of time to prepare."

"You've been a big help to us; do you have any other place to go?"

Lancelot shook his head. "Not really." He hesitated and then said, "All right. I'll stay and do the tournament."

Elen clapped her hands. "Oh, good! And I can be the queen! Will you wear my favor, Galahad?"


They held their small tournament the same time Arthur held his at Camelot. Lancelot thought of Gwenhwyfar as he dressed. A year had gone by now since he had seen her, three since he had talked to her. Everything about her, the gold and copper highlights in her unruly hair, the dark green of her eyes, the straight nose that usually had a smudge of dirt on it, and her lips, the softness of them until she demanded more . . . He closed his eyes. *Will I ever get her out of my mind?*

Elen knocked timidly on the door. "Are you dressed yet?"

Fleetingly, Lancelot thought about pulling her into the room. It had been too long since he'd had a woman. Clearly Elen had romantic notions, for she had not learned the art of subtlety. He doubted she knew what took place once a man was aroused; her father kept her too sheltered. He took no particular pleasure in claiming a girl's maidenhead. Lancelot remembered the orphaned Brigid, nearly raped by Saxons, whom his mother had wanted him to befriend. She had been the reason his mother had secured the courtesans for him. He had helped Brigid lose her fear of a man's touch. But Elen wasn't Brigid. He finished lacing his trews and went to the door.

Elen wore a silk gown and some sort of headdress he had never seen before. She was going to play "queen" today, he guessed. *Ah, Gwenhwyfar, I remember last year.*

"I made this for you," she said seriously, holding out a favor of red silk embroidered with pearls.

He backed away. He always refused any favors, since Gwenhwyfar was the only woman he would ride for, and he could hardly ask Arthur for his wife's favor.

Tears started to well up in her eyes. "Please, Galahad. Please. Let me pretend to be the queen for this day and you can be my champion."

"The king does not allow his queen to give favors," he choked out.

"Well, then, I will be a single queen." She tossed her head. "Will you take it?"

Reluctantly he put the thing on the band of his helmet. Only much later was he to realize the folly of that action.

She went from tears to a radiant smile immediately and took his arm as they went outside.


Lancelot had hesitated to participate in any of the events, but Tirre and Lavaine had insisted. He was too competitive not to try his best; as a result, he was the overall winner with the most tallies when the day was done.

Elen presented him with a silver wine cup. "This has been in our family for years," she said, "and this queen does grant a kiss." She glanced at her father.

"Go ahead, Galahad. You've earned it." Bernard slapped him on the shoulder.

Elen reached up for him, her arms going around his neck, blue eyes looking at him expectantly. The men started clapping and stomping their feet.

Clearly he was trapped. *A dutiful peck on the cheek would not satisfy anyone, maybe least of all myself.* The thought surprised him as he put his arms around her waist.

Lancelot kept his kiss gentle. He had almost forgotten how tender a woman's lips could be. She clung to him, begging another. He kissed her again, still keeping the pressure easy. He leaned back and looked down at Elen.

Her eyes were glazed and she swayed slightly. For a moment he wondered if she would faint, and he kept his hands lightly on her waist for balance. She shuddered a little, then drew a deep breath and her eyes cleared.

"Well?" he asked teasingly. "Was it what you expected?"

She stared at him. "I love you, Galahad," she whispered and turned and ran inside.


Three days later was Beltane. He had seen Elen only at mealtimes because Bernard had decided that she had reacted too seriously to the kiss. Mayhap he was right.

One of Bernard's men returned from a two-week absence that morning. He and Bernard spent a long time in private discussion. Afterward Lancelot had caught Bernard eyeing him on several occasions. That the man had gone north, he knew, because the man had said there was trouble with Hueil again. Had he found out anything else?

That evening Lancelot went up on the battlement. The low hills around Astolat rolled gently into each other, and he had a good view. Few bonfires were lit this close to the Saxon border. He thought about what the rider had said after he had emerged from the long talk in the study. If Arthur were fighting both Fergus and Hueil, he should be there. *Should I go back?*

He heard someone coming up the ladder and turned. Elen's head appeared and in a minute, she was beside him. She rested her arms on the barricade and looked out.

"Does your father know you're out here? Beltane is not a night for young girls . . ." he began.

"I heard this is a wild night," she said, not answering him directly.

"In some places Beltane is a religious night," Lancelot countered.

"Religious?" Elen questioned. "I thought this was a night when . . . when it was okay . . . to . . . to lie with a man."

Warily he looked over at her. "Some women do," he answered, "but ladies, brought up the way you have been, do not."

"Then what do ladies do?" she asked naïvely.

"Ladies wait until they are married to think of such things."

She was quiet for several minutes. He was turning to escort her back to the hall when she spoke.

"Will you marry me, Galahad?" she asked in a small voice.

Startled, he almost tripped. *By Mithras, what have I done?* He stared at her.

"I love you, Galahad," she said in that same small voice, but now it shook. "I've loved you . . ."

He put his fingers to her lips. "Stop. Don't say any more. Please." His voice was anguished. "You don't know what love is, really." He dropped his hand.

"I know what I feel," Elen said stubbornly. "When you kissed me the other day, I didn't want you to stop."

"Ah, Elen," Lancelot smiled at her. "What you felt was the beginnings of lust, not love; they are two different things."

She hung her head. "You don't love me, then."

His voice was full of pain when he answered. "I would love you if I could, Elen. You are beautiful and kind and gentle. But I cannot. In my heart, I love another."

He heard her draw a ragged breath. She hesitated, then whispered, "Why aren't you with her, then?"

Longing and aching soared through him. "She is not mine to have. She belongs to someone else." If Gwen had married anyone but Arthur, he would have spirited her away long ago and they would be in Benoic by now.

She stepped close to him and laid her hands on his chest. "Galahad, if you can't have her, then take me. You don't have to marry me," she pleaded, "just let me be with you." She stretched herself up against him and pulled his head down, kissing him eagerly.

Her body felt good against his. Lancelot wrapped his arms around her, lifting her, probing her lips with his tongue. She parted them willingly. He lost himself in her then, kissing her deeply, nibbling her neck, raining tiny kisses over her face, and finding her mouth again. When he started to slip his hand inside her dress to fondle a breast, he caught himself.

Shaking, he stopped. Elen groaned and opened her eyes. He removed her arms from around his neck and stepped away.

"I cannot . . . I will not . . . do this," he said.

"Why? Oh, Galahad, how can something that feels so good be bad?" She tried to put her arms around him again, but he caught her hands and held them. "Just this once? Please," she begged.

"Hush, Elen," he said and knew his voice was unsteady. "You don't know what you're asking. I will not take that from you which someday your husband will cherish."

"I don't want a husband. I want you!"

"Enough!" Lancelot took a deep breath. He walked to the ladder. "I'll help you down. Then you are going to bed. Alone."

She didn't say another word to him after that.


He was gone in the morning. He left the silver cup and the favor and a note. She held it crumpled in her hand.

*How he must have laughed at me, secretly, with all my talk about the king and queen and handsome champion. He was that champion! Lancelot.*

Then she thought of something else. *He had said not to*

*envy the queen, that duty came first. He had also said the one he loved, he could not have.*

*So that was it. The rumors were true. Still, I wish he had not stopped that night. Just once, I could have been with him.*

The final realization struck her and sent a searing pain through her heart. He had gone back to the queen. He would not be returning to Astolat. *I don't think I can live without him.*

# Chapter 14

# The Prodigal Champion

Gwenhwyfar was sitting on a bench in the flower garden, enjoying the late spring sunshine and listening to Medraut read his Latin. He was nearly thirteen and already his voice was acquiring a deepening timbre.

He had been at Camelot a little over a year. To her own surprise, once she had gotten over her anger, she'd found that she liked him. He looked so like Arthur, except for the hair, that she could see how Arthur must have been as a child.

Gwenhwyfar's thoughts drifted to Arthur. He had changed much this year, become hardened. He shared little of his comings and goings. He assigned Medraut's military training to Bedwyr, using the excuse that Uther had done him no favors and he would do none for Medraut. He spoke to the boy only when he had to. Medraut did not complain, but she knew that he was extremely sensitive. Whether he understood that it was Morgana Arthur hated, she didn't know.

The first few weeks after Medraut arrived, she barred her

door against Arthur, but he did not try it. Finally, once she had accepted the inevitable, she went to him.

*He was in bed when she knocked on his door and entered.*

*"To what do I owe this visit?"*

*She removed her robe, standing in her nightdress. "May I join you, Arthur?"*

*He didn't answer but lifted the covers for her to slide under.*

*"I'm sorry," she said, snuggling against him. "I've been so angry and I needed time. Will you forgive me?" She reached over and stroked his hair.*

*"It is I who need the forgiveness, Gwenhwyfar, not you."*

*She was surprised. "But surely, Arthur, you didn't know . . ."*

*"Incest is incest. What I've done cannot be forgiven."*

*"Have you talked to the priest?" she asked.*

*Arthur gave a bitter laugh. "Oh, yes. I've rubbed my knees raw from praying and I've filled the coffers well. Nothing's changed."*

*She trailed her fingers across his chest. He brought his arm around her.*

*"Nimue, then? What does her Goddess say?"*

*"The Old Ways are more tolerant. Nimue says the Goddess works Her will where She will; there are no accidents. Medraut is here for a purpose."*

*"And you can't accept that?"*

*His hand traced a pattern on her shoulder. "I don't know. When I look at him, I see Morgana. I have never trusted her; look what she did to you. I feel the same strangeness with her son."*

*"Give him time, Arthur. Mayhap if we all work with him, he will truly become your son—and mine—not Morgana's."*

*"You sound like Nimue. She and Myrddin think we can make an heir of Medraut, if need be. But, you would accept him as your son?" He looked puzzled.*

*"I have not given you a child, Arthur. I'm willing to try,
though."* She reached for him and found him soft. In all of
their nights together, that had never been a problem.

He sighed and lay back as her fingers worked on him.
After some while, he took her hand and held it against his
chest. She was startled.

He smiled wanly. *"Now you know why I haven't kicked
down your door."*

Medraut had finished reading. "My lady?"

She started. "Very good, Medraut, your cadence is coming together nicely." He gave her a delighted smile, and she
was reminded that Arthur thought he was besotted with her.
But really, why would a thirteen-year-old have a crush on
her?

He was an independent child. She was aware that he already had a reputation among the other boys as a person not
to be pushed too far. When he had first arrived, they had
teased him about following her around. Instead of striking
back, he studied each of the tormentors, looking for their
weaknesses. Nearly every boy in the fort had suffered some
loss of pride because of it.

He laid the book down and reached for a rose. Breaking
its stem, he offered it to Gwenhwyfar. "Its beauty can't do
you justice, Lady," he said gravely.

Gwen put the flower up to her nose. "Where did you learn
to talk like that, Medraut?" she asked with a smile.

His face reddened. "I . . . I meant no offense."

She reached out and patted his shoulder. "None taken,
child. I love the flower. Thank you."

He frowned and she thought he probably didn't like being
called a child, but she was not going to condone his flirting
with her.

"You see how smooth it is?" she asked, running her finger
lightly across the outside petals. "It feels like fine silk." She

held it out to him. "You must pick one for Elaine, too. It is her favorite flower." *And so like her. The smoothness belies the thorn.*

He started to reply but was interrupted by the gate guard. "Rider coming!"

Gwenhwyfar stood up. "Come, Medraut, let's see who it is. Mayhap Arthur is back from his errand."

As they reached the gate, a large red horse emerged from the cloud of dust that its hooves churned up. The rider sat easy in the saddle, one with the horse. Gwenhwyfar shielded her eyes against the sun.

"Lancelot!" she screamed and went running down the road, leaving Medraut standing by the gate, staring after her.

"Lancelot!" she screamed again, and the rider kicked the horse to full gallop, sliding to a stop inches from her. He slid off the horse and wrapped his arms around her.

Gwenhwyfar clung to him, giddy. "Lancelot, where have you been? We searched for you; I thought you were lost to us forever! Do not leave me again!" Pure joy washed over her as she clung to him.

He held on to her equally fiercely, his hands roaming her back, crushing her to him. Their mouths found one another, searching, relishing the taste of each other. "I thought I could stay away," he said between kisses, "but I can't. I love you, Gwen. May Arthur forgive me for coming back."

Arthur. Suddenly they realized they were standing in the middle of the road to the entrance of Camelot. Lancelot had retained enough sense to bring the horse between them and the gate.

Reluctantly they separated, but Lancelot kept his arm over her shoulder. They turned the horse and started walking to the gate. "How's Arthur?"

"Gone today," she said. "He should be back soon." Lancelot gave her a questioning look but didn't have time to ask any more.

Men were pouring into the bailey, all of them trying to get

to Lancelot first. He was pulled into the center of the cama-raderie, laughing.

Elaine hurried to Gwenhwyfar. "Is it really him?" she asked, her eyes shining.

"Yes! He's back!" Gwenhwyfar felt as light as a wisp of dandelion seed. "A feast, Elaine, tell the cooks. Everything must be the best tonight!"

When Arthur rode in, nearly an hour later, Lancelot was still surrounded by men, and Gwenhwyfar had rejoined him. Arthur slid off Valiant and they were in a bear hug, acting like two little boys, spinning each other around. When they parted, both had suspiciously bright eyes.

Gwenhwyfar had never seen either of them near tears. Lancelot was a passionate man, but Arthur always kept his emotions in check. She realized that they loved each other as much as she loved both of them. *And I do . . . I love both of them.* She was filled with wonder at this discovery, and then she noticed Medraut, standing near the wall of the herbal garden, fists clenched, and with a frightful scowl on his face. *He hates Lancelot. Why?* She didn't have time to go to Medraut, for Arthur was pulling her toward him. She linked arms with him and Lancelot, and the three of them pro-ceeded to the Great Hall.

She put Medraut from her mind. Lancelot was back and that was all that mattered.

Lancelot started to take the chair next to Gwenhwyfar at the high table that evening when Medraut tapped his shoul-der.

"I believe, sir, that seat is mine."

Lancelot turned around and Gwenhwyfar caught the look of disbelief as he looked at the boy and then at Arthur and back to the boy.

"What . . . who . . ."

Gwenhwyfar broke in. "This is Medraut, Arthur's son."

Lancelot was still nearly speechless, "But how . . . who is your mother?"

The boy gave him a tight smile. "Morgana, sir. I was Beltane-got."

*On his sister?* Gwenhwyfar read Lancelot's look and nodded slightly.

Arthur glowered at the boy. "Have a seat, Medraut. Not another word."

Elaine walked over and took Lancelot's arm. "There's a chair beside me, Lancelot. I would love to have your company at the feast."

*He belongs beside me!* But Elaine was already leading Lancelot away.

Medraut sat down beside Gwenhwyfar and smiled triumphantly. "You are looking especially lovely this evening, Lady."

"Thank you," she answered, but she barely heard him. *A curse on you, Cousin.*


"Tell me how in the name of Bel's fire this happened." Lancelot looked from Arthur to Gwenhwyfar.

They were alone in the map room the next morning. Gwenhwyfar knew Lancelot was still shocked, and Arthur had promised him last night that they would talk this morning.

"Our troops had just come back to Ambresbyrig . . . before you came to us . . . it was Beltane. I was walking back to the fort. She stepped out from behind some bushes; I thought I was seeing an apparition. I never saw her face, didn't know her name." Arthur turned his head away.

Cai appeared in the doorway. "Medraut's been in a fight."

Gwenhwyfar started to get up, but Arthur held her back. "I will handle this," he said. "You can tell Lance the rest. You believe in the boy more than I do."

After he left, Lancelot took Gwenhwyfar's hands in his

and looked into her eyes. "How are you coping? I wish I had been here for you."

She smiled and reached up to caress his face. *Ah, to touch you again.* "I wish you had been, too, but I've surprised myself, Lance. I may not have a child. If I raise this one to be like Arthur, I will have fulfilled a goal; he will have a proper heir."

"The boy is smitten with you, Gwen, if last night was any clue. I don't think I have ever been challenged for a seat before!"

"He's a child! Arthur won't allow Morgana near him and he misses his mother."

Lancelot leaned forward. "Gwen," he said seriously, "that boy was looking at you the way I would like to."

Abruptly she asked, "Why did you leave, Lance?"

He sighed and sat back. "I had to. Arthur told me to train Gaheris and come back to Camelot. I knew if I did, I would betray all three of us. I didn't want to be found. I thought I could start over, somewhere . . ."

"Where did you go?" Gwenhwyfar asked as Arthur returned. "We searched for you everywhere."

"I meant to go to Aelle and live among the Saxons, at least for a while," Lancelot answered as Arthur sat down next to Gwen. "But the wound I took festered, and I collapsed. When I woke up, I was at a place called Astolat."

"Astolat?" Arthur asked. "Isn't that a small holding near Aesc's borderlands? I think two boys from Astolat competed in a tournament a couple of years ago."

Lancelot nodded. "They wanted to come to court, but I trained them and the others to be a fighting unit, if ever needed. They now have a fortification for you to use. Their father's name is Bernard."

Arthur answered, "We'll have to visit this place. Bernard must be grateful to you."

"I did what I could." A strange look crossed his face and he changed the subject. "Tell me about Hueil, Arthur. Why is he still alive?"

Arthur grimaced. "The man keeps slipping across the sea to Eire. Last year, when I marched north, Fergus Mor brought his raiders close to Hadrian's Wall and I had to turn back. Hueil will begin raiding soon, and this time, I want to be in position, much as we were for Comoran."

Lancelot nodded. "When do you plan to move?"

"By the next full moon. While all the warlords were here, we counseled. We have northern Scotti allies, Angus and Cabran, who are established in their lands. They resent Fergus's invasion. The northern troops will be in place when we arrive." Arthur leaned across Gwenhwyfar and laid a hand on Lancelot's arm. "I'm glad we ride together again, my friend." He looked at Gwenhwyfar, then back to Lancelot. "We've both missed you."

Gwenhwyfar put an arm around each of them. "I'm just happy that I have both of you with me." She smiled and kissed Arthur lightly and then kissed Lancelot's cheek.

Gwenhwyfar saw the look that the men exchanged and then Arthur's jaw tightened. She sighed. *Forgive me, Arthur; I will always love him.*


"Why were you fighting?" Gwenhwyfar asked Medraut later as she looked at the bruise on his face.

"Ryons insulted you, Lady," Medraut said stiffly.

"Cai's son?" She was surprised. "What did he say?"

He smiled slyly. "He said now that Lancelot was back, Arthur needed to keep an eye on you."

Gwenhwyfar took his arm. "Come, have a seat." He complied with a big smile and she sat down next to him. "Medraut, Lancelot is a very good friend of mine," she began, "and Arthur is aware that we are friends. Lancelot and Arthur are the best of comrades. There is nothing for you, or the other boys, to concern yourselves about."

"I defended your honor, my lady." Medraut looked at her unbelievingly.

She smiled a little. "I thank you, but my honor doesn't need defending. Arthur and I were equally happy to see him; we didn't think he was coming back to us. Lancelot is the only one of Arthur's men who could be a king in his own land, if he returned to Benoic. He's chosen to stay with Arthur. In fact," she said, rising, "I think you should work with Lancelot. You could learn a lot."

Medraut smiled at her again. "Yes," he said, "I would like that." But something in his tone, or maybe it was his smile, made her think that he didn't.

Gwenhwyfar mentioned it to Lancelot the next morning as she watched him working Pryderi in the paddock. She was mounted on Safere.

He stopped next to her. "I don't mind," he answered. "I can meet with him this afternoon." He sidled Pryderi over to the gate. "But now, I haven't been on this brute for a while. Why don't we ride?"

She hesitated and he gave her a questioning look. She told him what Medraut had said.

"By Mithras!" Lancelot cursed. "Are the tongues already wagging?" He sighed. "I suppose you should have a proper chaperone, Gwen. I hadn't thought of it."

"Why don't we ask Medraut?" Gwenhwyfar suggested. "Having a child with us would be proper enough."

Medraut looked delighted. He asked for one of the stallions, but Palomides led out one of the palfreys. Lancelot and Gwenhwyfar hid their smiles.

They rode for several miles before they came to a meadow. The stallions were straining to gallop but had been held in check since Medraut's gelding would not be able to keep pace. The meadow looked like the perfect place to let them out.

"I'll race you, Lance!" Gwen laughed and she was off. Pryderi sprang into full stride behind her. Gwenhwyfar crouched low over Safere's neck, her hair flying behind her. Lancelot overtook her and they both pulled to a stop, laughing. They wheeled the horses and came racing back and then cooled them down by trotting in figure eights, meeting in the middle, then ambling sideways, the horses crossing their legs.

"How do you make them do that?" Medraut's eyes were huge.

While Gwenhwyfar demonstrated, Lancelot said, "The move is used in battle to get us out of some difficult spots."

"Can I try it?" Medraut asked Lancelot. "Can I use your horse?"

Gwenhwyfar laughed. "Medraut, Pryderi means 'trouble.' Only your father and Lance ride him."

He looked disappointed. "Yours, then? Or am I not a good enough rider?"

Gwenhwyfar hesitated and looked at Lancelot. He shrugged. "Why not? They've had a good run; he should be easy to handle."

Eagerly Medraut mounted Safere. Lancelot dismounted and stood beside Gwen while they watched Medraut.

"He sits a horse fairly well," Lancelot said.

Gwenhwyfar nodded. "Bedwyr thought so, too."

Medraut started to trot the horse in a circle; then, at the point at which he was farthest away from them, he turned Safere and gave him free rein, following the track they had made earlier.

He hadn't gone very far before Safere took the bit and his back legs kicked out. Medraut went flying over him and landed with a resounding smack.

"Are you hurt?" Gwenhwyfar reached him first.

"I'm fine," he said as he got to his feet. "That horse threw me."

Lancelot looked at him steadily. "The horse is not to blame. You let him get his head down."

Medraut narrowed his eyes. "I know how to ride a horse, sir!"

Lancelot reached over and Medraut took a step back, but he merely pulled a large twig out of Medraut's hair and handed it to him. "Yes," he said, "I can see that you do." He turned and went to collect the horses.

Medraut followed them home in stony silence.


Arthur's troops, along with Myrddin, left within the week. Gwenhwyfar stood outside with Cai and Medraut to see them off. Bedwyr looked at Medraut. "I expect to see improvement in both your riding and swordsmanship when I return. Cai will keep you fit."

Gwenhwyfar watched Medraut wince and sighed. Cai had a temper and a heavy fist. So far, Medraut had been able to avoid the blows that some of the other boys got. She knew he didn't much like being bossed around by the seneschal, either.

Arthur and Lancelot came over to them. "Take care of her for me," Arthur said to Cai as he gave Gwenhwyfar a kiss. He gestured to Lancelot.

Lancelot stepped forward and kissed Gwenhwyfar lightly on her mouth. She returned his kiss just as casually. She glanced at Medraut; he would have no way of knowing that Arthur had planned this after he had talked to Ryons about the fight.

Medraut narrowed his eyes. He scowled at Lancelot and then at Arthur.

Arthur smiled at him pleasantly. "Do you have a problem, Son?"

"No, sir," he said in a strained voice. He glared at Lancelot and moved closer to Gwenhwyfar. "I will protect the queen."

Lancelot appraised him a moment and then leaned down to whisper in Gwenhwyfar's ear. "What you need is protection from him, I think."

"Don't be silly, Lance," she whispered back. "I'll be fine."

Arthur studied Medraut, too. "The queen will have no need of your protection; Cai will be here."

Medraut didn't answer, but as they rode away, he smiled, a little secret smile that Gwenhwyfar wasn't sure she liked. Again she wondered what Lancelot had done to make Medraut hate him so.

Morgana, as though by instinct, arrived the next morning while Gwenhwyfar was out riding and collected Medraut.

"You must tell me everything," Morgana said to Medraut after she had him settled on the lounge beside her in her home. "What have you learned?"

"You tell me, Mother," he replied, "about the great Lancelot."

She picked up the cloak that she was embroidering. "He came back, then?"

"Yes." He gritted his teeth. "And he can't stay away from the queen."

Morgana laughed and patted his hand. "Medraut, he has always pined after her, but he will not act because of some code of honor. He makes himself miserable. He will not betray Arthur, nor will he find someone to take Gwenhwyfar's place."

"I hate him."

She put the cloak down and took her son by his shoulders. "Hate is an emotion that can cause you to err, Medraut. It is hard to control. When you seek revenge, you must always be in control. Look for the weakness. That's how you bring a man down. Do you understand?"

Slowly, he nodded.

"Why do you hate him so much, Medraut?" she asked.

"I love Gwenhwyfar," he whispered. "I want to be her champion."

Morgana shook him. "What you are feeling, Medraut, is a boy's first rise of moontide. We will find you an experienced wench and you will forget about her."

He stared at her. "That would be perfect; then I will be ready when she realizes I'm a man."

"Don't even think that way, Medraut," Morgana said sharply. "Your goal is to obtain the throne, not have Arthur kill you." She went back to her embroidery. "I gathered this wool and spun it myself for this special cloak. It has enchantments and spells to make it do its job quickly. No other hand has touched it."

"Is it to bewitch Arthur into making you the king's consort?"

Morgana smiled. "Something like that."

She kept Medraut with her that season, teaching him what he needed to know.

# Chapter 15

# The Confession

Arthur's troops arrived in Dalraida by mid-June and settled in to wait near Alclud. The fort was highly defensible,
situated on top of a caprock with three sides that dropped
vertically to the sea below. They would be warned of a sea-
ward approach by the screaming of thousands of rising
seabirds that lived in the estuaries. They waited nearly the
whole summer and Arthur began to wonder if Hueil had decided to raid farther south. He ordered patrols along the
western seaboard and sent scouts as far south as Glannaventa,
but all was quiet. Then, when the mornings were already
frosty, Hueil landed his ships farther north, in the protected
lands of Fergus Mor. From there he moved southward, not
expecting Arthur's armies to be spread between him and the
far northern Wall of Antoine.

The final battle was brief and when Hueil lay dead,
Arthur looked down at him sadly. "He could have lived," he
told Bedwyr and Lancelot, "if he had followed his father's

advice and accepted the land he was sent to. He could have ruled his own people."

"I wonder why he chose to come so late," Lancelot remarked.

Arthur shook his head. "Mayhap he thought we would be lulled by his absence and not expect him at all."

Bedwyr looked across the battlefield. "It isn't finished, though," he said.

"You're right. We need to pursue Fergus and put a stop to this for good, but the snows come early here and the land is rugged. It's too late in the season to plan a campaign and put it to use. We'll winter in Luguvalium," Arthur replied. "The fort is sound and the baths work. I would like to have Gwenhwyfar with me. Take an escort and bring her. And," he said as an afterthought, "bring Medraut as well. He might as well be exposed to the plans of battle."

Gwenhwyfar's party arrived as the first snow was falling. She laughed as she stomped the snow from her boots and handed her cloak to the chamberlain. Her cheeks were rosy with the cold. "I had forgotten how chilly it gets in the north."

Arthur wrapped his arms around her and held her close. "Warmer now?"

Elaine stepped toward Lancelot and put her hands in his. "My fingers are near frozen, I think."

He held them briefly and then he gestured. "Why don't you warm them by the fire?" Turning to Medraut, he asked, "Did you have a good trip?"

"I managed to stay on my horse, if that's what you mean," Medraut sneered.

A hand clamped down on his shoulder and spun him around. "You will keep a civil tongue in your head, Medraut, or you'll answer to me." Arthur frowned. "Lancelot and Bedwyr are my closest friends and are to be respected."

"Yes, sir. I'm sorry," Medraut said automatically as Lancelot kissed Gwenhwyfar.

She lingered on the kiss as long as she dared and then turned to Medraut. "Bring your father his gift."

He went outside and returned quickly, carrying a small white bundle. It wiggled and emitted a small bark when he handed the puppy to Arthur.

"One of the wolfhounds!" He sounded pleased. "A sturdy one at that. Is he Glena's?"

Gwenhwyfar stopped smiling. "Glena died with an infection after giving birth."

"I am sorry, Gwenhwyfar," he said simply.

She blinked the tears back. "At least I was able to be with her throughout. She gave her last breath in my arms." She felt Lancelot's hand on her arm and gave him a grateful look. "This pup is the only one that survived."

Arthur set him down on the floor and watched his antics. "I'll call him Cabal," he told Gwenhwyfar, "and teach him to be a war dog." He turned to Medraut, "Thank you, too."

Medraut merely scowled and turned away.


Later, when Arthur and Gwenhwyfar were getting ready for bed, he inquired about Medraut. "I don't like the surliness. Is he this way with you?"

"No," she said thoughtfully. "He's been pleasant the entire trip. I've not heard him use that tone with Bedwyr, either. He seems to dislike Lancelot, though."

"Medraut worships you, Gwenhwyfar. He's jealous," Arthur answered.

"He's a child. I take the place of his mother."

"Hmmm. How did his lessons go this season? Was Cai able to sharpen him?"

Gwenhwyfar stopped combing her hair. She had dreaded this moment.

"What is it?" Arthur asked. "Was he rude to Cai? No doubt Cai dealt with it."

She shook her head. "He didn't spend the summer at Camelot. He was with Morgana."

"What?" Arthur stood up, his trews half off. "How did that happen?"

"The day after you left, Palomides and I took the horses out. Morgana came while I was gone."

"Cai was there." Arthur looked puzzled. "He knows she's not to visit Camelot."

Gwenhwyfar hesitated. "Elaine told him that Morgana came to see her."

"What?" Arthur said again and started to step toward her, but tripped and fell back on the bed.

Gwenhwyfar went and sat down beside him. "I didn't realize it, Arthur, but apparently, Elaine has gone to visit Morgana several times. She said a mother had a right to know how her son was."

"Do I not make the rules in my own home?" Arthur asked angrily. "I will speak to her in the morning."

"What good would it do, Arthur? Elaine has changed. She has become distant to me. I don't approve of her friendship with Morgana either, but I can't deny she has a point. A mother should know how her son is."

"By Mithras, Gwenhwyfar, do you trust Morgana?"

"No, I don't. That's why I brought Elaine with me; I thought it would be safer."

"A wise decision, " he answered. "Still, I will speak to her."

"As you wish, Arthur." She reached over and tugged his trews off. "Now can I interest you in taking your wife to bed?"

He pulled her down with him, removing her robe as he kissed her. They spent some time exploring each other, but again, only his hand brought her release.

She held him as he fell asleep; then she let the tears come. Outside, the stars kept a cold, silent vigil.

In the spring Arthur's troops harried Fergus. Arthur's allies, Angus and Cabran, attacked from the northeast and east, Arthur from the south. Fergus held firm. They placed him under siege, but his ships were able to bring in supplies from Eire. The entire summer was a series of small victories and then retreats.

When autumn closed in again, the warlords met.

"We need a way to gain entrance," Arthur said.

Angus and Cabran looked at each other and then at Arthur. "The sea," Cabran said, "would be the most effective."

"We're not sea raiders," Arthur said.

"Sea raiders are available," Cabran answered with a smile.

"Mercenaries? Saxons? Vortigern tried that, remember!" Arthur said, somewhat sharply. "I already have Cerdic in the south, but he's half Briton."

Cabran shook his head. "No, I was thinking of the Visogoths. Clovis the Frank has taken Gaul. They need a place to go."

Arthur considered. "I would be willing to talk. How do we contact them?"

Angus answered, "Their sea captain, Theodoric, is already in Britain. He has been making inquires; that's how we heard of him."

"Then send for him."

When he came, Arthur drilled him for several weeks, asking about strategies, the number of men he had, what compensation he required.

A port, he had replied, for his people were seafarers and would protect the western shores.

So they agreed. Arthur appointed Bors, who had a love of the sea, to work with Theodoric, and ordered reinforcements from Camelot for the next campaign.

Agravaine was in the new group. Arthur attached him to a unit of the youngest soldiers, hoping he would provide some leadership. He also assigned Medraut to the unit.

For once, Medraut gave him a genuine smile, but his face darkened when he learned Lancelot was in charge of training them.

Lancelot worked them. In the mornings they cleaned the stalls and tack. Seventeen-year-old Selin protested that they were soldiers, not stableboys. They were cleaning all of the stalls for a week after that, not just their own. "Your horse will save your life. Remember that," Lancelot said to the boy, whose face turned scarlet.

He drilled them even harder. He made them ride without stirrups and sometimes without reins, using their legs for control and balance. Most of them fell off regularly, but no one said a word. One day, in disgust, when everyone had lain in the mud at least once, he pulled the saddle and bridle off his own horse and went through the maneuvers.

They had to care for their horses, brushing them down, picking the hooves, combing the manes and tails, after they rode. "Treat them as well as you would a woman," Lancelot told them one afternoon as they were leaving the stable.

Agravaine laughed at that. "Why would I treat a woman this well?"

Lancelot fixed him with a dark gaze. "Why wouldn't you?"

"Wenches like it rough."

"How many have you had, Agravaine?" Lancelot asked softly.

"I . . . I've had . . . my share," Agravaine blustered.

"Were any of them willing to return?"

Agravaine clenched his fists but remained quiet.

Lancelot turned back to the rest. "Each of you will do the chores of a serving woman this evening. Your supper will wait until the queen is satisfied that you have an appreciation of the work the women do."

In the afternoons they practiced weaponry.

Gwenhwyfar came down one day to watch the boys at swordplay. Their sword tips were wrapped, and Lancelot had devised a contest of sorts, pairing the boys, then having the winners of each set compete against each other until one winner remained.

Medraut was well skilled with the sword. As Gwenhwyfar watched, he added a few steps and swings, which threw the other boys into confusion. Finally he faced Agravaine as the only opponent left.

Lancelot came to stand by Gwenhwyfar. She smiled. "Medraut is rather good, isn't he, Lance?"

He glanced at her and back to Medraut. "He's showing off for you. He should be concentrating on what Agravaine is about to do."

Agravaine feinted to the right. Medraut, apparently sure that Agravaine would move to his left, cut right. Instead, Agravaine followed through and dealt Medraut a blow on his forearm, which sent his sword flying.

"Well done, Agravaine," Lancelot said. "Pick up your sword, Medraut. We're going to try that again." He turned away to get one of the blunted swords.

As Medraut bent over to pick up his sword, he loosened the wrap slightly.

"Now," Lancelot said as he took his position, "concentrate on me, not the queen."

They circled, Medraut's eye mere slits.

"Good," Lancelot said as he thrust and Medraut parried, then did a riposte. "Let's try that double feint you missed."

Only Lancelot did not do the double feint. He stepped to the left. Medraut cut low to his left, leaving his right side exposed. Lancelot delivered a light blow to his side.

Medraut spun, furious. "You lied to me! You did not double feint!"

Lancelot shrugged. "Anticipate, Medraut. You could have had a serious wound."

Medraut lunged blindly. Lancelot sidestepped him. Medraut swiped his sword point on the ground. When he brought it up, the wrapping was gone.

Lancelot grounded his sword; it was one of the rules.

Medraut lunged again, thrusting. With catlike swiftness, Lancelot brought his sword up, deflecting the other enough so it only grazed his left ribs. Blood stained his shirt.

The rest of the unit tackled Medraut. Only Agravaine watched impassively.

Gwenhwyfar was beside Lancelot immediately. Quickly she removed her overvest and pressed it against the wound, then moved his hand to hold it there. She draped his good arm over her shoulders, her arm around his waist, as they made their way to the hall. Calling for supplies, she sat him down and removed his shirt.

Gingerly she felt for broken ribs. She cleaned the cut gently and applied the salve the army medic had brought. She was finishing wrapping the bandage around his chest when Arthur came in.

His voice was grim. "What happened?"

Gwenhwyfar answered. "Lancelot was giving Medraut a lesson. The wrapping came off the tip of Medraut's sword, but he didn't stop. He lunged at Lance."

"Deliberately? With the point bare?"

She nodded. "I don't know why. Lance had already grounded his sword."

Arthur's face set. He turned to Lancelot questioningly.

"I goaded him, embarrassed him in front of Gwen. He lost control."

"It sounds more like he meant to kill you, my friend," Arthur answered.

Gwenhwyfar protested, "Oh, no, Arthur, it couldn't be . . . he may not like Lancelot, but I don't think . . ." Her voice trailed off.

Arthur raked his hair. "If it were anyone else, the man would be out of my army after a good flogging. I can't very well send him back to Morgana." He paced. "Well, I can take away his privileges. He will no longer spend any time with you, Gwenhwyfar." He raised a hand to forestall her. "He's far too besotted with you as it is. A week in the gaol won't hurt him, either. He'll have time to heal from his flogging."

He turned to Lancelot. "Do you want the privilege?"

Gwenhwyfar bit her lip. Lancelot looked at her and then at Arthur. He shook his head. "I goaded him, Arthur; mayhap the flogging wouldn't be necessary in this case."

Arthur raised an eyebrow. "I will not award my son any special favors. I will do it myself. Now." He turned on his heel and stomped off.

Gwenhwyfar was helping Lancelot put on a fresh shirt when they heard the first crack of the whip and Medraut's cry. She stiffened, her fingers on the shirt laces.

Lancelot touched her cheek. "Leave, Gwen. I can do this."

The whip cracked again and Medraut cried out a second time. She buried her face on Lancelot's good shoulder.

He held her until the beating stopped. Medraut had not cried out again.

"I can't believe Arthur can be so cruel to his own son," she whispered.

Lancelot released her then and tilted her chin up. "Arthur is the king, Gwen. He was right. He cannot excuse the behavior."

"But he's his father."

"He is king first."

\* \* \*

Theodoric returned in the late spring, his ships moored at Ynys Mon, and the fighting season began again. The troops harried and retreated, trying to lure Fergus ever farther from his fort. These were the first real battles Lancelot's young men had seen, and Arthur kept them in the second line. Agravaine was proving himself a strong soldier.

"But ruthless," Lancelot told Arthur one evening after they had shared several cups of wine in the deserted council room. "He enjoys the kill."

"How different he is from his brothers," Arthur said. "Gaheris follows commands to the letter; Gwalchmai enjoys the combat but would rather share a cup later."

Lancelot hesitated. "Agravaine spends so much time with Medraut."

After his public flogging and his week in confinement, Medraut had asked to go home. Arthur had refused. Medraut's former unit shunned him, except for Agravaine.

"He's about the only one who will talk to him," Arthur said philosophically.

Lancelot was skeptical. "Agravaine has no particular liking for you, Arthur, not since the night of your wedding feast. They breed foul ideas, I think."

Arthur sighed. "Medraut has not forgiven me for keeping Gwenhwyfar away from him, either. But what can I do? Mayhap he is my only heir. Incestuous bastard."

"Gwenhwyfar is young . . ." Lancelot forced himself to say. "You have time."

"I pray you're right, Lance. Incest brings its own punishment," Arthur said softly. "I feel that same sense of uneasiness around him as I do around Morgana."

"She's confined to her lands. What harm can she do?"

Arthur laughed then, but it had an unnatural sound. "So you don't know. Gwenhwyfar hasn't told you."

"Told me what?" Lancelot was genuinely confused. He wondered if they both had had too much to drink.

Arthur shook his head. "I can no longer give my wife what she wants, but I won't free her, either. Selfish of me. That's what Morgana has done."

Realization dawned. "You're not able . . ." Lancelot stopped.

Arthur put down his cup. "I thought you knew. I think I'm drunk." He stood and made his way to the door. "We won't speak of this again."

Lancelot stared at the door after Arthur left. *By the gods, Gwen, would it be wrong of me to satisfy you?*

# Chapter 16

# The Seduction

Cai prepared a feast for them upon their arrival back at Camelot. The court had been gone three years, and Palomides had many of the horses ready for battle; they now had foals, yearlings, and two-year-olds, as well.

Gwenhwyfar found that Morgana had left word requesting that Medraut be allowed to come and visit her on their return. Arthur grimaced when she told him.

"I don't want either Elaine or Medraut around her," Arthur said as a young man brought a platter of meat from the kitchen and set it down in front of the king and queen.

"Shall I taste it first, Sire?" he asked.

Gwenhwyfar didn't recognize him; he must be someone new. He certainly was a good-looking boy. Almost beautiful, if that term could be used for a youth. His hair was a halo of light curls, his eyes bright blue, his skin very pale. "What is your name?"

He blushed and bowed. "Sir Cai calls me Beaumains," he replied in a soft, musical voice, "because I am so fair."

"How long have you been here?"

"Nearly a year, my lady," he answered.

"Well, Beaumains," Arthur said, "we have no need for tasting. I have faith in Cai." The boy bowed again and returned to the kitchens.

"I don't think Medraut needs to go," Arthur continued his prior conversation.

"But Arthur, she is his mother. He hasn't seen her for three years. What harm can a few hours' visit do?" Gwenhwyfar asked.

Arthur looked at her cryptically. "A few minutes with Morgana can wreak havoc."

Gwenhwyfar turned away. *Arthur, you need to forgive yourself for the past.*

He sighed. "All right, Gwenhwyfar. I don't mean to make you angry. If you think he should go, then so be it."


Medraut took Elaine with him the next morning. No one was aware of it until Gwenhwyfar went looking for her. Arthur just threw up his hands in frustration and went to the stables.

Morgana was happy to see both of them. At sixteen, Medraut had grown tall and would be well muscled one day. When she learned of the flogging, she asked him to take off his shirt. Scars from the five lashes he had received were still evident.

"Was there no one there to treat you after? Where was Gwenhwyfar?"

"My father denied me the privilege of seeing his queen," Medraut said bitterly. "Yet he allows Lancelot access to her."

Morgana raised her eyebrows at that. "Access, Medraut? More likely, self-torture for all of them. I do not think that Lancelot's sense of honor has changed."

Medraut picked up his shirt and started for the door. "I would rather not talk about Lancelot."

Morgana waited until he had left. "You would, Elaine. I̶ that not why you are here?"

Elaine blushed. "I am dreadfully tired of watching Lancelot in a rutting state for Gwenhwyfar. I could ease tha̶ condition for him."

"Then why haven't you?" Morgana laughed.

"I've tried," Elaine said, exasperated. "But I can't seem t̶ get his attention for long. I thought maybe you could help."

"I see." Morgana said. "Tell me, Elaine, what exactly d̶ you want from him?"

The blush deepened. "Well, to lie with me. To bed me."

"I can make a potion that will make him desire . . . no̶ need . . . a woman. You must make arrangements for him to take it while he's in your presence, for it works quickly."

Elaine gave her a big smile. "I can do that!"

"And after, Elaine? What then?"

"Then he would have to marry me!" Elaine said happily.

Morgana chortled. "Are you so naïve as that? Ah, Elaine, take the pleasure of bedding him, of robbing Gwenhwyfar of her greatest desire, and be done. If even half the rumors are true, he gives his women an enjoyable time."

"But Lancelot would marry me; he is honor bound," Elaine cried.

Morgana considered. "Hmmm. But the potion will only raise the moontide in him. It will not make him love you."

"I can make him love me. I know I can!"

Morgana shrugged. "Give me a short while to prepare it."

While she was gone, Medraut returned. He and Elaine were talking companionably when Morgana reappeared.

She handed a small vial to Elaine. "Stir this in a cup of wine and have it waiting."

Medraut asked casually, "A little magic, Elaine? Who's that for? Lancelot?"

Morgana ignored her son and frowned. "Are you yet a maiden?"

Elaine became indignant. "Of course I am. I have saved myself."

"If you were going to your marriage bed, that would be a boon, Elaine. It presents a problem for what you have in mind."

She looked up quickly. "Why?"

"Lancelot will know you're a virgin. Also," she continued, "there will be pain the first time, and that will be hard to hide."

Tears welled up in Elaine's eyes. "I will have him," she said stubbornly.

Medraut leaned over and grinned. "Mayhap I can be of service. I could make sure the pain didn't happen on that night."

The implication took a short while. Elaine's eyes widened. "You mean . . . you would take . . ."

Medraut continued to smile. "Nothing would make me happier than to help you. I'm sure my father would be happy if you could lure Lancelot away." He moved closer. "Have you ever been kissed, Elaine?"

"Once," she whispered.

"Like this?" His mouth was demanding, forcing her lips apart, filling her mouth with his tongue. He drew back and looked at her.

She gulped. "No, I don't think I like . . ."

"You must like it, Elaine," Morgana interrupted, "and you must respond. Medraut, take her across the hall."

He grasped her arm and led her to a guestroom off the main hall. When he closed the door, Morgana settled herself on a chaise. *I hope I've trained my son well.* A short time later, she heard Elaine scream. She smiled.


Lancelot noticed them as they returned late that afternoon. Medraut was carrying a package wrapped in pale leather, and Elaine's face was glowing, a self-satisfied smirk on her lips. *She has the look of a woman who's just been bedded* . . . and then he shrugged. There was work to do before Arthur's tournament.

Nimue arrived the next morning, bringing Argante with her. She was nearly seven and delicately built with her mother's pale moonlight hair, but unmistakably, Arthur's clear grey eyes. Lancelot led them inside the hall where Gwenhwyfar waited.

Arthur walked in and picked up his daughter, hugged her, swung her around, and set her down. She giggled and then looked up at Lancelot. "You and my father are friends?"

"Very much so, Argante. My name's Lancelot."

She looked at Gwenhwyfar and back. "You're friends with the lady, too?"

He smiled slightly. "Yes."

With the straightforwardness of a child, she said, "You should be together."

Lancelot looked away, feeling himself getting red. He hadn't blushed since the first time he had bedded a woman, many years ago.

Arthur raised an eyebrow. "I think we have a new pony for you, Argante. Would you like to see her?"

"Certes," Argante answered. "Will you come, too, Mama?"

"The child has the blood of the Isle," Lancelot said when they left. "I hope she doesn't stay long or we will all be emptying our souls to her."

Gwenhwyfar reached for his hand and he clasped it tightly. "Mayhap," she said softly, "it wouldn't be a bad thing if we all bared our souls."

He grinned at that. "There's something else that I would see bare, Gwen." He heard her ragged intake of breath. "I'm sorry . . ."

"No, don't be." She turned to him. "I don't know how

much longer I can go on like this. I love Arthur, but I love you, too, Lancelot."

Pure joy washed over him. She'd said it. He'd known, but finally having heard it! He crushed her to him, and her hands were around him, kneading his back, pressing him even closer. He hungrily devoured her mouth, and she ravaged his. A great thwarted need had been building in both of them.

"Mama, are we going back in there?" Argante's voice warned them that they were close to the door.

With a groan, Lancelot released her. His eyes were pitch. "By all that's holy, Gwen, what are we going to do?"

But they were standing apart when Arthur and Nimue walked in.

A month later preparations were nearly in place for the late spring petition hearing and games. One night Gwenhwyfar asked Arthur to let Medraut sit at the high table as a reward for helping organize the games. Since Lancelot had gone on an errand to Marc in Kernow, Medraut had managed to sit next to Gwenhwyfar. They were waiting for the meat to be brought.

Beaumains brought it in, setting it down in front of Arthur and Gwenhwyfar as usual. As he looked up, his eyes met Medraut's.

"Gareth!" Medraut said. "What are you doing here? And why are you serving?"

Arthur looked at him sharply. "What are you talking about, Medraut?"

"That's Gareth," he answered. "Agravaine's brother!"

"What?" Startled, Gwenhwyfar looked from him to Beaumains. "Is that true?"

"Yes, my lady. I am the brother of Gwalchmai, Gaheris, and Agravaine."

Arthur went around the table and grasped the boy's shoulders. "Why did you not tell us?" he asked. "Cai! Come here!"

When Cai came out, Arthur fixed him with a look. "Why have you been working Gwalchmai's brother in the kitchen?"

Cai looked puzzled. "His brother, Arthur? I haven't been . . ."

Arthur pointed to Gareth.

Cai looked at the lad. "He came to me a year ago, said he needed to make his own way, wanted to work at Camelot. I thought him too soft for soldier's work."

"Medraut," Gwenhwyfar said, "get his brothers."

It was a happy reunion for them since they had not seen Gareth since he was a child. When everyone had calmed down, Arthur turned to Gareth.

"Now, young man, you have some explaining to do."

The boy gulped, growing pink, and went down on one knee. "I did not mean to deceive you, Sire. All my life I wanted to join my brothers and be one of your Cymbry. But I was too young, and my mother didn't want to let me go. So I finally ran away. None of my brothers was here when I arrived, so I thought I would prove myself by doing whatever I was assigned."

"We've been back a month," Gwenhwyfar said gently. "Why did you not tell us?"

Cai coughed and cleared his throat. Gwenhwyfar looked at him inquiringly. "Ummm, that may be my fault. I told him he was not to venture out of the kitchen if he didn't want to receive a blow."

Everyone was familiar with Cai's fists. Arthur frowned at him slightly, then turned to Gareth. "You want to be a soldier?"

"A Cymbry, like my brothers."

"You'll have to earn that, Gareth. I have a unit of young men training under Lancelot. No one could better teach you. You shall meet him when he returns."

\* \* \*

Lancelot arrived back shortly before supper two days before the games. Along with Tristan, he was escorting Marc and his queen, Iseult.

Gwenhwyfar and Palomides came down to meet them. The Saracen stared at Iseult, dumbstruck, and Gwenhwyfar felt a small ping of jealousy that Lancelot had been traveling with this black-haired, blue-eyed beauty who flitted as lightly as a butterfly between men. However, she soon saw the look of adoration on Tristan's face and she recognized the ache in the lingering of Iseult's fingers on his arm when he helped her up the steps to the hall. Gwenhwyfar shot Lancelot a sideways look. He grinned.

Custennin, Marc's son, also had come with them. Although he was young, his men accepted his orders willingly. He had dark hair and brown eyes that saw through a person. Gwenhwyfar had the feeling he didn't miss anything. She wasn't surprised when Arthur took him off to talk after he had greeted Marc. Custennin had an air of authority.

She didn't have a chance to talk to Lancelot until late. Elaine had all but pulled him to the seat beside her at the high table, and Gwenhwyfar found herself entertaining Marc. Next to him, his wife enjoyed Tristan's company. Gwenhwyfar already felt a kinship with the Eire beauty.

As they left the table, Elaine linked her arm to Lancelot's. "Would you walk with me?" she asked, her eyes big and blue. "I think I would like some fresh air."

Gwenhwyfar froze, half out of her chair. She hadn't seen him in nearly a month, but she couldn't very well go running after her cousin.

Tristan reacted quickly and smiled at Elaine. "Why don't you join me, my lady? Marc and his queen would like to walk; I'm sure they wouldn't mind if we went with them." For a moment Gwenhwyfar thought she had seen him wink when he passed her.

Iseult, in her soft, wispy voice, added, "Oh, please do. Tristan is good company."

"That's an excellent idea, Tristan," Lancelot said, disengaging himself from Elaine. "I have some things to discuss with Arthur and Gw . . . his queen, as well." He turned to Elaine. "I'll say good night."

She looked terribly disappointed. More so than usual. Gwenhwyfar wondered why, and then Lancelot was beside her, and she didn't care.

The next morning Nimue arrived and put her things in the old chapel/shrine that she now used on visits. Gwenhwyfar had long ago gotten used to her visits, and in a strange way, they had become friends. She knew Nimue would find her, so she stayed by the paddock, arms resting on the fence, watching Lancelot work one of the colts.

Nimue approached her a few minutes later. She watched Lancelot a short while and then turned to Gwenhwyfar. "How is Arthur?"

Gwenhwyfar glanced sideways. "Don't you mean, what is wrong with Arthur?"

"Is there something wrong?"

Gwenhwyfar shrugged. "Nothing new. He still can't forgive himself for having bred Medraut."

"It's been more than four years since he found out." Nimue inhaled sharply. "I would have thought . . ." She shook her head. "Argante said you were unhappy, and she is rarely wrong, in spite of her age."

Gwenhwyfar turned back to watching Lancelot. "Nimue," she asked, "why must it be so? I love Arthur, but he won't have me, nor will he let me go."

Nimue followed her gaze. "And yet, it is your *moirai*, your fate, to love Lancelot, too."

Gwenhwyfar was quiet for some moments. Finally she said, "I love Arthur for his strength, for his commitment to justice and peace. He is all that is good in a man, yet I feel there's a door that's closed to me. Maybe that's why we argue so much." Gwenhwyfar sighed softly. "With Lancelot there is no holding back. When I'm with him, even if we're just working the horses, everything seems so . . . so right."

"As a priestess, I have been taught to detach my emotions," Nimue answered. "It is the same for Arthur. He is king first, but even if he weren't, the difference is that Arthur thinks while Lancelot feels."

"I want them both, Nimue, but I can have neither. How ironic."

Nimue looked at her, her eyes as clear as the Kernow seas. "Oh, but you will, Gwenhwyfar. You will be blessed to have them both. One day, though, you will have to choose. Arthur's life will depend on it."

She smiled gently and walked away, leaving Gwenhwyfar to stare after her.


Rain riveted the tents the morning of the tournament. Lancelot swore, thinking of all the preparations that had been made. They moved the swordsmanship inside, and thankfully, the weather cleared during that time.

"I'm glad the rain lifted," he told Gwenhwyfar when they were able to move back to the outside benches. "This tournament has meant so much to Arthur. He wants the petty kings to meet at least once a year."

Gwenhwyfar nodded. "It makes good sense. We can tell if anything is brewing when they have to meet face to face."

Lancelot added, "And I'm looking forward to riding and not getting hurt."

She smiled at him. "I hope you're competing in everything. Arthur is awarding a wonderful silver cup to the overall winner."

Suddenly he was haunted by the memory of Elen for a moment. He hoped she had forgotten him by now.

"What is it, Lancelot?" Gwenhwyfar asked.

He shook his head and gave her his lopsided grin. "If I win, will the queen award me a kiss?"

"She might," Gwenhwyfar answered coquettishly, "but what if you don't win?"

"Then the queen should not award any kisses." He grinned again and left her as Tristan brought Iseult to sit with her.

The next event was hand-to-hand combat. Lancelot noted that Accolon stayed away this year. Cai, who loved a good brawl, easily won the hand-to-hand combat. Gwalchmai might have won, but his wife, Ragnell, called out good luck to him and he turned, allowing Cai to deliver a blow, sending him to the ground. The men all laughed.

Once again Lancelot managed to score the most points by the end of the day, and Gwenhwyfar smiled mischievously as she presented him with Arthur's silver cup, but she kissed him chastely on his cheek. He tried not to remember how eager Elen had been. He couldn't very well grab Gwen in front of all these people.

Now the guests were seated in the hall in the late afternoon. Gwenhwyfar entered and sat next to Arthur on the dais. Lancelot and Nimue sat a short distance away. The traditional opening of the gifts was beginning.

"Where's Medraut?" Lancelot heard Gwenhwyfar ask Arthur. "Shouldn't he be here?"

Arthur frowned slightly. "He gave Cai a problem earlier. He's nursing a bruise with the army medic."

One by one, either a chamberlain or a maid brought the gifts up and opened them in front of Arthur and Gwenhwyfar. The signature card was read for each gift.

Lancelot yawned. This was boring but necessary. The high king had to be paid tribute. He glanced at Gwenhwyfar sympathetically. She couldn't afford to look anything but interested.

The maid unfolded a cloak. He was close enough to see the careful embroidery and the use of many colors of fine thread. The design was a strange assortment of twists and spirals. The maid held it out carefully by its collar.

Gwenhwyfar looked delighted at something so beautiful and stepped up to try it on. As she did, Lancelot noticed the pale leather wrapping it had come in. *Where have I seen it?*

He turned to Nimue. "Stop her. Something's wrong . . . I don't know . . ."

Nimue didn't hesitate. Calmly she glided to Gwenhwyfar. "To try on this gift, Gwenhwyfar, would be an insult to the other gifts you have received."

Gwenhwyfar looked at her, puzzled. Nimue gestured ever so slightly to Lancelot, who shook his head. Gwenhwyfar turned to the maid.

"It's lovely. I'll try it on later."

"If it please my lady," the maid said, "I will don it for you."

Gwenhwyfar smiled and the maid took that as a "yes." She swirled the cloak over her shoulders.

And screamed. Loud, bloodcurdling screams as her skin developed blisters and burns wherever the powdered lining had touched. She fell to the ground, writhing in agony. Arthur shouted for guards to man the doors, and the Cymbry formed a circle around him and Gwenhwyfar, swords drawn.

Nimue managed to grab the girl's head, keeping it from pounding on the floor, and placed her hands at the pressure points, chanting in the Old Tongue. The maid lapsed into unconsciousness. A chamberlain brought riding gauntlets and very carefully, Nimue removed the cloak, keeping the lining on the inside, and rolled it in the leather covering.

She looked up at Arthur. "This powder is quicklime. It burns the skin. I must wash her first outside, before we take her to the infirmary."

Arthur barked out the orders. Nimue followed the litter. The rest of the Cymbry searched the courtyard and the battlements and sent soldiers to the campsites.

Gwenhwyfar's knees gave way suddenly, and Arthur and

Lancelot helped her walk to the map room. She lay down shakily on the cot.

Arthur's face was white. "Who would . . ." Arthur started and then, "Morgana. She must be involved in this."

"She wasn't even here, nor Accolon," Gwenhwyfar said weakly.

"I know I've seen that tooled leather wrapping before," Lancelot said, rubbing his forehead and pushing his hair back. "If I could just remember where."

Gwen sat up and gestured for both of them to sit down beside her. She turned to Lancelot. "You saved my life."

"Again," Arthur said. "I owe you once more, my friend."

Lancelot looked across at Arthur. "You don't owe me anything. I couldn't bear to think of Gwen hurt."

Gwenhwyfar slipped an arm around each of them. "Hold me," she whispered. "Both of you. I need to feel your strength."

Arthur encircled her waist and Lancelot slipped an arm over her shoulders. "We're both here for you, Gwen," he said.

"Yes," she answered and drew their free arms in front of her, Arthur's over Lancelot's. She placed her hands on top of them. "God help me, but I love you both."

Lancelot looked at Arthur, expecting him to be angry at the admission, but the look on his face was contemplative. *At least he knows how it stands with us.*


The supper feast was a subdued event. Nimue slipped in to eat quickly. Arthur seated her next to him, with Elaine on her other side. *Thank goodness I won't have to hold a conversation,* Gwenhwyfar thought. Lancelot was on her other side, but he would understand that she didn't feel like talking.

"The draught I gave the girl will cause her to sleep for

*Take A Trip Into A Timeless World*
*of Passion and Adventure with*
*Kensington Choice Historical Romances!*
## —Absolutely FREE!

Enjoy the passion and adventure
of another time with Kensington
Choice Historical Romances.
They are the finest novels of
their kind, written by today's
best-selling romance authors.
Each Kensington Choice
Historical Romance transports
you to distant lands in a bygone
age. Experience the adventure
and share the delight as proud
men and spirited women
discover the wonder and
passion of true love.

# Get 4 FREE Books!

We created our convenient Home Subscription Service so you'll be sure to have the hottest new romances delivered each month right to your doorstep—usually before they are available in book stores. Just to show you how convenient the Zebra Home Subscription Service is, we would like to send you 4 FREE Kensington Choice Historical Romances. The books are worth up to $24.96, but you only pay $1.99 for shipping and handling. There's no obligation to buy additional books—ever!

## *Save Up To 30% With Home Delivery!*

Accept your FREE books and each month we'll deliver 4 brand new titles as soon as they are published. They'll be yours to examine FREE for 10 days. Then if you decide to keep the books, you'll pay the preferred subscriber's price (up to 30% off the cover price!), plus shipping and handling. Remember, you are under no obligation to buy any of these books at any time! If you are not delighted with them, simply return them and owe nothing. But if you enjoy Kensington Choice Historical Romances as much as we think you will, pay the special preferred subscriber rate and save over $8.00 off the cover price!

We have 4 FREE BOOKS for you as your introduction to
**KENSINGTON CHOICE!**
To get your FREE BOOKS, worth up to $24.96, mail
the card below or call TOLL-FREE 1-800-770-1963.
Visit our website at www.kensingtonbooks.com.

## Get 4 FREE Kensington Choice Historical Romances!

❤ **YES!** Please send me my 4 FREE KENSINGTON CHOICE HISTORICAL ROMANCES (without obligation to purchase other books). I only pay $1.99 for shipping and handling. Unless you hear from me after I receive my 4 FREE BOOKS, you may send me 4 new novels—as soon as they are published—to preview each month FREE for 10 days. If I am not satisfied, I may return them and owe nothing. Otherwise, I will pay the money-saving preferred subscriber's price (over $8.00 off the cover price), plus shipping and handling. I may return any shipment within 10 days and owe nothing, and I may cancel any time I wish. In any case, the 4 FREE books will be mine to keep.

KN016A

NAME _____

ADDRESS _____ APT. _____

CITY _____ STATE _____ ZIP _____

TELEPHONE ( _____ ) _____

E-MAIL (OPTIONAL) _____

SIGNATURE _____

(If under 18, parent or guardian must sign)

Offer limited to one per household and not to current subscribers. Terms, offer and prices subject to change. Orders subject to acceptance by Kensington Choice Book Club.
Offer Valid in the U.S. only.

lll..l..lll....ll.ll.l.l..l.ll.l.l.ll.l..ll..l

**KENSINGTON CHOICE**
Zebra Home Subscription Service, Inc.
P.O. Box 5214
Clifton NJ 07015-5214

some time," Nimue told Arthur, "but I will spend the night with her. When she wakes, there will be pain."

"Will she be all right?" Elaine asked. "I was in the kitchen when it happened."

"There will be scarring," Nimue answered. "Tomorrow I need to get some sheep's fat for an elder rind salve that will help."

"But you'll spend the night with her in case she wakes up?" Elaine asked with a slight smirk on her face.

Nimue nodded and Gwenhwyfar wondered why Elaine was so interested; she was not known for being nurturing. And why that self-satisfied smile?

Gwenhwyfar put down her wine cup. "I think I have had enough excitement; I am going to retire early." Arthur and Lancelot both stood, pulling her chair for her.

"I'll come with you, Gwenhwyfar," Arthur said.

"You can't, Arthur. We have guests. It's impolite enough that I am leaving. I really need to be alone, to do some thinking." She patted his shoulder. "Don't worry about me; I'll be fine in the morning."

As she left, she noticed that Elaine was again wearing that smile of contentment, much like a spoiled house cat that had managed to get into the heavy cream. But she was really too tired to care.

Some time later, when all lay still and quiet, someone scratched on Lancelot's door in the officer's quarters.

Lancelot flung the door open, sword in hand. He stared at the old nurse, Brisen. "What are you doing here, woman?" he asked as he lowered the sword.

"My lady begs you to come; she cannot sleep after today's events."

His heart lurched. *Gwen had told them she wanted to be alone . . . Arthur would respect that. Was she really asking . . . ?*

Brisen held out a silk scarf of Gwenhwyfar's. "My lady asked you to take this."

He inhaled the lavender scent. "Where is she?"

"She is waiting in the old chapel."

"Nimue's room?" Lancelot asked in surprise.

Brisen smiled. "Nimue spends the night with the burned maid." She melted away into the shadows.

Lancelot looked after her. *I am about to violate everything I believe in, to dishonor my friendship . . . but Arthur no longer can . . . she told Arthur she loves us both . . . this is her decision, too . . . and she is waiting . . .*

Quickly he closed the door and slipped across the moon-patterned shadows to the chapel. He knocked softly.

"Enter." Her voice was soft and low.

He opened the door and stepped inside. A single candle burned in the far corner. As his eyes adjusted to the darkness, he could see the auburn hair spread across the pillow. The room smelled of lavender.

"Gwen? Love?" his voice was husky.

"There's wine for you," she whispered. "Drink it first."

"I really don't need any; why are you whispering?" He took a step toward the bed.

"Please."

*Mayhap it is a game she wants to play, with the whispering and wine.* He reached for the cup and drained it quickly. The taste was too sweet.

"Now come to me, Lancelot," she purred.

Quickly he pulled his clothes off, feeling slightly off balance. *I drank the wine too fast.*

He pushed the covers back and lay down, pulling her to him. When her breasts made contact with him, he shuddered, the urge, passion, and desire that had built up over the years overwhelming him. Her nails raked his back and he groaned, suckling on a breast. She pressed his head against her.

He parted her legs and his hand explored her. "I'm sorry

this is so fast, Gwen; I wanted our first time together to be slow, but I can't seem to stop."

Her whispered answer was quick. "Don't stop!"

He entered her powerfully, nearly in battle frenzy. A short time later, he realized she wasn't moving very much. He had thought Gwenhwyfar would be more active. He kissed her deeply as he found his release.

She clung to him and he rolled them on their sides. "We'll do this right, in a little while," he said softly. "I love you, Gwen. I always will. There will be no other."

Light flooded the room as the door opened, making it impossible to see who was behind the lamp. Elaine started screaming.

Lancelot reached for his sword, only to remember he had left it in his quarters. Elaine had pulled the sheet over her head but was still making a lot of noise.

He could hear footsteps, a lot of them, running toward the chapel in response to the screaming that was continuing.

Nimue lowered the lamp and he could see her now. Arthur and Gwenhwyfar arrived as he slipped on his trews. Others, too, were now crowding forward, looks of shock on their faces, especially Gwenhwyfar's.

*Gwenhwyfar? But she was in bed . . .* He felt as though Pryderi had just put both back legs into him.

He turned, slowly, to see Elaine emerge from beneath the covers. He leaped from the bed. *How in Bel's Fire had this happened?*

"Elaine! What . . . ? Gwen, I thought . . ." He turned from her to Arthur. "I . . ." He stopped. He had no excuse; he turned his head away.


Nimue took charge. Turning, she pushed Arthur and Gwenhwyfar out in front of her, closing the door behind her. Gwalchmai, Bedwyr, and Gryflet, as well as others waited. Medraut and Agravaine were in the back of the group.

"The secret is out now," she said serenely.

Gwenhwyfar didn't know how she could be so calm. Only Arthur's viselike grip on her arm restrained her from going back in there to deal with Elaine. *The brazen tart. And to think she felt Lancelot inside of her. I would give anything* . . . She nearly went mad thinking of it. Then horror filled her as she realized what Nimue was saying.

"Arthur was going to announce the wedding plans this afternoon, but then we had the accident. Lancelot has decided to take Elaine to be his bride." She smiled at the men. "I guess he couldn't wait for the wedding night." There were some guffaws among the soldiers. "I scared Elaine when I came back for supplies, nothing more." She added, "I think they would value their privacy now."

"Yes," Arthur agreed with a tight smile. "Lancelot shared his intentions with us." He put his arm around Gwenhwyfar and drew her close to his side. "We wish him well. Don't we, Gwenhwyfar?"

She could see the anger in his eyes. Arthur's hold had tightened, almost painfully. "Yes." She forced a nod. "I'm sure Elaine's a happy woman." She looked back at Arthur, her eyes points of steel. "And I hope their marriage is every bit as fulfilling as ours is!"

Arthur put his other arm around her and brought her to face him. "To happy marriages," he said aloud. To her, he whispered, "Make this good." He slipped her arms around his neck and kissed her deeply. She hesitated, hating to be on display, but Arthur was right. To protect Lancelot . . . to protect Arthur . . . she returned his kiss and ran her fingers through his hair and over his shoulders. The men goodnaturedly laughed and sidled away.

He released her only when the footsteps died away. He turned to Nimue. "If there is anything you can do to make them believe this pack of lies, do it. I will not have this kingdom brought down because of lust."

"Arthur, I did nothing wrong!" Gwenhwyfar exploded.

*You haven't satisfied me, yet I've remained faithful, even though
every fiber in my being yearns for him.*

Arthur's face was expressionless as he looked at her.
"Lancelot has never cared for Elaine. Obviously, he thought
he was meeting you, especially after your declaration this
afternoon." He caught her chin. "Tell me, Gwenhwyfar, if he
had made the arrangements for this meeting, would you
have gone?"

She jerked her head back and looked away.

Disgusted, Arthur turned and stomped off.

"What am I going to do, Nimue?" Gwenhwyfar asked
shakily.

Before she could answer, the door to the chapel opened
and Elaine stepped out, followed by a grim Lancelot. He
looked helplessly at Gwenhwyfar, pain on his face.

Elaine was smiling. "Why, Gwenhwyfar, shouldn't you
be with your husband?"

It was too much. In a rage, Gwenhwyfar flew at her.
Lancelot stepped between them and caught Gwenhwyfar's
arms.

"Let me go, Lancelot," she said in a cold, flat tone. "I will
kill her."

"I know you will," he said, not releasing her.

He turned to Nimue and nodded toward Elaine. "Get her
out of here." Elaine, big-eyed with fright, went without a
word. He turned back to Gwenhwyfar and wrapped his arms
around her waist.

"I'm not marrying Elaine."

For a moment she felt hope, but then she shook her head.
"Arthur will arrange it. He's as angry with me as he is with
you."

"You did nothing wrong, Gwen! I was the fool! I should
have known you wouldn't . . ." His voice trailed off.

Gwenhwyfar looked up at him. "He asked me a question,
Lance. He asked if you had made the arrangement, would I
have kept the meeting."

"And . . . ?" he asked, his eyes that smoky, inscrutable color.

"I could not tell him no."

He reached to stroke her cheek. "Come with me, then. We can go to Benoic. There is land enough for both Ector and me."

She caught his hand and kissed it. "I can't, Lancelot." Tears flowed down her face. "To leave—to admit to our desires—would destroy everything that Arthur has worked to build. I can't do that to him."

He studied her for some time. "No," he sighed, "nor can I." He stepped back. "You'd better go, Gwen, before I make another mistake and consummate this night."

# Chapter 17

# Redemption

Arthur was seated by the table in the map room the next morning when Lancelot entered. "Close the door," he said, working out logistics on vellum.

Complying, Lancelot stood and waited. Finally Arthur leaned back.

Lancelot took a deep breath. "I have no excuses, Arthur; I was a fool. Gwen knew nothing of this. She's innocent."

"So she said."

"But she is." Lancelot looked directly at Arthur. "I believed Brisen. I thought the events of yesterday had caused Gwen to . . . to need someone . . ."

"Other than her husband, you mean," Arthur said drily.

"No . . . Yes . . . Damnation, Arthur! You told me yourself that you didn't . . ." Lancelot clamped his mouth shut and stared straight ahead.

Arthur's eyebrow went up. "So I did." He sighed. "Mayhap I should be more surprised that you didn't take advantage of that information sooner. Or have you?"

"I have not."

"You have never been more intimate with her than those greeting kisses I allow?"

A muscle twitched in Lancelot's jaw. "I can't say that's true, either."

Arthur's eyes darkened momentarily, and then he slumped in his chair. "I suppose it's my fault as much as it is yours." *I've not been a husband to her. Damn you, Morgana.*

Lancelot glanced at him and then back at the wall. "I know the policy, Arthur. I take the flogging and face exile."

Arthur stood. "Too easy, Lance. Too many people witnessed last night, including Medraut and Agravaine. If you leave without marrying Elaine, they will assume you were already involved with Gwenhwyfar. A king cannot ignore his wife's adultery, even if the man could."

"We have not committed adultery!"

"The perception will be that you did. And it will tear this kingdom apart."

"I cannot marry Elaine."

Arthur stepped in front of him. "A cuckolded king is not one the people will follow. I am just now getting peace established in this land, and justice as well." He started to pace, running his fingers through his hair. "By Mithras, it might be good to put the two of you in the same gaol cell for a week and let you rut yourselves raw." He came to a stop in front of Lancelot again. "You will marry Elaine. Nimue's idea was good. You will take her to Joyous Garde and I will make that her dowry. You'll send Gaheris back. The tongue-waggers will be quiet if I keep you in the army. You will be away from here and Gwenhwyfar's reputation will be saved."

"The irony of this strikes me, Arthur. I'm supposed to marry Elaine because I didn't go to bed with Gwen?" Then he said softly, "Gwenhwyfar's reputation must be saved." He sighed. "I suppose Elaine will go along with all this?"

Arthur laughed a sharp bark. "Need you ask? She is planning the wedding."

Lancelot set his mouth in a tight line. "And when will I get that sentence?"

"The day after tomorrow. Everyone is here for the tournament; they might as well stay for a wedding, especially since you've already bedded her." Arthur watched him closely. "You see why this must be done, my friend?"

Lancelot looked at him. "Are we still friends, Arthur?"

"We're friends. We shouldn't be. You would have taken my wife last night. But can I blame you, brother?" Arthur asked. "Gwenhwyfar affects you the same way she does me. Neither of us can help loving her."

"I have not had the pleasure of showing her that love," Lancelot said bitterly.

Arthur studied him, then turned and went back to the table, sank down in the chair, and held his head in his hands. "There is a cottage," he said at last, not looking up, "by the circle of stones. Be there tomorrow morning. I will bring her to you."

"You're going to do it, aren't you, Arthur? Make him marry that twit!" Gwenhwyfar came storming into the map room shortly after Lancelot had left.

Arthur rubbed his neck and looked up from his writing. He was in no mood for an argument, and Gwenhwyfar was spoiling for one. "It has to be done. You know that."

She put her hands on the table and leaned on them. "She's been chasing him for years; he's not interested. Why do you have the right to meddle in people's lives?"

"Because I am high king, Gwenhwyfar. What other solution is there?"

"You can send her back to her father! She's disgraced herself."

Arthur asked, "What answer will you have for those who say that he really wanted to lie with you?"

"No one would dare!"

"Mayhap not to our faces, Wife, but the rumors are already spreading. I must have them squelched. You are the queen. There can be no doubt that we are a . . ." he paused. "What did you call it . . . a fulfilled couple, and happy."

"Mayhap I'm tired of being the queen!" She bit off the words. "I'm tired of these responsibilities! Where does Gwenhwyfar, the person, count?"

He came to her and took her shoulders in his hands. "Gwenhwyfar, I get tired of these responsibilities, too. You must remember, we are seeing peace and justice prevail. Where would our people be if this work fails? Massacred by the Saxons? In civil war again? I won't have this country destroyed. We must squash the rumors."

"Rumors. All that matters to you is kingship," Gwenhwyfar shot back, and then she paused. She sank down into the chair and buried her head in her arms on the table. When she rose back up, her eyes were red with unshed tears. "I agreed to help you lead the people. I am the queen; duty comes first. My life is not my own."

He breathed a sigh of relief. *Finally she understands my obligations.* In that moment, Arthur didn't think he'd ever loved her more. Taking her to Lancelot in the morning was going to be the hardest thing he'd ever done.

The next morning, as they were breaking their fast, Arthur turned to Gwenhwyfar. "I doubt that you wish to stay and help with the wedding preparations. Why don't we take some food for our noon meal and go for a long ride?"

She nodded. *I can't abide seeing Elaine today.* "I would love to get away from here. A ride sounds wonderful."

Shortly, they were trotting through the gates, food and drink packed in Safere's saddlebags. The late spring day was warm, with a cloudless sky and a zephyr.

"There's a meadow not too distant," Gwenhwyfar said,

"where we could race the horses. Do you think you can still win?"

Arthur laughed. "You know I could. Valiant's the fastest horse we have, but let's just ride for now."

As they neared the circle of stones, Arthur reined in his horse.

Gwenhwyfar pulled up next to him. "Did you want to stop here, Arthur?"

"No." He shook his head. "This is where I leave you."

"Leave me? Why? What are you talking about?"

"I must find Myrddin," he answered. "I will be back for you at Nones."

She was bewildered. "Arthur, you are making no sense. You wanted to ride with me today, but now you are telling me that you want to find Myrddin. You want me to stay here until midafternoon? I can go home."

"I don't think you're going to want to do that," he said softly. "Turn around."

She turned in her saddle. Lancelot was standing at the top of the hill. She looked back at Arthur, her eyes wide.

"Are you . . . giving . . . permission . . . ?"

"I love you, Gwenhwyfar. I will do this only once." A look of pain flashed across his face as he backed Valiant away and put him to the full gallop.

She stared after him until he disappeared at the next bend. Then she trotted Safere up the hill and slid off into Lancelot's arms. When they finally separated, Gwenhwyfar asked, "How did this come to be, Lancelot? He was angry with both of us."

"A gift, Gwen, in exchange for my sentence. And I suggest we not waste a minute." He kissed her softly.

Behind the cottage the River Cam gurgled over large rocks, the sound refreshing. Lancelot tilted his head to one side. "Care to go for a swim, Gwen? Last one in has to catch the other." He grinned as she turned and ran, but he tethered

Safere before he joined her. She crouched down in the pool that formed before the river turned, aware that the water just covered her breasts. She watched him quickly shed his clothes and realized she had never seen him naked. His body was beautiful: lean and hard and exquisitely sculpted. Already she ached to touch him and make the magic happen.

He plunged in and surfaced beside her and ran his fingers lightly over her shoulders and to her breasts. "Ummm, the water makes your skin feel silky."

She trailed her fingers across his chest, loving the feel of his smooth, tight muscles. He gave her throat a series of small kisses. She nibbled at his ear; he pushed her underwater.

"What was that for?" she shrieked when she rose.

"That's what a wench gets who bites!" he teased.

Gwenhwyfar slanted a look at him. "And what does she get for this?" She gave his neck a small nip.

"This," Lancelot said as he bent and lightly pulled at her nipple. "And this," as he took the other one in his mouth.

Gwenhwyfar pushed his head down, but he had hold of her and they both went over. They wrestled playfully until Lancelot finally lifted her in his arms.

As they emerged, Lancelot brought her down on the embankment. The grass was springy beneath her back and smelled of clover. The sun warmed her wet skin. She spread her hair to dry and stretched her arms over her head.

Lancelot caught them there, crossing her wrists and holding them easily with one hand. Very lightly, his fingertips barely touching her skin, he traced a path on the tender underside of her arm. Gwenhwyfar closed her eyes blissfully.

Slowly, his lips just grazing her skin, he trailed along the other arm, mouthing her armpit, his tongue warm and pliant. She shivered in delight and tried to bring her hands to him, but he held them in place.

She opened her eyes to find him watching her. "Let me hold you, Lance."

"Not yet." He played with her nipples, flicking them with

his fingertip, making her squirm. He began kissing her neck, nibbling at her ear, and then leaned across her to reach the other side. Gwenhwyfar moaned and tried to move her hands again, to no avail.

She wiggled. "Let me kiss you then!"

Obligingly, Lancelot brought his mouth to her, kissing first her top lip, then her bottom one; then he drew back, kissing her chin and her throat.

"Lancelot! Stop teasing me!" Her breathing was shallow.

He grinned. "I've only just begun." He moved to her breasts, cupping the one, kneading it gently, then more firmly as he suckled on the other. She moaned again, tossing her head from side to side.

He moved down to her stomach, finally releasing her arms. She reached for his shoulders, but he took hold of each hand and placed them at her sides.

"Lie still, Gwen." His voice was soft as his velvet tongue ran over her belly, tickling her. "I want to explore all of you." His hands moved slowly over her ribs and caressed her stomach as he slid lower, switching positions.

She felt a quiver as his tongue made circles down her thigh, his fingers following the path as he moved down to her calf. He suckled a toe. Gwenhwyfar restrained the urge to sit up and pull him back to her by his hair. She pulled out turfs of grass instead. He draped the foot over his shoulder and kissed the underside of the other one, near the instep, and began his journey back up the other leg. She gave herself up to the total sensuality of her entire body being stimulated.

Lancelot lingered on her inner thigh, caressing with his hands and lips, nibbling as he worked his way closer to the golden mound that glistened moistly. He lapped at it softly and Gwenhwyfar gasped. As he dipped into her and swirled his tongue, her back arched and she moved into the ancient pattern. Lancelot pressed her hips firmly to the ground as his mouth played with her. He found the sensitive spot and suckled hard.

Gwenhwyfar shuddered as her body spasmed. She thrashed, but still he didn't release her from the ecstasy. She gulped for air. Slowly the vibrations began to subside.

Lancelot slid her legs off his shoulders and continued his way back up her stomach, to her breasts and neck. Finally he rose up on either elbow and looked down.

"Now you may kiss me, if you wish," he said.

Gwenhwyfar pulled his head to hers, ravaging his mouth, her hands raking his back, then holding him tightly. She wrapped her legs around his thighs, not able to get close enough to him.

Then he plunged deeply inside her and she felt his fullness with every thrust. They found their rhythm immediately and Lancelot drove himself into her until they were both at the point of madness. Gwenhwyfar trembled as she peaked, feeling wave after convulsive wave flow through her. Dimly she was aware of feeling his release, and slowly their rasping breaths turned to panting and then to normal.

He made no effort to free himself, burying his face in her neck.

After some time, she whispered in his ear, "We should go inside the cottage." She stroked his back gently.

Reluctantly he pulled himself from her and sat up.

"If I never have you again, Lancelot, this was worth it," Gwenhwyfar sighed contentedly as she looked up at him.

He grinned down at her. "I thought to try some other ways, but if this is all you want . . ." He let his voice trail off.

Gwenhwyfar's eyes widened and she playfully slapped at him. He caught her hand and brought her to a sitting position. "Well?" he asked.

"I understand there's a bed in there," Gwenhwyfar answered in mock seriousness.

"Hmmm. Conventional," Lancelot answered, "but it will do for a start."

He pulled her to her feet and she slipped on her shirt while Lancelot got the food from the saddlebag. They entered the cottage. Gwenhwyfar had not been here before. She briefly wondered if Arthur and Nimue had used the bed, then put the thought out of her mind. The cottage was a snug stone building, and small, with just the hearth, some shelves, a table with two straight chairs, a comfortable, oversized lounge chair, and a feather bed. A linen sheet covered the bed to keep the blankets clean. Nimue's work, no doubt.

She set the food on the table. "Would you like some wine?"

"Mayhap later. I want a clear head today," Lancelot answered. "I intend to remember every single thing I do with you."

Gwenhwyfar wandered over to the shelves and examined some small jars. She chose one and walked over to Lancelot, smiling. She reached for his hand and nudged him toward the bed. "On your stomach, please."

"Is this going to hurt?"

"Only if you want it to," she retorted.

"I'm your obedient servant, Wench. Do what you will." He stretched out, folding his arms under his head. Gwenhwyfar settled herself on his buttocks.

"So far, it feels good," he murmured.

"Silly." She hit him lightly on his shoulder. "I'm going to give you a massage."

"We'll see," he answered as she poured some of the sandalwood oil and began to stroke it in. She kneaded his shoulder muscles, tracing the scar from the Saxon ax, and worked down the large arm muscles and then gently up the middle of his back. He gave a contented moan, and she wondered if he would fall asleep, but when she started to move herself, he told her to stay in place.

"Ah, but you'll like this, Lancelot," she said as she slid down on his thighs and nibbled his buttocks before beginning to massage them. He groaned.

She worked down his legs and feet and stood. "Time to turn over."

He rolled over obligingly. He pulled her to him for a kiss, but she resisted. "Not until I'm finished." She smiled as she sat beside him and rubbed the oil across his chest.

"The scar from the lance healed nicely," she said as she ran her fingers over it. "Someone did good work." She picked up his hand and worked each finger.

"Bernard's daughter. She has a healer's touch," Lancelot answered.

Gwenhwyfar glanced at him and reached for the other hand. "Was she pretty?"

"She was," he said, "but I did not bed her. Is that what you wanted to know?"

Blushing, she bent her head. "I'm sorry. It really isn't any of my business."

He tilted her chin back up. "I love you, Gwen. No matter what has happened or will happen, I will not renege on that."

She kissed him quickly. "Thank you, my love."

"Now," he said, propping the pillows up behind him, "I'd like to finish this massage, please. I am interested to see what else you have in mind."

Gwen let her fingers glide over his taut stomach and stop just short of the part of him that suddenly seemed to have a mind of its own. Very lightly, she let her fingers brush the tip of him. Lancelot trembled as she went on massaging his thighs.

Kneeling beside the bed, she gently began stroking him and watched him spring to life. Lancelot moaned softly and ran his fingers through her hair. She licked the sweet droplet that appeared and saw his stomach muscles tighten. When her mouth closed over him slowly, he inhaled sharply and began a gentle thrusting. Gwenhwyfar found she could use her tongue as well, causing him to growl, low in his throat. She rose up at the sound, not sure if he wanted her to stop or continue.

"Come here," he said, his voice raw, "and get rid of that damned shirt." His fingers feverishly worked with the laces of the shirt. He stripped it off, pulled at one nipple with his teeth, and caught the other between his fingertips. "Mount me, Gwen," he whispered and lifted her so she could fit over him. He reached for her breasts again, kneading both of them, keeping her in a sitting position, and began a rocking rhythm.

*Like riding a horse, only better.* She gasped as she felt his full penetration deep within her, then realized she could control much of the movement and started experimenting, caressing his chest as she rode him. She felt the pulsation of his release strongly this time, and it brought on her own. She collapsed against him, panting.

He wrapped his arms around her. "I thought that might be a favorite position."

"I've never done it before," she replied before she had time to think.

She didn't see the look of surprise on his face. "Well," he said, kissing the top of her head, "then I'm glad I was the one to show you."

He rolled her over on her side and they lay together for some time, quietly, content to hold each other and exchange small kisses. Eventually, they got up, put on their shirts, and went outside to check the horses.

Gwenhwyfar looked at the sun's position. Arthur would be coming for her by midafternoon. The sun was directly overhead.

"We still have time, Gwen," Lance said as he read her thoughts.

She broached the subject first. "Is there no way you can avoid this marriage?"

"I told him I would take exile in Benoic, but he said that would make certain that everyone knew it was you I desired instead of . . . her."

"He said the same thing when I told him to send Elaine back to her father for disgracing herself." Gwenhwyfar turned to him. "I don't think I can bear losing you."

"You'll never lose me, Gwen. You may not see me for a long time. Arthur wants us separated and he's probably right. How can we go on like this?"

Gwenhwyfar nodded. "Arthur would never have agreed to this, had he thought you would stay." *But, my love, now that I've known you, how can I let you go?*

"Let's not talk about it anymore," Lancelot said. "I'm hungry. How about you?"

They walked back to the cottage. Lance sat at the table while Gwen laid out the dried venison, hard cheese, and soft bread. She opened the crock of honey and poured a cup of wine.

"Want to share it?" She stood in front of him, offering him the cup. He took a sip and set it down; then he grasped her buttocks, pulling her toward him until she straddled the chair and him.

"Sit."

She smiled devilishly as she did. "I thought you were hungry."

"I am," he answered as he slowly untied the laces of her shirt. "But I see no reason not to enjoy the meal like this." He opened the shirt and draped it behind her. "I think I'll help myself to you first," he said as he flicked his tongue across her breasts.

"Me, too," she laughed and quickly undid his shirt.

He broke off a piece of cheese and offered it to her, and then he took his bite from hers, their lips brushing. Taking a piece of bread, dipping it in the honey, and allowing her the first bite, he finished it, licking her lips completely afterward.

"An interesting way to have a meal," Gwenhwyfar observed.

"Hmmm," Lancelot murmured. "Let's make it more interesting." He took another piece of bread, dipping it well into the honey crock and letting golden liquid drip on her breast. She giggled as he bent to lap at the stickiness.

Gwenhwyfar inserted a stick of dried venison in her mouth, inviting Lancelot to take a bite from the other side. The taste of their kiss was salty when their lips met.

"And now," Lancelot said when they had finished eating, "a minor adjustment . . ." He shifted her hips and probed slowly. "We can share dessert."


Sometime later, they stood in the doorway in a full body kiss, beginning with their thighs and pressing upward along their bodies to their necks, enjoying the slow, easy, sensual embrace. Gwenhwyfar opened her eyes; over Lancelot's shoulder she could see the tops of the stones that were just visible over the hill.

"Have you ever been inside the circle, Lancelot?" she asked, tilting back from him.

He shook his head. "The circles are consecrated and used for ritual. I have not had the training."

"I forget, Lancelot, that your mother is a high priestess." Gwenhwyfar ran her fingers through his hair lightly.

"The circle protected you from the Saxons, Gwen."

"Yes, if only I had not been foolish enough to leave it. They were scared of the magic. You would have arrived before . . ."

"Hush, Love. It's done and in the past."

"How did you kill them, Lancelot?"

"The killing was easy. Neither of them was good with a sword."

"Did you . . . were they still alive when . . ."

He traced her cheek with his finger. "They were when I took out my dagger. Aelle made me wait until they were dead."

"I'm glad you waited," Gwenhwyfar said. She turned back to look at the stones again and leaned against him. "Arthur and Nimue created Argante in that circle."

He wrapped his arms around her waist. "Does that still bother you, Gwen?"

"No." She shook her head. "He had to perform the rite for the people, but Arthur had this cottage built for her." She sighed and looked outside. "The circle is a sacred spot. Was Nimue's child a gift from the Goddess?"

"I don't know. The ritual is symbolic of the king's marriage to the land."

"Do you think the Goddess would grant me a child if I lay with you in the circle, Lancelot?" Gwenhwyfar did not look at him, but she felt him take a deep breath.

He turned her around. "Do you want a child so badly, Gwen?"

She looked back steadily. "I would love to have your child."

"What of Arthur? Would he be so willing to accept it?" Lancelot asked.

"I think he would, Lance. He wants an heir who is not Medraut."

He gave her his lopsided smile. "You may already bear the seed, Gwen. We've been rather busy today."

Her eyes widened at the thought. "I hope so, Lancelot, for if you must leave, your child would remind me of this day." She looked at him pleadingly. "But your Goddess smiles on these rites; the Church does not. I have committed mortal sin today, whether by Arthur's leave or no. Mayhap the Goddess would bless me."

"The rituals are not meant to be selfishly enjoyed. I don't know . . ."

"Oh, please, Lancelot. What must I do?"

Lancelot held her close. "We cannot approach the Goddess without purification."

They went down to the river again, this time without banter. Quietly they washed each other and walked back to the cottage. Gwenhwyfar took the blanket from the bed and they walked up the hill.

As they entered the circle, Gwenhwyfar felt that same

pulse of energy she had the first time. "Do you feel it, Lancelot?"

He nodded. "Each time a circle is used, the residue lingers." He led her to the altar stone. "Nimue and Arthur would have performed the rite here."

"Not on the grass? The stone looks awfully uncomfortable."

"Using the circle isn't for personal pleasure, remember." He laid the blanket on top of the stone. "I will hold you. Come."

He lay on his side and lifted her partially across him, her head resting on his shoulder. The lovemaking was slow, gentle, and easy.

Gwenhwyfar inhaled contentedly as her body moved with his and felt the power of the Goddess.


As they prepared to leave, Lancelot knelt at the altar and chanted soft and low. "I'm asking for the Blessing for what has taken place," Lancelot explained as he stood. "One of the few things I remember from my time with Myrddin."

"When were you ever with Myrddin?" Gwenhwyfar asked, surprised.

He looked down at her. "When I was about ten. My mother thought I might make a bard." He stopped, an odd look on his face.

"Gwen, did you ever come to the Isle when you were small?"

"No, not the Isle," she replied. "But I was at the abbey of Ynys Gutrin with my father when I was about six. There was a resurgence of the Pelagian Theory and he had come to debate."

A slight glaze crossed his face.

"What is it, Lance?" she asked. "You look strange."

"Gwen," he said as he turned to her, "do you remember

nearly slipping into the water and a boy with a sword? You told him you knew how to use a sword, too?"

She thought and then smiled. "Yes, and a monk in brown came and scared me and I ran." Her eyes grew huge. "Was that you, Lance?"

He nodded. "The monk was Myrddin, in disguise, for the debate. He sent me away because he wanted to keep us separated. My mother told me that he was afraid we would destroy Arthur's dream." He turned to Gwenhwyfar. "What have we done?"


Gwenhwyfar watched as Elaine stepped down from the carriage, radiant in a hastily assembled but well-fitting white silk gown. *It has been eight years since I stepped from that carriage to become Arthur's bride. Did Lancelot feel this pain then?*

She didn't think she could bear this. Not after yesterday. At least Arthur had taken pity on her and not made her ride with Elaine.

Lancelot emerged from the little side room that the priest used. His face was pale beneath the tan, and there were dark circles under his eyes. She wondered if he had slept.

He offered Elaine his arm. As they approached the church door, they stopped in front of Arthur and Gwenhwyfar. Elaine made a proper curtsy, but her smile was smug. *Slut.* Gwenhwyfar fought the urge to slap her. Lancelot bowed to Arthur and dropped to one knee in front of Gwenhwyfar, taking her hand and kissing it. She felt the trembling of his fingers. When he looked at her, she was reminded of a stag that had been brought down when she had gone hunting with her father as a child. She had reached the animal first; it had looked at her with pain and acceptance in its eyes. She had never hunted again.

She put her hand over Lancelot's. "You will forever be the

queen's champion." *My love. I cannot endure this.* Then Arthur's hand was beneath her elbow, turning her.

Arthur and Gwenhwyfar took their places in the first pew. As the vows were read, Gwenhwyfar blocked the sound. She didn't want to hear anything about until death parted them or the promises he would have to make. Even though she knew he didn't want this marriage, he would be honor bound to uphold it. *Elaine will be enjoying those caresses, that sensuous mouth, the fullness of him inside . . .* She made a strangled sound and looked up to find Arthur watching her steadily. She lifted her chin and squared her shoulders. *Forget this is a church. Damn you, Elaine.*

Arthur was relieved. It was over. Gwenhwyfar had held up, although there had been that one moment.

Great revelry followed the ceremony. The incident with the cloak had dampened the tournament, but now the guests who had stayed were enjoying this banquet to the fullest. Ryden had composed a song in which he sang of the accomplished feats of Lancelot, and Dagonet was more energetic than usual.

Lancelot and Elaine had their own table at the center and in front of the high table. Elaine clung to Lancelot's arm, but with his free hand he made sure his wine cup was not empty. By midafternoon, he was already half-drunk.

" 'Tis not the way to start a marriage," Gwalchmai said to Arthur as they watched him. "A pity. My Ragnell has made me a happy man."

"It's time the man was married and bedded in a nightly manner," Myrddin said sharply, his hawk eyes taking in the picture as he popped a hazelnut into his mouth.

"Is it bedding you're wanting?" The faerie tickled Myrddin's ear, her green eyes glittering.

"Bedding a woman nightly wasn't ever his problem,"

Arthur said, unaware that Myrddin was preoccupied. "Keeping his interest was. I hope Elaine will be able to hold his attention."

*Dear Lord,* Arthur prayed. *Let this marriage work. I want Gwenhwyfar back.*

The evening wore on and the time came to see the couple to bed. Lancelot was in a near stupor. Arthur hauled him to his feet. He tottered for a minute and got his balance. Gwalchmai came around the other side, and together they were able to get Lancelot to walk toward the room that had been made ready. Brisen and a handmaid accompanied Elaine. Gwenhwyfar desperately needed a walk in the fresh air, but Elaine called out.

"The king is attending my husband. I would like the queen to attend me!"

Gwenhwyfar turned to stone. Arthur glowered. Lancelot swore.

Elaine approached Arthur. "Surely the queen, my cousin, wishes us well and would want to see us to our bed, properly married?"

Arthur's eyes turned the color of slate. "I'm sure the queen does, Elaine, but you have ladies to attend you."

Gwenhwyfar began to breathe again. *Thank you, husband.*

"It would be a shame for me to admit that I was raped, while my husband sought the queen." Elaine's tone was soft and low, but her eyes bore into Arthur's.

"Damnation, Elaine! Is there no end to your bitchiness?" Lancelot stared at her.

She smiled sweetly at him, then turned to Arthur. "Well?"

Arthur drew a deep breath. "Gwenhwyfar," he called. "A moment, please."

Gwenhwyfar slowly came closer, dreading every step. "Yes?"

"Elaine has a proposition for you. I will abide by your decision." Arthur's tone was flat and Lancelot, again, looked like a wounded animal.

Elaine repeated herself. Arthur was prepared and caught Gwenhwyfar's hand as she swung. They had a moment of silent argument; then Gwenhwyfar's shoulders slumped.

"As you will." Gwenhwyfar mightily wished she had one of Morgana's potions to use. *Hemlock would be good.* The women entered the bedroom and she slammed the door furiously behind them.

Brisen helped Elaine out of her wedding gown and smock and Gwenhwyfar held out her nightdress. "I doubt that I'll be needing that," Elaine giggled as she slipped naked under the covers and settled in the bed. She spread her hair over the pillow and smiled at Gwenhwyfar.

Gwenhwyfar snorted. "He doesn't love you."

"No?" Elaine arched her brows. "But I'm his wife." She accented the word. "I'm sure I'll find him man enough to take care of my needs. If you like, cousin, we can talk in the morning."

In the adjoining room, Gwalchmai was making an attempt at getting Lancelot sobered. "It's your wedding night, man. You are expected to bed her."

Lancelot peered at him through bloodshot eyes. "Hmmm." *Like I care.*

Arthur handed him a robe. "You need to get undressed. Let's get this thing done before Gwenhwyfar tries to kill her."

"I can always hope for that, I guess," Lancelot muttered. *I'm surprised I haven't heard any noise over there.*

"What ails you?" Gwalchmai asked, exasperated, "She's pretty enough; she looks a lot like Gwen . . ." Lancelot's unsteady blow missed him, just cuffing his jaw.

"Enough," Arthur said as Gwalchmai's arm came up.

"We'll not be brawling." He held out the robe again and Lancelot grabbed it.

When they entered the room, Gwenhwyfar tried to slip out, brushing against Lancelot coming in, as she did. For a brief second he squeezed her arm. *One last touch.*

Arthur pulled her back into the room. "We'll leave as soon as we see them both in bed," he whispered, holding her to his side. She glared at him.

Lancelot slid partially under the sheet and leaned against the backboard. Elaine pressed against him immediately and pulled his robe off his shoulders.

"Kiss me, my husband, and hold me," Elaine purred, "that these folks may leave and let us have our privacy."

*Yes, let's get this charade over with.* He pulled her across him and placed his lips on hers. Elaine threw her arms around him, trying to pry his mouth open with her tongue, but he wasn't cooperating. He hadn't even closed his eyes.

With a sigh, Arthur motioned everyone out of the room. He tugged at Gwenhwyfar. "It's time."

Reluctantly Lancelot watched her go. *Please, Gwen, don't believe any of this.*

When the door shut, Lancelot let his arms drop. "That, my dear wife," he said, "is the last kiss you'll be getting from me."

"What do you mean? We're married! You're supposed . . ."

"Do not tell me what I am supposed to do, Elaine." He lifted her off him. "If I had ever wanted you, I would have taken you years ago."

"But I love you, Lancelot!" She started to cry.

"No tears. You duped me into this marriage, and that witch Morgana probably gave you something for the wine, or I would have realized you weren't Gwen."

She looked at him furiously. "So, you have bedded her! Honorable Lancelot!"

He gave her a tight smile. "Let's talk about bedding for a minute, Elaine. You were no maiden. Whose soiled goods did I inherit?"

She tried to slap him, but he caught her hand. "Whose?"

"There's never been anyone but you, Lancelot. I've never loved . . ."

"I didn't ask if you loved him. Who was it?"

"It was just once." She started sobbing again. "So there wouldn't be any pain. So I would know what to do."

Lancelot dropped her hand and looked at her incredulously. "You are telling me that you asked . . . asked? . . . some man to show you?"

"No!" she protested, "he offered."

"A gallant thing to do," he said sarcastically. "Who was it?"

"Med . . . Medraut," she replied in a small voice.

For a moment he was nonplussed. Then he started to laugh. When he was finally able to stop, Elaine had moved to her side of the bed, fuming.

"I don't see what is so humorous."

"Of course not." Lancelot was still amused and nearly sober. "Medraut has won for now; I will be out of his way for a while. But he's besotted with Gwenhwyfar, too. You really need to find someone who isn't."

"Are you going to bed me this night or not?"

Lancelot reached over then and turned her to him. "I want you to understand this clearly. The only coupling you will get from me has already been done. I will take to wenching again before I take you." He removed his hand and turned over, pulling the covers up. "Think on it, Elaine. A lifetime of no love and no lustful expressions, either. I suggest the priest annul this marriage, for it is nothing but a shambles. I will confess to any sort of abuse you can create."

The next morning Lancelot and a disgruntled-looking Elaine departed for Joyous Garde; his cousins, Lionel and Bors, and Gareth went with them.

Lancelot put a hand on each of Gwenhwyfar's shoulders

and leaned down for his kiss. "I've asked for an annulment," he whispered.

Gwenhwyfar could hardly contain herself. An annulment was the perfect answer! The rumors would be squashed since the marriage had taken place. Lancelot would be a free man again. She tried very hard not to show her joy, but took his hands and squeezed them hard as she said aloud, "I pray that you return to Camelot soon." *And come to me.*

# Chapter 18

# Revelations

Gwenhwyfar and Arthur were ensconced in the comfortable chairs in front of an unlit hearth one evening in high summer. She watched him finish his wine, hoping he was relaxed. Her courses had not come for three moons.

"Arthur, can we speak of Medraut?"

"What has he done now?"

"Nothing that I know of," Gwenhwyfar answered. Medraut was making friends with a new group of recruits that had been hard to train and discipline. Bedwyr had his hands full without Lancelot. "He mentioned to me the other day that Morgana wishes him announced as heir."

"I'm sure she does," Arthur said bitterly, "but it's not going to happen."

"If you aren't planning to name Medraut heir, who then?"

Arthur gave her a pained look. He was quiet for some minutes and Gwenhwyfar didn't press him. "Custennin," he finally said. "If we have no child, I will appoint Custennin.

He is young and already a strong leader. The men will follow him."

Gwenhwyfar hesitated. "And if I could give you a child now?"

Arthur laughed humorlessly. "It takes two to do that and . . ." he stopped and stared at her. "Lancelot?" he asked softly.

She nodded and went to sit on the floor beside him. "Please don't be angry, Arthur. This means so much to me . . . for us . . ."

She watched a range of emotions cross his face. Momentary anger. Jealousy. Despair. Sadness. Hope.

He stroked her hair. "So he's done what I cannot."

"I believe the Goddess helped, Arthur. I asked Lance, the last time that day, to lie with me in the circle and he . . ."

Arthur silenced her. "I don't wish to hear the how of it, Gwenhwyfar. Spare me that, at least."

She bit her lip. "I asked for Her help, Arthur, even though I am a Christian. Another mortal sin I've committed."

"Praying to the Goddess is not wrong, Gwenhwyfar. I'm not surprised that it worked for you and Lancelot. He has his mother's fey blood; the Goddess would hear that call."

"Will you accept the child, Arthur?"

"Come here." He sat her on his lap, an arm loosely around her. "Lancelot may want to recognize the child as his own. Have you thought of that?"

Her eyes widened. "He can't, Arthur. Such acknowledgment would do everything you were afraid would happen if he didn't marry Elaine." *Yet, once his annulment is announced, he'll be able to return and see his child.*

"A man could change his mind, though, to get his child," Arthur said.

"Lancelot wouldn't do that to you, Arthur. He understood why he had to marry."

Arthur arched an eyebrow. "The rumor there is that he abuses her."

"Lancelot?" she asked in genuine surprise. "He couldn't; he is the most . . ."

"I am well aware of how he treats you." Arthur caught her chin. "But you haven't ridden with him in the field or seen him when the battle frenzy is upon him. I would think him capable if she goads him and he has no liking of her."

She took his hand. "I think you're wrong, Arthur. But even so, on that day, when we talked about a child . . ."

"Hush, Gwen." His arm tightened around her waist and he closed his eyes. "I will accept the child and raise him as my own. He will be my heir."


Several weeks later one of Lancelot's soldiers came to them with a routine status report from Joyous Garde. He was given a seat with them at supper.

Gwenhwyfar wanted desperately to ask if an annulment had been announced, but dared not. "Landinus," she asked, "how is my cousin Elaine?"

"I believe she is with child, lady," he smiled.

Gwenhwyfar put a hand over her own slightly swollen belly. *If that was true, there could be no annulment.* She felt the blood draining from her face.

Arthur moved quickly and brought her head down to her knees. She began to breathe normally again.

Landinus looked confused. "Is she ill, my lord?"

"No." Arthur shook his head. "She is with child, too, and women are sometimes affected this way after they have eaten."

"You must congratulate Elaine for me," Gwenhwyfar managed to say as she straightened. "Lancelot must be very happy; does he treat her well?"

Arthur threw her a sharp glance, but she ignored it. *I have to know; is it really over between us?*

The younger man squirmed. Arthur asked quietly, "Is there something wrong?"

He looked at Arthur, a trapped expression on his face. "The Lady Elaine says that Captain Lancelot misuses her. I don't believe it, though!"

"In what way?" Arthur's tone was inviting.

"Must I say, Lord? The queen is present . . ." Landinus's voice rose.

"He is my champion, Landinus," Gwenhwyfar said. "I would hear what the rumors are."

He swallowed and whispered, "She says that he brutally rapes her nightly, that she fears she might lose the babe."

"Has anyone seen any bruises?"

He shook his head. "No . . . well, one time, she had a bruise close to her eye. Captain Lancelot said she hurt herself on her spinning wheel as she bent down."

Arthur exchanged glances with Gwenhwyfar. "Well, that's easy enough to do," he said reassuringly. "I want you to give them a message. Tell them the king and queen look forward to seeing both of these births."

One frosty morning at the start of the fall season, a rider came to them from Venta. Arthur brought him to the council room. Natanlaod was a distant relative of Ambrosius, but he had been one of the last to pledge allegiance to Arthur.

"Cerdic causes trouble," the warlord told Arthur shortly.

Myrddin looked up from a scroll he was reading. The faerie stopped dancing across the page, her attention riveted on the newcomer. "This is going to be bad . . ."

"Hush!" Myrddin hissed.

Natanlaod turned to him, an eyebrow raised. "Are you asking me to be quiet?"

"Ah . . . no," Myrddin answered, looking annoyed. "I was talking to myself . . ."

Arthur gave him an odd look before turning back to Natanlaod. "Cerdic? Has he grown ambitious?"

"Not only does he want more land, but he brings more men. I think it wise to ride against him."

"Now? The winter season is nearly here."

"His troops are still raw. Better to attack than wait until they are well disciplined."

Arthur thought for some moments. He could not allow the Saxon to establish a stronghold. Too dangerous. "What is your plan?"

"There is a village, Hamwih, across from Clausentum, that would make a good camp. We would outnumber him at least eight to one at this time." Natanlaod shrugged. "We would have this finished before the weather turns."

"How many troops have you?"

"Three hundred horse, three thousand foot."

"You would take them all?"

"A show of force, mostly," Natanlaod answered. "The cavalry will make quick work of his men, for they all fight on foot."

Arthur considered. "That area is swampland. Mayhap your infantry would be a better choice."

"They can back the horse, if necessary," Natanlaod replied.

"What do you need from me?"

"Nothing except your permission. You're the high king."

"You have it," Arthur said, "provided you bring Cerdic to me alive. I would treat with him."

"I prefer to take no prisoners."

Arthur straightened. "That may be so, but a man beaten can be kept in bounds. Cerdic is good at keeping the seas open; I would not have him killed unnecessarily."

Natanlaod stood defiant. Arthur waited.

"As you wish," the warlord finally said and bowed to take his leave.

When he had gone, Myrddin shook his head. "That attitude will get him killed."

Arthur called Gryflet to him and explained the situation. "I want you to go to Clausentum. Find out how matters lie. Attach yourself to the Venta army when it arrives. I'm not sure if Natanlaod will heed me. I will have the truth of what happens."

Six weeks later, in the wind-driven cold of a late autumn rain, Gryflet returned. His horse was near exhaustion. Gwenhwyfar and Arthur had just finished the noon meal as he ran into the hall.

"Natanlaod is dead, Arthur. Cerdic prepares to march on Venta."

"What in all the gods' names happened?" Arthur asked as Gwenhwyfar brought Gryflet some wine. He gratefully accepted and sat down.

"Cerdic withdrew into the swamp—Nettley Marsh, I think they called it. Natanlaod foolishly sent his cavalry into that bog. They mired down. Cerdic's men harried them until there was nothing but confusion. Cerdic had men hiding in the streams and brushes and they came at him from all sides."

Arthur's face was dark. "Did Natanlaod's men not rally?"

Gryflet shook his head. "They had all they could do to get the horses out. When the infantry saw the look of them and learned their warlord was dead, they retreated."

"Damned cowards!" Arthur started pacing. "Over three thousand of them to Cerdic's what? Five or six hundred? Bel's fires!" *I should have forced Roman training on them when Natanlaod swore allegiance!* He turned to Gryflet. "You said Cerdic marches? Is there any way we can stop him and treat?"

"I don't know, my lord. Cerdic's troops were ready when I left."

Arthur considered quickly. "If we ride to Venta at first

light, we might intercept them there, but it will be close. Gryflet, tell Bedwyr to make the preparations. Make sure that Medraut and Agravaine ride with us."

After he had gone, Arthur turned to Gwenhwyfar. She was in her seventh month and getting large. "I'll not have those two at home with you. I hate to leave you, Gwenhwyfar, but this must be stopped. Do you want me to send for Nimue?"

"No," she said, "I am not ill. The babe is not due for another two moons; you will be well back by then."

He gave her a kiss and then quickly kissed her belly, too. "I will miss holding you and the little one," he said, for he enjoyed feeling the child kick. Then he was gone, looking for Bedwyr.

Arthur arrived too late to protect Venta. Cerdic had already entered the city, although he was willing to treat, since he had no desire to be Arthur's enemy. The process was long and drawn out. Cerdic would keep the land, but reaffirmed his allegiance to govern in Arthur's name, just before the summons from Camelot came. But by then the damage had been done.

A fortnight had passed since Arthur had left. Gwenhwyfar was sitting by the fire late one December afternoon, enjoying its warmth and, half tranced, watching the flames leaping blue and yellow amid the orange. Outside it was sleeting and the wind screeched. Contentedly she lay her hands on her belly, feeling the baby move.

She did not hear Lucan approach as he motioned the guest forward. Suddenly, though, she sensed someone near her. She sat up and turned slowly.

Lancelot stood behind her, that lopsided smile she loved so well on his face. Euphoria filled her. She struggled to get up; he moved to lift her and then she was in his arms. He smelled of fresh snow and his cheek was cold, but his lips were warm.

"What are you doing here, my love?" she asked when both of them could talk.

"Landinus brought me the news; I had to come." He kissed her again, making her breathless.

"How did Arthur take it?" he asked after they were seated and wine served.

"He was worried that you would come for the child." Gwenhwyfar watched as his face momentarily clouded. "He will claim the babe as his heir."

"Will he let me know him, do you think?"

"I don't see why not, Lance. Uther trained Arthur, not telling him who he was. It could be the same for you."

The cloud lifted and he grinned again. "And I would get to see his mother."

"You still find me attractive then?" She kept her tone light. "I feel like a cow."

He left his chair and knelt down on the floor beside her, placing his hands on her fully rounded belly. "You will be attractive to me when the shadow of the Crone is upon you, Gwen." He gently moved a hand across her abdomen. "This is our child." The baby kicked hard at that moment and he looked up in wonderment. "Does that hurt you?"

She laughed, "Not really, but he is an active child. I think I will be ready to hold him in my arms instead."

His face clouded again. "And Arthur will be the man who holds him."

Gwenhwyfar studied his face. "Won't you have another babe to hold?"

Lancelot sighed. "If I am allowed near him."

"What does that mean, Lance? She cannot deny you the right to your child."

He picked up Gwenhwyfar's hand and kissed the palm, then continued to hold it. "Elaine has put out that I rape her in order to destroy the child." He tried to laugh. "The priest has forbidden me to enter her room. She has posted a guard. I told the soldier not to worry since it will be the easiest post he's ever had."

"We have heard those rumors, Lancelot. I don't believe them."

"I swear to you, Gwen, I have not touched the bitch since that first night when I thought I was meeting you."

"Not even on your wedding night?" Gwenhwyfar blurted before she could stop. *My love, I've tortured myself with thoughts of your coupling with her.*

He kissed her hand again. "Especially not on the wedding night. I was hard-pressed not to throttle her when I had to go through with that exhibition so you would leave." He looked into the fire. "I would not harm a babe, even if it is hers."

"And yours also, Lancelot," Gwenhwyfar said gently.

He shrugged. "She threatens to take him home to her father."

Gwenhwyfar inhaled deeply. "Let's wait and see. How long can you stay?"

"A day or two at most. I must get back before the snow closes the roads. I would never see that child if I weren't there for its birth." He let his hand lightly roam the roundness. "But Gwen, I want to be with you when our child is born."

*Our child, yet Arthur's too. I love you both.* "That can't be, Lancelot. For your sake and Arthur's." She pressed his head against her stomach and he kept her hand to his chest. They stayed like that for a long time, gazing into the fire.


Lancelot stayed three days. While he was there, he worked Safere in the paddock. Gwenhwyfar stood near the fence the first day, watching.

He brought the horse to the rail and dismounted. Safere tossed his head and raised his front hooves. Lancelot brought him down sharply with a resounding smack. The stallion stood quietly after that. "He's becoming a handful, Gwen. Mayhap Arthur should start using him since you can't ride."

"That's a good idea," Gwenhwyfar said as they handed the reins over and walked back to the hall. "I'll ask him when he returns."

The company of men that Arthur had left behind to protect Camelot were glad to see Lancelot as well and quickly arranged for some weaponry matches. On the third day he practiced with some of the recruits from Bedwyr's new unit.

"They've got an edge to them that I don't like," he told Gwenhwyfar. "They hesitate before they take an order, as if deciding on their own whether to obey."

She nodded. "Arthur feels the same way. I wish you were here to help Bedwyr."

He draped an arm over her shoulder. "Let's see what the spring brings."

On the fourth morning he had to leave. Gwenhwyfar had said her farewell privately and still felt warm from the intensity of his kisses. He would come back in the spring; she knew he would. And she would have a son to show him. A small crowd surrounded him now and she stood back. He turned to wave as he cantered away.

She watched him disappear as the road rounded into the trees. She was crossing the bailey when she heard a horse neighing shrilly. It sounded like Safere. She walked as quickly as she could in that direction.

A stableboy was frantically trying to beat something with a broom at the door of Safere's stall. "It's a hare, lady. Gotten into the stall and is scaring the horse."

"Get that broom away," she ordered. "Move back."

Gwenhwyfar took his place, crooning softly. The whites of the stallion's eyes showed, but his ears twitched toward her, a sign that he was listening. Slowly, he stilled, occasionally pawing the ground with one hoof and blowing.

She moved in and began stroking his neck, still speaking

softly. She grasped his halter, and the hare took that opportunity to escape, running in front of the horse.

Safere reared, pulling Gwenhwyfar up along with him. When he came down, she was slammed against the stall as he broke free and bolted out the open door. She reeled, falling to the ground.

"Catch the horse," she managed to say before she passed out.

When she recovered consciousness, she saw Nimue's worried face looking down at her.

"What are . . . you . . . doing here?" she managed to ask in a weak voice. *Why am I in so much pain? My stomach feels on fire. The baby . . .* She tried to sit up.

Nimue gently pushed her back. "Don't try to move yet. Clear your head first."

"Is the baby . . . all right? I can't feel it." Gwenhwyfar searched Nimue's face and then turned away. "He has to be . . . he has to live," she whispered.

Nimue placed a cool cloth on her forehead. "You've lost a lot of blood."

"How long have I . . ."

"Nearly two days, Gwenhwyfar. We've sent for Arthur."

"Is the babe . . . dead?" she finally asked.

"There has been no movement the whole time."

Gwenhwyfar grabbed her hand. "Is there nothing you can do? The babe was a gift from the Goddess. You are Her priestess."

"I cannot command the Goddess. She does as She wills," Nimue said softly.

Gwenhwyfar began to cry then. "But he is still in me. He must be . . ."

Again the cool hand stroked Gwenhwyfar. "He must be brought out."

"No." She placed her hands over her rounded abdomen.

"You will die if the babe does not come out." Nimue handed her a cup of thick, cold white broth with crushed leaves in it. "Drink this."

"What is it?" She eyed it suspiciously.

"Brooklime," Nimue answered. "If the child is dead, this will expel him."

"No."

Nimue sighed and put the broth down. She picked up two other vials and added a few drops to another cup that held wine. "Then drink this; it will take the pain away."

Gwenhwyfar sniffed and picked up the odor of fresh hay. "It won't harm me?"

"It will not harm you."

Slowly, Gwenhwyfar took several sips.

Nimue sat with her, holding her hand, as she watched the woodrowel and horehound's hypnotic effects take hold. Gwenhwyfar's eyes slowly glazed.

"The . . . pain . . . is . . . gone," she said slowly.

"Yes. I told you it would be." Nimue began chanting softly in the Old Tongue. Gwenhwyfar stared at her, entranced.

"Now," Nimue said, "drink this. It is what you need."

Unquestioningly, Gwenhwyfar drank the broth.

Several hours later, the child came—a boy. His name would have been Llacheu.

Another week passed before she was able to sit up or recognize Arthur. He had nearly killed his horse racing home when the note came. He sat by her bed and prayed. She was gaunt from the weight she had lost, and she had no appetite. Arthur took to feeding her himself to make sure she swallowed the food. *I almost lost you, Gwenhwyfar.*

"I have sinned, Arthur, and that is why the babe was killed. I should not have lain with Lancelot." Her voice sounded sorrowful.

"Gwenhwyfar. Look at me." He waited. "The babe was killed in an accident. Whether the child was mine or his does not matter. Do you want me to send for Lancelot?"

"No." Her reply was firm. "There's nothing he can do, and if he comes now, he'll miss Elaine's birthing. She'll make sure he never sees the child."

Arthur grimaced. "She can't do that."

"Well, don't send for Lancelot. I have sinned; this is my penance."

"I gave you permission for that day, remember? How can that be sin, then?"

She whispered, "I asked the Goddess for a child, Arthur. The Church forbids that, but I did it anyway. That's why God took him from me."

"Don't do this to yourself, Gwen. I let my guilt take control of me, and we know what's happened. God does not hate."

With those words, a great stone seemed to be lifted from him. *It is true. With all my pleading for Gwenhwyfar's life, this is the answer. God does not hate; I have only hated myself!* For the first time in years, he felt the stirring of desire in his groin, and now Gwenhwyfar was not in any condition to participate. Relief and happiness flooded him. *I will wait.*

Her recovery was slow. The harsh winter did nothing to help matters since Arthur didn't want her to go outside. He told her he feared she would become ill again.

As spring arrived, so did Landinus. He handed the status report to Arthur and a note to Gwenhwyfar.

The note was from Elaine. She had a son, she wrote, and had named him Galahad. She hoped Gwenhwyfar had been delivered as well. She ended by saying that if Lancelot should choose to visit them, she and the child would be gone when he returned.

Gwenhwyfar silently handed the note to Arthur and watched his jaw set.

Landinus spent several weeks with them while Arthur thought what to do. Finally he let the man go, saying simply that their child had been stillborn.

After that, Gwenhwyfar became more despondent. She picked at morsels of food and rarely left her room. Arthur had come one night and broached the subject of another babe, but she became hysterical. He left her alone after that.

One day in early summer she went to Arthur as he was plotting a map for another campaign. "I think I need to leave for a while."

He came to her, taking her hands. "Where would you like to go? All is quiet right now. We can—"

"No," she interrupted. "I need to find some peace. I would like to visit Ygraine."

Arthur looked surprised. "She has taken her vows. I don't know how much visiting she can do."

Gwenhwyfar shook her head. "Ygraine has always been content within the confines of the Church. Mayhap I can find forgiveness there for my mortal sins. I must try, Arthur." She looked at him hopelessly. "I must try."

Ygraine embraced her happily. "I am glad, my daughter, that you have come to us; the reason is not important," she said as she led Gwenhwyfar to the small cell that would be hers. "You will find the peace you seek here."

Life at the abbey was simple. The sisters each had tasks: working in the vegetable gardens, preparing the food, washing the clothing, making soap, carrying in new rushes for the floors, cleaning and polishing. Gwenhwyfar rotated through each position, finding it satisfying to sweat and work with her hands. She recited the offices with the nuns and prayed at length each day, asking for forgiveness.

Arthur came to visit after she had been away a month.

"More trouble with Cerdic," he told Gwen when they

were seated in the abbey's small courtyard, a sister standing a discreet distance away. "He's moved north of Venta."

"What will you do?" she asked.

He raked his hair. "I still think we can live together in peace. Cerdic has no desire for war, but he wants the land. He's testing me. I don't know. Most of this season will be spent in treaty, I think."

Gwenhwyfar smiled complacently. "Do not feel you must visit me, Arthur. I am content. I may even be forgiven one day."

He kissed her chastely. "Do not plan on staying here, Gwenhwyfar," he whispered. "I miss you too much."

She watched him leave. She could not return to him now; she had found her place. With enough hard work, she could receive absolution. She refused to see him the next time he came.

In the spring of the following year, a young priest named Gildas came to visit the abbey. He had the unbridled passion of a zealot. Gwenhwyfar listened to his emotional speeches in a detached manner until he began to criticize Arthur.

He had no way of knowing that she was Arthur's wife, for she had taken to wearing the simple dress of the novice.

"The king keeps a pagan priestess and calls himself a Christian. His wife left him because of it and rightly she should, the queen being a Christian woman. Who knows where she went? He taxes the Church, can you believe? He harbors a half-mad druid who talks to himself. It is time we look for a real Christian king, I tell you!"

The speech bothered her. Had she brought Arthur to this? How much damage could these rumors do? Did Arthur need her? Should she return to her duties?

She no longer felt the guilt that had brought her here. She had confessed to the abbess and been convinced that God loved all children, regardless of their conception. And Lancelot . . . Elaine would not allow him to come to them. It would be safe to return.

The next day she had a long discussion with the abbess, and then she sent a messenger to Arthur. She was ready to come home.

Several days later Gwenhwyfar was about to begin working in the vegetable garden. She was dressed in her trews, which she preferred while crawling around on the ground. Even some of the novices had adopted them. Looking up, she saw the abbess approach.

"Your escort is here, my lady, to take you home."

*Arthur!* They walked to the small office at the front of the abbey. "Thank you for letting me stay and for your help," Gwenhwyfar said sincerely as the abbess smiled and opened the door, motioning her through.

"I will be your escort, my lady," Lancelot said formally.

Startled, Gwenhwyfar tripped. Instantly he was at her side, his hand under her elbow, steadying her. His touch sent a shock impulse through her. She drew a ragged breath, aware that the abbess was watching them.

"Thank . . . thank you. Did you come by yourself?" she blurted, still short of breath.

His eyes had gone smoky and she could see he was trying not to smile. "That would not be proper, my lady. Gareth and the rest of the escort wait outside."

She struggled for some semblance of dignity, very much aware that he was still holding her arm. "What I meant was . . . is Arthur not able to come?"

He released her arm. "Cerdic is after ever more land. Arthur has taken his cohort to Calleva. I had just arrived when your message came." He tilted his head a little. "Have you objections to your champion coming for you?"

"No, of course not," she said quickly. "I am willing for

you to take me." She saw the smile begin again and realized what she had said. She felt herself blush. She had forgotten how easily they could exchange innuendoes. "Home. Take me home."

When he offered her his arm, her fingers trembled. *A year and a half since I've seen you and the attraction is even stronger. Has this daily prayer done nothing for me?*

They walked outside and he helped her mount. As they trotted down the road, she turned back to see Ygraine watching from the small window of the chapel. *She doesn't think I'm strong enough not to betray Arthur. Well, I am. I am his queen.*

Lancelot remained formal for the duration of the two-day ride, so it wasn't until their first night home that Gwenhwyfar was able to question him. They were playing chess, their chairs close together by the hearth.

Lancelot moved his queen across the board and stopped three spaces ahead from her king. "Check."

Gwenhwyfar studied the board and sacrificed her last bishop. It would give her one move before checkmate.

"You're not concentrating, Gwen," Lancelot said. "What's on your mind?"

She asked the question that had been on her mind for two days. "Did Elaine change her mind on your visiting us?"

His face set. "I imagine she's gone to Pelles by now."

Gwenhwyfar was startled. "Then why did you come, Lancelot?"

"Just before Arthur left for Calleva, Gaheris brought a message." He set the board aside and took her hand. "Arthur asked me to come talk to you since you were refusing to see him."

"Arthur asked you to abandon Galahad?" she asked, shocked.

"I doubt that he thought of it." His fingers played lightly

over the calluses on her palm. She closed her eyes, giving herself to the sensation.

"Come sit with me, Gwen."

Gwenhwyfar opened her eyes. "I should not. I would not commit more sin."

The corner of his mouth quirked. "I think it more of a sin to torture me, which is what you're doing." He began kissing her palm, his tongue supple and pliable.

She felt herself weakening. She tried to pull her hand away, but his grasp was firm. He slipped out of his chair and tugged her onto the floor with him, his mouth over hers. She gave in momentarily, savoring the taste of him; then she pushed against him.

He raised his head. "What is it, Gwen?"

"This is sin, Lancelot," she whispered.

"You've spent too much time in that convent, my lady." He nuzzled her neck, nibbling at it. "Have you forgotten how good this feels?" He brushed her lips with his.

"Yes . . . no . . ."

"Let me remind you then," he said as he continued to play with her mouth, his hands deftly undoing her shirt. She groaned softly as his touch scorched her flesh, sending flames of passion through her.

He lowered his head to suckle her breast gently and then with increasing pressure. "I would have you, Gwen," he whispered as his mouth found hers again, this time demanding, as the pent-up desire built.

She pushed at him as hard as she could. "Stop, Lancelot. Please. Stop."

He stared at her for a moment and then sat up. "What in your God's name is wrong with you?"

She pulled her shirt together and struggled to sit. Automatically he helped her. "Please don't be angry, Lance," she said with a raspy breath, wanting nothing more than to tear off his clothes and join with him. "I love you as much as I ever did. I don't know if I can explain . . ." and she told him the whole story of Safere kicking her, the stillbirth, the depression and the time at the convent, where she felt she had received absolution.

"What a strange religion that bids its people to feel guilt about receiving pleasure," he said.

"I am married to Arthur."

"Arthur sent me to you."

"To talk."

He sighed. "In my mother's religion, women have thigh freedom, the right to choose their partners at will. What happens between a man and a woman should be as easy and natural as play. There is no guilt. Maybe that's the real absolution."

Gwenhwyfar fiddled with her shirt laces, puzzled.

"Let me make amends, Gwen," Lance said, reaching for the laces. "I can dress you as well as undress you." He brought them together and tied them. He placed a kiss on the tip of her nose. "Now leave me before I lose control again."

Gwenhwyfar found him near the stables the next morning, preparing to mount. "You're not going back to Joyous Garde, are you, Lance?"

"No," he answered, checking the girth and tightening the cinch after Pryderi blew. "Gaheris mentioned that Agricola and Theodoric want to pursue a campaign against the Scotti of Dementia. I thought to offer my sword to Arthur."

"He has no need of your sword while he is treating with Cerdic. Why not wait for him to return?" She smiled. "You know I enjoy your company."

His eyes became unreadable. "Gwen, the crime that I'm accused of committing with Elaine, I would commit with you if you refused me again." He turned back to the horse, making an adjustment on a saddlebag. "I have never raped a woman, but you came too close last night."

"I would not call it that," she said in a small voice.

He took a step toward her. "Tell me you'll be willing, and I'll stay."

She was silent, looking down at the ground.

"Do you want me to force you, Gwenhwyfar? To not stop when you tell me to?"

"You would not hurt me," she replied, still looking at the ground.

He was beside her then, his hand not gentle as he took her chin and tilted her head up to meet his eyes. "Games can be played, Gwen, where force is used, but I don't think that's what you really want." He lessened his grip. "I think you still feel that damnable guilt. If I simply took you, it wouldn't be your fault, would it?"

He was as frustrated as she had ever seen him. She could feel the potency building. She removed his hand. "You would be satisfied."

He shook his head. " I want you to come to me freely and enjoy what we do."

He mounted Pryderi and leaned down toward her. "The only force I might consider using, Gwen, is to turn you over my knee when I get back and swat that religious guilt out of you." He straightened. "The gods help us both if you like it."

The horse leaped to full stride, churning small stones in his wake.

She watched him ride away. *Even that, my love. Your touch is like a fire, branding my soul.*

# Chapter 19

# The Plotting

Over the next three weeks Gwenhwyfar got to know Gareth a lot better. Lancelot had left him behind in his haste to be gone.

Clearly he worshipped Lancelot. She chided herself for taking advantage of the youth, but she was also learning what life must be like at Joyous Garde with Elaine.

"He never goes near her," Gareth said the first evening when she had asked him to sit with her after supper. "The man who guards her door sniggers that it is the easiest post he's ever been assigned."

That was music for her soul. Elaine wasn't enjoying him. Gwenhwyfar couldn't resist saying, "Well, many men take their pleasure of the wenches that wait about."

Gareth blushed. "Not Captain Lancelot. Oh," he boasted proudly, "there's plenty of them following him, and pretty ones, too, but he doesn't notice. I think he must be very devout, to remain so pure."

She almost choked on that.

Gareth was on one of his stories about a training session one morning when the gate guard sounded the gong. "The king returns!" he shouted.

Together they got up and went to the gate. The familiar red and gold dragon banner floated above the first horses, and she could see Arthur and Lancelot riding together. They were a handsome pair, she thought, resisting the urge to run to them. A very blond young man rode between them.

Lancelot saluted her as they rode through, and Gareth followed him. Arthur dismounted and walked to Gwenhwyfar and took her hands. "Lancelot tells me you were ready to come home on your own."

She smiled. "I was. I would like to make up for my absence to my king and lord." *I will be your queen again; we will work together.*

"It is enough that you came back," he said softly, and then he wrapped his arms around her tightly. She felt him tremble.

Gwenhwyfar linked her arm through his as they walked toward the hall where Lancelot was waiting with the young stranger.

"Who is that?" she asked Arthur.

"Cynric. Cerdic's son," Arthur replied. "He will be our hostage."

She looked at him in surprise. "Was there trouble?"

"No." He shook his head. "I sent Gwalchmai with a troop to Clausentum as we proceeded to Calleva. He found Cynric wenching in the local tavern. You know how Gwalchmai can charm a pig into smelling sweet. Once we had Cynric captive, Cerdic was willing to negotiate. I think there will be no more land raidings."

The young man looked at Gwenhwyfar appreciatively as she approached.

Lancelot cuffed him. "Keep your eyes in your head, boy."

He met Lancelot's glare, unfazed. "Surely the lady cannot object if a man finds her beautiful." He turned back to

Gwenhwyfar and bowed. "I am Cynric. I understand I am to be a . . . guest . . . here." He gave her an easy smile.

Gwenhwyfar observed him. He was extraordinarily handsome, with golden tanned skin, light hair, and ice blue eyes, but a little too sure of himself. He must be about twenty, not much older than Medraut.

"You are welcome to our home, Cynric. I pray that all goes well for you." She looked at Lancelot. "And how does my champion?"

Lancelot stepped closer and bent over her hand formally. Laughter was in his eyes. "Your champion is ready to take care of any problem, my lady."

Her eyes widened slightly. *Is he referring to our last conversation?*

"You will be given your own quarters, Cynric," Arthur was saying. "Under guard, of course, until you earn some privileges. I expect you to uphold the honor that your father has placed in you. You are to cause no trouble, and we stay at peace. Lancelot, would you see to it?"

He turned to Gwenhwyfar with a grin. "We have other business to take care of."


Arthur opened the door to his quarters and ushered her in. Once the door was closed, he crushed her to him.

"I've missed you, Gwenhwyfar. Over a year is a long time," he said, and then held her away. "Why would you not see me?"

*Why? How to explain that cocoon of protection?* She met his earnest gaze. "I'm sorry, Arthur. The convent was so peaceful. You wanted me to leave, so it was easier not to see you at all."

"Did you find what you were searching for?"

"I worked hard, Arthur, and I denied myself pleasures. Eventually I received absolution. I was forgiven for calling on the Goddess and using pagan ways."

"Did I not tell you that as well?" he asked.

"Yes, but Lancelot says . . ." she stopped.

"Lancelot says what, Gwenhwyfar?" His grey eyes watched her steadily.

"Nothing. It's not important." Gwenhwyfar reached for him, but he stepped back.

"Finish it."

For a moment her eyes smoldered. "He says women should have the right to choose, and that real absolution is to feel no guilt about taking pleasure."

"And is Lancelot in the business of granting absolution these days?" Arthur's voice was deceptively calm.

She looked at him apprehensively, for she recognized the tone. "I have not lain with him, if that's what you're asking, Husband."

"Do you want to?" His voice had gone flat.

She remembered the last night with Lancelot and her temper flared at the implied accusation. "Are you giving me a choice?"

"No," he answered, his eyes the color of slate. "You are my wife. Mayhap it is time I remind you of it."

She knew she was making him angry, but she couldn't stop. It had taken every ounce of her willpower to deny Lancelot, and now Arthur was accusing her of giving in. He had no idea. "Please do," she said sarcastically. "It's been years . . ."

He grabbed her and spun her around, ripping at the fasteners on the back of her gown. He pushed it down and seized one breast with either hand, pinching the nipples.

"You're hurting . . ." she said, and he turned her toward him, his mouth savage, his hands gripping her back. He held her against him with one hand as he undid his trews.

They fell together on the bed, and he clamped his mouth over her breast, his teeth finding the nipple, while his hand roughly pulled on the other. She winced in pain and began striking at his shoulders with her fists.

"Stop it, Arthur. You're hurting me!"

He looked up then and she felt a tinge of fear. His eyes were glazed and she knew she was seeing the face of the warlord king, a man that might very well plunder, not her husband. She pushed at him, but he pressed her down.

"I will not be denied what is mine any longer." His eyes blazed and his voice was raw. He ravaged her mouth again, and she tried to twist away but only succeeded in hitting her cheekbone against the side of his head.

He rammed himself into her, his mouth never leaving hers, plunging deeper with ever-more-forceful stabs. She could only lie there as a receptacle for his anger. When he finished, she rolled over and cursed him silently.

Sometime later, she felt his hand on her arm, gentle this time. She did not move.

"How much did I hurt you, Gwenhwyfar?" he asked hoarsely. When she did not answer, he slowly turned her over on her back. Leaning on an elbow, he looked down at her. With his fingers, he caressed her face, lightly touching the bruise that was forming on her cheek.

"I'm sorry, Gwenhwyfar," he whispered. "I didn't mean for this to happen. I had planned, after all this time . . . then all I wanted was to make you forget Lancelot. I was battle frenzied. By your Holy Virgin, I would never deliberately hurt you. Please believe me. Forgive me."

"You raped me, Arthur." She got out of bed, wrapping the sheet close. "Right now I cannot bear your touch. I only pray that one day I will change my mind." She swept out of the room without looking back.

Gwenhwyfar was brushing Safere when Lancelot appeared the next morning. He leaned against the stall door. She kept her back to him, not wanting him to see the bruise.

"You didn't break your fast with us this morning," he said, "and Arthur was in a foul mood. Are you all right?"

"Certes," Gwenhwyfar replied without looking up. "Now that you're back, Lancelot, we need to meet with Palomides . . ."

"Why aren't you looking at me?" he asked.

"I'm brushing the horse." Then she felt his hand on her arm, drawing her toward the stall door. She kept her head down.

"Look at me, Gwen."

"I can't. I mean, I'd rather not. Please go, Lance."

"No." He put a hand under her chin and tilted her face upward. She heard the sharp breath he took when he saw the bruise. "Arthur did this?"

"It was an accident."

"How? Men don't hit women."

"I mentioned what you'd said about thigh freedom and he went mad. I got the bruise when I tried to stop him. I couldn't. I've never seen him like that." Tears welled up in her eyes and slid down her cheeks. She stamped her foot in irritation.

Lancelot drew her to him and kissed a salty teardrop off the corner of her mouth. "Battle frenzy. I've seen Arthur that way only once, myself. I'm not defending him, Gwen, but I almost raped you the last time."

"You stopped . . . and you didn't try to hurt me."

His mouth set in a tight line. "No. And if he does it again, he'll answer to me, even if he is the king. I am your champion."

Gwenhwyfar pressed closer to him. "Promise me you'll never hurt me, Lancelot."

He wrapped his arms around her tightly. "I promise, not ever," he said as their lips met for a long and tender kiss.


Morgana watched Medraut pacing back and forth in front of her where she was handtooling a piece of leather in the tannery. "You're excited this morning."

"Something is wrong between Arthur and Gwenhwyfar," Medraut announced.

"In what way?" she asked.

"She had a bruise and a swollen face the morning after we came back. She has hardly talked to him since then."

"What do you think took place, Son?"

He laughed. "Probably the same thing that takes place with you and Accolon every night. Only Gwenhwyfar seemed not to like it."

Morgana smiled. When he was a child, she'd let him hide behind the tapestries sometimes when she and Accolon played their semisadistic games. Knowing he was watching had heightened her excitement.

He leaned forward. "Lancelot the Great is angry at Arthur, too, and they're planning a campaign against the Scotti in Dementia soon. How well will Lancelot defend Arthur if he's angry at him?"

She put down her tooling needle and smoothed the leather. "They have a strange bond between them. They may fight over Gwenhwyfar until they are all too old to do anything about it, but each would give his own life defending the other in battle." She looked intently at Medraut. "However, if one or both of them were to die in battle . . ."

"Should Arthur die in battle, I would be king and I could have Gwen . . ."

"Forget Gwenhwyfar, Medraut. You will have your pick of women. Being king . . . having the power . . . is the important thing. That should be your goal."

"And yours, Mother. I haven't forgotten that you want to be consort."

"That's true." She smiled at him as her hands caressed the soft leather.

He sighed. "Anyway, Arthur can't be killed in battle, not while he is wearing his scabbard. It prevents him from losing too much blood."

"Sometimes, Medraut, I truly think you have the Old Blood in you." She held out a hand to him. "Come see what I'm working on."

He walked over to the table. "A scabbard."

"Look closely at it, Medraut."

"It's beautiful work, Mother, very intricate. Lots of pagan symbols."

"When it's finished, it will be a replica of Arthur's," she said, watching him.

Slowly, he smiled. "You're planning an exchange? This one won't protect him?"

"That's right. I will wait for an opportunity to obtain a hostage, then draw Arthur out and have Accolon challenge him in hand-to-hand combat. He will have to remove the swordbelt." She did a sensual, catlike stretch and then straightened on the chair again. "I will make the switch while no one notices."

"Excellent plan, Mother. Are you planning to abduct Gwenhwyfar again?" Medraut sounded half serious, half sarcastic. "I'll help."

She ignored the barb. "No. Lancelot."

"What?" Medraut nearly grew hysterical, laughing. "Are you just going to take him by the hand and lead him some- where?"

She remained unruffled. "Something like that."

Medraut dried his eyes. "You forget, Mother. Lancelot looks only at Gwenhwyfar. I doubt that even you could pro- duce a charm to seduce him."

"I did once," she answered placidly, "but that isn't what I had in mind."

"What, then?"

"Wait and see." She smiled. "Now tell me about the new guest you have."

"Cynric? He's Cerdic's son. Arthur got tired of Cerdic's land grabbing, so now we have a hostage. It's odd, but I feel a kinship toward him. He told me about a hideaway he has about a half day's ride from here. He offered me its use in return for supplying wenches for him since he can't leave."

"He may be a possible ally one day," Morgana said. "You need to begin to build your own base of supporters. The Saxons have no reason to be loyal to Arthur."

"Yes," Medraut said, his eyes gleaming, "and if Arthur refuses to acknowledge me, I could take the land with my own men!"

In preparation for a western march to stop the Scotti raids, Arthur drilled his cohort long hours, and finally Lancelot and Bedwyr both approached him after one particularly strenuous session.

"The men are ready, Arthur. Let's not weary them of battle until we reach it."

Arthur began to pace. "You think I don't know how to direct the cohort, Captains?" He turned to Lancelot. "You drill your men harder than anyone else. I'm doing no more than that." *By Mithras, I will have control over something!*

"May I speak bluntly?" Lancelot asked.

Arthur eyed him. "Is this about Gwenhwyfar?" When Lancelot nodded, he shook his head. "I don't want to discuss it." Raw pain seared through him. After all those years of being unable to perform, now his wife wouldn't let him anywhere near her. Not that he blamed her.

Doggedly Lancelot continued. "For the first time since I've known you, you are letting your personal feelings interfere with your command."

Arthur narrowed his eyes. "I could have you flogged for that!"

Lancelot looked straight ahead, his jaw set.

Bedwyr threw up his hands. "If anyone needs a thrashing, it's that sister of mine. Look at what she's done to both of you. Lancelot, you act like she needs protecting from Arthur. Why?" He turned to Arthur. "I don't know what happened, but she is your wife and she needs to start acting like it. She must be brought to heel."

"NO!" Arthur and Lancelot said together. They stared at each other, neither backing down. Finally Lancelot turned and left the room.

Arthur sighed. "He's right. I have let my personal problems get in the way, but I wronged your sister." He changed the subject abruptly. "I stand corrected. Give the men two days' liberty. They've earned it."


"How many ships, Theodoric?" Arthur asked again in the council room the next day. "I forgot what you said."

Myrddin sighed and closed his eyes for a nap. The faerie gave him a rueful look and fluttered over to Arthur. "Concentrate," she whispered in his ear.

He looked around. "What was that?" *Am I beginning to hear voices?*

Theodoric exchanged glances with Agricola and Lancelot. "Ships, over one hundred, if we need to put them all into service. But I think with a two-pronged attack that it won't be necessary," the sea captain answered.

"Still, I want them all on the horizon, ready to move," Arthur said. "I'm tired of these Scotti raids. If we can capture coastal Porth Mawr, we can stop them from landing."

He turned, "And you, Agricola? You'll be marching from the east, through the mountains. Do we have time to mount this campaign before winter sets in?"

"If we leave within the fortnight, there should be no problem. Brychan has assured us clear passage through his lands."

"All right," Arthur said as he dismissed them. "I think we can be ready in two days. I guess I'd better tell Gwenhwyfar." *If only I could make things right with her before I go.*

\* \* \*

Gwenhwyfar watched the preparations covertly. Four moons had passed since Arthur had returned home, and the leaves had turned color, ready to fade away.

The morning they were ready to leave, Bedwyr approached Gwenhwyfar. She expected his usual kiss-on-the-cheek farewell, but he wasn't smiling.

"I don't know what has happened between you and Arthur, but it's carrying over to the troops. Do you understand what that means, Little Sister?"

She narrowed her eyes a little. "I don't think what Arthur and I do concerns you."

"You're wrong, Gwenhwyfar. And don't lose your temper with me. You put all of us in jeopardy if Arthur makes a flawed decision."

"That is not my problem, Bedwyr!"

"What if it were Lancelot who didn't come home?" His eyes were piercing. "He's the most vulnerable of all, for he rides beside Arthur."

She stared at him. "I . . . that wouldn't . . ." She looked around for Lancelot.

Bedwyr grabbed her arm and gave her a shake. "Remember you are Arthur's wife, not Lancelot's. By Mithras, Gwenhwyfar, they nearly came to blows over you a few nights ago. Do you know what can happen in the field? If you cannot put Lancelot from you, then ask Arthur for a divorce." He dropped her arm. "Anastasius will, no doubt, have Symmachus grant papal dispensation from Rome. I am only surprised that Arthur hasn't considered it himself."

She was stunned. Divorce. Arthur would be within his rights to do so, since she was refusing him. She stared at her brother.

"Are your men ready, Bedwyr?" Arthur asked, coming up to them.

"Yes. I was just saying good-bye." Quickly Bedwyr kissed her and left.

Arthur faced Gwenhwyfar. "You have told me you cannot

bear my touch, Wife, but I think a public farewell must be in order. The troops expect to see the queen send her husband off to battle."

"Mayhap I have been too harsh with you, Arthur," Gwenhwyfar said quietly.

He raised an eyebrow. "Then I may touch you without fear of being struck or made a fool of?"

"You need not have that fear, Husband." She smiled a little.

He tilted his head, regarding her. "Why the change of heart, Gwenhwyfar?"

She met his gaze evenly. "Would you divorce me, Arthur?"

His face paled beneath the tan. "Divorce? Is that what you want?"

"No!" she answered vehemently. "I didn't mean . . . you would be within your rights to send me somewhere."

"You are the most difficult woman I have ever met, Gwenhwyfar, but I still prefer to have you with me than away."

"I have not treated you well since I've been back," she said softly.

"I deserved it. What I did was inexcusable."

She stepped closer to him and put her arms around his neck. "Now, do you want your queen to see you off warmly or not?"

He didn't waste breath on an answer as he crushed her to him.

They had been gone some weeks, and Cai was serving Gwenhwyfar a light supper when Cynric's guard appeared in the doorway to the hall.

"He requests a word with you, my lady."

Gwenhwyfar looked at Cai. "You will be close by?"

Cai smiled benevolently. "Just tap your cup and I'll come."

"Bring him in, then," Gwenhwyfar answered.

She had forgotten how handsome this golden stranger really was, or how cocky, she thought as she watched him walk toward her, his sky-colored eyes looking her over. Momentarily she wondered if she had done the right thing.

He bowed, reaching for her hand. She put it in her lap and he straightened, an almost amused expression on his face.

"May I sit, my lady?"

"You may. Why did you wish to see me?" She laid down her linen napkin.

"With so many of the men away, I would like to offer my services."

Gwenhwyfar eyed him warily. "I doubt that Arthur would approve of my letting you roam the fort, Cynric."

"Not roam. My guard would be with me. I could help your seneschal."

Gwenhwyfar smiled at that. "You are obviously not aware of the heavy hand Cai takes with the boys who work for him."

"I am not a boy. " He looked into her eyes.

She looked away. "I doubt this is a good idea."

"I grow tired of sitting in my quarters, my lady, when I could be useful somehow," he said seriously.

"I suppose I could send some work for you to do," she answered cautiously.

His eyes flickered. "Whatever your wish. Medraut said you had a kinder soul than your husband."

"Medraut?" Gwenhwyfar looked at him then. "How do you know him?"

Cynric gave her his Adonis smile. "Medraut has taken pity on me. We are close to the same age, and we share some interests."

Gwenhwyfar wondered if Arthur knew about this. He would not approve. Medraut was not well accepted by Arthur's men, although he seemed to have made friends among the newer, younger recruits. But the Saxon hostage?

"I could help your man—the Saracen—with the horses, now that Captain Lancelot is gone." Cynric went back to his first topic.

She studied him. "You ride well?"

He shrugged, "Not as well as your champion, but who does?"

Gwenhwyfar smiled. "Lancelot is one with the horse when he rides."

Cynric nodded. "You are quite accomplished as well. Mayhap you could teach me a thing or two."

She looked at him sharply, but his expression was bland. She felt herself weakening. Palomides could use the help.

"You are honor bound to your father not to try to escape," she said, considering.

He leaned forward, looking earnest. "I am aware of the hostage treaty, my lady. My own father would have me tortured if I were to break the oath."

"Let me think on it," Gwenhwyfar said and tapped her cup for Cai.

Cynric rose and bowed. "As you wish." But his smile was slightly cynical.

Gwenhwyfar watched him wink at a serving girl as he left, then grin as she blushed. Young Cynric needed to be kept in check.

Arthur sent word near Yule that Porth Mawr had been taken, and in early spring the cohort came home. Arthur and Lancelot had gotten over their differences, for they were both laughing and exchanging stories at the supper table. But when Arthur slipped an arm around her waist as they prepared to leave, Gwenhwyfar noticed Lancelot's smile did not quite reach his eyes. He promptly excused himself and left.

They were quiet on their way up the stairs, and Gwenhwyfar did not hesitate at the door to her room this time. Without a word, they sat on his bed and rediscovered each other, kissing gently, teasing with their tongues, hands exploring over the clothing they both still wore.

Finally Arthur lay back with her on the bed. He undressed her slowly, stopping to savor the softness of her skin. This time, he was tender and gentle in his lovemaking. Gwenhwyfar found herself responding and realized how much she had missed the bedding.

Later he propped himself up on an elbow. "I take it you don't mind my touch?"

She didn't answer but reached for him, and they came together once more.


Lancelot stayed away from the Great Hall the next day, so it wasn't until the second morning that she saw him.

As he sat down to break the fast he said, "Palomides tells me that Cynric has been helping work the horses."

Arthur looked up. "How did that come about, Gwenhwyfar?"

She shrugged and told them the story. "I was skeptical, but he has kept his word." Gwenhwyfar turned to Lancelot. "Didn't Palomides agree that he's been useful?"

"He did," Lancelot answered. "Have you also noticed how many of the serving girls have swollen bellies this spring? Mayhap he's been useful in more ways than one."

"But he should not have time and his guard should always be with him."

Lancelot cocked an eyebrow, "He may have been. I've done some asking; the girls didn't mind telling me. It seems Cynric doesn't mind sharing."

Gwenhwyfar was shocked. "At the same time?"

"I didn't think it polite to ask for the details, Gwen." Lancelot's eyes crinkled. "But there is a term the Breton courtesans used: *ménage à trois*." He turned to Arthur. "Remember?"

Arthur changed the subject and Lancelot grinned. "We may have a new breed for the land, then," Arthur said. "Saxon and Briton, native born. I'm not sure I am displeased, although that guard needs to be whipped."

"Did I tell you that Cynric and Medraut are friends?" Gwenhwyfar asked and had their undivided attention for the next hour as they discussed the repercussions.

Spring rolled gently into summer. A promise of peace was in the air; all was quiet. Gwenhwyfar arranged some flowers that Lancelot had brought in one morning, while Arthur played with Cabal. It was one of those rare, perfect days. None of them had an idea of how shattered their world would soon become.

They had just finished the noonday meal and were sitting at the table, enjoying the slow drifting of the day, when one of the gate guards appeared in the doorway, along with a mute old man.

Lancelot stared at him, his fingers losing their grip on his cup. It crashed on the tiles. His face turned pale.

"What is it, Lancelot?" Gwenhwyfar asked.

"You'd better come, my lord," the guard said to Arthur. "This man has something on his barge that you must see."

# Chapter 20

# Trail of Madness

A strangely quiet crowd had gathered by the time Lancelot forced himself to walk to the river. He wondered why Elen had sent Erec and if she were with him.

He stopped when he saw the barge, unable to take another step. Elen, but just a shell of her, wrapped in white silk, lay on a bier. She was dead.

"No . . ." He sank to his knees. "How did this happen?" *Elen, so gentle, so innocent.*

Erec handed him a letter, but Lancelot passed it to Gwenhwyfar. She read:

> *Dearest Galahad: I know you are the queen's champion, but I loved you.*

Gwenhwyfar stopped. "Lance, I think you should read this first." He shook his head and she knelt down to continue, for his ears alone:

*I know you could not love me back. Nothing is left for me. I am writing to bid you farewell. If I may be granted a request, it is that I am buried at Camelot, the place I once dreamt about. I will love you always, Elen.*

Gwenhwyfar handed the letter to Arthur and put an arm around Lancelot's shoulders. He leaned against her, eyes closed.

Arthur scanned the note and then ordered the group to disperse, sending Gwalchmai and Bedwyr to find a litter.

"This was the lady with the healer's touch, Lance?" Gwenhwyfar asked quietly. He nodded, his eyes still closed. Slowly a tear rolled down his cheek.

"You cared about her."

He opened his eyes then and looked at her. "I would have married her, Gwen, had I not already met you."

Arthur took a sharp breath and bit his lip, staring into space above their heads.

Bedwyr and Gwalchmai returned with the litter and lifted her carefully onto it. "Take her to the church," Arthur said.

Erec stopped the litter and removed a faded, crumpled note and a bit of red silk from Elen's hands. It was embroidered with pearls. He handed them to Lancelot.

Lancelot stared at the favor, mesmerized. He got up without a word and staggered off like a man with too much drink in him.

Lancelot disappeared for three days. When he returned he was dirty, unshaven, and disheveled.

"I must leave," he told Arthur and Gwenhwyfar, saddling one of the geldings.

His eyes held a glaze that Gwenhwyfar didn't recognize. "Where will you go?"

"Eventually, to Astolat. Before that, I don't know."

"When will you be back, Lance?"

He mounted and swung the horse around. "When I have been forgiven."

Morgana had asked Medraut to keep her apprised of Lancelot's business, for she was ready to implement her plan. So she wasn't surprised to see her son gallop in on a nearly winded horse one June morning.

"This is your opportunity, Mother." Medraut waved his hand expansively as he dismounted. "Lancelot is half mad and wanders alone to Astolat."

"You are right, Medraut." She chuckled when she heard the story. "How strange that a woman besides Gwenhwyfar has done him in!"

"What exactly is your plan, Mother?" Medraut asked curiously as they entered the house.

She smiled, went to her embroidery basket, and returned with a fine, hollow-pointed needle. "I'll lace this with wolfsbane," she explained, holding it up. "All I need to do is prick his skin. He will lose consciousness quickly. Once Accolon has him tied, we can move him."

"What makes you think Lancelot will let you get close enough for that, Mother?"

"Really, Medraut," she frowned. "Do you think me completely without wiles?"

He laughed. "Not at all. A lot of women have tried using their . . . wiles . . . but it doesn't seem to work. Not even his wife can hold him."

"I warned Elaine," Morgana said simply. "Let me deal with Lancelot, Medraut."

He grinned. "I'm sure you will. Where are you planning to keep him?"

"Maelgwyn has a . . ."

"That's the first place Arthur will look, once he knows Lancelot is a hostage."

". . . hidden dungeon," Morgana continued. "I doubt that Arthur knows of it."

Medraut leaned forward. "Arthur is thorough. He will tear the place apart, right after this one. I have a better idea."

"Oh?" she asked.

"Cynric's hideaway that he's not able to use. He stocked it well because he meant to use it as a wenching haven." He grinned slyly.

Her interest was piqued. "How far away is it?"

"A half day's ride from here, deep within the forest."

Morgana nodded. "A good location. Would you ride with me tomorrow and show me this place?"

"For certes. And then what?" Medraut asked.

"Then go back to Arthur and wait."

The serving woman leaned across Lancelot to replace the empty cup with a full one. *She's undone another lace since the last time she brought my wine.*

She straightened slowly, giving him a good view of her full breasts. "Is there anything else I can do for you?"

*Why not?* He pulled her to his lap. She would be a warm body to hold him, like the others had done every night for the past three months. He drank enough so he wouldn't remember names or faces. He wasn't even sure where he was. He focused on her momentarily. She was past her prime, plump, the face slightly puffy from late nights. The brown hair was not yet streaked with grey, and her green eyes were alluring . . . *green eyes . . . no, blue eyes . . . Elen's eyes had been blue.* Lancelot shook his head.

"Do you feel all right?"

The sound of her voice brought him out of his vision. *Older women are more accommodating.* He cradled her head and kissed her. She parted her lips willingly for his tongue. "I could feel better with your help."

She smiled slowly and slipped from his lap, taking his hand. "I'll do my best. What's your name?"

"Is my name important?" he asked, his other hand fingering the laces.

She frowned. Then her face softened as he began to caress her breast.

He stood. "If you want some privacy with this act, you had better lead me to it."

She glanced sideways at him. "Come with me."


Morgana and Accolon had been trailing him for weeks. They had heard of a dark-headed warrior who went by no name. He was gathering a reputation for appearing in a village, challenging anyone to swordplay for a wager, and then drinking and wenching well into the night.

"The drink probably makes them all look like Gwenhwyfar," Morgana told Accolon. "The fact that another woman died for love of him has sent him mindless. He always had that damnable code of honor, and now he bears its guilt."

Lancelot had wandered north at first, and then turned east toward the Fens, skirting the Saxon territory on his way back south.

Now he was in Venta. Morgana watched him as he left the tavern the next morning and went to get his horse. He turned on the road toward Astolat, holding the gelding to a walk.

"Perfect!" she said. "We circle ahead." She pulled the hood of her riding cloak over her head. "He won't know it's me until it's too late."


Sometime later, Lancelot's gelding tossed its head, scenting the wind. "What is it, boy?" he asked, his hand soothing the horse. He drew his sword.

As he passed a dense copse of beeches, he saw the mare.

Its rider was sitting at the side of the road, holding her ankle. He sheathed the sword and dismounted.

"Can I help, my lady?"

"Please . . . will you help me stand?" she sobbed into her hood. "It hurts . . ."

He stepped closer, putting a hand under her elbow to help her up. He extended the other hand for her to grasp. A needle pricked his skin.

"What . . . ?" He jerked his hand back and stepped away, then began to stagger. "Who . . . are . . . you?" he managed to say before he slumped to the ground.

When Lancelot woke, he had a headache. He tried to rub his head, but his arms were tied. Staked, he realized, as the fuzziness lifted. He was lying on a comfortably soft bed, his hands and feet tied to the four posters. The thought flitted through his still-dazed mind that he may have been involved in a special game some woman had wanted to play, but he was fully clothed, except for his boots.

He looked around the room. Wherever he was, the owner had spared no expense in making it enticing. A thick, fleecy rug covered the floor in front of the hearth. A huge upholstered chair that would easily hold two people stood close to the fireplace. Each of the tapestries on the walls depicted various scenes of lovemaking. On the ceiling above him was a piece of highly polished tin. It offered a blurry, cloudy picture of him. He began to grin in spite of his situation.

The door opened then and Morgana walked in. The smile left Lancelot's face as she came and sat down on the bed next to him. She looked up at the tin.

"An interesting device, isn't it?" she asked, putting a hand on his chest.

"Why am I here?"

She feigned surprise. "Look around, Lancelot. What do you think?"

He stared at her for a minute and then laughed. "You

don't want me, Morgana. So, where am I and why am I tied?"

She leaned close to him, her face inches from his. "I might want you, Lancelot. You've managed to drive Gwenhwyfar insane for years, even though Arthur is quite capable of keeping a woman happy. What is it you do?" When he didn't answer, she sighed and sat up. "But you're right," she said, reaching into a pocket for a small vial and a needle. "I haven't come for that." She dipped the needle in the vial, carefully siphoning the liquid into the hollow point, and held it up. "This will make you feel almost as good."

"By Mithras, what are you doing?" Lancelot pulled on the ropes. They held. He felt a twinge of anxiety. *Damnation, to be totally helpless!* He tugged on his bonds.

"Don't worry," she crooned as she slipped the needle under his skin. "This is highly prized in the East. It will make you manageable and mayhap a little fuzzy." She sat beside him while the poppy juice took effect. "Dream of Gwenhwyfar."

He lived in a fog after that. Accolon would come and untie him so he could attend to himself; they would rouse him enough to eat, and he would drift back to his swirling, hazy world, very comfortable inside his head. Vaguely he was aware that Accolon and Morgana were together in the room, on the floor or in the chair, and once he thought he had felt her hands on him, opening his trews, but she was pulled away. Sometimes the tapestries came alive. He dreamed of Elen and knew she was serene and happy in the Otherworld. Mostly, though, Gwenhwyfar was with him in this lovely room of unlimited games. He smiled in his stupor.

"I think you're giving him too much," Accolon told Morgana.

She lifted an eyelid. Lancelot's eyes were totally dilated.

"He must be kept manageable, Accolon. He's too strong to handle any other way. You must protect your hands for combat with Arthur."

"Com . . . bat . . . Arth . . ." Lancelot mumbled.

She sighed. "I'll give him less. Does that make you feel better, Accolon?"

Lancelot's muddled brain began to clear somewhat. His hearing became more acute. He overheard a conversation that made little sense at the time.

"I had Maelgwyn send the messenger to Arthur yesterday, along with Lancelot's dagger. Arthur is to meet us tomorrow afternoon at the edge of the forest."

"He won't come alone."

"He doesn't have to. All you have to do is challenge him in direct combat, so he'll remove the scabbard. I can make the switch while everyone is watching you."

The next morning as Accolon was getting ready to retie a pliable Lancelot, Morgana walked in. "Let him stand, Accolon. Tie him to the one post only." She looked up at the tin and Accolon followed her gaze. He grinned and quickly tied Lancelot's hands, leaving him slumped against the wall.

Morgana laughed as she and Accolon undressed each other. "It is a pity you wouldn't let me have him . . . maybe later?"

"You won't need him later," Accolon growled as they tumbled onto the bed.

*Thank the gods for that.* Lancelot tried to clear his head while pretending to be unconscious. *I must follow them when they leave. Arthur is in danger.*

Arthur read the note and handed it to Gwenhwyfar. "God's thunder!" He began pacing in front of the dais. "How in Bel's fires could this have happened?"

Gwenhwyfar's hand flew to her mouth. Morgana had abducted Lancelot. She was holding him as hostage until Arthur made her king's consort.

"This can't be true, Arthur. Lancelot would never . . ."

Arthur held up the dagger the messenger had left. "His, is it not?"

She stared at the athame, recognizing the engraved spirals of druid tradition on the ebony handle. His mother had given the knife to him when he had joined Arthur's army.

"How could Morgana have done it, Arthur?"

"Who knows? The woman's a sorceress."

"This meeting . . . it's some kind of plot." Gwenhwyfar felt a dread coldness wash over her.

"No doubt, but what choice is there? The gods only know what condition Lance is in. He would have escaped if he could." Arthur began pacing again.

"I'm going with you." *Dear Lord, protect Lancelot. Keep him safe.*

"You are not."

She glared at him. "He could be hurt and need attention."

"I'll take the medic, Gwenhwyfar," Arthur said drily. "And I will tell Cai not to let you out of his sight, or would you prefer I lock you in the gaol?"

She spun on her heel and walked out. *I'm going anyway.*

Arthur's party left two days later. Once they had disappeared, she made her way to the stables.

"I'm sorry, Gwenhwyfar," Cai said from the shadows, "but you aren't leaving."

She jumped, the bridle in her hand. "Oh, Cai . . . I'm . . ."

He came closer and she could see he was troubled. He held the key to the gaol. "Arthur said to use this if I needed to. Would you want to be responsible for the flogging I'll get if I disobey that order?"

She stared at him and then her shoulders slumped; he was her friend. "No," she said miserably and hugged him. "I won't have you whipped because of me."

* * *

Arthur and his troop waited a short distance from the forest's edge. All was quiet, but each was straining his senses to detect anything unusual.

"There," Gwalchmai pointed.

Morgana and Accolon rode to the edge of the tree line and stopped. Arthur rode forward with Bedwyr, Excalibur drawn.

"What craziness is this, Morgana? Where is Lancelot?"

"I have him safely confined," she answered. "Am I your consort or not?"

"I will never make you my consort."

Accolon rode forward. "A challenge then, my lord. I'll champion Morgana for the consort title. If I win, you acknowledge her. If you don't accept, we kill Lancelot."

"You want to fight me?" Arthur asked.

"Yes. Morgana deserves the title," Accolon answered.

"Then name your weapon, time, and place," Arthur responded.

"Here. Now. Bare fists."

Arthur handed Excalibur to Bedwyr and dismounted, motioning for his men to stay where they were. He walked to Morgana. "If Lancelot is hurt, you are both dead."

She smiled. "He lives, Arthur."

Accolon handed Morgana his sword and scabbard, along with his cloak. She held out her hand for Arthur's. He undid the scabbard and tossed it on the ground.

She picked it up and moved everything to a clump of holly bushes that grew at the tree line's edge. She threw Accolon's cloak over the scabbards as she sat down.

Arthur and Accolon circled, each watching the other's face. Accolon swung as Arthur turned, the blow glancing off his shoulder. He punched Accolon's stomach.

Morgana reached through the thorny leaves for the scabbard she had made. Using the cloak as a shield, she quickly made the exchange, pushing Arthur's scabbard far back in the bush for retrieval later.

The sound of a lone horse pounding the road through the forest caused Arthur's men to surge forward. Arthur took a step sideways. A root stopped his boot.

Accolon was on him like a striking snake.


Lancelot came bursting out of the trees, seeing Arthur on the ground and horses galloping toward him. His brain was still fuzzy and he had no time to determine who they were. Raising his sword, he bore down on Accolon. The blade sliced true. Arthur rolled and was on his feet as Accolon fell. Lancelot wheeled his horse, putting himself between Arthur and the oncoming men.

"They're Cymbry, Lance!" Arthur shouted. "Bedwyr, hold the men!"

They pulled up short in a cloud of dust, swords drawn. As the adrenaline receded, Lancelot recognized them and sheathed his sword. Only then did he become aware of Morgana's screaming.

"He's dead! You've killed Accolon!" She charged at Lancelot.

Arthur caught her. "This blood is on your hands, Morgana. No one else's."

She looked at him, wild-eyed, and began to laugh. Higher and higher, her voice rose. He slapped her then and she crumpled to the ground.

Arthur walked over to the bushes, picked up the scabbard, and wearily strapped the belt on, recovering Excalibur from Bedwyr. "Take her and Accolon back to Camelot," he said as he handed Accolon's sword and cloak to one of the men.

He turned to Lancelot. "Are you ready to come home?"

Lancelot nodded. "I've made my peace, but I don't think I . . ." and he slumped over in his saddle.

Arthur caught him. Lancelot was pale and shaking. "What did they do to you?"

"Some kind of drug . . . very strong . . ." He laid his head against the horse's neck and closed his eyes.

Arthur mounted, took the reins of Lancelot's horse, and started home slowly.

Lancelot opened his eyes once and thought he saw a youth step from the trees, holding Arthur's scabbard. But Arthur had his scabbard. The world became fuzzy again, and he sank into oblivion.

Gwenhwyfar was waiting. She recoiled in shock at seeing Accolon dead and Morgana unconscious. Then she saw Arthur, trailing behind the rest, leading a horse with a body slumped over it. Lancelot's body. Her throat constricted and she felt as though she couldn't breathe. *Lancelot, my beloved!*

She ran to meet them. "Oh, Arthur, no! Is he . . . he can't be . . ." She saw a small movement in the fingers that were intertwined with the mane. Lancelot rolled his head toward her and opened his eyes with an effort.

"Gwen?"

Relief overcame her so suddenly that her legs nearly gave way. She took his hand and walked beside the horse. "I'm here. We'll take care of you now." He smiled feebly.

Arthur sent Gwalchmai for Nimue. As they settled Lancelot on a cot in the infirmary, Gwenhwyfar sank to the floor beside him.

"What have they done to you, Lance?" she asked, stroking his cold, clammy forehead. He started to tremble and she held his hands to steady them.

The medic quickly undid his shirt. "No wounds," he said as he examined him. He turned one of Lancelot's arms over, exposing small red marks. The other arm had the same marks on it. He looked worriedly up at Arthur.

"I've not seen this before. He has been stuck with something small and sharp, mayhap a needle, but I don't know why. I need to check the rest of him."

"Gwenhwyfar, will you step outside?" Arthur asked, placing a hand on her shoulder.

She didn't look away from Lancelot's face. "I won't leave him."

Arthur bent over and spoke in her ear. "Do not flaunt your love so openly." She felt his hand under her elbow, lifting her up. She fought the urge to pull away, but even as she did, Arthur's other arm went around her waist. She stepped hard on his foot as she stood, but she allowed him to propel her to the door.

"I expect to find you on this side of the door when I return," he told her as they stepped into the hall and he released her.

"Where are you going?"

His mouth was set in a straight line. "To see Morgana."

Later that day, Lancelot was moved to his own quarters since the medic knew of nothing that would help with the tremors. He sat propped against his headboard. Gwenhwyfar watched as he tried to keep his arms from shaking. All she could do was hold his hands steady. Inwardly she cried for him. His strength had been drained.

Gwenhwyfar was wiping his face with a cool lavender-scented cloth when Nimue arrived. She sat down on the other side of Lancelot and turned his arms over, counting the marks. "How long were you there, Lancelot?" she asked.

He shook his head slightly. "The last thing I really remember is leaving Venta and finding a woman who had been thrown from her horse . . ." He stopped as the tremors racked his body again and then he shivered. "After that, it was all hazy. I just drifted."

She looked at Arthur, standing behind Gwenhwyfar.

"Morgana said this was poppy seed extraction? It seems similar to the reaction the young priestesses have when they've taken too much of the sacred mushroom."

Lancelot broke into a sudden sweat and Gwenhwyfar dipped the cloth again and applied it across his chest. He tried to smile and then squirmed.

"What is it, Lance?" Gwen asked.

"My back feels as though something is crawling on it."

"Turn over. Let me see."

With an effort he rolled over. Muscles twitched all along his back. Gwenhwyfar tried to smooth them with her hands.

Nimue dug through her bag. She held out a vial. "Here, use some of this."

Gwenhwyfar applied a few drops. As she worked in the sandalwood oil, the spasms became less. Rhythmically she worked her way across his shoulders and down the center of his back, spiraling outward and then working upward again.

Nimue began to chant softly. Gwenhwyfar began stroking in accord with the rhythm of the chant. Eventually Lancelot relaxed and slept.

"It's the best thing he can do," she said.

Gwenhwyfar settled in a chair next to the bed. Arthur raised an eyebrow.

"I'm staying, Arthur."

He turned away from her and looked at Nimue.

"I'll stay, too," she said.


A week later Lancelot was well enough to walk around. "I feel like a newborn foal," he told Gwenhwyfar as he thankfully sat down on a bench in the enclosed herbal garden. "It's a good thing we're not riding on campaign." He held out his hand to her.

Gwenhwyfar put her hand in his and turned her face up to catch the late autumn sun's waning warmth. Arthur and Nimue had ridden out earlier to visit some of the tenants who still had crops in the fields. *I wonder if they are at the cottage.*

Lancelot draped an arm around her, and she settled herself comfortably against him. "I've missed you, Gwen. When I was . . . there . . . I dreamed of you. This room I was kept in was made for a man and a woman to spend the day." Lancelot described it, finishing with the polished tin above the bed. Her eyes widened as she listened.

"The place is mine. I'm glad you liked it." Cynric startled both of them as he leaned against the entryway, one of the scullery maids behind him. "I was just looking for a place to . . . well, this spot is obviously taken." He winked and was gone as Lancelot struggled to his feet.

Gwenhwyfar stood, too. "Why do we always seem to get caught when we are doing nothing wrong?"

"Do you still think having me is wrong, Gwen?"

"I don't know, Lancelot. I don't want to hurt Arthur. I wish he would give us permission to make love again," she said plaintively.

Lancelot laughed at that. "If I were you, Gwen, I wouldn't ask," he said, kissing her forehead lightly. "I have few places to go if he exiles me."

That night at supper Lancelot remembered Morgana's conversation about the scabbard and his vision.

"Arthur," he asked. "Are you still wearing the same scabbard?"

Arthur gave him a puzzled look. "Yes. It was a gift from the Lady. Why wouldn't I be?"

As Lancelot repeated as much of the conversation as he could remember, Nimue went and retrieved the belt from the hook by the door. She came back to the table with it.

"This is not the Lady's," she said. She ran her fingers over the tooling. "The power isn't there."

Arthur paled. "So that's why Morgana planned all this. A

ruse to exchange the Lady's scabbard for one which won't protect me in battle." He looked at Lancelot. "That's why she took you hostage; she knew I wouldn't accept any other challenge."

"She didn't take your scabbard, though. She was unconscious," Lancelot said. "Maybe the boy left it there."

They rode out the next morning but found nothing. Lancelot's "vision" hadn't been a hallucination. Whoever the boy had been, he was gone, and so was the scabbard.

# Chapter 21

# Temptation

"So Lancelot is recovered?" Morgana asked Medraut on one of his winter visits. Arthur had sent her home, but with his own guards posted at her gate.

"Lancelot invents reasons to be close to her," Medraut said bitterly as Morgana steeped some goldenseal tea. "Why does my father allow it?"

"Mayhap Arthur is growing weak." Morgana handed him a cup.

Medraut laughed. "He is as fit as any of the younger men."

"But is he fit to be king if he allows himself to be cuckolded?" She took a sip.

He stared at her. "What are you saying, Mother?"

"Think. If you could find Lancelot in Gwenhwyfar's bed, Arthur could not deny it. You would need witnesses. Reliable ones. Maybe even Arthur's friends."

"He would have to get rid of Lancelot then." Medraut smiled, a faraway look creeping over his face.

Morgana grabbed his arm and pinched hard. "Stop thinking about Gwenhwyfar. Exposing them would bring Arthur down, for he would protect her. His men will not appreciate a king who has two sets of laws."

He looked at his mother appreciatively. "If Arthur were deposed, the way would be clear for me. The power and the land would be mine."

She leaned back and smiled. *Yours and mine, my son. I would be the queen mother. There is power in that.*

With a grim face Lancelot listened to the messenger that Arthur had sent north. Quintas Carucius, the Dux Britanniarum from Diera, wanted to establish a hold in Eboracum. His army consisted mostly of Saxons exiled from their native lands by Clovis.

Arthur would have to stop him. That meant marching through the rugged Pennine Mountains to get to him. Lancelot resigned himself to spending the winter with Arthur and Bedwyr, planning the campaign and stealthily moving troops northward. Arthur had the idea to use the spring tournament as a foil. Quintas would not know most of the troops were already in place. The element of surprise would be theirs.

Iseult sat next to Gwenhwyfar under the awning at the tournament. They were watching Lancelot compete in swordsmanship. His opponent was Medraut.

"Your champion is very fast," Iseult said in her wispy voice as she watched him parry and riposte.

"Yes," Gwenhwyfar answered. "He taught Medraut at one time."

Lancelot sidestepped a thrust and Medraut made a savage low cut. Lancelot just managed to parry in time. The look on Medraut's face was murderous. "Your stepson seems too serious, Gwenhwyfar. Isn't this supposed to be sport?"

Medraut had been surly lately. Gwenhwyfar wished Lancelot had not drawn him as an opponent. She turned to Arthur. "I don't like the look on Medraut's face."

"Lancelot can handle Medraut. Don't worry."

Then it happened. Medraut pulled the wrap from the sword's tip and he advanced with catlike svelteness on Lancelot. Lancelot said something to him, but he laughed, circling.

Gwenhwyfar put her hand to her throat. *Not again, Medraut! Oh, Lancelot, be careful!*

Lancelot pulled his own wrap. Their swords clashed as they engaged, and for a moment they struggled before springing apart. Lancelot went on the offensive, swiftly raining blows, advancing quickly, not giving Medraut time to anticipate, backing him toward the stands. Gwalchmai and Bedwyr quickly positioned themselves to tackle him.

Medraut stepped back, his ankle turning just a bit. His sword arm wavered for a split second just as Lancelot cut high. Medraut's sword went flying, and Lancelot's blade bit deeply into Medraut's arm.

Medraut was already being carried away when Arthur gained the field.

"What was that about?"

"I don't know," Lancelot said between deep breaths. "He's been difficult lately, but I didn't expect . . ."

"For him to be so stupid," Arthur finished. "I had better go see how bad the wound is." He gestured for the games to continue as he left the field.

Gwenhwyfar waited for Lancelot as he came around the stands. She fought the urge to throw her arms around him because there were too many people near.

"Why did he do it, Lancelot? Why does he hate you so?"

"He's jealous. He's in love with you, Gwen."

She was taken aback. "No, you're wrong. He had a small boy's fondness for me when he first came, a slight crush; that's all."

Lancelot's eyes crinkled just a little at the corners.

"Fondness, Gwen? Fondness?" He became serious again. "More like lust and obsession. And he's not a boy any longer. He's a man."

"But that's madness, Lancelot."

"It is madness, Gwen." He laid a hand on her shoulder. "You need to be careful not to be alone with him."

Arthur approached and Lancelot turned to him. "How is he?"

"He'll live," Arthur answered, "but that arm will be useless for several months. The gash severed some muscles."

"I had not meant to injure him seriously."

"I know," Arthur answered. "I saw you forcing him toward Bedwyr and Gwalchmai. Let me think on what to do with him. We'd better return to the games."

The jousts were just about to begin. "Look," Iseult said, pointing to Tristan. "He's going to ride against Agravaine."

They made the first pass with glancing blows, keeping their horses to a canter as the rules dictated. Agravaine nearly unseated Tristan on the second pass, but miraculously he stayed in the saddle. Iseult clapped her hands. "He is good, isn't he?"

Gwenhwyfar forced herself to smile. Agravaine did not like losing. As he began the third pass, he kicked his horse to full gallop. Tristan reacted instantly, giving his horse his head.

"They're closing too fast." She clutched Arthur's arm. "Agravaine will kill him."

The lances shattered with full force, unseating both riders. Agravaine's foot caught in the stirrup as his horse kept going. He tugged it free, his leg twisting horribly. Tristan's horse slipped and fell, landing on Tristan's thigh as he tried to roll away.

Iseult screamed and stood. Gwenhwyfar held her back.

"Let me go!" she cried.

"Your husband is watching you, Iseult. You must not show how much you care."

Iseult groaned. "But I must be with him! You understand, don't you?"

Gwenhwyfar hugged her. "That I do." *More than anyone, I understand.*

Gwenhwyfar sat beside Lancelot in the map room, watching Arthur fidget with his quill across the table. He did that only when he was worried about something.

"We have three casualties," he began. "Tristan and Agravaine both have broken legs, and Medraut's arm muscle is severed. None of them will be able to ride on this campaign." He paused. "I will not leave Medraut and Agravaine with Gwenhwyfar."

"Cai will be here, Arthur," Gwen said.

"Yes, and there are two of them," Arthur answered. He took a deep breath and turned to Lancelot. "I want you to stay and protect her. You will act as regent."

Gwenhwyfar inhaled sharply. *Did he have any idea of what he was asking?*

Lancelot met his look. "Wouldn't Bedwyr be a better choice, Arthur?"

Arthur's smile was tight. "A safer one, no doubt." His voice sounded resigned. "Bedwyr commands my right flank of cavalry. I need him in that position. You once commanded it yourself, Lance, so you know how strategic it is." He continued, "Gwalchmai commands the left; Gryflet has taken your old company. This campaign will be won on those strengths. I can't afford to switch captains on the men now."

Lancelot made one more try. "My old company would follow me."

"They would," Arthur agreed, "and Gryflet would do his best here. But would he be willing to defend Gwenhwyfar with his life, if need be?"

"Arthur, surely you don't think I am in such danger, do you?" Gwenhwyfar asked.

He took her hand. "You might be. I suspect my son is not balanced in his thinking, and Agravaine is brutal and cold-blooded. If I could, I would postpone this campaign until I could take them with me, but I cannot. All is in place and we must go. A king's duty overrides that of a husband."

He turned to Lancelot. "I know you will protect her," he said sardonically, "because you love her as much as I do."

A muscle in Lancelot's jaw twitched. "Arthur, mayhap I can ease your mind. Gwenhwyfar and I have not lain to-gether save for the one day you granted. Not that I haven't wanted to," he added when Arthur gave him a calculated look. "Your wife would not have me. And I will not take her unwillingly."

Arthur looked at Gwenhwyfar, hope in his eyes. "This is true, Gwenhwyfar?"

"I do not want to commit more mortal sin, Arthur." She brought her chin up. "But I cannot deny that I love Lancelot as well as you."

"Well"—Arthur sighed as he stood—"I can't change that; we don't choose whom to love. May the gods favor me." He did not look back when he left.

Lancelot and Gwenhwyfar stared at each other.

"May your God give you strength, Gwen," he whispered.

Gwenhwyfar was on her way to the kitchens when she heard Iseult in the dining hall. She paused in the doorway.

"Gwenhwyfar may need my help." Iseult touched her husband's face gently. "I would like to stay."

"Does she not have help enough?"

"Yes, the servants, of course," Iseult agreed, "but with her husband gone, and with other men about, might it not be bet-ter that another lady be with her?"

Gwenhwyfar watched Marc eye his pretty young wife. "Would it be Tristan you're thinking about, rather than Gwenhwyfar?" he asked.

"Husband," Iseult said in her soft voice, "Tristan will be confined for weeks. Gwenhwyfar must spend much time with her seneschal and her champion. A chaperone would be most well received. Do you not think Arthur would be most appreciative if you let me stay?"

Gwenhwyfar repressed a smile; she could see Marc weighing the advantages of Arthur's favor.

He smiled. "Mayhap he would, at that."

*I might as well help her out,* Gwenhwyfar thought. She stepped through the doorway. "There you are, Iseult. I have a favor to ask of you."

Arthur had reestablished the old Roman Posting Service, which was a system of relays. He placed two men every twenty miles along the route to the north. Messages could be carried faster and riders travel longer distances in a day than by trying to wear out one man and a horse. As a messenger rode in, another rode out with a fresh horse.

The initial news was good. Arthur's troops were well received by the Verterae fort, the first along Pennine Road. The second fort, Lavatrae, offered resistance, but had been subdued. Lamorak and Gaheris were harrying Quintas at Corstopitum, and Arthur was proceeding to Mons Arvaius to open the route through the mountains. He had been on campaign nearly six weeks.

"It's taking longer than Arthur thought," Lancelot said to Gwenhwyfar when they heard the news. "Once they break through, Quintas won't be able to advance."

"Do you miss not being there, Lance?"

He glanced over at her. They were sitting in the council room at the Round Table. Seeing her sitting in Arthur's chair seemed strange, but this was where they received all messengers. "A part of me does," he said. "Any able-bodied man, trained by Arthur, knows his duty is to fight. But," he smiled at her, "I can't say I mind my duty here, even if you do make me sleep alone." *I'm near mad. For six weeks, I have resisted touching you.*

She looked away. "I'm glad you're here, too, especially with Medraut up and about and sulking all the time."

The smile left his face, and his eyes became troubled. Medraut avoided him, but he was often seen talking to small groups of the young recruits Arthur had left behind. Medraut also made sure Cynric was not denied any privilege, except the right to leave.

"Medraut bodes trouble, Gwen. I don't like that he and the Saxon are friends."

Gwen looked thoughtful. "Cynric takes advantage of that situation, for he does not like being confined to quarters."

Lancelot said wryly, "Half our maids would break down his door if he were."

"What I meant was, I think Cynric is his own man. He is as much the charmer as Gwalchmai, but beneath that easy smile of his, I think he is always watching, waiting, and looking for the right opportunity. I don't think he's foolish, either. He does not follow Medraut. I think, rather, it might be the other way around."

"That makes him doubly dangerous," Lancelot said. "He will replace Cerdic."

She walked to the window and went back to her original subject. "I wish I could do something about Medraut's sulking, though."

"He sulks because I told him to stay away from you." Lancelot came to stand beside her. He caught a faint whiff of lavender from her hair. *Silky hair. So soft.*

Gwenhwyfar looked up at him. "I'm bothered that he hates you so."

"Why do you suppose that is?" Lancelot grinned.

She blushed. "Well, he knows I care for you."

"Care, Gwen? You care about me?" He kept his tone light.

"Certes, Lancelot . . . stop teasing me."

"I don't want to tease you, Gwen." He became serious. He stroked her cheek lightly with his finger.

She protested. "We shouldn't . . ."

Throwing caution to the winds, he wrapped his arms around her. "You don't like this?" he murmured, his breath light in her ear.

"You know I do, but . . ."

His lips brushed hers, barely. "And this? Does it feel good?" He kissed her again, still gently.

"Yes," she sighed, "but you promised Arthur . . ."

"I told Arthur only that I would not take you unwillingly, Gwen," he said softly, nibbling her lower lip. "If you wish me to stop, you must say so." He covered her mouth, prodding with his tongue. Slowly, she parted her lips, inviting him.

They lingered over the kiss. Finally Lancelot leaned back from it, his arms still around her. "I didn't hear you tell me to stop."

"I wasn't exactly free to speak!"

He studied her. "Tell me, Gwen, that you do not want me and I will not touch you again."

"I . . . I don't think I could bear it if you never touched me again," she whispered.

He tightened his arms around her. "Then, my love, I think it's time we took our pleasure of each other."

Their kiss was interrupted by a loud crash in the hall outside the door.

"Damnation!" Lancelot swore as he went to the door and swung it open.

Cai and Medraut stood on the other side.

Gwen peered around him. "What happened?"

"I was simply coming to ask . . . my stepmother . . ." Medraut made a point to say, "what the news was from my father, when this clumsy oaf dropped the pots and pans."

Cai reddened, his fists balling.

"That's enough, Medraut," Lancelot said sharply, although he was tempted to let Cai at him.

"You cannot tell me what to do, Lancelot!" Medraut challenged him.

Gwenhwyfar slipped in front of Lancelot, preventing further escalation. Quickly she told Medraut what the messenger had said. "I'm glad you're interested, Medraut. We will keep you informed in the future."

He stayed in the doorway.

"You've been dismissed," Lancelot said.

He opened his mouth, but Cai's hand clamped down on his weak arm. He winced and grudgingly turned and left.

Lancelot looked at Cai, questioningly.

"I caught him standing by the door, listening," Cai said, picking up the pots. "I was taking these back to the kitchens; I thought it best to make some noise, lest he hear something that was not meant for his ears."

"Thank you, my friend," Lancelot said.

Cai gave him a straight look. "Aye. Arthur is my brother. I did this for Gwenhwyfar," he said as he walked away.

Lancelot waited until they were alone in the hall. "I will find a way for us to be together, Gwen. Somehow. We've been apart for much too long."

The opportunity came within the week, one evening after supper. Iseult was sitting at one of the trestle tables talking to Gwenhwyfar, and Lancelot was lounging in a chair next to the hearth.

"Tristan will have to go back soon, now that his leg is healed," Iseult said, "and I would like . . . I mean . . . if we could spend some time . . ."

Gwenhwyfar patted her hand. "You'd like some privacy, away from here?"

Iseult nodded.

"There is a cottage not far from here. We could take you to it." She and Lancelot had thought about using it but were afraid Medraut would follow them. He would have no reason to follow Tristan and Iseult, though.

Iseult hugged Gwenhwyfar. "Wonderful!"

They set out early the next morning, shortly after dawn, for Iseult wanted to spend the whole day. When they reached the stone circle, Gwenhwyfar pointed. "You'll find the cottage just over that hill."

Tristan gave Lancelot a slap on the shoulder as he and Iseult turned their horses and trotted away.

Gwenhwyfar watched them, recalling the long-ago day of memories. She sighed and turned her horse toward Camelot.

Lancelot cocked an eyebrow at her. "Where are you going, Gwen?"

She stopped. "Home. The cottage is being used, remember?" She smiled gently. "I don't think it wise to try and find somewhere out here . . ."

"Nor do I." He tugged on her rein and Safere obligingly wheeled around. "If you don't mind a hard ride, I think I can make it worthwhile."

"Is that a promise?"

"It is." He allowed Pryderi his head and Safere streaked behind him, Gwenhwyfar's hair blowing wildly in the wind.


They approached Cynric's place in just over two hours, the horses having run most of the way, with short periods to cool down.

Lancelot located the key and opened the door for her. Gwenhwyfar looked around. The room was sparsely furnished: a table and two chairs, shelves, a cooking hearth, and a small cot in one corner. She looked at Lancelot questioningly.

He shrugged. "I did not spend any time out here." He took her hand and led her to the door on the other side of the room. "I think you'll like this better."

Gwenhwyfar gasped and walked to the bed. She looked at the polished tin on the ceiling. Lancelot stood behind her, arms circling her waist. "Would you like to try it?"

"I've . . . never seen anything like that," she said, still not taking her eyes from it.

"I think we actually need to be on the bed to appreciate that mirror fully."

She turned in his arms, suddenly shy. "I don't know if I want . . ."

"I think you do," he answered, giving her a thorough kiss. He undid his sword belt, kicked off his boots, removed his shirt, and stretched out on the bed. He patted the place beside him. "Join me, Gwen."

She sat down and tugged off her boots. He brought her down beside him. The bed swayed gently on its rope and leather webbing. They both looked up at the mirror.

"It makes us hazy," Gwenhwyfar said, "as though we're in a fog bank."

"Hmmm," Lancelot said, undoing her shirt laces partially. "Remember the first time we saw each other? It was foggy then, too."

"That was magic fog, from the Isle," she answered.

"This can also be magic, Gwen. Just watch." He turned on his side, slowly finished undoing her laces, and slipped the shirt halfway off her shoulders. Her eyes widened as she watched him expose one of her breasts and then the other. He tucked the shirt beneath her but didn't remove it. In a very pleasant way, she felt as though she were being offered as a ritual sacrifice. She gasped as she watched his dark head bend over her and suckle on a nipple. His hand was sensually circling the other breast, his fingers tracing lightly over it and then across her ribs and stomach.

She groaned when he undid her trews and inched them down, a bit at a time as she stared into the mirror. It seemed to take forever before he had them off, and she began to tremble as he stroked her inner thighs and then explored further.

"Are you liking this, Gwen?" he murmured in her ear as he nibbled on her neck.

For an answer, she worked feverishly to remove his trews until her hands found what she was seeking.

He groaned as her fingers worked more magic and brought himself over her. She sighed with pleasure and closed her eyes as she felt him begin to enter her. She had waited for this moment for three years.

"Keep your eyes open, Gwen," Lancelot whispered, waiting for her. He tilted her chin over his shoulder. She stared upward, watching the ramming action of his tight buttocks and the muscle strain of his thighs as he thrust.

Lancelot rolled over, bringing her with him. They slowed to a rocking-horse rhythm. He was playing with her breasts, keeping her upright, watching her above.

"Look up, Gwen. Share this with me." His voice was liquid fire, inflaming her.

She threw her head back and they lost themselves in wild, hard bucking, finally peaking as wave after vibrating wave of sheer sensation racked their bodies.

They lay, exhausted, side by side, watching themselves above, their fingers tracing patterns on each other's bodies.

Eventually they gathered their clothes. Gwenhwyfar reached for a poster to steady herself and noticed the ropes. "Why are these here?"

Lancelot glanced at them. "Morgana used those to restrain me; not that I was going anywhere once the poppy took effect." He reached for his shirt.

Gwenhwyfar looked at the other three posters. "She staked you out, Lance?"

"That's right," he answered offhandedly, his shirt half on.

"What did it feel like?" she asked.

Lancelot stopped dressing and looked at her. "What do you want to know?"

She fingered the rope, rolling it in her fingers. "The idea . . . you couldn't move . . . you were helpless . . ."

"Being helpless is not a pleasant feeling," he said quietly.

She colored and dropped the rope. "I guess not."

"Gwen, is . . . is that what you want?" he asked when she had not moved.

"I . . . there would be no guilt . . ." she whispered.

Lancelot stared at her. "Are you still feeling guilty? After what we did today?"

"Mayhap because of what we did," she said in a small voice.

He spun her around then and draped her over his knees before she could think and slapped her sharply on her buttocks.

It stung. "What are you doing?" she cried, struggling to sit up.

He had one arm over her back, holding her firmly in place. He swatted her again, more gently this time.

"I told you once, Gwen." His voice sounded anguished. "I'd take you over my knee to swat that Christian guilt out of you. Now I plan to do it. Go ahead and struggle, until you've let it all go. I will not have you feeling guilty each time we make love."

She kicked and tried to pummel him as he administered a series of quickly repeated, small smacks to her bottom until it was red and hot and his hand felt cool. She squirmed and twisted to no avail. Finally she lay still. "No more."

Lancelot gently massaged the area. "Are you still feeling guilty, Gwen?" She growled low in her throat and he turned her over in his arms.

"I will repay you for this, Lance."

He grinned. "My lady, you can spank me anytime you wish."

She struggled to sit up and reached for her shirt. "That isn't what I meant."

Lancelot sobered and stayed her hand. "I don't want to have to wonder if you are holding back in your heart or in your mind."

Gwenhwyfar kissed him. "I love you, Lancelot; if that's wrong, then so be it. From this time forward, I will have thigh freedom."

"Then prove it!"

She smiled and pushed him back on the bed. "Now it's my turn."

# Chapter 22

# The Lady of the Lake

The Lady of the Lake was dying.

Nimue sat beside Vivian, bathing her face softly with a cool cloth dipped in essence of myrrh. Twilight was beginning to fall this Midsummer's Eve. Candles glowed softly around the bed. Outside the priestesses were singing the Song of Passing. The Rite of Purification had begun.

Nimue chanted softly, using the Old Language. *Mother, Goddess, if she can be spared, to stay with us yet awhile longer . . .*

Vivian opened her eyes slowly and smiled at Nimue. "My daughter, pray not that I remain here; I am tired. I would find my rest."

Nimue choked back a sob. "I love you, Lady. You have been mother to me since I came. I am not ready to take your place."

The Lady's hand found Nimue's. Her rheumy eyes were full of compassion and her voice just above a whisper. "I have something to say."

"Save your breath and your strength, Lady. You may tell me in the morning." Nimue clutched the frail hand tighter.

Again the smile came with an effort. "I will not be with you by morning."

Nimue pleaded, "Try, Lady. I've sent for Myrddin. He'll be here by dawn."

"He is already on his way. Never fear," Vivian answered. "I plan to say good-bye to him as well. Now tell me why you have been chosen."

"I don't know why, Lady. I know I have the Sight."

Vivian's eyes cleared somewhat. "You would not have been chosen just for that. You, like Argante, are a gift of the Great Rite."

"I don't understand, Lady." Nimue was puzzled. "Uther never used the Rite."

"Ambrosius did, though, when he was king," Vivian said.

"With whom? Weren't you the Lady then?" Nimue blurted and then stopped, staring at Vivian.

"That's correct." Vivian smiled. "You are my daughter, Nimue, and his."

"Mother?" Nimue gasped as the full realization struck her. She placed her hands on Vivian's thin shoulders. "Why did you not tell me sooner? The things we could have done together, shared . . ."

"No." Vivian's voice was once again strong, as if the Goddess were speaking. "That could not be. I am the servant of the Goddess; I had to train you as such. I could not afford to be too close."

"I am close to Argante," Nimue argued, "and she is to succeed me . . ."

"Mayhap I made a mistake." Vivian's voice was a whisper again. "But Argante is the daughter of a live king; she must stay in contact with him."

"She does," Nimue said softly. "Arthur visits with Argante often."

"Yes," the tired voice came back. "I am aware of your affections as well, Daughter. You must be careful not to bring his kingdom down."

"I?" Nimue forgot the situation for a moment. "Gwenhwyfar will be the one who will ruin it!"

Vivian patted her hand. "Gwenhwyfar can no more stop her love for Lancelot than he for her. She was never meant to be Arthur's."

"That is what Myrddin said, many years ago!"

"He was right," Vivian answered. "But the Goddess made no move to stop Gwenhwyfar from marrying Arthur because she has a part in Camelot's destiny."

Nimue's eyes glazed and she heard the answer she had given Gwenhwyfar long ago: *You will have them both. One day, though, you will have to choose. Arthur's life will depend on it.* It had been the Sight.

She sighed as the words faded from her mind. "As the Goddess wills."

Myrddin arrived a short time later and Nimue hurried out to see him. "The messenger could not have gotten to you so quickly," she said as she took his cloak. For the first time she noticed the amount of silver in his tawny hair.

He smiled at her. "Did you not think I would know her time?"

Nimue looked at him pleadingly. "Can you not do something? Mayhap the power of an arch-druid combined with that of the Isle could save her."

"Nimue," Myrddin said sternly, but his hands were light on her shoulders. "You are a priestess. Soon you will be the high priestess. We are forbidden. We must let the Goddess take her back."

She held back the tears. "Come then, quickly."

Myrddin followed her in and sat down beside Vivian, taking her hand, stroking her face gently.

"Ah, Myrddin, I always have enjoyed your touch," Vivian murmured.

"My dear and oldest friend, Vivian." His tone was mesmerizing. He turned his hawk look on Nimue.

Nimue came to the bed, bent down, and kissed Vivian. "May your journey be peaceful and you find your rest." She looked tearfully at the arch-druid.

"I will take care of her," he said. "Now go and prepare the others."

She joined the semicircle of priestesses and acolytes that had formed outside the Lady's chamber. She raised her voice in the ritual chant of passing, calling on Rhiannon, the Goddess aspect that would escort the Lady. Tonight the earth and heavens must seek balance to bring the Lady safely through, so she might one day return to a new world. The torches embedded in the ground responded, the firelight leaping high and burning low.

The moon was dark that night, and Nimue felt the static charge before she looked up and saw the firedragon fly, the long tail lighting the sky. Slowly she sank to her knees, her head in her hands.

A short time later, a gentle but firm hand raised her. She looked into Myrddin's golden eyes. The raven was perched on his arm. She blinked her eyes once at Nimue and then rose silently, the great black wings lifting her into the night sky.

"Vivian wanted you to have this," he said, handing her a wrapped parcel.

Nimue knew what it contained. The Lady's sickle, short and curved, both its edges sharp, the carved ivory handle bearing the symbols of the Maiden, Mother, and Crone intertwined with the swirling lines of the dragon's breath. The blade reflected the light from the fire.

"You see," Myrddin said, enclosing her hand in his and moving the blade to catch more light. "Earth and fire seek balance. Did the firedrake fly?"

Nimue nodded. "It was beautiful, her soul leaving," she said softly.

"Yes." He held her close for a minute. "Now we must release her body to follow."

Dawn was breaking by the time they had finished the ritual washing and wrapping of her body. They laid the Lady of the Lake in her hallowed oak, and Myrddin sealed the entrance to the inner cave. When he emerged, he brought the dark blue cloak to Nimue and held it open.

She backed away. "I can't wear that. It was hers."

"You are high priestess now, Nimue. You are the new Lady of the Lake." His voice had taken the melodic timbre of the bard. The other priestesses bowed in supplication.

She allowed him to drape it over her. As he did, she felt the power radiating from it, giving her strength.

She raised her arms and cast the circle, calling the four elements. Facing east, she chanted the greeting of the sun, even as the sky lightened; she turned then and faced west.

"I call upon you, Rhiannon, to escort the spirit of Vivian, Lady of the Lake, safely there. May the wind that rushes over the western sea carry you both into Annwn. May the rich soil protect her, the warm waters renourish her, and the eternal sacred fires create a new life that Arianrhod will bring back to us one day." She lowered her arms.

The priestesses sank into a circle on the ground, each with her own private prayers.

Nimue sat in the Lady's chair, turning it around so she could see the white hart on the tapestry behind her. The textures of its fabric glowed richly this night. Quietly she reflected on how she had come to be there.

As a child, she had found life in the forest peaceful. Her foster mother, Dyonas, had taught her to hear the windsingers in the trees, to distinguish the messages of the oak and beech and hazel. She had met the tree dryads and water naiads and learned to recognize the air sylphs that looked like butterflies, as well as the asrai, the mist faeries with long green hair and webbed feet. The elementals had not played their tricks on her. But she had known the forest was not her home.

Dyonas had brought her to the Isle when she was ten, but she hadn't met the Lady until she was ready to be initiated, four years later.

"This is our newest daughter?" the Lady had asked Meg, the healer, before its start.

Nimue had been terrified. The Lady's voice was majestic, resonating over the earth and bouncing back from the Lake. She seemed to grow tall in Nimue's eyes, and a white light emanated from her. *What if I do something wrong?*

"This is she, Lady," Meg answered.

"Come." The Lady extended her hand. "Do not be afraid, Nimue. The Goddess has chosen you . . ."

Nimue had no idea of what that really meant, but she desperately wanted it to be true. They proceeded up the path to the stone circle at the top of the Tor. The other priestesses formed a circle and the Lady placed her in the center and removed her cloak, leaving her sky clad.

"Feel the coolness of the Goddess's light wash over you, Nimue," the Lady said before she withdrew. "Absorb the energy, become one with it. Lose yourself in it."

Nimue became aware of a soft chanting and realized the others were nude as well, turning in place to let the moon's rays wash over all of them. The sweet smell of incense wafted to her. It seemed natural to raise her arms and turn in rotation. She relaxed into the ritual, eyes closed, listening to the music of the night.

The Sight came. She was still in the circle, but no longer a part of it. *She was watching a battle scene: a warlord . . . no, a king . . . tall, broad of shoulder, his sword flashing in the sunlight. He was battling another, a black-haired man who bore a striking resemblance. . . . The king was wounded. She*

*saw his clear grey eyes look in her direction before he slumped
to the ground.*

Nimue screamed, breaking the vision. The Lady wrapped
her in her cloak and held her close. The priestesses closed
the circle around them.

"Wh . . . what . . . happened?" she stammered. She sagged
against the Lady.

"Tell me what you saw," the Lady answered.

"A king . . . he fell wounded . . ."

The Lady breathed a sigh of relief. "Not dead, then. There
is hope."

"Who is this king, Lady?" Nimue dared to ask.

"His name is Arthur," the Lady answered. "He will be our
hope to keep the darkness from taking over this land."

And so her training had begun. The next ten years were
filled with arduous learning: rituals, herbal healing, enchantment, scrying, and accepting the Sight.

She loved the Isle. The fog bank that shut Avallach off
from the rest of the world created a realm of peacefulness
and bliss. Then Myrddin had come, and she was bid to perform the Great Rite.

She stared at the white hart now. It seemed to move on the
tapestry, its limpid eyes wise. Her life had changed when she
met Arthur.

She had never expected to love him. She knew as priestess what duty she must perform; she knew that she would
play a role in helping him. Even carrying the child was a sacred thing, for Argante would be Lady one day and more
powerful than she. To love Arthur, to want him physically,
she had not anticipated. Every priestess was supposed to remove herself from raw desires. What would she do as high
priestess now?

Nimue continued to muse. Gwenhwyfar loved Arthur,
too, but she did not long for him as she did for Lancelot.
Lancelot and Gwenhwyfar made each other whole, no doubt
the bond made stronger from other lifetimes. Arthur and

Gwenhwyfar were attracted to each other like opposite ends of those little pieces of ore Nimue sometimes used. Myrddin had been right, so long ago, before Arthur was married. *If only I could make Gwenhwyfar forget Lancelot . . . or Arthur forget Gwenhwyfar . . . !* That was beyond her power, even if the Goddess would approve.

Slowly she got up, walked outside and down the Processional Way to the Sacred Pool. The white hart stood there, waiting for her.


Myrddin came to her the next morning as she was walking back from the pool. She felt, rather than saw, how old he had become.

"You are welcome to stay," she said gently, seeing his bag beside him.

He shook his head. "I am ready to leave."

"Are you going to join Arthur?"

"I have ridden on Arthur's campaigns for nearly thirty years," he answered. "Arthur rules in his own right now. My work with him is done."

She looked at him, startled. "Where will you go, then?"

"I go to be with Vivian." He smiled at her and there was a softness in his golden eyes she had never seen.

"You would take your life, Myrddin?"

"No." He shook his head. "That which the God has given me cannot be forsaken, but in the world between worlds, I may be with Vivian. The faerie queen has gone to prepare my way. She has promised that I may lie in trance at Avalon."

"I wondered where she was." Nimue smiled at him. "So you tolerated her all these years for this?"

"It was a pact we made long ago, although I think that I annoyed her as much as she did me. She was ready to go back to her own consort."

Nimue raised a delicate eyebrow. "The Horned One?"

"Aye. Cernunnos," Myrddin answered. "She has missed

the Wild Hunt." His eyes glowed with golden light. "And I can finally put aside my own vows."

"You have loved Vivian that much, this whole lifetime? I used to think . . ." she paused, "that you were my father."

"Ah, child, were it true! But no, that fate was to belong to Ambrosius, for you needed the blood of kings as well as that of the Isle. For me to have lain with Vivian would have been to violate my soul."

"Yet you bid me perform the Great Rite. How is that different?"

Myrddin hesitated. Finally he answered, "Male and female energies are opposites. When they come together, they balance each other, yet they also cancel one another. To a druid that is squandering the life force, our prana, that allows our souls to grow."

"All souls grow," Nimue responded, "according to their life's lessons."

"Yes," Myrddin replied, "but I am talking about recognizing Truth and seeing the difference from Illusion, which is what most humans toil under."

"Ah, Enlightenment," Nimue answered. "Once we know Truth, it is wrong to live under the excuses that those who are not ready would make." She paused, thinking. "Yet the Great Rite made the land prosper and grow; it did not neutralize it."

"That was its purpose, Nimue. The rite was symbolic for the people. As you said, those who are not ready to see Truth must have something to guide them." Myrddin shrugged. "That is why the followers of the Christos have so many laws governing their religion."

"Their way is to rule by fear and guilt," Nimue said. "I wonder if that is what the Christos really meant when He spoke?"

"Jesu trained as druid on our Holy Isle," Myrddin answered. "His message was one of peace and tolerance that each may walk on his own path toward Annwn." He paused.

"The Romans changed that when they combined their laws with religion."

Nimue looked at him, her eyes wide. "Arthur's goal is peace and tolerance."

"Yes," the arch-druid answered. "He is our hope. Freedom will fade away and be replaced by the darkness of bigotry and hate if Arthur doesn't succeed."

"But Myrddin, that is why you must stay. To help Arthur!"

He smiled, "Arthur has you now, Nimue. My work is done."

"I don't know if I am strong enough," Nimue answered. "I have trouble remaining apart from him. His is a lonely soul."

"You should be able to hold yourself above primal pleasures, Nimue," Myrddin said sternly. "Does your training not sustain you?"

"It has." Nimue's eyes flashed. "I am priestess first! Arthur has always respected that, but I wish to soothe the wound that Gwenhwyfar has given him."

"Ah," Myrddin said. "I warned Arthur before he married her. He chooses to keep her, even though she bears him no child and he allows Lancelot permission to her, although he would deny it."

Nimue shook her head. "He loves her and he loves Lancelot, and she loves them both. They can't be separated, but I fear it will bring his dream to an end."

Myrddin looked at her sharply. "That is why, Nimue, you will be there for him."

"Yet I feel the urge to join with him," she answered softly.

He sighed, "Who is to foresay the Goddess, Nimue? Be guided by Her; what will come of it, will come."

Nimue closed her eyes. *I submit my will to you, Arianrhod. You are the Goddess aspect who spins the threads of life and weaves the fabric of what will be. I can do nothing to stop the Wheel of Fate.*

She opened her eyes. "I cannot convince you to stay?"

"No, child," he answered. "I have taught you all I can." He handed her the small bag of hazelnuts he always carried. "I always told Arthur eating these made me wise. Mayhap they will work for you." He gestured toward the Lake. "Walk with me this last time."

She followed him down the path to the barge. He gave her a kiss. "Remember that Gwenhwyfar has a destiny to fulfill as well. Let all of them seek their own paths."

Nimue clung to him for a moment and he hugged her back; then he stepped into the barge. She watched as the fog began to roll toward it, gradually enveloping him until there was nothing but the gray, swirling mist and the sound of faerie laughter.

# Chapter 23

# Entrapment

A little more than a fortnight after Nimue had sent news of the Lady's passing to Camelot, a messenger came from Arthur.

They had taken Mons Arvaius, and Arthur had captured its captain, a man named Retho. He was sent to Luguvalium with a heavily armed escort. Before Arthur's men could advance, however, Frollo, Quintas's second-in-command, met them on the open field just beyond the hillfort. Bedwyr had been injured.

"How badly?" Gwenhwyfar interrupted. *Dear God, I've always feared this.*

"He will live," the soldier said quickly, "but his left arm is . . . may be . . . useless."

Gwenhwyfar sagged against Lancelot. He put an arm around her. "Gwen, your brother is a fighter. This will not stop him." He turned back to the messenger. "Is he coming home?"

"No. He will stay at Luguvalium," Clarence answered.

Lancelot frowned. "I'd rather have him here. Nimue could look after him."

"The king suggested that." The man nodded. "Bedwyr would not come. He wishes to return to fighting as soon as he is able."

Gwenhwyfar raised her head then and managed a weak smile. "He's more stubborn than I am."

"And the rest of the battle?" Lancelot asked.

"Frollo was forced to retreat," the messenger said. "The king sent Gwalchmai to parley with Quintas. The first relay left at that point and it is all I know."

After the man was dismissed, Lancelot pushed away from the Round Table and went to stare out the window. Gwenhwyfar watched him, thinking how much he reminded her of the horses when they had been left in their stalls too long. He was ready to bolt.

"You want to go join Arthur."

"I can't," Lancelot answered in a desperate tone. "Medraut and Agravaine are still recuperating, or so they say. I won't leave them here with you . . . and Cynric is here. Cai can't handle everything."

He sank into a chair and closed his eyes. She walked behind him and leaned his head against her stomach. She started massaging his temples, her thumbs working the frown lines from his forehead, brushing the stubborn strands of hair back.

"I certainly hope I'm not interrupting." Medraut stood in the doorway.

Gwenhwyfar stepped back quickly and then chided herself. *I have been doing nothing wrong.* She resumed her massage.

"What is it you want, Medraut?" Lancelot opened one eye.

Medraut stared at Gwenhwyfar's hands as if mesmerized.

"Medraut?" Gwenhwyfar asked, continuing to stroke Lancelot's forehead.

His voice had a raw edge. "The messenger. What is the news?"

"Bedwyr has been injured." She told him what had been said.

"I'm sorry, my lady," Medraut replied.

Lancelot turned his head, still leaning against Gwenhwyfar. "I find it interesting that you are so eager for news of the battle but unwilling to fight. Why is that?"

Medraut clenched his fists. "I am willing to fight, but I will take my own troops with me when I go."

"I don't remember Arthur designating troops to you," Lancelot answered languidly.

"Mayhap you should take more of an interest in what takes place on the practice field than what the queen does with her time!" Medraut said between clenched teeth and walked away.

Lancelot sat up and stared after him. "He may be right, Gwen. It is time I start watching him."


A month later Arthur sent for reinforcements from Camelot. Of the one hundred trusted veterans he had left behind, only twenty remained, Cai and Gareth among them.

"I am uneasy doing this, Gwen," Lancelot told her as he watched them ride out.

She looked up at him. "We have others here. Camelot is still well defended."

He shook his head. "Defended, yes, but by loyal men? They're mostly new and many of them are young. Some of them have never fought with Arthur."

"But you work them, Lance. They know you."

"And they have no love of me," he sighed. "Medraut spends time with them."

"That can't be stopped?"

"It seems Medraut has finally decided to become a soldier, and he implies he's Arthur's heir."

"How many of these men follow him, Lance?"

"I'll show you." He held out his hand. "Come with me to the battlements."

Once there, she gasped. Well over a hundred men, in rank and file, were practicing maneuvers. Medraut sat on his horse, shouting commands. Agravaine was beside him.

"How long has this been going on? Why didn't we know?"

He gestured to the field. "This has just started. Medraut has become so bold only lately. I have been investigating. He's paid more attention to our training than I had thought. He's been working them in units of ten, after supper. Then he takes many of them wenching and pays for it."

"Have you questioned him?"

Lancelot gave a short laugh. "I tried. He swore he's only training them to defend Camelot."

"You don't believe him?"

He smiled slightly. "I would believe the Saxons before I do him. The longer Arthur is gone, the more these young recruits will attach themselves to Medraut. When he's not with them, he spends his time with Morgana. It is not a recipe for trust, I think." He took her arm. "Let's go back to the hall; I've seen enough."

"Arthur has been gone much longer than he thought," Gwenhwyfar said as they walked across the bailey in the crisp autumn air. "From the messages he's sent, Arthur still hasn't gained the narrow pass. Frollo appears to retreat and then blocks the way."

They reached the hall and proceeded straight through to the map room. Lancelot shuffled some papers, looking for the map of the Pennine Mountains.

"Here," he said when he found it. "This is the pass that has given him so much trouble." Gwenhwyfar came to stand beside him, looking over his shoulder as he leaned on the table. "It is narrow and an invitation to an ambush. Arthur can send his men through only in a wedge formation, which is the worst thing to do in this situation. He won't have enough men on the other side for defense, if need be, and no room for the horses to charge. Arthur doesn't want to risk his men."

"Why don't you send a message to Arthur and tell him how things stand here?"

Lancelot straightened and threw the map down. "Arthur trusts me to be in charge. What would I say? Ask him to retreat and come home because his son grows too bold and I can't handle it?"

"I did not mean to make you angry, Lancelot." Gwenhwyfar moved closer to him and pressed against his shoulder.

He put his arm loosely about her waist. "I'm not angry," he answered, kissing the top of her head. "Frustrated, maybe."

She reached up and touched his cheek. "I can solve your frustration."

He pulled her closer. "Medraut spoils even that. We never know when he's likely to put in an appearance."

Gwenhwyfar sighed. "Arthur doesn't know it, but he has a good chaperone in Medraut. I am afraid to be near you half the time."

Lancelot nuzzled her neck. "I would like to spend the night with you."

"We've never spent the night together," Gwenhwyfar said wonderingly. "What would it be like, waking up to you?"

"I pray that one day we will find out," Lancelot said.

*To hold you all night, to have the warmth of your body next to mine.* Gwenhwyfar felt a tingle begin in her stomach and course its way through her veins. She pulled his head down for a kiss. "Find a way, Lancelot."


Just before the winter solstice, the next messenger arrived. He was one of the newer members of Arthur's Cymbry, a young man named Patrise. He asked for Gareth and Agravaine to join them in the council room. Medraut came with them.

"I rode the route myself, stopping only to exchange horses and rest a bit. Arthur has finally broken through and taken the pass, but the battle was costly. Gaheris is dead."

Gareth immediately clung to Gwenhwyfar. Agravaine's swarthy face turned even darker, and he and Medraut left without a word.

"How did it happen?" Gwenhwyfar asked, one arm around Gareth.

Patrise looked at the floor. "A tactical error."

"That doesn't sound like Arthur," Lancelot remarked.

Patrise shook his head. "Gwalchmai returned from his parley with the message that Quintas would talk to none other than Arthur himself. He swore him safe passage."

"Arthur went?" Lancelot asked, unbelievingly.

"Yes," the man answered. "He left Gryflet in charge, since Bedwyr was not there, and Gwalchmai went with him." He paused, but Lancelot said nothing. "Gaheris was getting impatient. He talked Gryflet into launching a full effort to take the pass before the snow would close it and trap Arthur in the north." He turned to Lancelot with a paradoxical smile. "Arthur's parley was a ruse to purchase time for Hoel and Lamorak to converge. But they didn't wait for that command."

Lancelot slammed a fist on the table. "Damnation! Arthur could have used me. I would not have let that happen." His face was stormy.

"Patrise," Gwen quickly suggested, "why don't you take Gareth and find his brother. Tell him how brave Gaheris was."

"Gaheris was foolish, Gwen, not brave," Lancelot said when they had left.

"Gareth doesn't need to know that."

He pushed the hair back off his forehead. "I know," he said more quietly, "but Gaheris should have known better than to lead a wedge in those quarters. What was Gryflet thinking?"

"I think Arthur needs you," Gwenhwyfar said softly. "I will go to Amesbury Abbey. I'll be safe there."

He sat down beside her. "Never, Gwen. I will not lose you to the convent again. I must stay. I didn't like Agravaine's and Medraut's reaction to the news. Who knows what they are plotting?"

On an early spring day, Medraut ran the men through the drills. This time Lancelot sat his horse beside him. Over the winter, Lancelot had decided the best way to know what Medraut was doing was to stay with him.

Medraut said offhandedly, "I am thinking about doing overnight maneuvers."

Lancelot glanced at him warily. "I'll ride with you."

He looked disappointed; then he shrugged. "As you will, Lancelot." He wheeled his horse and went to join his men.

Lancelot watched him join Agravaine and they both looked in his direction. *Now what is Medraut up to?*

As Fate would have it, Lancelot was to stay at Camelot. Marc rode in with an escort the morning Medraut's men were to leave.

"Welcome, Marc." Gwenhwyfar met him in the courtyard. "This is an unexpected pleasure."

He bowed stiffly, for he was not a young man, nor lean. "I am sad to say the visit is not for pleasure, my lady. Forgive me for bringing my troubles to you."

"Arthur is not here, as you know, but Lancelot acts as regent," she said as Lancelot joined them, carrying his hauberk. "Come, let's go inside."

"Iseult left me," Marc said when he was seated and had been served wine.

"Where did she go?" Gwenhwyfar asked. *Foolish girl. And yet, if I could . . .*

He spread his hands. "I do not know." He looked at her and then at Lancelot. "Tristan went with her."

Gwenhwyfar shot Lancelot a questioning look.

"Do you think she is here?" Lancelot asked evenly.

Marc looked embarrassed. "No, no. I just thought, since Arthur is away, that Tristan might have been bold enough to seek the queen's favor for a night's lodging, that is all. Iseult liked you, my lady."

"I'm sorry, Marc," Gwenhwyfar said. "We have not heard from them. I pray she comes to her senses and returns to you." She ignored the quirk at the corner of Lancelot's mouth.

"I will have her put away," Marc said in an angry tone.

"You would not seek her so diligently if you did not want her back, I think," Gwenhwyfar said gently.

He was silent a moment and then he slowly nodded. "You are right, my lady. I know that she and Tristan lust after each other, but I love her."

Gwenhwyfar looked at the floor. *Is this what I've done to Arthur?*

Medraut appeared in the doorway. He was wearing full armor and carrying his gauntlets. "I see you have a guest," he said as he walked over and greeted Marc. He turned to Lancelot. "You're not prepared to ride."

Gwenhwyfar said quickly, "I have asked him to stay, Medraut. Marc will be our guest for several days since I have to send out some queries. It would not be proper for me to entertain him alone."

Medraut's eyes narrowed as he looked from Lancelot to Gwenhwyfar. "Then, by your leave, we will be gone." He turned to Marc. "If you're still here when we return, I will be glad to entertain you. You might be interested in the games we play here."


Gwenhwyfar sat on the chaise in her bedroom, trembling with anticipation. She had fresh linens on the bed that still smelled of sunshine. The sweetly scented oil lamps burned low, casting a golden glow to the room. She had bathed in lavender-scented water and let her hair dry naturally. She loosened the laces on the fine silk nightdress that she wore under a soft woolen robe. Compline. Lancelot should be here at any moment. *We'll have all night and I can wake up to you in the morning!*

She heard a soft step on the stair. He had no need for silence, really, since Marc had insisted on riding on that afternoon, after all. The servants were in their quarters; she was alone on the second floor.

Lancelot opened the door and stepped inside, bolting it. He removed his sword belt and hung it by the door before he came to her. "So much clothing," he murmured as he removed her robe. He pulled the string on the nightdress and it fell open.

"Very nice." He slipped it off her shoulders and kissed a breast.

She smiled and knelt, helping him with his boots. He shed his shirt as she worked on the trews' laces.

"You had better let me do that, Gwen, unless you have a notion to be taken before we get to the bed."

"Nay, my lord," she giggled, lifting her hands. "I would hope you take more time than that."

He made an unintelligible sound low in his throat as he kissed her. Together they tumbled onto the bed, their hands and mouths seeking each other's pleasure spots.

When their first passion was spent, he whispered, "Now, we play easy. All night, if you'd like."

"I'd like," Gwenhwyfar answered as she turned in his arms, pressing her breasts against him, entangling her fingers in his hair, and teasing his mouth with her tongue.

He growled. "All night, my love . . ."

Much later, they fell into exhausted sleep, their arms and legs intertwined.

\* \* \*

They were jarred awake by the sound of an ax shattering the wooden door, splintering the bolt. A blaze of light came from the hallway. Gwenhwyfar drew the covers up as Lancelot reached for his sword, but it was hanging by the door.

The lanterns moved in and Gwenhwyfar could see the looks of horror on Cai's and Gareth's faces and the fiendish one on Medraut's. Behind him were at least ten of the young recruits he had trained. All of them were armed. Dimly she was aware of Cynric in the background.

She never would be able to say what happened next; it was all so sudden. She remembered Lancelot springing out of bed, fighting the first men who reached him, knocking two or three to the floor. Then someone hit him over the head with the pommel of a sword and he slumped. Several of the men quickly wrapped a rope around him and dragged him, half-conscious, out the door. Two of them caught Cai and forced him along as well.

Gwenhwyfar tried to get out of bed. Agravaine caught her arm, and she flailed at him with the other, striking him across the face with her hand. He slapped her, making her head snap back. Momentarily stunned, she didn't realize he had anchored one of her wrists to the corner post of her bed and had a rope around the other.

"Don't hurt her!" Medraut shouted, "I want to be able to enjoy her!"

"Take this then," Agravaine replied, handing the second rope to Medraut. "Tie her to that post." He moved to her legs, grabbing an ankle and securing it. She tried to kick at him, but he was out of reach. Deliberately, he pulled the rope painfully tight on the second ankle before slipping the loop over the post. He pushed past Medraut, who was already undoing his shirt.

"There'll be time for that later," he snapped. "Attend to Lancelot first."

Medraut hesitated, his eyes devouring Gwenhwyfar's

naked body. He grinned slowly and demonically. "Yes," he said. "I believe I will torture him first. Let him know everything I plan to do with the queen." He looked into her face. "I have waited so long for this, Gwenhwyfar." He spoke her name slowly, as though he savored the sound. "When I come back, I will make you forget both Lancelot and Arthur. It will be so good, just the two of us . . ." His voice became childlike. "I love you, Gwenhwyfar."

An icy terror flooded Gwenhwyfar. She had no feeling in her wrists or feet and was past the point of humiliation from being spread upon the bed. Medraut was truly mad; there would be no rescue. *Holy Mother of Our Lord,* she prayed, *help me bear this.*

Agravaine gave Medraut a shove. "Go." He looked down at Gwenhwyfar. "If there's any fire left in you, when Medraut is through, I'll take my turn." He leaned down, inches away from her face. "I have always wondered why Arthur and Lancelot both tormented themselves over you. I think I will find out later."

She hissed at him and he gave her a diabolical smile. "Mayhap there are other young bucks who would also wait in line." His face became hard. "Think about it, Gwenhwyfar, while you lie here and wait." He turned on his heel and pulled Medraut out of the room with him.

*Dear Christos, spare me the pain. May my death be merciful.* She tugged at the ropes desperately, her eyes shut, trying to hold back the tears.

"That will only make them tighter."

Gwenhwyfar's eyes sprang open as she stifled a scream. Cynric stood beside her.

"Not you, too," she whispered in despair.

"No," he answered as he took a sheet and covered her. "This is not a game I enjoy playing."

"That . . . that's what Lancelot said once," she choked out. *That day at the cabin, when I so foolishly thought that being helpless . . .*

Cynric shrugged. "At least Lancelot will die a happy man."

"Save him, Cynric. Please." Her voice was a whisper. "He must live, even if I don't. Arthur needs to know . . ."

The guard at the door eyed them suspiciously as he leaned over her.

"You will live. Medraut wants you too much. He spent hours telling me his fantasies about you." Cynric's brow furrowed for a moment. "You must tell him, though, that you don't like pain. I think he'll listen." He took a deep breath. "I ride for my father's lands tonight. But I have no wish to be Arthur's enemy; tell him that."

"Help Lancelot, please! It will be my last request of you." *Dear Mary, Mother of God, let him do this for me. Arthur must be told.*

His blue eyes looked into hers. "I hope, one day, that I find a woman capable of such love." He sighed softly. "I will do what I can. Now, forgive me." He tilted his head toward the guard. "I must act like another man in lust." He kissed her then, hard and passionately.

"That's enough of that!" The guard was in the room, tugging at Cynric's sleeve. "Medraut gets her first! That's an order."

Cynric smiled lazily and stood, slapping the guard on the shoulder. "Ah, Manassen, you know Medraut and I are friends. He would not begrudge me a kiss." He leaned closer to him. "But I think the queen would enjoy Medraut more if she could feel him."

Manassen grinned.

"Look," Cynric said, taking one of Gwenhwyfar's wrists, "how limp and white it already is. The ropes must be loosened some."

The guard backed away. "I don't know. . . ."

"You do the other side." Cynric didn't wait for an answer but quickly loosened the rope a bit. As the guard reluctantly moved around, Cynric loosened the rope enough for her to work out of it after he left. He gathered up Lancelot's clothes.

Gwenhwyfar stayed still, beginning to feel a glimmer of hope.

"He'll have no need of those," Manassen said, frowning.

"Even the Saxons would not deny a man the right to die with his clothes on," Cynric said reprovingly.

The guard looked embarrassed then and glanced at Gwenhwyfar.

"Please," she said. "Show the Saxon that we are not barbarians at Camelot."

Manassen gestured for him to go.

Cynric bowed to her. "Good-bye, my lady," he said formally, but he winked as he turned to leave.


Lancelot lay as though unconscious on the cold floor of the gaol cell. Medraut was clearly mad and he needed time to think. *Gwen. Great Mother, where is she? Please keep her safe.* He heard the outer door open and cracked one eye slightly.

Cynric tossed the clothes into a corner as he entered. Medraut looked up and motioned for the guards to leave. "He doesn't look so appealing now, does he?" He pointed to Lancelot. " He doesn't like what I'm going to do." Medraut laughed again, more shrilly this time, his voice rising. "I told him I would come back and tell him how much Gwenhwyfar liked it. Then I'll kill him."

"And Arthur will kill you. Slowly." Cynric's voice rang with certainty.

Medraut stopped laughing. "He should thank me, I would think."

"Not so." Cynric shook his head. "Don't you think he will want to avenge this situation himself? Wouldn't you?"

"Mayhap," Medraut said slowly.

Cynric leaned down. "Arthur will not take kindly to you raping his wife."

"But she wants me. I know it. She'll love me, once I've been with her." His voice was childlike, his face earnest.

"Medraut," Cynric said patiently, "you wanted to catch Lancelot with the queen so Arthur would get rid of him, correct?"

His eyes slithered to Lancelot and back to Cynric. "Yes, but . . ."

"You have done that. Now you must wait for Arthur. He is on his way home. Let him kill Lancelot. I would wager that he will be so angry with the queen for having shamed him, that he will send her away."

*Please, Great Mother, let him believe it,* Lancelot prayed.

Cynric played his trump card. "Then you will be able to take her and make her your rightful wife."

Some of the madness left Medraut's eyes. "My wife?"

"Yes, Medraut," Cynric spoke softly, as though to a child. "If you wait for Arthur, he will give you Gwenhwyfar. But Arthur will be very angry with you if you take her first, without his permission."

"But I want her," Medraut said stubbornly.

"I know," Cynric said soothingly. "Think about how much better it will be if you wait for her to be your wife. And she'll want you more if you make her wait as well."

Medraut began to smile a natural smile, and Lancelot began to hope Cynric's lies were sinking in.

"Gwenhwyfar will want you more if she has time to prepare herself, don't you think?" Cynric asked.

"I . . . I guess I could wait," Medraut finally said.

Lancelot breathed an inward sigh of relief.

"Good," Cynric replied, and he sounded relieved, too. "Then why don't you look to your soldiers? They will be awaiting your command. Have you secured Camelot?"

"Agravaine is seeing to them."

"Why don't you go find him? Tell him you've decided to protect Gwenhwyfar from everyone because she will be your wife."

Medraut threw a triumphant glance at Lancelot, who lay still.

"Go," Cynric said. "I have no love of Lancelot either. I will guard him for you."

Slowly Medraut moved to the door. He turned just before he left. "One thing, Cynric," he said in a clear, sane voice. "I have other guards posted outside this door."

Cynric retrieved Lancelot's clothes after Medraut had left and pushed them into the cell. "I wasn't able to bring any weapons," he said as Lancelot sat up.

"Is Gwen all right?" Lancelot asked weakly as he struggled into his clothes.

"For a while." Cynric explained the situation to him quickly.

Lancelot studied him. "I was wrong about you. I owe you our lives."

He shook his head. "I was planning to ride away from here, but Gwenhwyfar asked me to try and save you, even if she died. I couldn't say no." He looked at Lancelot. "You've been a lucky man."

"I know," Lancelot said softly. "I must find a way to get to Arthur, to put an end to this."

"Well," Cynric said with his easy smile as he settled into a chair. "That may take some doing. It seems we are both prisoners here."

# Chapter 24

# Escape

Nimue sat up in bed. *Camelot is in danger. Someone is on the way to Avallach.*

She dressed quickly and made her way to the storage room. She opened a great chest and pulled a convent sister's habit and a monk's robe from it, not questioning why the garments were important. She simply donned hers over what she wore. The monk's robe she carried.

By the time Gareth pounded down the path to the Lake, she was waiting.

"My lady." Gareth flew off his horse and half knelt, half fell at her feet. "Medraut found Lancelot with Gwenhwyfar."

Nimue felt cold fear in her stomach. *The Wheel was spinning, the beginning to the end of Camelot.*

Barinthus appeared with two fresh horses, although she had no recollection of asking for them. She handed the reins of a fresh horse to Gareth and mounted her mare. "Where are they, Gareth?"

"I don't know," he shouted over the steady rhythm of the

hooves. "Someone hit Lancelot; they were dragging him away when I ran. Gwenhwyfar was still in the bed."

*Dear Mother, let us not be late, let there be time.* She gave all her attention to willing the horses to go faster as she bent low over the neck of hers.

Camelot was drowsing in the heat of the noonday sun as the monk and sister approached the gate, their tired horses plodding with hanging heads. The guard waved them through, not bothering to look at them.

Cai came to meet them in the bailey. "You are welcome, friends of the Lord Christos," he said loudly enough for the guard posted by the Great Hall to hear. "We have two prisoners in need of shriving." He pointed to the gaol. "That way."

One of the guards eyed them suspiciously as they approached. "I would see the prisoners to offer what comfort we may," Nimue murmured, her head bowed.

"Neither of them is Christian, Sister," the guard answered.

"Even so, the lord Cai has sent for us. Allow us to do what we can."

The guard hesitated and looked at the other, who shrugged.

"All right, then, but don't take long. We will be replaced at this post soon." He unlocked the door and followed them inside.

Nimue went to the cell where Lancelot was propped against the wall. Gareth followed but tripped as he passed Cynric, who was sitting on the floor. The guard spun around.

"Will you open the door so I may give him the Lord's blessing?" Nimue asked.

The guard turned back and laughed. "The only time that door will be opened is when we take him out to kill him, Sister. Bless him from where you stand."

The monk kept his head lowered as he stood beside the guard while Cynric hid the dagger that had fallen into his lap.

Nimue made the sign of the cross. "Very well, then." She turned to Lancelot and extended a hand through the iron bars; the other she raised in blessing. "Take my hand, sir, with both of yours, that I may bestow the Christos's mercy."

Lancelot knelt before her and covered her small hand with his. Nimue slid the cool metal of the dagger toward him. Slowly his fingers stretched above her wrist and edged the knife down into his own sleeve.

"Bless you, Sister," he said reverently.

She began chanting the litany, "*Jubilate Deo . . . Salvi nos fac, Domine . . .*" Instinctively the guard bowed his head for an instant.

Cynric sprang, making a clean slice through his throat with one stroke, and caught the man as he slumped to the ground. He pulled the keys from the guard's belt and threw them to Gareth.

Nimue glanced down at the man on the ground, the blood pooling around him, and chanted the Passing blessing in the Old Tongue.

Lancelot came to them. "We don't have much time. Gareth, get the other guard."

Gareth pulled the hood lower and opened the door. "Some trouble in here . . ."

The guard peered past him, then pushed the door wider and stepped in.

Lancelot's arm came around his neck, silencing him as Cynric ripped the man's belly wide before he had time to struggle. Lancelot eased the guard to the floor. Hastily he strapped on the man's swordbelt.

Gareth removed the monk's robe and handed it to Lancelot.

"Pull it over," Nimue said, averting her eyes from the blood and intestines on the floor. "We will walk out of here as Christian clergy."

Gareth poked his head outside cautiously. "All is still."

They slipped out, carefully closing the gaol door behind

them. Nimue said to Cynric, "Stay in the shadows while Gareth relieves the guard at the postern gate and he will let you through. Tell your father we may have need of him before this is done."

Cynric knelt before her. "Lady, my father's people will be ready." Then he disappeared with Gareth behind the gaol.

Lancelot started across the bailey with his long stride. Nimue tugged him back. "Slowly, Lancelot. You are a monk, remember? Keep your head down and bend a little." She wrapped her hands in her sleeves and bowed her head.

Crossing the bailey was painfully slow. Lancelot showed some semblance of shuffling. Once inside the hall, he whispered, "One guard? I can take him."

"No," Nimue hissed. "Too much noise. You wait here. I go up alone." She softened somewhat. "Trust the will of the Goddess." Then she was gone.

Lancelot fidgeted beside Cai, nervously fingering the beads on his robe. He would have to ask Gwen what these were used for. By Mithras, where were they? His fingers traced the hilt of the sword beneath his robe.

Finally Nimue returned. She walked with her head bent even lower, the wimple completely hiding the rest of her face. Lancelot leaped up.

"Where is Gwen? Is she hurt? Can't she walk?" He headed toward the stairs, but a hand restrained him. Her covered head lifted slightly, and Gwenhwyfar's green eyes looked out. "Thank the gods, Gwen." He wanted nothing more than to crush her to him and never let go. "Where is Nimue?"

"She will come," Gwenhwyfar answered. "Her orders are for us to ride out of here slowly, with a great show of piety."

"Piety is not my strong suit, I think," Lancelot smiled crookedly.

"Then learn," Cai said harshly. "Take her to the Isle and ride for Arthur. I will hold Camelot while I can."

"You and Gareth need to go with Nimue when she leaves. Better that none of us remain here until Arthur can bring his troops."

Cai nodded. "Aye. Now go."

The gatekeeper was still leaning idly against the parapet as the horses passed through, walked sedately around the turn, and were lost from sight.

Agonizingly Nimue waited in Gwenhwyfar's room, making sure Lancelot had time to get away. A loud commotion was taking place in the bailey. She hurried to the window. Medraut was down below, shouting at the men standing by the open door of the gaol. The dead guards had been discovered.

She summoned all the power she had and brought the cloak of illusion down. Opening the door, she expanded her aura until white light shimmered gently around her.

The magic had the desired effect. In her pale blue robes, with the magical glamour surrounding her and making her somewhat misty, she projected the image of the Holy Virgin. The guard fell to his knees, his mouth open in awe.

Nimue barely got down the stairs and to a seat beside Cai before Medraut burst through. He hardly noticed her as he bounded up the stairs, his men behind him. She heard his tormented scream as he discovered Gwenhwyfar missing and braced herself.

Medraut thundered back down the steps. "Where is she?" he yelled at Cai.

Cai looked up from his cup as casually as if nothing were amiss. "I am not her guard, Medraut. You forbade me to go near her room, remember?"

Medraut glared at him and then noticed Nimue. "What are you doing here?"

She smiled. "Gwenhwyfar sent for me."

"Yesterday, when Marc was here, Medraut," Cai said

quickly. "The queen thought the Lady could help find Iseult."

*Bless you, Cai.* "Has something happened?" Nimue rose.

"Ha!" he barked. "Lancelot was found in the queen's bed last night, in front of witnesses. Naked as newborns." His voice was bitter. Suddenly his face softened and his voice became childlike. "Once Arthur finds out what she's done, he will put her away, and I will marry her."

*The man really is mad.* Nimue gave Cai a worried glance, but he just stood calmly beside her, one hand resting carelessly on his sword hilt. "Yes, Medraut. When Arthur returns, all will be well."

Medraut continued to look at Nimue. Some of the madness left his eyes. "Mayhap I should have a hostage until Gwenhwyfar is returned to me. Would you like to be my guest, Nimue, and take her place?" His smile became sinister. "Seize her!" he shouted to the guards who had accompanied him.

Nimue drew inward and tried to expand a protective aura, but she had used too much energy with the other guard. A slight glitter was all she could raise, just enough to make the men hesitate.

Cai drew his sword and immediately two of Medraut's men found their mark, piercing him both in the stomach and thigh as he collapsed.

*You dear fool, Cai. No quick moves . . .* Nimue dropped and tried to stanch the blood. The tips of several swords were inches from her face. "You won't need those," she said coldly. "I will stay willingly if you let me help Cai."

"Willingly?" Medraut drawled. "You will do as I command?"

"If you allow me to care for Cai."

He began to smile heinously. "You give me your oath as high priestess?"

Nimue hesitated. She had no choice if she were to save Cai's life. "Yes," she answered. "My oath."

"Leave her be then," Medraut said to his men. "I've never had the pleasure of a priestess in my bed." They laughed a little too loudly. He turned back to Nimue. "I hope you'll make it interesting."

"That," she said in a deceptively calm voice, "I can promise."

The barge was waiting as Gwenhwyfar and Lancelot reached the Lake. His fingers gently traced the bruise on the side of her face where Agravaine had hit her. "I will make him pay for that, Gwen," he said as he took her hands in his. He stroked the rope burns on her wrists. "You will be avenged, Gwen. You have my geis."

They clung together, savoring the taste of their kiss. Reluctantly he released her. "I must ride."

"Yes," she answered, as Barinthus came forward with Gareth's rested horse.

Lancelot mounted and leaned down for one more quick kiss. Then he wheeled the horse around, urging it to full gallop.

*Godspeed. May Arthur forgive us both.* Gwenhwyfar closed her eyes in prayer.

A lone priestess waited as the barge scraped against the sandy shore. Ceridwen, whose vows included silence, gestured for Gwenhwyfar to follow.

She was given the same room she had nearly fourteen years ago when she had come for healing from Morgana's poison. She rested awhile, then made her way to the apple orchard. This time the trees were filled with the white blossoms that lent their sweet fragrance to the air. The sky was an ethereal blue here, and she wondered if it were as brilliant on the other side of the encircling mists that ever hovered over the Lake. She lay back on the soft new grass, enjoying its clean scent as well.

Deliberately she pushed the nightmare of her capture away and lost herself in the swirls of memory, remembering the feel of Lancelot's arms wrapped about her, the slightly salty taste of his tongue inside her mouth, and the unique, pleasant odor of soap and leather that clung to him. She loved the silkiness of his nether hair compared to the hardness of him. She hugged herself, thinking of the many different ways that they had made love last night.

Then Arthur's face appeared in her mind. Blond streaks where the sun had bleached his brown hair; his direct, clear grey eyes, always searching for truth and honesty; the tanned face with its strong jaw. His face with its hard lines was transformed into youthfulness when he smiled. He had not smiled often in the past few years, except when he was with Nimue. *How much of that is my fault? I never meant to hurt him.*

Reluctantly she wondered what he might do. Being Arthur, he would try to understand. But he was the king and she was his queen. *Treason? Possible death if he chose?* A chill went through her, remembering the flogging he had given his own son, her own rape, and the times when he had not shown mercy. He could easily remove himself from emotion. *Will he put me away, instead? What of Lancelot? Will Arthur unleash his fury on him? Exile or death?* She doubted that Arthur would take revenge for their coupling; he had been aware of their love, but the cost to his kingship was another matter.

*I may never see Lancelot again.* She lay down and buried her face in the grass and wept for all the wrongs she had ever done.

"You fool, Medraut! You absolute fool!" Morgana slapped him and began pacing the length of her dining hall.

He put a hand to the welt that was rising. "You told me to find them together!"

She stopped. "Yes. When Arthur would be close by. He could not deny it then! What were you thinking?"

He did not answer and she suddenly comprehended. "Have you taken her?"

He laughed mirthlessly. "I didn't have time that night."

She breathed a sigh of relief. Medraut looked at her with a puzzled expression. "Of all people, why would it matter to you, Mother?"

Her voice was flat. "Arthur would never allow you to live if you had raped Gwenhwyfar." *By the gods, could her son not understand that?*

"Then he'll have to kill Lancelot, too," Medraut said triumphantly.

"Don't be stupid, Medraut. I doubt that Lancelot came close to anything like rape," Morgana replied. "Don't you think Arthur knows about them?"

"If he does, why doesn't he do something about it?" Medraut asked angrily.

She sighed. "I don't know, Son. When you were young, I had spies watching him because I wanted you to be acknowledged one day. The rumors my scouts brought me were that he and Lancelot shared the same women. It appears they still do." She shrugged. "My point is, as high king he cannot afford to be cuckolded. He will either have to condemn them both or he will have to violate his own code of honor. Either way, a door opens for you to take leadership." She paused. "And, with luck, the throne."

"Arthur will have to pursue him, since Lancelot abducted the queen."

Morgana laughed. "Where do you suppose Lancelot has gone, Medraut?"

"I don't know. He's probably trying to catch a ship to Benoic. He won't risk facing Arthur now."

"That is exactly what he will do," Morgana said with conviction, and Medraut opened his eyes wide in surprise. "That's the charm of him; he has never hidden his love of Gwenhwyfar from Arthur. He must have the Christian devil's own blood in him to get by with it."

"I can hold Camelot," Medraut said stubbornly. "My men control it now."

Morgana sniffed. "Arthur will take Camelot. You have less than one hundred men, and he will bring his full cohort back once Lancelot reaches him. You need to be gone before he returns." She sank down in a chair despondently. "My hopes, my own dreams . . . ruined because you are besotted with that whore."

"She is not . . ." Medraut stopped, then brightened. "Nimue is still my hostage."

"What?" Morgana felt her face pale. "How did that happen?"

"She came to see Gwenhwyfar, she said. I didn't believe her, but I asked her to stay as my . . . er, guest. She agreed after Cai was wounded. She gave me her oath as priestess that she would come to my bed."

"If you value your own life, you will not touch Nimue," Morgana said coldly. "She is not only priestess, she is the Lady of the Lake. Have you forgotten?"

He grinned insolently. "Would that not make her a good choice for me? I could gain much power, I think, from coupling with her."

"If you force Nimue, it will be the last time you have a woman."

He was silent, brooding.

After several minutes, Morgana said thoughtfully, "However, keeping her as a well-treated hostage may be your only hope. Set her free when Arthur grants you and your men safe passage. Beg his forgiveness; remind him you are his son, his only heir, and that you meant to save the queen, not harm her."

He stood to leave. He turned at the door. "I will not retreat like a coward, Mother. My father has taught me well. I will stand against him."


Arthur marched his cohort double time, Roman style, since Lancelot had met him on his way home. Camelot was now within a half day's ride; he signaled his men to halt. Gwalchmai rode up to him.

"Rest the men here. Take a unit and fetch Morgana." He smiled at Gwalchmai's questioning look. "I think we will fare better if we have bargaining leverage. Who better than that bastard's mother? We ride tonight, to be in place before dawn tomorrow." Arthur turned Valiant west. "I must see Gwenhwyfar first."

He reflected as he rode. Lancelot had not minced words; Arthur had sent him to wait at Joyous Garde. He needed time to think. He told his men only that Medraut had rebelled and tried to take the queen hostage and now held Camelot. *I've been a fool not to realize how unbalanced Medraut's infatuation has become and how deep is his hatred for Lancelot.*

As he arrived at the Lake, he sensed something amiss. The fog that continually lay low across the water was seeping inland. It crept like a snake on the road toward Camelot. No sound, not even the gentle ripple of the water lapping the edges of the bank was heard. Neither gulls cried nor herons croaked. The fog slithered around the horse's hooves, and he snorted and pawed the ground.

Arthur pulled Excalibur and held it high. He knew its vibration would reach the priestesses on the Isle. He waited.

The barge became visible. One of the small, dark people from the mud huts nearby came to take his horse as the boat scraped bottom. Barinthus bowed to him but seemed uneasy.

"I must go across," Arthur said. "Gwenhwyfar is here, is she not?"

Barinthus nodded silently and gestured for Arthur to step

aboard. He poled off the flat bottom, turning the barge into the dense wall of mist.

They broke from the fog bank and the lush green Tor of Avallach loomed ahead. Even from here the sweet smell of the orchard wafted on the air, overriding the odor of the brackish water. He had visited Ynys Wydryn only twice in his life. He felt the same magical pull now as he had then.

Ceridwen came to greet him. Arthur followed her silently up the hill. She led him to Nimue's greeting chamber and offered him a chair. He removed his swordbelt and sat facing the tapestry of the white hart. Its luminous eyes gazed at him.

He heard a soft footstep in the doorway. Gwenhwyfar approached him and sank to her knees, her eyes on the floor.

"Meekness does not become you," Arthur said flatly. "Look at me, Gwenhwyfar." She raised her eyes to his, and for a moment he saw the old defiance flash in them; then it was gone. He raised an eyebrow. "Have you nothing to say, Wife?"

"I have been unfaithful to you, Arthur." Her voice was shaky. "I am sorry."

A muscle twitched in his jaw. "Sorry you got caught, you mean?"

"No! I am sorry for hurting you, sorry for ruining your dreams. I love you still."

"A very strange way you have of showing it, Gwenhwyfar." *How I want to believe you.* He took a deep breath and his grey eyes penetrated hers. "How could you have been so half-witted? What possessed you to openly invite Lancelot to your bedroom?"

She flared then and stood. "You should never have left me with Lancelot. What did you expect would happen after a year?" She turned away. "We tried to stay apart, partly fearing that Medraut would find us." She gave a short laugh. "Your son, the chaperone. The mad chaperone. That night . . . that one night, Arthur." She turned back and stared into his face. "We had never spent the night together. Never in fourteen years had I ever awakened to him."

Arthur felt his anger rising and he stifled it. *I had no intention of being gone a year!* "You are right, Gwenhwyfar," he finally said, and his voice sound tired. "This was not unexpected. Lancelot tried to warn me. I have been the fool."

She laid her fingers across his mouth gently. "Stop, Arthur," she begged. "The fault is mine. I was not strong enough to withstand . . . I do love you, but I love him, too." She sank to the floor in front of him.

He reached out and touched her face. "I know," he said sadly. "I never thought to be in such a situation."

She grasped his hands. "What will you do, Arthur?"

He shook his head. "I don't know, Gwenhwyfar. I will try to salvage this dilemma somehow." He changed the subject. "I need to speak to Nimue. Where is she?"

There was silence. "Gwenhwyfar? What is wrong?" The sense of foreboding he had sensed earlier returned.

She took a deep breath. "Nimue is still at Camelot. A hostage, we think."

"What?" Arthur was on his feet, bowling Gwenhwyfar over. "Lancelot told me she followed you here!" *By Mithras, I'll kill Medraut if he's touched her.*

"She was supposed to," Gwenhwyfar said as he helped her up. "When she didn't arrive by that evening, the priestesses scried for her; they saw her with Medraut."

He was already buckling his swordbelt on. He paused for a minute as the white hart's eyes seemed to follow him. He turned at the door. "Pray for her, Gwen, and for me, to whichever god you choose," he said, and he was gone.

As he made his way to the barge, he tried to block what his son might do. Nimue had power, but could she stand against Medraut? *Don't let me be too late, dear Lord. I wish Myrddin were here.*

His thought was picked up by a windsinger. Far away, on

Avalon, in a cave reflecting light off the crystals, the queen
of Faerie whispered in Myrddin's ear.

The fog was thick this morning, a dark grey that lay
folded like a blanket, encircling Camelot. The first bursts of
red and orange gathered on the horizon and the swirling mist
drifted slowly back. Emerging from that pale light was the
golden banner with the red dragon. Arthur saw the guard appear and then he heard him sound the alarm. "The high king
is without! We are besieged. God have mercy on our souls!"

He knew men would be stumbling out of barracks, some
dressing as they came, others struggling with their weapons.
Then he saw Medraut and Agravaine appear on the battlement.

Arthur's men remained immobile. The front line stood
still as statues and as silent. Eerily the mist rose and fell behind them. They faded in and out of sight.

In the stillness the muffled footsteps of marching men
could be heard. Cynric emerged from the mists with his father's troops.

Medraut shouted across the field. "Father! Nimue is our
hostage."

Arthur gave no response from the field.

"She will see the banner," Cynric said as Nimue was
brought on the battlement.

*I hope so.* Arthur dared not move; part of his plan was to
make those inexperienced troops nervous by remaining still.
His men were well out of arrow range; they would wait.

"Lancelot told me that you saved Gwenhwyfar," he said
out of the corner of his mouth.

Cynric, too, looked straight ahead. "I saw no sport in
what they planned to do."

"You have my gratitude for that, Cynric. And your freedom. May your people and mine continue to live in peace."
Arthur paused. "You also saved Lancelot?"

Cynric grinned. "The queen asked me to. She is a hard woman to deny."

"It would seem so," Arthur said drily. " 'Tis the reason we are here."

Nimue was removed from the battlement and Arthur sighed. "Pray to Woden, Cynric, that no harm befalls her, or I will destroy Camelot myself to get at Medraut."

Arthur's army continued to stand throughout the day. As night fell, small fires were lit, ringing Camelot in a halo of red, yellow, and blue flames. "Leave a portion near the postern gate unlit," Arthur commanded Gryflet. "Some men will try, foolhardedly, to escape. Let them through. Wait for them. Take no prisoners."

Gryflet hesitated. "Even Medraut and Agravaine?"

"Agravaine will die fighting, Gryflet. Medraut knows, I think, that his only hope is to keep Nimue alive and well. He doesn't know we have his mother."

The next morning Arthur led Morgana forward, just short of arrow shot.

From the battlement Medraut shouted, "Your terms, Father?"

"Bring Nimue; you and your men come out."

"Do you grant safe passage, Father? For my men, as well?"

"Once I know Cai, Gareth, and the rest are alive, yes."

"Your oath, Arthur," Agravaine yelled.

"My oath that your passage will be safe in return for your hostages!"

Slowly, then, the men filed out, their weapons taken away. Arthur's medics rushed in to find Cai. Agravaine and Medraut came last with Nimue.

She ran to Arthur and he wrapped his arms around her. He was surprised when she reached for him and kissed him. He didn't hesitate in returning that kiss.

Morgana took a step toward Medraut, only to have Cynric firmly grip her arm.

"Arthur's oath didn't include you," he said with a lazy smile.

She tried to slap his face and he grabbed the hand, bending both arms behind her in one fluid motion. "Did anyone ever tell you how Saxon men treat hostile women?"

Arthur turned to Medraut. "Your mother stays as she is until you and your men have disappeared. Do not plan to return."

Medraut nodded. "Just bring us our horses."

"No horses. You walk."

"Go," Morgana told him, "before this fool breaks my arms."

"If you call me another name I don't like, Lady, I may do that." Cynric pulled her arms up a bit and she gasped. "It is an easy thing to do."

Arthur watched impassively and then turned to Medraut. "Why are you still here? I won't stop Cynric."

Agravaine grabbed Medraut and dragged him to the few men who waited.

After they left, Arthur turned to Morgana. "You will remain my prisoner."

The Cymbry gathered around them as Cynric released her. Morgana stepped away, rubbing both of her arms.

"Why on earth would that fool rebel?" Gryflet asked. "Only an idiot would try to take on Arthur's cohort with those few men!"

"He thought he could hold Camelot!" Gwalchmai replied. "Against Cymbry!"

"And he tried to abduct the queen!" Patrise shook his head in amazement. "What was he thinking?"

"I'll tell you what he was thinking!" Morgana moved in the midst of them before either Arthur or Cynric could stop her. "He did not mean to rebel. The queen was caught in bed, coupling with your brave comrade, Lancelot! Medraut thought only to hold them for Arthur's return, so justice could be done. That is all!"

Stunned silence followed her remarks.

"There is no proof of that!" Gwalchmai said in the void. "You accuse people who are not here to answer for themselves!"

Arthur said sharply, "I will not have the queen insulted."

"Hear, hear!" the men said, but Arthur sensed some doubt in their voices. He glanced at Nimue; her eyes were glazed and he knew she had gone into a trance.

"The Wheel has begun to turn," she whispered.

# Chapter 25

# Tribulation

Although his arm was not completely healed, Bedwyr brought Gwenhwyfar home several days later. She stared straight ahead although she noticed that Arthur's men avoided looking at her.

Arthur came down the steps to greet her. She was grateful for the support of his hand under her elbow as she dismounted, for she felt her legs trembling. Bedwyr had told her on the ride back that the men were divided about Morgana's accusations.

Arthur leaned toward her and whispered, "We will make this look good in front of the men. I will not have a bad situation made worse by your refusing me."

He pulled her into a crushing embrace and kissed her roughly, demanding entrance to her mouth. *All right, I'll play along.* He responded more gently as she acquiesced and put her arms around his neck, but then he returned to a near brutal kneading of her back with his hands, his lips bruising hers. She knew they were on display for the men watching. *The high king claiming his property.*

She managed to move her mouth slightly away from him. "Can we not move inside?"

Arthur stepped back but grasped her arm tightly. "These men will see that I am only taking what is rightfully mine."

Gwenhwyfar forced herself to smile, conscious of the stares. "If it's your intention to humiliate me, then do it and be done, for you are hurting me."

Arthur's eyes were steely as he looked down at her; she raised her chin and refused to look away. He relaxed his hold but did not release her arm until they were alone in his quarters upstairs with the door bolted.

He pushed her toward one of the chairs by the table and sank into the other one. "I think," he said, "that you had better tell me about you and Lancelot, although I really don't want to hear it."

When she finished, he was silent for some time. "So," he said wearily, "you not only condoned Marc's wife's being unfaithful, you encouraged it. Wars begin over things like this, Gwenhwyfar. Marc is still looking for them, but you don't know where they are?" He glanced at her sharply as she shook her head. "And Cynric has a place of . . . pleasure . . . that Lancelot took you to. Cynric was our hostage all this time?" He gave a bitter laugh. "It seems to me there has been too much freedom at Camelot."

Gwenhwyfar looked down at the floor. So many things had gone wrong.

"All I have to do now," he finished sarcastically, "is convince my Cymbry that you are still a lady of honor and respect; that you had a weak moment and were overcome by our heroic Lancelot." Arthur's jaw set. "That will be hard to do, Gwenhwyfar, when I know otherwise."

"You were the one who made him my champion, Arthur! You were the one who asked him to give me his geis." She felt herself growing angry. *I tried to be faithful. I tried.* "You were the one who left him here with me. Do you have any idea of how hard it has been for me to stay away from him? To content myself with . . ." Too late, she stopped, horrified at what she had said.

Arthur's face hardened, and his eyes went cold. He sat down on the bed and tugged off his boots. As he undid his shirt, he looked up.

"If you aren't out of those clothes by the time I am out of mine, I will tear them from you," he said simply.

"Arthur, I am sorry . . . I didn't mean . . ." Gwenhwyfar stopped, for he had taken his shirt off.

"One way or the other, Gwenhwyfar. It matters not to me. But you will join me on this bed." His tone did not change.

She turned from him, feeling humiliated, as she tugged her boots off and worked her trews open and slid them off. She undid the ties to her tunic and then turned to sit down beside him on the bed, clutching the shirt to her.

Arthur shook his head. "I said off." He ripped it open. She gave a slight gasp as he pushed her back on the bed, pinning her body with his.

He did not hurt her, although there was no tenderness in him, only a reclaiming of her body. Methodically, he explored her, eventually penetrating, but in no hurry to set a rhythmical pace. Slowly he withdrew and probed again. She began to respond to him, her body asking for quicker movement, but he retained his leisurely tempo. She felt no warmth from him, only the steadiness of his measured thrusting. Eventually she began to chafe and still he kept on.

"Arthur, will you please finish?" she whispered, her body aching from need.

He rose up and looked down at her. "If I thought I could erase Lancelot from your mind," he answered, "I would continue until you screamed for mercy."

"I am asking for mercy! I am sore, Arthur."

"Did you tire so easily of Lancelot, Gwenhwyfar? Or is it just me?" He caught the hand she swung at him and pinned both arms to the bed.

She glared at him. "I will not discuss Lancelot with you, Arthur! It is unfair of you to ask."

"Unfair?" he rasped. "I am getting tired of bearing the blame here. But since you want this to be over . . ." He forcefully rammed himself into her, the thrusts hard and fast.

Gwenhwyfar shuddered and held him to her and together, they let the blessed relief flow. *I love you, Arthur. Forgive me.*

They were seated at the high table, being served supper, when Morgana was brought in. Arthur watched her warily as she was led to her table at the far end, but she did nothing more than merely glance at Gwenhwyfar. She was docile throughout the meal, and Arthur became more uneasy.

The meal had been quiet, too quiet, for the nearly one hundred cavalry that were seated. Where men should be talking and laughing, there were subdued conversations. He saw the looks that were quickly averted if Gwenhwyfar's gaze turned on them. Tension filled the room. Bedwyr, Gwalchmai, and Cai stayed close.

Arthur made a show of treating Gwenhwyfar well. Finally he stood. *This is going to be hard; can I convince these men to accept her?* "I would like to have my wife made welcome in her own home." His voice was filled with authority. "What has taken place need not concern anyone but me. Gwenhwyfar is your queen." *And my wife, whom I still love.* "I remind all of you that your allegiance with me includes her."

"What of Lancelot?" Someone, bold in the far shadows, called out.

Arthur's voice was calm. "Lancelot will remain at Joyous Garde. He will no longer have a place at Camelot." *Even with all that's happened, I will miss him.* The men murmured at that, but it sounded as approval, not disgruntlement.

Arthur held his hand to Gwenhwyfar and raised her to stand beside him. "Have you something to say, my wife?"

"Only that my husband and my king," she said clearly, "has shown greatness and mercy in forgiving me for my mistake. I beg you to honor him and respect him for it."

"Honor and respect, Gwenhwyfar?" Morgana's voice rang out amid total silence. She came forward to stand in front of them. "You have dishonored the high king, not just your husband, by coupling with another man. That is treason by any name." She turned to Arthur. "How can we respect a king who would allow this?"

"Enough, Morgana! You are not the person to speak of respect and honor." Arthur's voice was tightly controlled.

"Mayhap not," Morgana shrugged. "Your own system of justice demands action to be taken. Or is justice applied differently if you are the king?"

The grumbling of the men began to swell. Gwalchmai and Bedwyr grabbed Morgana to lead her away.

She glared at them. "Is this also the king's justice? To drag me away because I speak the truth?"

"Truth is not something you would recognize," Arthur replied angrily, aware of the low rumble. "But, in the name of justice, I will let you speak your piece and have done with you." The hall quieted again.

Morgana turned to the men. "All of you have fought with Arthur. You have followed him willingly because you thought he was a fair man." She paused as many of them nodded. "I ask you then, does the queen's adultery with a trusted captain of the king fit your code of honor?" Many of the men avoided looking at her, but some did not. "Do any of you believe that this was a mistake, as the queen claims?" She began to walk around the room. "Have you been blind that you did not see the two of them, always together, always touching? Was Lancelot not overly protective of her? Has he not even forsaken his own wife for her?" She raised her voice. "This has been going on for years and Arthur has known and condoned it. Behold," she finished triumphantly, "your very cuckolded king!"

"Are you finished, Morgana?" Arthur asked coldly.

Morgana slid a sideways glance at him and turned back to the crowd. "I am not finished. My son, Arthur's son . . ." she hesitated and sighed. "Medraut has been exiled for bringing the queen's indiscretions to the king's attention. Is that justice?" The noise level had become a low roar. Morgana turned back to Arthur. "I demand that you enforce your code. The sentence for treason is death at the stake, is it not?"

Gwenhwyfar closed her eyes and leaned against Arthur.

Gwalchmai spoke then. "There is a way to settle this." He looked about the room and the men waited. "Trial by combat. The queen's champion against whomever Morgana chooses to champion her. If Lancelot is victorious, both their names will be cleared." The soldiers made sounds of approval. Arthur nodded slowly.

"Not Lancelot." Morgana's voice was firm. "You said he was banished from Camelot. Or are you willing to break another rule for the queen's sake?"

Arthur stared at her. *How could one woman have so much hate in her? Certes, I know. Medraut. The throne. Consort to the king.*

"I will champion her myself," he said.

"You cannot. You are the king!" Morgana laughed. "Is this your day for changing the laws, my brother?"

His mouth set in a straight line. "Who will champion the queen?" he called out.

An embarrassed silence followed as no one stepped forward. Gwalchmai had suggested the match; he could not volunteer now. Bedwyr's arm still had not healed properly, and Cai was too stiff. Gryflet was not present; the other men shuffled their feet, no doubt thinking Bertilak would be

Morgana's choice and he was still a powerful fighter, the best in Rheged, now that Accolon was gone.

Arthur glared at all of them. "Are you the Cymbry or are you slaves to Morgana's evil?"

"I will do it, Sire!" Gareth struggled through the crowd to the front. His face was shining with devotion. "For Captain Lancelot and for the queen."

"You will be killed," Gwalchmai hissed at him. "Bertilak has years of craftiness and experience on you, little brother!"

"He is right," Arthur said quietly. "You and the queen will both be dead."

"I'm better than you think, my lord. Lancelot taught me," Gareth said stubbornly.

Arthur sighed. "Let it be Gareth then. When next the moon is full." He turned back to the crowd. "Now be gone, all of you."

The hall cleared quickly; he knew none wanted to face his wrath. Morgana's slant-eyed face bore a most satisfied expression. Like a cat sitting in front of an open birdcage. For a moment he could almost see her licking her whiskers. *Witch.*

Arthur was breaking his fast alone the next morning. He had not slept well and he doubted that Gwenhwyfar slept at all, although she had lain quietly in his arms all night.

He had opened the bedroom door earlier this morning to find a guard posted in the hall. Embarrassed, the man explained that he had drawn the short straw. The majority of the council felt that if the queen were charged with treason, she should be guarded.

Arthur's concept of the Round Table allowed his council to speak freely and rule by majority. For the first time he saw a flaw in that policy. The matter was out of his hands. Gwenhwyfar was now confined to her room. Moodily, he toyed with his food.

Patrise approached him. Arthur looked up at him questioningly.

"I wanted to apologize for not volunteering to champion the queen, my lord." Arthur made no reply, and he continued, "I did not feel that my skill with the sword was great enough to save her." He looked around to check if anyone was within hearing distance. "I do want to volunteer for something else."

"What would that be?" Arthur asked, motioning for him to sit.

"The queen needs her champion. I will ride to Lancelot."

"Did you not listen last night, Patrise?" Arthur grimaced. "I would be changing the rules if I sent for him. Or so I am told."

"You will not have to send for him. I go on my own," Patrise said earnestly.

"Do you not have duties here? Abandoning them is a serious offense," Arthur said mildly.

"It is, and I'll take the flogging." Patrise shrugged. "I never told anyone what I heard when I went in search of Agravaine the day I brought the news of Gaheris's death. Medraut was plotting to find them together and I laughed it off. I must do something to compensate for that."

Arthur felt a flicker of hope. "I think," he said at last, "I will let your commanding officer know you have been moved to Bedwyr's company, effective this morning. Mayhap Bedwyr won't notice you are gone."

Patrise grinned. "I will ride like the wind, Sire."

Arthur stared after him as he left. The full moon was less than a fortnight away; there should be time. *Can I allow Lancelot to fight? The council would not accept it now that Morgana had made such an issue of honor and justice. If Lancelot rescues her and takes her away, Gwenhwyfar's name would not be clear, but she would be alive. That's what really matters. Once this is past, I will somehow bring my men together.*

He breathed a sigh of relief, having made the decision.

\* \* \*

Heavy black clouds hung low over the bailey on the early summer day of single combat. Gwenhwyfar was unable to eat and her palms were sweaty as she waited for Arthur to escort her. She was dressed in her usual trews and shirt, for Arthur had told her she must be ready to ride. *Please, sweet Jesu, let me survive this day.*

She watched the men assemble the kindling and logs around the flogging post, thinking that if it rained, the wood would not light quickly. But the smoke would kill her as surely as the flames. *And less painfully.* She almost prayed that it would rain.

Gwenhwyfar turned when Arthur entered the room with the guards behind him. He was dressed in his finest tunic; the golden cloak with the red dragon hung from his shoulders, and the torque, which he seldom wore, around his neck.

He handed her torque to her. "You are still the queen," he said softly. "If you did not have to ride today, I would have you dress the part." He fastened the torque for her. "This will remind everyone that it is the high king and high queen who stand before them." His hands rested lightly on her shoulders. "Are you ready?"

"Is Patrise back?" she whispered.

Arthur hesitated. "I have not seen him."

Panic set in. She clutched Arthur's arm. "I don't want to burn."

He leaned over to kiss her. "Lancelot won't let you down."

Her arm still trembled and her legs felt weak as he escorted her down the stairs. She pulled back slightly as they reached the door. Arthur waited. Taking a deep breath, she lifted her chin and squared her shoulders.

"I love you, Arthur. Do not ever forget that," she said as they stepped outside.

The bailey was crowded with soldiers and villagers. A

pathway opened for Arthur and Gwenhwyfar and the guards. Her hands were tied in front of her and the rest of the rope looped over the pole, for Arthur had insisted she need not be strapped to it until the outcome of today's events.

"Remember to step away and pull that rope tight if Lance rides for you. He will have only one chance to cut it," Arthur whispered as he kissed her. Then he was gone.

Nimue appeared from the crowd. "Will you accept my blessing, Gwenhwyfar?"

"I would accept all blessings on this day." She tried to hold her voice steady.

Nimue took her hands and she felt the touch of cold metal as Nimue's little sickle frayed the rope. A spark of hope ignited. Gwenhwyfar held the ends together with her fingers. She was actually free of the post. If nothing else, she could always run. *I wonder how far I could get before someone runs me through? Still, a sword wound would be swifter than fire.*

"Take care of Arthur for me, Nimue?"

Nimue held her gaze, her eyes as clear as the sea. "That I will always do."

The match was about to begin. Bertilak was talking to Morgana, who sat under heavy guard. He was grinning and held his sword nonchalantly. Gwenhwyfar hoped he was bluffing.

Gareth acknowledged the king and was now approaching her. *Poor Gareth; he looks so scared.*

He knelt in front of her, his eyes on her face. "I have begged the Christos for help today," he said fervently, "for a strong arm and clean cuts. I will do all that is in my power to save you, my queen, but I wish Lancelot were here to do it for me."

*I wish he were, too. I must keep faith.* "I know you will do your best, Gareth, but you must lose the fear. It will slow you. Bertilak is older and heavier than you are; he will tire more easily. Keep him moving." She smiled slightly. "Is that not what Lancelot would tell you?"

His face lit up. "It is. And I will remember the rest of his training as well." Quickly he stood and walked to where Bertilak was now waiting.

They began slowly, circling each other. Gareth lunged and Bertilak retreated easily. He feinted and cut low; Gareth parried. They continued, each holding his own. Bertilak did not show signs of tiring; he was becoming more aggressive. Gareth quickly took several steps backward to avoid a thrust and stumbled. Bertilak quickly cut low; blood trickled from a light wound on Gareth's thigh.

No one noticed the tall hooded monk emerge from the old chapel and edge toward the destrier tied to the paddock fence.

*Engage him, Gareth, riposte, and make him move back. Stay on your feet. Find your balance.* Gwenhwyfar could feel Lancelot mentally coaching him. *Where are you, my love?*

Suddenly Bertilak spun and dealt a blow that sent Gareth to the ground, dazed. Before he could recover, the point of Bertilak's sword was at his throat. He would have to yield or die.

The warhorse leaped under Lancelot's touch. He was near Gwenhwyfar when men started to react. He slashed to the right and left, and the men fell back.

Lancelot pulled Gwenhwyfar up behind him. Soldiers closed in again. He struck down the first two that approached.

Gareth was up and running toward him, brandishing his sword. He was close when Lancelot wheeled the horse. The horse's back hoof kicked forcefully, making contact. Gareth thudded to the ground as the horse jumped clear of the remaining soldiers and thundered through the gate.

Chaos ensued. Arthur shouted for the men to cease.

Bedwyr and Gryflet barred the gate, preventing anyone else from leaving.

Gwalchmai knelt beside Gareth, cradling his head. He was breathing, and slowly his eyes opened. "I . . . can't . . . feel my legs," he whispered as the medics arrived.

Arthur reached them as they lifted Gareth. "I failed you," Gareth said weakly.

"You did not." Arthur swallowed hard and put his hand lightly on Gareth's shoulder. "You did well. You helped Gwenhwyfar get away. Now rest."

He watched as Nimue walked with Gwalchmai beside the litter. The cost had been great today: nine of his soldiers lay dead; Gareth might never walk again. He had lost his wife as well as his best comrade. He would refuse to follow them. Gwenhwyfar and Lancelot would stay alive if they stayed away.

Wearily he started back to the hall. He noticed Morgana's chair was empty. Bertilak was nowhere to be seen, either. They must have escaped in the midst of it. He really didn't care anymore.

*How will I live without Gwenhwyfar?*

# Chapter 26

# Joyous Garde

They were on the road over a fortnight. Lancelot managed to procure another horse, but he did not want to use the Fosse Way where they easily could be seen and possibly recognized. They skirted the marches, the land to the northwest, and stayed close to the forest lines most of the time.

The first morning, near Glevum, Gwenhwyfar woke early and lay listening to the soft rustling of leaves swishing against each other in the stirrings of a dawn breeze. She was using Lancelot's shoulder for a pillow, and she burrowed up against him now.

He stirred and brought her closer to him.

"This is the first time I have been able to wake up next to you, Lancelot," she said softly, her fingers tracing his cheek.

He rolled over, facing her. "This wasn't exactly what I had in mind for our first morning."

"I don't care, Lancelot. It is so peaceful here, so very quiet."

"Too quiet. Why aren't the birds singing?" he whispered and put his hand to her mouth. He was on his feet even as he reached for his sword.

Silently Gwenhwyfar rose with him. He handed her a dagger.

A twig snapped near Gwenhwyfar and instinctively she crouched. The man who sprang from the bushes missed her, and Lancelot made short work of the swordplay.

Neither of them recognized the dead man. They held their silence for several minutes until the forest came to life around them.

"He may have been just a thief," Gwenhwyfar said shakily.

"Mayhap," Lancelot said, wiping the blood from his sword on the grass, "but I will feel better once we have put some distance between us and Camelot."

As they moved on that day, Lancelot planned. "We will ride closer to the fells; the Sidhe may protect us."

A waft of cool breeze caught Gwenhwyfar and she shivered, looking at the jutting hills with their crumbled, ragged edges. Morning mist shrouded parts of them. "Sidhe?"

Lancelot nodded. "The small, dark people of the Old Blood. Nimue would be able to contact them directly, but I have not had the training. Wait," he said, sidling his horse to the side of the road and breaking two good-sized twigs off the branch of an oak tree. Opening his saddlebag, he rummaged and finally brought out a piece of ragged red silk, a few pearls still clinging to it.

Elen's favor. Gwenhwyfar watched as Lancelot made a square cross of the twigs and bound the center with the red cloth.

"I will offer this at the next well we come to," he said as they proceeded on. "Mayhap the Sidhe will accept it."

"Will they acknowledge you?" Gwenhwyfar asked.

"No." Lancelot shook his head. "They have no wish to be

seen. The tips of their arrows are poisonous, though. If they are between us and whoever follows, we will be safe."

They came to a spring two miles later. The doire, keeper of the spring, waited, as if expecting him. Lancelot dismounted and knelt, pouring an oblation for the Goddess. He stroked the silk talisman once before presenting it to the maiden. She pointed up the slope of the hill where a single hawthorn grew. A portal for the Sidhe. He nodded before he returned to his horse.

They traveled in silence for several miles before Gwenhwyfar spoke. "You kept her favor all of these years."

Lancelot glanced over at her. "Had I not accepted her favor, mayhap she would be alive today."

"Do you want to talk about it?"

"Someday. Not now. All I did was say good-bye." He kicked his horse to a canter.

The soldiers outside the fort of Joyous Garde stopped their drills as Lancelot and Gwenhwyfar rode toward the gate. Silently they filed in behind them. Lionel and Bors emerged from the hall as they stopped in the bailey.

Lancelot sighed. He had hoped to have some time before giving an explanation to his men. Lupin came to take their horses, but Lancelot held up his hand. He glanced at Gwenhwyfar once before he spoke.

"Accusations have been made against the queen. Arthur has asked me to protect her until such day as there is no danger." Lancelot looked around at his troops. "If there is anyone here who is unwilling to acknowledge the queen, you are free to leave. See Lupin for your wages, take your horse, and be gone by sunup."

Lancelot waited. Slowly, the men closest to them knelt. Then, as one, the others bent their knees as well. Lancelot nodded curtly and helped Gwenhwyfar dismount.

His elderly housekeeper, Augusta, was waiting for them. She curtsied to Gwenhwyfar. "Welcome to Joyous Garde, my lady." She turned to Lancelot. "Which room, my lord?"

"The one next to mine," Lancelot answered, and noticed the disapproving pursing of the old woman's lips. He tilted his head and grinned at her. "You do not approve?"

She reddened a little. "Don't think you can change my mind, my lord, with that smile. It's not fitting for the queen to be so close to you."

Lancelot answered her teasingly. "How else can I be sure she is protected?"

"Humph!" she answered staunchly. "You might think to appearances."

"You are right, my dear chaperone," he said seriously. "I would not have the queen's name tarnished here. You choose the room then."

Augusta looked at him suspiciously, but he merely gestured for her to proceed. She led Gwenhwyfar to a room at the back of the hall, as far from Lancelot's downstairs room as she could get. He laughed and dismissed her.

Lancelot shook his head after she had left. "I inherited her from Hoel, before he left to go back to Armorica. She decided from the start that none of my soldiers would bring their wenches home. I guess she was tired of the camp women who trailed Hoel."

Gwenhwyfar glanced sideways at him. "Are you telling me that I am to act in a chaste manner and stay in my own bed?"

Lancelot's eyes crinkled as he walked over to her. "You might try acting chastely sometime to see how long it takes me to change your mind." He wrapped his arms around her. "As for your bed or mine, it matters not, except that I do not intend for you to sleep alone . . . or unmolested," he added with a grin.

She pressed up against him, running her fingers through his hair. "How would you molest me, Lance?"

"You'll have to wait until tonight to find out," he answered, stepping back.

"Lancelot, we have been on the road for days without . . ."

"You think I need reminding?" Lancelot stroked her breast lightly over her tunic. "This time, my love, I want nothing to go wrong. Is that not worth the wait?"

"Just a kiss then," she said, reaching for him.

"Ah, no." He moved away and opened the door. " I don't have that much resistance. Now, let me show you around this place, in the most honorable manner."

He laughed as she deliberately avoided touching him as she walked out the door.


As the next six months passed, word was routinely received about activities in the south. Arthur liked the relay system he had established during his war with Quintas and he kept it intact.

"Medraut has found a place with the Saxons," Lancelot read from the letter that Bedwyr sent. Arthur was not taking the chance of communicating directly. Lancelot knew he'd had enough problems convincing the Cymbry not to pursue them.

"Not Cynric?" Gwenhwyfar asked. She poured tea for both of them and settled in next to him on the chaise in the small living area that overlooked the gardens.

"No. Cerdic and Cynric remain allies . . . or neutral, anyway." Lancelot could not bring himself to fully trust Cerdic.

"Who then? Aesc?"

"Yes, and his son, Eormenric, as well. But Aelle is dead, and his son, Cissa, has joined with Aesc."

Gwenhwyfar inhaled sharply. "Who stands by Arthur?"

Lancelot looked up. "Marc, since Arthur found Tristan and Iseult in Clausentum, waiting for a boat. Once Arthur sent Tristan to Armorica and Iseult home, Marc repledged his allegiance. Cador and Agricola are loyal . . . Owain in the north and your father's people. Hoel, unfortunately, is fighting his own battles in Armorica now that Clovis has decided to move west."

He handed her the letter and took a sip of tea. She glanced through it. "Medraut commands his former units from Camelot . . . a pity you trained them."

"I trained Medraut, too. He hated me, but he learned his lessons well," Lancelot replied grimly.

She put the letter down. "It says nothing of movement. Mayhap Arthur can hold them, especially if Cerdic and Cynric stand fast."

"I have always felt that Cerdic merely bides his time, like a cat waiting for the bird to light. Land is what matters to the Saxons; that, and the begetting of sons to keep it." Lancelot took a deep breath. "Arthur will depend on the Cymbry, his countrymen. They will be who keeps Britain whole." *My brother, I wish I could join you.*


A dove cooed its dawn song as Gwenhwyfar became aware of Lancelot's fingers tracing a delicate pattern across her stomach. Lazily, she stretched, arching her back. He grasped a nipple with his lips and pulled gently. She pressed his head to her breast, sighing contentedly. They moved slowly into a natural, easy rhythm, caressing each other and leisurely bringing each other awake.

The sun shone through the window, silhouetting the fresh new leaves on the tree outside when they finally lay quietly again.

"I wonder," Gwenhwyfar said, "if I might still get pregnant?"

Lancelot stopped twining her hair around his finger. "I had not thought to use precautions, Gwen. Are you afraid you might be?" He pulled her over on top of him.

"It's a little late to ask now, isn't it?" She smiled. "I would like to give you another child, Lancelot. One that would be ours." She shifted her weight, pressing her soft flesh against his chest.

His hands worked their way down her back, kneading her buttocks and holding her against him. "I'll be glad to try if you'll give me a few minutes."

Gwenhwyfar nibbled his neck. "Would you not like a child?"

"Gwen, if you want a child by me, I would be happy to have one. It isn't necessary for me, though. I want you." He paused. "Remember, I have not been much of a father to Galahad."

"Galahad is nearly eight now." She brushed back his stubborn strands of hair. "When was the last time you saw him?"

"I haven't, since Elaine took him to her father's."

"You've not seen him?" Gwenhwyfar was shocked. "Wouldn't you like to?"

"I suppose that would be nice," he said, staring past her at the ceiling. "He's old enough to begin to learn a soldier's work, but I can't just go and see him."

"Why not? He's your son. Surely Elaine will grant you a visit."

"Elaine would see me in the Christian hell before she would grant me a favor." He made a grimace. "For certes, she would not want me as a guest in her home."

Gwenhwyfar was quiet for some time. At last she rolled over and sat up. "Have Arthur send for him, Lancelot," she said excitedly. "Elaine cannot refuse the king!"

Lancelot traced the side of her cheek with his thumb. "Have you forgotten that we are all but in exile? I am not in a position to ask Arthur for favors, either."

"It's not a favor! Say that you would like to begin working with the child here at Joyous Garde, and you would send him to Arthur in two or three years for court training."

Lancelot stared at her. "You would be willing for him to live here?"

"Certes. I accepted Medraut under much worse circumstances and learned to like the child, although not the man. Arthur can tell Elaine the boy needs to be fostered."

"To work with my own son . . . I could teach him how to fight; how to handle a sword, the lance . . . horses . . ." He turned to her, his eyes shining. "I had not thought about this. Gwen, I love you!" He sat up quickly and kissed her soundly. "I'll send the messenger this morning."

She pulled the sheets up and watched him dress. She smiled to herself. Having his child nearby would be so much fun. She wondered if Galahad looked like him.

Arthur's tournament that year did not go well. Several of the lesser kings had declined to attend, stating various reasons.

"This is but the first step toward resistance, if not rebellion," Arthur fumed, pacing the council room.

"The reasons were all logical, Arthur," Nimue pointed out.

He raked his fingers through his hair. "The rumors are that I could not control my own son nor my wife, and not even all the Cymbry support me." He turned to Gwalchmai and Bedwyr. "And if my own cohort is not loyal, the Saxon unrest will soon turn to war."

"The men are restless, so they look for trouble," Gwalchmai commented.

"It has always been that way when there is no war," Gryflet said. "A year has passed since we stood against Medraut."

"What a disaster that was." Arthur sat down suddenly and slammed his fist on the table. "Now he flits from Cissa to Eormenric, stirring the young blood. Would that I had stopped Medraut and that bitch mother of his when I could."

"You treated with them, Arthur. You gave them your oath," Nimue said.

"What would it have mattered, Nimue, once I knew you were safe? I broke my own code to save Gwenhwyfar; I should have finished it."

No one replied to that; they all knew what was really bothering Arthur. There was no solution; if he brought Gwenhwyfar back, the fragile unity that remained at Camelot would be broken. Without her, he was despondent and his temper was short.

"I received a letter from Gwenhwyfar," Bedwyr finally said.

Arthur stopped. "What does she have to say?"

Bedwyr hesitated. "Lancelot would like Galahad to return to Joyous Garde. He wants to work with him."

"And Gwenhwyfar would like to raise him," Arthur replied bitterly. "It was what she wanted of me and Medraut, when there was still a chance for goodness in him."

Bedwyr shuffled uneasily and Arthur sighed. "If he wants Galahad, let him take him. It is his right."

Bedwyr looked back at the letter. "Elaine will not allow it. Gwenhwyfar is asking that you issue the order."

Arthur stared at him and then broke into laughter. "Elaine has finally gotten her revenge. There is something that Lancelot cannot have." He sobered. "By all the gods, I wish that marriage had worked. I had hoped—" He stopped abruptly.

"Isn't she still his wife?" Gryflet asked. "Why don't you send them both back?"

Gwalchmai and Bedwyr exchanged glances. "They hate each other, Gryflet," Gwalchmai said. "That would do Galahad no good."

"Gwenhwyfar and Elaine have no love of each other, either," Bedwyr added. "Lancelot would have his hands full keeping the two of them from each other's throats. You all know my sister's temper."

"I doubt that my wife has ever turned that temper on him." Arthur gave him a thoughtful look. "Mayhap he should experience that as well. Issue the order. Tell Elaine that she and Galahad are to move back to Joyous Garde or face indictment from the king."

"Keep a tight rein!" Lancelot called as the colt Gwenhwyfar was riding tried to break away from her. The young horse had nearly gotten the bit in his teeth, and she was straining not to let him get his head down. They were in the paddock behind the barns, but Lancelot had the rope ready, should the horse win.

Gwenhwyfar sawed on the reins, easing the bit back to the soft part of the colt's mouth. He quieted and stood trembling.

"Now ask him to canter," Lancelot said, but she had already done so.

They were so intensely focused on the horse that neither of them heard the guard call that riders were approaching. A brambleweed blew across the ground suddenly and the colt slipped and Gwenhwyfar kicked free of the stirrups and threw herself from the saddle, landing in a heap at Lancelot's feet.

Lancelot knelt beside her. "Lie still," he said, running his hands lightly over her shoulders, arms, and legs to feel for broken bones. "Do you think you're hurt anywhere?"

"Just my pride," she answered, lying on her back. "Let me try again."

With relief he lifted her and held her to him. "The horse is limping. No more riding for you today," he murmured in her ear.

"I see things haven't changed much, Husband."

Startled, Lancelot whipped his head around. Elaine and Galahad were standing by the paddock fence. At least he assumed the boy was his son; he had Elaine's blue eyes. A dark lock of unruly hair brushed across his forehead.

Lancelot got to his feet and helped Gwenhwyfar up. She brushed off the dirt as they walked to the fence.

Galahad moved nearer to his mother, who put her arm around his small shoulders. As Lancelot came closer, the boy clutched at Elaine's skirts.

A muscle in Lancelot's jaw twitched. *The boy is afraid of me. Why?* He crouched low under the rail of the fence, bringing his face even with the boy's.

"Galahad. I'm your father and I'm glad you are here." He held out his hand, but the child shrank farther behind Elaine.

Lancelot stood and frowned at her. "I see you have already done your work, Elaine. What have you told him?"

"Not now, Lance," Gwenhwyfar laid a hand on his arm.

Elaine gave a short, harsh laugh. "You still can't keep your hands off him, can you, Gwenhwyfar?"

"By Mithras, Elaine, we do not have to go into that in front of the boy." Lancelot's voice was low. "Why are you here? You did not have to come."

She raised an eyebrow. "I think I did. I have no wish to face Arthur's wrath."

"What are you talking about? I asked only for Galahad."

"I wondered why Arthur was sending me back to you." She pulled a paper from her cloak and handed it to him. "I didn't realize Gwenhwyfar was here. Apparently I am to take up my wifely duties and keep you two apart." She smiled sweetly at Gwenhwyfar. "I am still married to him."

"In name only," Lancelot answered and skimmed the order and handed it to Gwenhwyfar. His face could have been chiseled out of marble. Gwenhwyfar went pale.

"How could Arthur do this?" she whispered. "Now, we won't be able . . ."

"Justice," Lancelot interrupted grimly. "He has found a way for us to pay back what we have done to him." Lancelot sighed. He might have to treat the bitch well in front of the household, but no one would keep him from Gwenhwyfar's bed. Deliberately he draped an arm over her shoulder. "And yes, we will," he answered.

* * *

"The boy is hopeless," Lancelot complained as he sank down on a bench near the freshly dug garden bed.

Gwenhwyfar looked up from the buttercups she was planting. Galahad had been with them nearly six months. He excelled at his book learning and playing the harp; he had even warmed to her, in spite of Elaine, but remained aloof with his father.

"What has he not done now?" she asked. It wasn't that Galahad was defiant; he just didn't progress the way he should.

"The sword," Lancelot said wearily. "I have gone over and over the importance of anticipation, but he still lets himself be taken on the first move."

"You have worked with him only a few months. Galahad is not quite nine, Lancelot; he is still a child."

"Do you remember when we met, Gwen? I had a wooden sword in my hand and I was near his age. You were only six and already knew how to hold one."

She put her supplies down and went to sit beside him. "Galahad is different from us, Lancelot. He has not been taught to be a leader. His is a gentle soul."

"He's a dreamer. I dread the day I try to teach him hand combat."

"How does he with the bow?"

"He hasn't the strength to pull much, but that can be overcome. I have already begun giving him work that requires lifting weight."

"And his pony? He seems to do well enough with that," Gwenhwyfar said.

Lancelot brightened a bit. "The one thing he does well is take care of that animal. Usually I have to beat that into the recruits, but it comes naturally for him."

"There. You see?" Gwenhwyfar smiled. "He pleases you in something."

"But he still fears me, Gwen. I don't know how to change that. I have tried talking to him. He gives me short answers and volunteers nothing. He skitters away if I get too close; he hates my touch when I show him how to hold the sword."

Gwenhwyfar sighed. Much of this was Elaine's fault. She filled the child's head with her own version of the wrongs that she perceived Lancelot had committed. "He probably still thinks you hurt his mother," she said softly.

"I have not touched the woman," Lancelot answered. "I'm with you every night."

*And you have to leave before dawn.* "Yet I think Elaine feels both love and hate for you, Lancelot." Gwenhwyfar tried to avoid Elaine as much as she could, but they had to have the evening meal together in the dining hall. More than once, she'd caught Elaine watching Lancelot with something akin to longing.

"I return only one of those emotions," he answered. "I told her I would admit to any kind of abuse if she granted me an annulment. She has not done that."

"And I will not." Elaine walked up behind them. "Why are you discussing me?"

"We were discussing Galahad," Gwenhwyfar replied calmly, for she knew Lancelot was seething. "You've been filling his head with stories."

"Stories? No. Only that his father has misused me, which is true. He still refuses to fulfill his marital obligations; instead, he whores . . ."

"Enough, Elaine!" Lancelot was on his feet. "You will not insult Gwenhwyfar!"

"Did I mention her name? Didn't you and Arthur used to share the women who ran after you?" Elaine gave Gwenhwyfar a venomous look as she retreated from Lancelot's wrath. "They've always enjoyed besting each other. You're no more than a trophy wench to either of them." She turned and fled.

Gwenhwyfar blanched. Lancelot sat down beside her and took her shoulders. "You must believe that I love you."

"But you did share women?"

Lancelot sighed. "Sometimes. You have not been exposed to camp followers, Gwen. Most are filthy and diseased. Other women were available if a man knew where to look: married women whose husbands didn't take the time to pleasure them, older women with experience, but often ignored. Clean women. And women who could hold a conversation. Arthur pretty much wanted those same things." Lancelot took her face in his hands. "I never thought to compare. For most men, coupling is a need. I tried to make a game of it, so the women would feel pleasure too. But if you think that I enjoy you in bed because I wish to compete with Arthur, I will stop . . ."

"For heaven's sake, Lancelot, I don't want you to stop!" She inhaled deeply. "I am no blushing maiden or even young anymore. I never thought to compare you and Arthur either; each of you completes me in a different way. If that makes me a willing wench, then so be it." She settled herself against him and brought his arms around her. "We must ignore her. Now, we were discussing Galahad before all this started."

"Yes," he said, nuzzling her neck. "I wonder if Galahad will ever enjoy this as much as I do?"

The air was bracing and the autumn day crisp, but Lancelot watched Galahad wipe sweat from his brow and then circle warily, sword ready. His son had been at Joyous Garde a year, and he was still afraid of him.

He parried now and Lancelot pushed his sword aside. He saw Galahad struggling with the humiliation of it; then suddenly, the boy lunged faster than usual. His sword made contact with Lancelot's leg.

Lancelot sidestepped quickly, surprised. "Very good, Galahad. You caught me unprepared. That is not easy to do."

The boy smiled lopsidedly. "I am glad to please you, Father."

"Pleasing me is fine." Lancelot looked down at him, his dark eyes serious. "But you should want to learn these skills. You don't want to go to Arthur unprepared."

Galahad's smile disappeared. "Queen Gwenhwyfar said I can stay here."

"So you and the queen are friends?"

Galahad nodded. "She's always nice to me and listens to me read. She likes my harp playing, too."

"She also expects you to learn a warrior's skills, Galahad." Lancelot watched as a faraway look crept into his son's blue eyes.

"What are you thinking about?" Lancelot asked.

"About you."

Lancelot cocked an eyebrow. "What about me?" This was probably the longest conversation he'd had with Galahad. *Be easy.*

Galahad blushed and looked down. "You are different around her. Not so hard." He cringed as if expecting a blow. Finally he looked up.

*Am I that transparent?* "I push you, Galahad, to make you strong. You must, at least, be able to defend yourself. Do you think me cruel?"

The boy hesitated. "I . . . my mother says you are." He looked away.

"Have you seen me hurt your mother, Son?" Lancelot asked quietly.

"No," he replied, his voice barely audible.

Lancelot put a hand under his son's chin. "I will not harm her or you. Your mother and I simply do not like each other."

Forced to look at his father, he blurted, "Why don't you like her? Why don't you talk to her like you do the queen?"

Lancelot dropped his hand to his side. "You will not understand why for some years yet. The queen and I have been friends since we met, nearly sixteen years ago. We are comfortable with each other."

Galahad took a deep breath. "Why has the king sent her away? Mama said she did a bad thing."

*Hopefully Elaine had enough sense not to be graphic.* "Someone who did not like Gwenhwyfar made accusations. Her life was in danger," Lancelot answered. "The king expects me to protect her."

"He must trust you," Galahad said.

Lancelot stared into space and was silent.

"The king is not brutal and ruthless then?"

"Where did you . . . no." More from Elaine, no doubt. He looked at his son seriously. "Arthur is a warlord, true. Excalibur was bloodied many times. He demands much from his men, but he is not heartless. He spares the lives of those overtaken if they will swear allegiance to him. There is nothing barbarous about him." *He gave up Gwen.*

"But he will expect me to fight?" Galahad looked down.

Lancelot sighed. "What is it you would rather do, Galahad?"

"I . . . I enjoy playing my harp," he answered. "It calms me when I am afraid."

"You play well," Lancelot admitted. "Is it a bard you want to be?"

Galahad stared at him. "That is not what I see in my vision."

Lancelot gave him a sharp look. "What do you mean? Have you the Sight?"

"I don't know what you mean by the Sight, Father," Galahad answered. "Sometimes, when I play the harp, a picture comes inside my head. It is always the same . . . a silver cup, but the hands that hold it glow white. When I see it, I feel at peace."

"Well," Lancelot said and tapped the sword Galahad was still holding. "You can talk to Nimue about the vision, but bard or not, you will still need to be able to defend yourself. I will have you worthy for Arthur. Let's try again."

"You had a dream, Arthur," Bedwyr said. "Nothing more." They had finished breaking their fast but were still at the table, neither of them wanting to go out into the bracing cold winter day.

Arthur was skeptical. "I was flying. The eagle soared beside me. I looked down and the earth was green and fertile, the sky clear and blue. And then . . ." He closed his eyes. "Then a blackness—a cloud—appeared on the horizon, rolling toward me, getting bigger and bigger. I felt a cold blast of wind—it was icy, Bedwyr—and suddenly I was spinning, over and over, crashing toward the earth. The eagle tried to fly under me, to support me, but I was too heavy for her. Then there was silence. Total silence and darkness." He looked at Bedwyr. "Do you think I foresaw my death?"

"I don't know. I do know that you cannot fly, so why worry?" Bedwyr tried to make light of the subject.

Arthur gave him a tight smile. "Look around you, Bedwyr. Camelot is fading. Many of the Cymbry have left. Some are looking for the silver cup of the Last Supper that the Bishop Dubricius claims to have seen in a vision, but I fear the men no longer have faith in me. We have had no rain for our crops, and the cattle and sheep are thin from lack of good grass." He sighed deeply. "Medraut's strength grows. It is only a matter of time before he moves against me. I am separated from my wife and I am separated from the land. Both my marriage and the Great Rite have been destroyed."

Bedwyr changed the subject. "Isn't Nimue bringing Argante with her today?"

Argante. What would she do when she saw him like this? He was gaunt and unshaven, and his tunic was dirty. He straightened and rubbed his stubbled chin. "I guess I had best send for the barber."

"Yes," Bedwyr replied, rising. "And forget about that dream."

Arthur did not fool Argante. When she arrived with Nimue later that afternoon, she went to where he was sitting by the empty hearth. Her touch was cool and soothing.

"You are hurting, Father." Her crystalline grey eyes searched his face.

"I have failed the land, my daughter." He suddenly felt very old.

Argante shook her head. "You have blocked your energy with the land, Father. You must seek to undo that."

"Argante," Nimue said firmly, coming to stand beside her. "Remember that Arthur is the king. Is it your place to tell him what to do?"

Daughter and mother stared at each other. "The blockage concerns something that you are trying to postpone, Mother. What is it?"

Nimue broke the stare and looked down at the floor. She was silent for so long that Arthur finally spoke.

"Would one of you please tell me what you are talking about? If there is something I can undo, I will undo it!" *I've lost my wife. If I can hold the land . . .*

"Gwenhwyfar must come back," Nimue said in a low voice. "I performed the Great Rite with you, but she is your true link with the land. The queen always has been; it is she who heals the earth while men plunder it." She sighed. "You must send for her."

His eyes blazed with a deep hunger. "Do you know how many times I have wanted to? But she and Lancelot are as youth at their first Beltane. Galahad has just brought them closer together. Even Elaine's presence makes no difference." He stopped and his voice dropped to a whisper. "She will not want to return."

"That is not her choice." Nimue inhaled deeply. "I will go and bring her back."

He shook his head. "She must come willingly; I doubt she will leave Lancelot."

"Arthur, you loved her enough to send her with him," Nimue said impatiently. "She cannot forsake the land. Lancelot must love her enough to let her go."

Faintly, Arthur saw the shimmer of gold and silver light around her. For the first time in months, he was willing to hope. *If she came back, they could restore Camelot.*


Lancelot stomped the snow off his boots and hung his cloak on the peg by the hall door. "I'm half frozen," he said as Gwenhwyfar wrapped her arms around his neck.

"Hmmm," he said as she pressed the warmth of her body against him. He buried his cold face in her silky hair. "I gather Galahad is elsewhere?"

For an answer, she giggled. "You may kiss me without fear."

"When my lips thaw, I will," he answered, but she didn't wait.

"Warm now?" she asked several minutes later.

"More than that," he grinned. "To what do I owe this privilege?" He kept his arms around her, caressing her back.

"Elaine took Galahad to the village earlier. The first tinkers have broken through the pass and Elaine had to see what new wares they had. They will not be back for a while, I think." She smiled seductively at him.

"Lead the way to my room, Wench, before I embarrass you out here."

"Before Augusta catches us, you mean." Gwenhwyfar laughed and took his hand.

As they stepped into his room, she kicked off her slippers and started to remove her shirt. Lancelot stopped her.

"We have time today. Let me do that." His fingers played with the shirt laces as he led the way to the bed.

They spent some time teasing each other, removing one piece of clothing at a time, tantalizing the exposed skin. Gwenhwyfar groaned when, at last, his tongue found that exquisite spot between her legs that so easily sent pulsations throughout her. The sensation was agonizingly sweet and nearly unbearable. She was already at the point of frenzy, knowing the series of small spasms would soon culminate, bringing her blessed release, but he did not stop. She gulped for air, and her entire body clenched, erupting into one glorious explosion. Lancelot rolled her over on her stomach and covered her body with his, lifting her hips as she shifted her legs to accommodate him. His deep, hard ramming inflamed the still throbbing center he had just left, an excruciatingly delicious torture. She was pinned beneath him and he caught her hands and held them still as she tried to claw the sheets. She gave herself up then to the pure enjoyment of receiving him. Wave after wave of pleasure flowed through her.

"I have missed these games, Lancelot," Gwenhwyfar said as they cuddled later. "We must find a way to have more privacy, more time."

He kissed the tip of her nose. "Galahad is old enough now to send to Arthur," he said. "Once he is gone, we will not have to hide what we do."

Gwenhwyfar burrowed into his shoulder. "And Elaine will leave?"

"It doesn't matter," Lancelot answered. "She can watch for all I care."

"Lancelot!" Gwenhwyfar slapped his other shoulder lightly. "I will not . . ."

"Hush, I didn't mean it." He nibbled a trail to her breast. "I think we may have time for another game. What will it be?"

She reached across him to retrieve a small key from behind the bedpost; then she rose and padded across the room to open a locked cabinet. She studied the contents and removed a blindfold, the bundle of ostrich feathers, and a softly padded leather strip.

Lancelot grinned and rolled on his stomach, putting his hands behind him. Gwenhwyfar tied them with a slipknot and flipped him onto his back, then covered his eyes with the blindfold. The feathers worked their way across his face and throat and lingered on his chest. He shuddered slightly. Gwenhwyfar brushed his arms lightly and then trailed the feathers across his belly and watched him grow. He began to squirm as she brushed them along his inner thighs. Gwenhwyfar giggled and lifted the bundle.

Lancelot moaned. "Don't stop, for God's sake."

She remained silent, giving him time to anticipate. The feathers dropped again, this time teasing the tip of him, and then she swirled the bundle around his genitals. He began to struggle against the bonds. She stopped suddenly and he gave a low groan.

Gwenhwyfar stood up and walked to the cabinet. Lancelot turned his head in her direction, but the blindfold stayed in place.

"Let's see what else we have." She returned with a silk scarf and let its cool smoothness glide across his body and then started sliding it back and forth gently around what was now the center of attention for both of them. His arm muscles were straining to loosen the knot and Gwenhwyfar smiled. "You know that's not going to work."

Lancelot grinned. "If I get loose, Gwen, you'd better be prepared."

"I know how to tie a knot, Sweet." Gwenhwyfar leaned over and teased him with her tongue, causing him to gasp. Slowly she began to suckle him until he was thrashing wildly. Then she sat up and he growled in frustration.

"Ummm," Gwenhwyfar murmured as she straddled him

and eased him inside of her. She reached under him and slipped the knot loose. "Take me for a ride, Lancelot."

"Ah, Gwen," he answered as he began bucking, "what would I do without you?"

# Chapter 27

# The Return

Nimue and Bedwyr arrived late the next afternoon with a small escort. Gwenhwyfar could not believe they had struggled through the late snow that lingered into spring this far north.

"What brings you here at this time of year?" she asked after she hugged Bedwyr. "Have you come for Galahad? We were going to send him when the snow thaws."

"Yes, we will take him with us." Nimue looked directly at Gwenhwyfar. "Arthur needs you. It is time to come home."

Gwenhwyfar froze. A searing pain tore through her. After so long, she thought Arthur would leave her in peace. "Lance . . ." She reached for him but his arm was already around her shoulders.

Lancelot looked over her to Bedwyr and Nimue. "Follow me." He led them to a smaller version of the council room like the one that was used at Camelot. "What is this all about?" he demanded when he had thrown the bolt and they were all seated.

Bedwyr talked long to them of the drought, the near famine it had caused, the departure of over half the Cymbry from the Round Table, Medraut's strengthening numbers, the Saxon unrest, and the lesser kings' lack of support.

"We have heard all of this before," Gwenhwyfar said angrily. "What does that have to do with me? Let us be." *I've finally let go of the guilt. Let me be content.*

Bedwyr leaned forward. "Have you forgotten, Sister? You would probably be dead if Arthur hadn't sent you away." He ignored Lancelot's smoldering face. "Arthur broke his code for you. Do you have any idea what that meant for him?"

Gwenhwyfar frowned. "I cannot make a difference. My presence would drive a bigger wedge into Camelot."

"The division has been made, Gwenhwyfar. Those who were not loyal have gone; the others will accept you back," Nimue said calmly. "Arthur's wish is for his queen to return home."

"His wish!" Gwenhwyfar shot back. *Arthur always has been arrogant!* "It was his wish that Elaine be sent here to try and torture us; now it is his wish to take me back . . . for what? Has he thought to become a god, that he acts so?"

"Stop it, Gwenhwyfar." Bedwyr's voice had the ring of struck steel. "You are still the queen and still his wife."

"I wish to be neither! You can tell Arthur that!" *I'm not some poppet that can be flung back and forth!*

Nimue interrupted. "Gwenhwyfar, the marriage to the land must remain intact. You were consecrated that day in the circle of stones. The land will accept healing only from its queen, and that must be done by reuniting with Arthur. You cannot deny, or give, that responsibility away. If you do, you will destroy Britain for all time."

Gwenhwyfar covered her face with her hands. "How can one person . . . a woman . . . have the entire fate of Britain placed on her, Nimue? It is too much." *Sweet Mary, the burden is overwhelming. I never asked for this!*

Nimue knelt beside her. "Myrddin tried to prevent your marriage. Arthur refused to listen. Now we no longer have a choice. We teeter on the brink of Darkness. We must fight it a while longer." She looked over to Lancelot. "If you still share Arthur's dream, you must make her go. If you love her, you will let her go."

"No."

Bedwyr leaned forward. "Yes. Arthur wants her back. You cannot refuse the king. Gwenhwyfar will come with us."

"I will not let her go."

The men stared at each other. In a moment they were both on their feet.

"We will take this outside," Lancelot said in a flat tone. "One of us will return."

"No!" Gwenhwyfar was on her feet, too. "I cannot bear to have one of you dead because of me." She grasped Lancelot's hand and brought it to her lips. "Arthur has won, Love. Queens must perform their duties. I will go to him."


They left the next morning. Galahad, on a palfrey from the stable, looked bewildered. Nimue sighed. Yesterday they had arrived unexpectedly. She supposed he'd seen Gwenhwyfar run, crying, from the council room. She knew he'd seen Lancelot's stormy face as they emerged from the talk because Galahad had turned around and sought shelter in his own room. He had not come out all evening.

Nimue glanced at Elaine, standing close to his father, trying to link her arm to his. Lancelot was standing rigid as stone, staring only at Gwenhwyfar. Finally Elaine stopped trying.

Gwenhwyfar was walking toward her mare now, her face blotchy from crying. Lancelot suddenly rushed to her, grasping her arm. She stopped but did not turn. Lancelot leaned close to her and whispered something. Gwenhwyfar shook her head slightly and looked at Lancelot quickly. Watching Galahad, Nimue sensed his puzzlement. One day he would understand.

Lancelot turned and walked to the hall, entering without looking back.

Gwenhwyfar remained stoically silent on the trip south, although she took a little comfort that Galahad appeared delighted with the changes in scenery. The rugged mountains and heather moors gave way to flat forestland and straight Roman roads; then the hills began again, this time freshly green from the spring rains. The countryside gave way to gently rolling fields of grain and pastureland. When the huge hillfort of Camelot finally came into view, Gwenhwyfar stopped her horse and Galahad rode alongside.

"Is that your home, my lady?" he asked. She glanced at him. He had played his harp for her each night, and slowly she had become less desolate.

"It was," she said gravely. "I suppose it will be again." *Leaving you, Lancelot, is the hardest thing I've ever done.* She took a deep breath and signaled the mare to walk.

As they rode into the bailey, Arthur came down the steps of the hall. His gaze, as clear as a northern rock spring and piercing as an eagle's, stopped on Gwenhwyfar. She studied him. There was a gaunt hardness to him now. She wondered what the past two years had really done.

The escort rode on to the stables, leaving them. Arthur stepped to Gwenhwyfar's horse. He lifted a hand to help her dismount, but she swung out of the saddle herself.

The king looked from her to Nimue and back to Gwenhwyfar. "You did not come willingly?"

"I accept my responsibility to return to you, Arthur. I know what my duties are."

He sighed slightly. "I had hoped you would be glad to see me."

*Oh, Arthur. You tore me away from happiness.* "I am rather tired from the ride, that is all," she replied stiffly. "I've brought Lancelot's son to you."

For the first time the king seemed to notice the boy. Galahad brushed the unruly lock of hair off his forehead and looked back at the king.

Arthur smiled a little at the familiar gesture. "So you are Galahad," he said. "Your father is a fine soldier. One of my best. Are you seeking to find a place among us here at Camelot?"

"I am, my lord." His voice quivered a little.

"You might dismount, if you're planning to stay." The king sounded amused.

Galahad reddened and scrambled down from the palfrey.

"What weapons do you favor, Galahad? You look a bit young to handle the lance well, but the sword maybe? Or the bow? I see neither on your saddle."

"He knows both, Arthur. Lancelot was not remiss in his training," Gwenhwyfar came to them and smiled at Galahad now. "But his gift is his music. He has soothed my soul on the ride here."

Arthur lifted an eyebrow. "So the son is like the father?"

"Don't be rude, Arthur," she snapped, the smile gone, "or we will be in an argument before I set foot in the hall."

Arthur grinned then. "So not all of the fire has left you," he said. "Mayhap I can still spark a desire?"

"Would it matter?" She glared at him. *He still has that arrogance about him.* "We must reunite, they tell me, for the sake of the land."

The smile left his face. "So, we are back to that?" Arthur said softly and turned away. "Your room has been prepared and I will leave you now." He took the reins to her horse. "Do not bar the door tonight, Gwenhwyfar."

She turned without answering and walked away.

\* \* \*

The rain came down in wind-driven sheets, but Lancelot sat in front of the unlit hearth, not noticing the damp, chilly air on this late spring night. He poured the last cup of wine from the flask and drank half of it before he set it down.

He felt Elaine watching him from across the room. Gwenhwyfar had been gone nearly three months, and he knew he was sinking deeper into the churning depths of black despair. He no longer cared.

Elaine walked over to him. "Is there anything I can get for you?"

He stared moodily into the ashes and remained silent. She was about to turn away when he looked up at her. "Why the change of heart, Elaine? I think I prefer the shrew; at least you left me alone then. Now you sit and watch me like a she-bear over her lone cub." He turned back to his study of the ashes.

She picked up the empty flask. "Let me fill this for you."

When she returned, she sat down in the chair next to him and refilled his cup. "Lancelot," she said, "mayhap we have been given a second chance to make this marriage work."

"What marriage? I do not love you, Elaine. I cannot make it more plain than that." He shrugged. "I do not even hate you anymore. You are free to stay or go. Just leave me alone." He drank some of the wine.

He didn't see her smile. "What I did was wrong," she admitted. "But you have a fine son in Galahad, haven't you?" When he didn't answer, she continued, "Gwenhwyfar was already Arthur's wife when you came to my bed."

"You tread on boggy ground, Elaine."

"I do not mean to insult her, Lancelot," she soothed him. "She is not here." She paused, then leaned closer. "I am."

Deliberately he finished his wine. "Are you trying to seduce me? I have already told you . . ."

She lightly touched the leather laces of his trews. "Have you no need for a woman, Lancelot?"

"By Mithras, how many times do I need to say it? I have no need of you." He removed her hand.

She replaced it on his thigh, letting her fingers trail upward. "Are you sure?" She smiled sweetly.

Despite himself, he grew hard at her touch. He stared at her and then at the wine cup as if it had suddenly become animate. "You have done it again, haven't you?"

"Morgana gave me the recipe long ago." She pouted a little. "The potion will only make you enjoy me more."

Lancelot pushed her hand away and rose. Elaine held on to his arm.

"Please give me a chance, Lancelot. I have learned the ways to please a man. Let me show you."

He looked down at her. "You've no honor, Elaine. Have you no pride as well?"

"I cannot be made warm with pride, Lancelot, nor can you." She stood then and pressed against him, putting her arms around his neck and trying to kiss him, but Lancelot turned his head. She sank to her knees and opened his trews.

Lancelot started to push her away, but Elaine had already taken him in her mouth. He moaned a little and then gripped her shoulders hard. *If this is what she wanted* . . . He thrust into her and felt her try to pull back, but he did not loosen his grip. *You asked for this* . . . She began to choke as he filled her.

Lancelot dragged her up. "Have you had enough or do you want more?" he rasped, feeling the drug lust.

She whimpered. "I want you. Please. Take me. I'll do whatever you want. I am begging . . ."

"Don't." He reached for her gown and ripped it open. She clutched the two pieces together, but he pulled her hands apart. "If you are going to be a whore, Elaine, then act the part." He took her to the ground. "Let's finish what you started."

He didn't kiss her or touch her in any manner save to ram

himself into her like a crazed bull, not caring when she cried out. He drove himself forcefully, plunging deeper and deeper, the potion in full effect. The rage of the last three months was causing him to satisfy himself cruelly, but he scarcely noticed. There was only anger and despair and the carnal thirst for consummation. With an agonized roar, he thrust harder and faster, pummeling her. She tried to slap him, but he simply pinioned her arms. When he finished, sweating and exhausted, she was bruised and raw. She lay on the floor, clutching her stomach and crying softly. Only then did he come to his senses.

"I am sorry," he said at last, laying a hand on her shoulder.

She crawled away from him and struggled to her feet, holding her torn gown in front of her. "I was a fool to ever want you, you brute!" she screamed. "Come near me again and I will kill you!"

"I would not have come near you in the first place, were I not drugged," he pointed out, calm now that the frenzy had left him. "But I did not mean to hurt you."

"I am going to Carbonek in the morning," she snarled. "Will I be safe until then?"

"From me? Unless you plan to put something else in my drink, you have no need to worry."

She glared at him. "I want nothing more to do with you. If I never see you again, that will be fine with me." She stalked off to her room and threw the bolt.

Nine months later, he received a terse note. Elaine had died in childbirth, bearing him a daughter.


Gwenhwyfar read the letter from Lancelot and handed it to Arthur. "Elaine finally got what she wanted," she said softly. She was sorry that Elaine had died, but also felt a ping of jealousy, both for the fact that Lancelot had finally succumbed to Elaine—*not that I can fault him when Arthur takes me to bed*—and that she had given him a daughter.

Arthur looked at her quickly. "He has named her Elen," he said. "Wasn't that the name of the girl from Astolat?"

She nodded and smiled satirically, remembering his story of how perfect Elen thought everything was at Camelot. *Would that she could see us all now.*

"Lance plans to raise the child. He will probably have her on a pony before she can walk."

Arthur laughed and then grew serious. "Have you told Galahad?"

Gwenhwyfar shook her head. "I have sent for him; I think he was finishing grooming his horse." Even as she spoke, the boy came through the door of the hall to the table where they were seated.

"You wanted to see me?" he asked, and Gwenhwyfar noticed how much deeper his voice had become in the year they had been at Camelot. He not only looked like Lancelot, but he was also acquiring Lancelot's timbre.

"You have a sister, named Elen. Sit down, Galahad." Gwenhwyfar told him about his mother. He swallowed hard and blinked back tears.

Arthur laid a hand on his shoulder and squeezed it. "No need to hold back."

The boy shook his head. "I think I would like to be alone, if I may leave."

"For certes." Gwenhwyfar hugged him.

A few minutes later they could hear the sad, slow plucking of his harp.

Arthur listened for several minutes. "If Galahad had the interest in weapons that he does in music, he would surpass even his father."

Gwenhwyfar shook her head. "Lancelot would like nothing more, but he would accept Galahad's becoming a bard."

"A hard thing for a priest to do," Arthur said.

"A priest?" Gwenhwyfar echoed. "What are you talking about?"

"Galahad told me he wanted to enter the priesthood. Something to do with that vision of the Grail that both he and Bishop Dubricius have seen."

"The Grail is ever elusive. Your men seek it because it is supposed to be worth much. Galahad thinks there is something spiritual about it." Gwenhwyfar paused. "Nimue would call it magic. Is there anyone who can tell us what it really is?"

Almost a year to that day, the gate guard called out that a stranger was approaching. Arthur and Gwenhwyfar had just returned from the Pentecost Mass.

"A rider?" Arthur called.

"No," the guard called back. "A man on foot, dressed oddly."

Arthur and Gwenhwyfar exchanged glances as the young man approached. He was not much older than Galahad and lean, not overly tall. He was wearing armor of sorts: a rusted, bronze hauberk that appeared too large for him, leather bracers on his arms, though he carried no bow, and greaves on his shins. His trews were of the plaid that the Scotti were so fond of wearing, but the man himself had the darker hair and skin of the native Britons. In the crook of his arm he carried an old Roman helmet.

He stopped and gave Arthur a Roman salute. He bowed low to Gwenhwyfar. She could not help smiling for the young man was taking himself quite seriously.

"My lord king," he said formally. "I have come to offer my services to you. I wish to be a part of the Cymbry."

"Many of the Cymbry have left," Arthur replied. "From where do you come?"

The young man faltered. "My home is in Gwynedd, but I was raised by Dyonas, the forest woman of the South."

"I see," Arthur said, with a sideways glance at Gwen-hwyfar. "Have you any experience with weapons?"

"I can learn, Sire," he said earnestly. "I know the stories of your great men."

A sad expression crossed Arthur's face. "I am afraid you will be disappointed, for those days are past, but will you join us for supper, lad?" he asked. "It might do me good to remember how Camelot used to be."

It was a healing meal. Gwenhwyfar had not seen Arthur show so much enthusiasm in the two years she had been back. Even though the fields had become prosperous again and the cattle and sheep sleek and fat, many of Arthur's men had not returned, and she knew he missed the camaraderie that used to take place in the evenings. *How I miss Lancelot at my side at times like this.*

"I found the hauberk years ago, by a campsite," the boy explained. "The lady who raised me had this helmet. I don't have much, my lord, but my body is strong and my heart seeks a place at your table."

"Then," Arthur said as he rose, "follow me. I will show you the Round Table of the Cymbry."

The young man stopped in awe in the doorway. "This is the table in my dreams."

"Dreams?" Arthur asked.

"I dream sometimes of a goblet carried by a woman who shines with light. She sets the cup down on *this* table." He moved around, his hand brushing the polished wood. "The names of your men are carved into the chairs?"

"Yes," Arthur replied, "although most of them are gone."

The youth wandered. "Here is Lancelot's," he said in delight. "I saw him once. He was wonderful to watch on his horse."

Gwenhwyfar had a sudden image of Lancelot on Pryderi and herself on Safere, racing across a meadow. *Ah, that was so long ago.* She refocused and smiled warmly at the youth. There was something so inoffensive about this strange man-child . . . as though he had no idea of the evil and hurt of the world.

He continued around the table, reading names. He halted suddenly.

"What is it?" Arthur asked.

"This name . . . Lamorak," the boy said.

"Yes? Lamorak lives in the far north now, as does Lancelot."

"He is my brother."

"What?" Arthur looked at Gwenhwyfar, then back to the oddly dressed young man. "You are Pellinore's son? Sit down, for I think we have some talking to do. No, not there . . ." He was too late, for the boy was sitting in the chair named "Perilous."

Nothing happened. The boy appeared to be unharmed. *Mayhap Myrddin's prophecy has lost its power,* Gwenhwyfar thought.

"What is your name?" Arthur asked.

"Peredur," he replied.

Arthur smiled. "I wish Pellinore were still alive; he would appreciate that his son made it to my court, in spite of his mother's intentions." He turned to Peredur. "The Lady's magic must have touched you, lad, for you sit in a chair that has been empty for over twenty years, waiting for a man who will not shed blood."

Peredur jumped up at that. "That surely isn't I," he cried. "I will be a soldier, such as my brother."

Gwenhwyfar laid a hand on Arthur's arm. "Mayhap it's time you recall the Cymbry to Camelot." From the glow on Arthur's face, she somehow had the feeling that Peredur would be a blessing.


Gwenhwyfar was delighted that many of the Cymbry answered the call over the next two years, bringing younger recruits with them. They were trained according to the old

Roman methods that had been so successful in Arthur's first twelve battles. Slowly Camelot was being reborn.

She also took a special interest in the naïve young man who had survived the Siege Perilous. Peredur took learning his skills seriously, although he was clumsy. The young lieutenant training him taunted him mercilessly. Most days he went limping to the infirmary to be bandaged for some nick or cut. He could be seen, however, doggedly practicing by himself with his sword, even with his hands bandaged.

His ability with a horse wasn't much better. One day, he had just gotten a foot in the stirrup when the nervous horse began circling in the paddock. He hopped alongside the horse on the other foot, trying to gain enough momentum to haul himself up. Gwenhwyfar started toward him, but Galahad strode over and grasped the bridle first. Peredur gratefully put both feet on the ground.

"Thanks," he said sheepishly. "You've saved me from another ridiculing."

"I've had plenty of them myself," Galahad replied. "Here, let me show you how to make the horse stand still."

Gwenhwyfar placed her arms on top of the fence and watched. He did have a natural way with horses, like his father.

Galahad tightened the right rein and took hold of the horse's mane, his other hand on the pommel, and pulled himself forward, swinging a leg easily over. He dismounted and handed the reins to Peredur.

Peredur tried it several times. To his delight, the horse stood calmly.

Galahad eyed him. "Why is this so important to you, Peredur? If you don't like riding, don't do it."

"I can't be a member of the Cymbry if I can't handle a horse!" He sighed. "I am a fool. I can't handle a sword or throw a lance or sit a horse. The king will be disappointed in me when he finally sees me."

Gwenhwyfar was about to reassure him when she realized that both of them had forgotten her presence. Mayhap these two would become friends, she thought.

"I understand," Galahad said. "Once I got here, I did not dare disappoint the king either, but it was for fear of my father, not because I wanted to excel in weaponry."

"You were more afraid of your father than the king?" Peredur looked puzzled. "Who is your father?"

"His name is Lancelot."

"Lancelot?" he breathed reverently and Gwenhwyfar smiled.

Galahad grimaced. "I am expected to enjoy fighting and going to war. But I don't. Bedwyr and Gwalchmai tell me to wait; the battle frenzy will take me the way it does my father." He looked at Peredur. "I don't want to kill men. I would rather teach men to soothe the beasts within themselves with music or through prayer."

"Soothe the beast . . . I have felt that sense of peace, too, but it is always in a dream. Then I awaken and I remember I want to be with the king."

"What is your dream?" Galahad asked.

"A silver grail . . . it glows . . ."

"Like a goblet?" Galahad repeated, "And it glows?" When Peredur nodded, he continued, "I see the same thing when I play my harp; it comes to me! If more people could feel its joy, there would be no need for war!"

"Do you think it exists?"

Galahad considered. "It might. You are the third person I have heard who has seen a vision of it. I would seek it, but I don't know where to begin to look."

"When we become Cymbry, we can ask King Arthur to let us search for this cup," Peredur said. "It will be our quest."

"Yes," Galahad agreed excitedly. "The grail will be our gift to the fellowship of the Round Table."

*Mayhap,* Gwenhwyfar thought as she watched them walk

away with the horse, *Camelot will have something to believe in again.*

Arthur hosted a tournament that year, the first in five years. "We will know who stands with us," he told Gwenhwyfar, for the Saxon unrest was becoming more noticeable.

Marc, Agricola, Cador, and Owain came first; some of the other lesser kings arrived more slowly, but overall, Arthur said he was pleased with the attendance.

Lancelot came also, and brought Elen with him. Gwenhwyfar hadn't seen him in the four years since she'd returned. She ran out to meet him, throwing her arms around his neck, not caring what anyone thought. *I was so afraid I'd never see you again!* She inhaled the scent of him contentedly. *You feel so good, my love!*

Lancelot lifted her and spun her around. "Ah, Gwen, I don't want to let you go. It's been too long . . ."

They were interrupted by Augusta's cough. With a grin, Lancelot set Gwenhwyfar down. She saw the toddler then and caught her breath. The child had nothing of Elaine about her. She had Lancelot's dark hair and the same smoke-colored eyes. The child tilted her head, studying Gwenhwyfar seriously; suddenly, she held out both small hands.

Laughing, Gwenhwyfar picked her up. "Come," Gwenhwyfar said, "and meet your brother." She could see Galahad waiting by the hall and she wished she'd had time to prepare Lancelot.

Lancelot looked toward the hall and inhaled sharply. Galahad was fifteen now, and tall, with a lean build. He was wearing the short black stole of an acolyte for the priesthood. A gold cross hung around his neck. His bright blue eyes met his father's dark ones.

"What is the meaning of this, Gwen?" Lancelot whispered.

"He wants to be a priest," she answered, "but he can't take Holy Orders until he's twenty-five. Mayhap he will change his mind."

Galahad reached them. He extended his hand to his father. "I can see from your face that you are not happy with my decision."

Lancelot shook his head. "We will discuss this later. Meet your sister."

Elen took that moment to try and launch herself onto Galahad. He scooped her away from Gwenhwyfar and tossed her up. She squealed with delight and clutched at his cross as he turned and carried her into the hall, Augusta hobbling in his wake.

Gwenhwyfar was aware that Lancelot had stepped closer. Every fiber of her body ached for him. Then his hand was on her shoulder and heat blazed through every vein.

His voice was filled with longing. "Have you been well, my love? Are you happy?"

"Happy?" Her voice trembled. "I am reconciled. I am the queen; my life is not my own. Arthur treats me well enough; we still argue." She took a ragged breath. "But at this very moment, I'd like you to take me into the nearest building and tumble me like any common wench."

He made a sound, low in his throat, but before he could say anything Bedwyr, Gryflet, and Patrise interrupted them, among others. Gwenhwyfar lost him as the men crowded around Lancelot.

She walked back to the hall to find Galahad and Elen. She could take some comfort in his son and daughter. Seeing Lancelot again flooded her with memories she had tried to squelch; she was shaking. How was she going to survive the next three days?

Galahad looked up as she came in. "He will never understand, will he?"

She sat down beside him and took Elen on her lap. "I

don't know. He is pagan. He has always thought that I carry guilt needlessly because I am a Christian."

"What would you have to be guilty of, my lady?"

Gwenhwyfar's face became haunted. "I committed mortal sin, Galahad." *Given the chance, I will again before Lancelot leaves.* She was ashamed of the thought, but it persisted. "Mayhap your father will understand."

"He wants me to be a soldier."

Gwenhwyfar laid a hand on Galahad's arm. "Lancelot is a warrior, but there is a bit of poet in his soul." She smiled gently. "Did you know, when he was small, he thought to be a bard himself?" She handed the child back and rose to leave.

Galahad stared at her. "My father?"

"Yes. When you talk to him, remember that."


A month after the tournament, Arthur received an urgent message from Hoel. Clovis, the Frank, was marching west. Hoel's lands in Armorica were threatened. Could Arthur send troops? Gwenhwyfar read the request with a sinking feeling.

"I cannot refuse," Arthur told her and Bedwyr and Gwalchmai, "not after all the help he gave us, but the timing couldn't be worse. Medraut hangs like a vulture on the borderlands, and Eormenric brings in fresh troops from across the Narrow Sea. Only Cerdic and Cynric stand between us and Cissa."

"Let Bedwyr lead them, Arthur," Gwenhwyfar interjected suddenly, the uneasiness growing.

Arthur shook his head. "Hoel led his own men; I must lead mine. Gwalchmai and his company will stay at Camelot."

"That leaves you only four hundred of your own men, and the rear flank will have to take the left," Gwalchmai said. "Send for Lancelot, then. His men will be ready and you will have a full cohort. Ban's lands are close to Hoel's. He will want to go."

"I would rather leave Lancelot where he is, in case you need reinforcements here while I am gone," Arthur replied. "I will take men from Marc and Cador; they stand to lose much if our seaports in Armorica are taken."

Arthur mustered an additional two thousand troops within a week. He reinforced Camelot with Agricola's men.

"I wish you'd reconsider." Gwenhwyfar made one last attempt to get Arthur to stay and send another captain.

"What is it, Gwenhwyfar? I've ridden off on campaign many times. War is war. Why are you so worried this time?"

"I don't know," she replied. "But it feels like I'm saying good-bye."

Arthur laughed. "We're going to reinforce Hoel's troops, not lead the charge. But if the Saxons march, I want you to go to Joyous Garde. Do not wait for me to return."

She laid her hand on his arm. "Thank you for loving me that much, Arthur."

He gave her a tight smile. "I'm aware that you and Lancelot managed to be together during the tournament." He held up a hand as she started to reply. "I've accepted that you'll never be able to put him from your heart. Yet you stayed with me when he left." He took a deep breath. "I would rather lose you to Lancelot than to have the Saxons find you, Gwenhwyfar. I could not bear that thought, especially if Medraut is among them."

*What a fortunate woman I am to have the love of two great men. And I'm sorry, too, that I cannot love only you.* "I will go if the need arises." She kissed him deeply.

He gave her a last hug and mounted his horse, signaling his captains. He set his stallion to a canter. Within minutes, he was lost to her sight.

# Chapter 28

# Cam's Landing

During that summer, while Arthur was with Hoel, Morgana helped Medraut recruit forces from the Scotti who had settled in Lleyn but were confined by the boundaries of Gwynedd and Powys. Their captains were Padraig and Salaigh, both sons of men whom Arthur had defeated years ago. They still thirsted for blood and more land.

"We will be ready when Arthur returns," Medraut told them as they met at Padraig's holding. "Eormenric's cousin, Chelric, brings twenty keelboats. That is eight hundred more troops. Eormenric's two thousand will march from the east. Your thousand will march from the west. We will create a vise that will grip Arthur tightly."

"Doesn't Cerdic prevent the advance from the east?" Padraig asked. "He has been Arthur's ally."

Morgana smiled. "He has acted as an ally. Even now, Cissa persuades him to expand north, to take Londinium in Arthur's absence. Our passage will be clear, for he will be busy settling his men. Arthur will return the way he left, from Isca Dumnoniorum. Portus Adurni cannot hold his number of ships. We will lie in wait for him on the road home."

"Aye," Padraig said to Salaigh. "Better to force him to fight in the open, rather than behind the solid walls of Camelot."

Medraut added, "I want your men to take part in the ambush, along with mine and Maelgwyn's. Cissa will lay siege to Camelot, but only to prevent Agricola's army from coming to Arthur's aid. We will take Camelot when Arthur has been defeated. Once through Cerdic's territory, Eormenric will move northward, to Aquae Sulis. That will create a block for any reinforcements from the north, especially from Lancelot."

"Lancelot?" Padraig asked. "He remains loyal to Arthur after taking the queen?"

Morgana snorted. "A strange bond holds the three of them together."

"Then your king is a fool," Salaigh laughed, "if he trusts the man."

"Make no mistake, Salaigh." Morgana narrowed her eyes. "Arthur is no fool. If you think that, you will be dead as soon as the battle commences."

Medraut interrupted, "Have a healthy respect for both of them. Lancelot, in battle frenzy, will overshadow even Arthur. I've seen it. They must not be allowed to unite." He continued, "Chelric's men will sail behind Arthur's landed troops, blockading the harbor." Medraut turned to Morgana. "Have I been remiss in any of these plans?"

Morgana smiled, proud of her son. "Only that I want to be on the battlefield to watch Arthur die."

"Lancelot was right." Gwenhwyfar looked across the Round Table at Gwalchmai. "Cerdic was merely biding his time."

One of Gwalchmai's scouts had just returned with the

news that Cerdic's army was advancing northward, armed for battle.

"He heads for Londinium," Gwalchmai answered. "It borders the Saxon lands to the northeast. If we send Agricola's troops, we leave ourselves vulnerable to Eormenric and Cissa. If we allow Cerdic's advance, he will be settled by the time Arthur returns."

Agricola looked grim. "The timing was good on his part."

Gwenhwyfar turned to the scout. "Does Cynric march with him?"

He shook his head. "I did not see his banner."

She breathed a sigh of relief. "Then there is still a defense in place." She saw Agricola look at her skeptically and knew he was unused to a woman discussing battle strategy. *Celtic queens have always led!* She lifted her head.

"Cynric will defend his land but won't force himself into war," Agricola said.

"He rallied to Arthur once!" she retorted.

Agricola raised an eyebrow and looked at Gwalchmai. "You know him. What do you think?"

Gwenhwyfar felt herself becoming a storm about to break. Cynric had saved Lancelot's life!

Gwalchmai glanced at her and quickly replied, "Gwenhwyfar is right. I think Cynric will hold steady." He added to pacify Agricola, "We need to prepare for the Saxon advance."

Agricola nodded. "We can defend Camelot. The harvest is done; our stores are good. We will bring the cattle and sheep in early. We can sustain ourselves until spring."

"Surely Arthur will return before the snow falls," Gwenhwyfar exclaimed. "Did the last messenger not say Clovis had retreated?"

"He halted, Gwenhwyfar," Gwalchmai answered. "Claudus harried him from another direction. If Arthur returns this autumn, he will, for certes, leave troops behind."

"Where is Medraut?" Gwenhwyfar asked suddenly. "Has anyone heard?"

Agricola replied, "Medraut has been seen in Siluria, conversing with the Scotti."

Gwenhwyfar's brow furrowed. "Why?" Her eyes widened in comprehension. "He stirs trouble in the west as well? We will have to fight on both sides, then. We will need more men. Send for Lancelot."

"No." Agricola's voice was firm.

Gwenhwyfar stared at him. *Is he worried that I'll betray Arthur on his watch?*

"Mayhap we should send you to Joyous Garde, Gwenhwyfar," Gwalchmai said reluctantly. "Arthur did say if there was danger from the Saxons . . ."

"I am not going to Joyous Garde," Gwenhwyfar said emphatically.

Both men looked surprised. "It was Arthur's order," Agricola said stiffly.

"Arthur is not here. Lancelot is needed." She glared at both men. "If I go there, do you suppose he will leave me unguarded and bring his men down?"

Agricola sighed. "I guess we could send for Nimue. She has the Sight; mayhap she can be of help."

"That," Gwenhwyfar said, "is the only good idea you have had thus far. Nimue will simply reaffirm what I have already said. She will tell you to send for Lancelot."


Nimue arrived two days later. She listened gravely to their suspicions.

"We've had a messenger," Gwenhwyfar explained. "Arthur is on his way home; if the Saxons are going to move, they'll do it soon."

"Can you induce the Sight, Lady?" Gwalchmai asked.

She looked up. "I've brought water from the sacred pool and a vessel from the Isle. I will go to the old chapel and fast." She rose, the light beginning to shimmer around her as she projected her aura. "Mayhap the Goddess will bless me."

* * *

Gwenhwyfar was awakened near dawn. She automatically reached for the dagger she kept under her pillow, but Nimue's voice stilled her.

"Come quickly," she said. "We have no time to lose."

Silently Gwenhwyfar threw on a robe and followed her down the stairs. She heard the horn, calling the men to battle formation.

Agricola and Gwalchmai were in the hall, both of them half-dressed.

"The Saxons march." Nimue's voice was strong. "Some will lay siege to Camelot; others lie in wait for Arthur. You must act now or you will be surrounded."

"Where does Medraut wait?" Gwalchmai was tugging his boots on as he asked.

"Medraut waits on a ridge off an old Roman Road . . . there is a river with a ford . . ."

"The old Fosse Way," Gwalchmai said. "A river winds round near Lindinis. Arthur will be returning through Dumnonia."

"Both sides can plan an ambush." Agricola smiled tightly. "I will take my men out and circle behind them when they approach. Your men can defend from the battlements, Gwalchmai. Once we have finished, we ride for Arthur."

"I am riding now," Gwalchmai answered, strapping on his sword. "A man alone will not be noticed. I can, at least, warn Arthur." He turned to Gwenhwyfar. "Patrise is on his way for Lancelot."

"Lancelot may not get through," Agricola said.

"He will come," Gwenhwyfar said simply.

"Until he does, I want Nimue to take you, Galahad, and Peredur to the Isle," Gwalchmai said firmly. "No arguments."

Nimue shook her head. "Gwenhwyfar knows the way. I am riding with you."

"You are not. You will slow me down."

"I can protect Arthur." Nimue looked at Gwenhwyfar. "I must go to him."

The feeling of dread overcame Gwenhwyfar again. "Go. Protect him, Nimue."


The horses had galloped several miles before the three of them slowed to a walk, Gwenhwyfar riding in the middle.

"I don't know why Agricola wouldn't let us stay and fight." Peredur sounded petulant. "How will I become a part of the Cymbry if I stay hidden away during war?"

Gwenhwyfar glanced at him. "Arthur's orders were that neither of you be forced to shed blood. He still believes in Myrddin's prophecy."

Galahad frowned. "Why does the king put faith in pagan beliefs?"

"Arthur is tolerant of all faiths. It is one way to unite the people of Britain," Gwenhwyfar answered. "He even sees no harm in the Saxons and the Scotti having freedom to worship their own ways, as well."

"But that is not what Holy Church teaches, Lady," Galahad protested. "To be saved, we must believe only in the Christos, who made the ultimate sacrifice for us."

"Mayhap," Gwenhwyfar answered, "but the Lady of the Lake gave Arthur his sword, Excalibur. I held it once; I felt its power." She added wistfully, "I just wish that he had not lost the scabbard years ago. I would like him to have that protection against blood loss in battle."

"How can a scabbard protect anyone?" Galahad looked puzzled.

"Nimue said much ritual had gone into the making of it. The ancient symbols held spells and enchantments of healing and protection. Macsen Wledig wore it before Arthur. The scabbard was very old, even then, the leather soft and smooth and an odd burgundy color."

Peredur pulled his horse to a stop, eyes wide and his mouth open, his face pale.

"What is it?" Gwenhwyfar asked. "We must keep moving. Are you ill?"

He shook his head. "The scabbard," he whispered. "I think I know where it is."

"What?"

"The day I saw the king—and Lancelot—and the others meet with another man and a lady. There was a fight and after it was done, I found a scabbard."

Gwenhwyfar remembered the conversation they'd had after Lancelot's return from being held captive. "What did you do with it? Where is it?"

"I took it to Dyonas. She put it away. I forgot about it." He wheeled his horse around. "I'll get it and bring it back."

"You can't, Peredur. The Saxons will be crawling throughout the forest," Galahad said. "You'll be killed."

"He's right," Gwenhwyfar said. "We are nearly to the Lake. We must ride on."

"No." Peredur looked at her earnestly. "I will be a member of the Cymbry. If the king does not wish for me to shed blood, the least I can do is keep him from shedding his. I will return." He thundered off, not hearing Gwenhwyfar's protests.

"I'll ride after him and talk some sense to in him, Lady," Galahad said.

"No." Gwenhwyfar grabbed his reins. "Lancelot would not forgive me if I let you ride to your death as well."

Galahad drew himself up in his saddle, his mouth set. "I am sixteen and no longer under my father's thumb," he said, sounding just like Lancelot. "He trained me. I can protect myself."

"I'm sure you can," Gwenhwyfar said soothingly. "But are you forgetting the king's order?" He hesitated and she added, "I know of no man who would be fool enough to defy both Arthur and Lancelot."

Reluctantly he turned around. "A monastery sits near Ynys Wydryn, doesn't it?"

"Yes. Ynys Gutrin. Why?"

"I would prefer to stay there, Lady, rather than on the Isle."

Gwenhwyfar slowed her horse. "Do you think the Saxons will spare the monks?"

"Certes!" Galahad said in surprise. "They live on holy ground. The barbarians must respect that."

She grimaced. "Saxons are not as merciful as Arthur. They would relish the killing, more so because it is a Christian place. Death would not be quick."

"Why would they spare the Isle then?"

"They would have to get to it first." Gwenhwyfar pointed. "Look. Do you see wisps of fog beginning to form along the road?"

His eyes opened in amazement. "Why would there be fog on a clear day?"

Gwenhwyfar smiled. "Some say it is dragon's breath, instead of fog, meant to protect those who still believe in the dragon."

The grey mist gathered around them, shrouding the sunlight. In the dampness, Galahad pulled his cloak more closely about him.

A man loomed in front of them suddenly, as though rising from the fog itself. Galahad drew his sword.

"What is this evil place?" he asked.

"Not evil," Gwenhwyfar answered. "Across the Lake lies Avallach. Put up your sword. Barinthus has come to take us over the water."

"I don't like it here."

Gwenhwyfar leaned over. "You must learn tolerance, Galahad. If your father can accept your becoming a priest, then you must be open to the way he was raised."

"You must hurry, my queen." Barinthus was holding the bridle of her horse.

They walked their horses onto a flat barge. Barinthus silently poled away from shore, entering a fog so dense, there was no sound.

Gwenhwyfar felt Galahad reach for her hand. Gently, she squeezed it. She hoped she was right. The Saxons would not find Avallach.


Arthur's army marched north on the Fosse Way. They had just parted from Marc's and Cador's men.

"It will be good to see Camelot again," Arthur said to Bedwyr.

The crossing had been rough, the seas tossing, causing the ships to pitch and roll. Many of the men's faces were tinged with green as they walked, but none dared to break ranks to relieve their churning stomachs.

Noting Bedwyr's silence, Arthur continued, "We will not have to return. Between Claudus and Hoel, they can hold Clovis in check." He watched his men struggling to stay in file. Even his archers, the sturdy men from Powys, had their bows hanging low. "When we reach the river near Lindinis, we will rest before we cross."

They rode along in silence, the steady clopping of the horses' hooves on the graveled road helping to keep the rhythm of marching men. Idly, Arthur watched an eagle soaring overhead. It suddenly swooped low, flying over them, and then it was gone.

Arthur pulled his cloak about him, for the air suddenly turned chill, even though the sun was shining. The leaves were nearly off the trees and the harvests in. The snow would fly before too long, but he would be home, able to sit in front of a warm hearth.

"I do not see much activity," he said as he looked about the empty fields.

Bedwyr shrugged, "The work is done; the crops are in."

"Still," Arthur said, straightening in the saddle. "There

*Cynthia Breeding*

should be people about." He sounded a note on his horn and the lead rider turned back. "What is the news from the outriders?"

"I do not know, my lord. No one has returned yet."

They rode for several more miles, Arthur scanning the gently rolling hills brown with dead grass.

"What is it?" Bedwyr asked.

"I don't know," Arthur replied, "but something is not right."

Bedwyr surveyed the countryside. "I see nothing but thickets and bracken. A few copses that could hide only a man or two. Nothing more."

"Exactly. Where are the people? The cattle?"

"Relax, Arthur. You have been at war too long."

"I suppose you are right." He smiled. "Mayhap I need a rest, too. How much farther to the river?"

Lancelot halted his men. "Damnation!"

His scout had just returned. The Saxons were massing just north and east of Glevum, blocking passage of the Roman road.

"How many?"

The scout hesitated. "Hundreds, maybe a thousand."

"They're not in battle formation? We haven't been seen?"

"I don't think so."

"Can we go around them? Off the road?"

The man shook his head. "There are too many; they are spread wide."

Lancelot swore again. "Then we will have to charge. I hate risking my men before we even reach Arthur." He turned and went back to his lieutenants.

"Wedge formation. Do not join in battle. Slash only for clearance. They are on foot, so we keep riding."

Silently the men formed behind him. In another minute they would be committed, out in full view of the Saxons.

Lancelot raised his hand. The only sound was of metal scraping against leather as swords were drawn.

He dropped his hand and his horse leaped, full out, reaching its battle stride.

He saw the look of surprise on the closest faces as the Saxons quickly reached for their axes and formed their line. He tore through, slicing and cutting as two huge men fell to the ground. In a short time, his sword and greaves were red with blood; he wasn't sure if any of it was his. He felt nothing but the movement of his horse under him, using its teeth and hooves to help him.

He was through the line, but the Saxons were running to surround him. More and more, his men were joining battle now; they had no choice. He saw a horse go down to his right, but he had no time to look for the rider. They were outnumbered four, maybe five, to one, and more men were coming. The blond heads looked like a strangely colored sea, rolling in waves toward him. *We must pull free.*

Space and motion seemed to blend. He was no longer aware of the movement of his arm, the sword hewing down men like a sickle through stalks of grain. He heard a blood-curdling cry and, from some dim place in his memory, realized it was his own voice.

An ax swung at his leg and he spun the warhorse around, its huge hindquarters sending the man sprawling. Another reached for the bridle and Lancelot gashed the man's throat, a scarlet ribbon appearing where the sword had touched. He saw Eormenric running toward him, screaming like a berserker.

Then he was free. The space was clear in front of him. His men were pulling away, lying low over their saddles to avoid being hit from behind.

Once out of sight, they slowed to a trot to give the horses a rest, but Lancelot did not stop until much later.

"What's the toll?" he asked the medic who was attending him after they made camp for the night.

"Sixty-two injured, twenty-three missing, nine horses gone."

"Fewer than three hundred able-bodied men, then," Lancelot said, "and still another two days to Lindinis."

*I must reach Arthur. One more time, to fight beside him.*


Arthur's infantry halted near the western bank of the river, where they gratefully sank to the ground to rest. The cavalry halted, too, and the men dismounted.

The air was rent with the sound of the Scotti war cry. Suddenly men were scrambling over the eastern slope, starting across the ford in the river. The tired archers fell into position and the sky rained dark with arrows, halting the Scotti's progress. Arthur's foot soldiers rushed into the water. Within seconds, it ran red.

Arthur wheeled his horse, shouting for his men to fall into rank. Bedwyr and Gryflet tried to form their flanks, but the area was too narrow.

"We've got to get across where we have room to fight. Watch the ridge!" Arthur pointed to woody section across the river to the north. "Let the infantry cross here. We can swim the horses over farther downstream." Minutes later, his horse plunged into the water, followed by Bedwyr's company. Only a few of them had reached the far bank when Medraut's horsemen appeared on the ridge. With a wild shout, they charged.

Excalibur flashed once in the sunlight before it was dulled with blood. Bedwyr fought to Arthur's left; Gryflet struggled to close behind him. The battle took on the sounds of soft thuds as horseflesh met horseflesh, and the hard clamor of steel against steel. The ground was soon littered with bodies as Arthur sought the higher ground of the ridge. *Medraut's men, once mine,* he thought in a moment when time seemed to have no meaning. *They had been trained only too well.* Then he was engaged again, concentrating only on the next man to appear in front of him. Excalibur felt light in his hand, as if it had a spirit of its own.

He saw Medraut, fighting some distance away. A part of his mind detached itself, watching his son objectively. He could find no weakness in him. He sat his horse with ease, his shield was up, his arm still strong. He sliced a foot soldier open from chest to groin and laughed as the man's intestines spilled out. A chill went through Arthur. *What witch's spawn have I produced?*

Medraut looked across at him then, as though he heard the thoughts, and gave him a mock salute. He turned and started hacking again.

Arthur's men were being pressed back toward the water, the most vulnerable place to fight. Desperately they struggled to hold their ground.

More horsemen appeared on the ridge. Arthur groaned. *How much longer can my men hold out? If Medraut has more reinforcements coming . . .* and then he saw the silver and blue of Lancelot's banner.

Medraut's men whirled to meet this new challenge, giving Arthur the opportunity to advance. Outnumbered now, Medraut sounded the retreat. Lancelot's men charged, running down the hapless infantry who were not quick enough to run at first sight.

Arthur motioned a halt and Lancelot called his men back reluctantly. He rode over to Arthur.

"Let me finish the job, Arthur. For once and for all time."

"I don't know how many more are out there, Lance. I will not risk your men when so many of mine have already died."

Lancelot sighed. "Rest then. My men will stand the watch from the ridge."

"I will rest once our dead are buried," Arthur said tonelessly. "I will not leave them here like this. Tomorrow we march for Camelot."

"With the River Cam to cross," Lancelot said. "Let's hope there are no surprises."

* * *

The troops were nearing the ford at Cam's Landing the next day when two riders approached at a gallop.

Lancelot's sword flashed. Arthur already had Excalibur in hand. Neither of them was prepared for the sight of Nimue, her tunic torn and her long silver hair flying out behind her. Gwalchmai was leaning over his horse, wounded.

Lancelot leaped to the ground and caught him as he fell. He eased him down, propping Gwalchmai's head up, and assessed the massive sword wound to his thigh.

Arthur lifted Nimue down. "What in the name of heaven and hell are you doing here, Nimue?"

"We came to warn you," she answered as she sank down beside Gwalchmai. "We meant to meet you much earlier, only a band of Saxons caught up with us. We just managed to escape." She stuffed a part of her ripped tunic against the wound and placed Lancelot's hand on top of it. "Hold this," she said, "and close your eyes. Listen to me, for I will need to meld your fey energy with mine if we are to save his life." She took his other hand in hers and began chanting softly in the Old Tongue.

Arthur knelt beside them. Gwalchmai looked up at him. "The Saxons . . . behind us . . . a seadog named Chelric follows you . . . Medraut . . ."

"Shhh," Arthur said. "I know where Medraut is. Save your strength. Let Nimue do her work."

Bedwyr and Gryflet knelt also. Gwalchmai gave them a weak smile.

"Cissa besieges Camelot."

"Gwenhwyfar?" Arthur asked. "Did she go to Joyous Garde?"

"No." Nimue finished her prayer and bound the wound with more of her ripped tunic. "She is at the Isle with Peredur and Galahad. He must rest. No more questions."

"We will camp here, then, for the night," Arthur said. "If

Gwalchmai can travel in the morning, we will make for Camelot and take care of Cissa. If not, we make our stand here at Cam's Landing."

Gwalchmai's wound became infected and he was running a high fever the next morning. Nimue gathered some reeds and sedgegrass to make a poultice. "I do not have the herbs I need," she said in frustration to Arthur, "and he cannot be moved."

"Leave me then. Arthur must get to Camelot." Gwalchmai's voice was a whisper.

"I won't do that." Arthur looked around. "Can he be moved as far as that?" He pointed to a copse of trees some distance from the river. "You will need to hide, too, Nimue. I'll not let the Saxons see a woman out here."

Lancelot and Bedwyr placed the cavalry on revolving shifts. Foot soldiers dug trenches, and archers built barricades of branches. They camped across the river from the crested forest. If anyone were to attack, they would have to cross the river.

They waited throughout the day and night. Most of them slept little. To the north, the night sky was alive with sweeps of pink and green.

Arthur stood beside Lancelot. "Myrddin would say those lights are a portent."

Lancelot nodded. "Do you want me to fetch Nimue? She might know . . ."

Arthur shook his head. "It matters not if they signal victory or defeat. We will fight; the rest will be."

The next morning, just after dawn, Arthur felt the earth vibrate. "They come."

Chelric's eight hundred foot soldiers marched in front of Medraut and Maelgwyn's three hundred cavalry. They stopped out of arrow distance.

Arthur's men fell into formation.

Medraut rode forward on a large black horse, with Morgana beside him.

"He brings his mother to war?" Gryflet asked in surprise.

"Do not be fooled, Gryflet," Lancelot ground out between clenched teeth. "That woman bodes ill. Do not hesitate to kill her if you get the chance."

Arthur raised the flag for parley and nudged his horse forward. Lancelot followed.

"Does it take both of you to talk to me?" Medraut asked as they met halfway.

"I have no quarrel with these men you bring, Medraut," Arthur said calmly, ignoring the remark, "and I would not quarrel with you. Go back to the east and live in peace." *Too many men have already died.*

Medraut laughed. "That would be too easy, Father. But if you will do as my mother asks, I will not kill you."

"Morgana?" Arthur forced himself to smile pleasantly. *If there is a chance to end this peacefully . . .*

"Grant Medraut the lands to the west of here . . . Cador's, Marc's, Agricola's. Make him your coregent. Make me your consort." Her eyes bore into his.

Arthur sighed. He should have known better. "I cannot do any of that."

The smile left Medraut's face. He pulled a dagger.

Lancelot reached for his sword, but Arthur stopped him.

Medraut made a small cut on his finger and sucked the blood. "Before this is over, Father, I will have tasted yours." Abruptly Medraut turned his horse, and Morgana's followed the other's lead. They cantered back to their troops.

"That would have been the best chance to end this. Why did you stop me?"

"I still fight with honor, Lance," Arthur answered.

They said nothing more as they joined their men.

"Now what?" Bedwyr asked as Medraut's men made no move.

"They wait," Arthur said, glancing uneasily at the forest above the river.

"Let's engage them before more troops arrive," Gryflet urged.

"No. I will not start this war." Arthur held firm.

Two hours later the forest came alive as Eormenric's men broke through. They rushed the ford. Arthur's archers volleyed arrows at them.

Behind Arthur, from the east, Cissa's men marched. The armies surrounded Arthur's men on three sides. The Cam soon flowed red.

Then, from Camelot, came Agricola's army and Gwalchmai's company. Slowly, they fought their way through. At the sight of five hundred fresh horsemen, Chelric's and Eormenric's foot troops retreated. They melted away into the forest where the horses could not follow.

The battle turned quickly. Within the hour, the battlefield was still, save for the moaning of the wounded and dying.

Lancelot leaned heavily on his sword. His horse had been slashed from under him, and he had lost sight of Arthur while fighting on foot. He looked up at Bedwyr.

"Where is Arthur?"

Bedwyr shook his head. "I've been looking for him since Agricola gave chase. I found Valiant dead, some time ago."

Lancelot looked at the strewn bodies that littered the field. The massacre was the worst he had ever seen. Hundreds upon hundreds lay dead.

"Did Medraut escape?"

"Yes. Morgana, too," Bedwyr answered, and then he turned to see Nimue coming toward them. She was crying.

Lancelot turned to her. "Gwalchmai?"

"The fever took him." Nimue looked over the massive destruction. "I must talk to Arthur."

"We haven't found him, Nimue. He may be . . ."

"No." Her sea-colored eyes glazed. "I would know if he were."

They spread out then, overturning bodies one by one, checking the faces of those who lay beneath. Near sunset, a groan came from a thicket near the edge of the forest crest. Nimue raced up the small hill, followed by Lancelot and Bedwyr, and pulled apart the bramble.

On the ground, a gaping wound in his side staining the ground red around him, lay Arthur. Nimue dropped to her knees beside him.

He struggled to open his eyes. His breath came in ragged gasps, but he smiled faintly. She grasped his hand in hers.

"Take me home, Nimue, to Camelot," he whispered as he slipped into unconsciousness.

# Chapter 29

# The Way to Avalon

Within three days of his leaving, Peredur returned with the scabbard.

Gwenhwyfar said a silent prayer of thanks.

"The power is still strong," Argante said, tracing the ancient symbols lightly with her fingertips. "Arthur will need this soon."

Gwenhwyfar nodded. "I plan to take it to him."

"We will escort you," Galahad said and turned to Peredur. "Was there fighting in the countryside?"

"Cynric's lands are peaceful. The road to Clausentum was clear. On my way to the cottage, I saw the Saxons moving west. On my way back, Agricola was in pursuit."

They set out the next morning. "The lights danced last night," Gwenhwyfar said.

"You must not let the superstitions of a dead druid shake your faith, my lady," Galahad said when she told him of her concerns.

She smiled wanly. "Not just Myrddin. Cynric told me

once that his people believe the lights reflect off the armor of the Valkyries as they ride to collect the souls of the dead."

They rode silently for a while. As they skirted Maelgwyn's borders, they turned off the main road to follow a trail to the Cam.

"If we follow the river, we may find them sooner," Galahad said. "An army will want to camp by water."

Later that afternoon Peredur stopped his horse. He pointed to the stream flowing toward them. The water had taken on a pinkish hue.

"Be alert," Gwenhwyfar warned. "Let's see what's around the bend." All three of them drew their swords.

They came to a ford where an old crone was washing blood-soaked clothing in the river, but there were no wounded about.

"Why is the clothing so bloodied?" Gwenhwyfar called out.

The woman straightened and turned. She was not so old, after all. Her face was unlined and though her hair was white, her eyes were black as raven feathers.

Instinctively Galahad and Peredur drew their horses closer to Gwenhwyfar's.

The ageless woman laughed, a hollow ringing sound. Her voice sounded tired when she spoke. "No need for fear, young ones. I wash the clothes of those who are already dead. The battle is done."

"Have you seen King Arthur?" Gwenhwyfar asked.

The strange eyes turned on her, flickering dark blue as the sunlight flitted over her face. She pointed up the river. "The battle joined there. I have not seen the king this day."

Gwenhwyfar shivered suddenly for, although the sky was cloudless, shadows were falling across the water. "What is happening?" she asked.

The Morrigan turned toward the water. "Those are the souls of the dead. Rhiannon waits for them on the other side."

The water was nearly black now. *So many souls,* Gwenhwyfar thought.

"Aye." The Morrigan answered her unspoken thought. "The king is not among them yet. But you need to hurry if you're going to put that scabbard to use."

Gwenhwyfar stared at her in astonishment. "How did you know . . . ?"

"Go," the Goddess said gently, "before you are too late."


They rode on for some distance before they came upon the first bodies. Galahad dismounted and turned them over. "Saxons," he said. "No one has taken the time to plunder the bodies. The weapons and armbands are still on them."

"They were probably overtaken by Agricola's men. There would have been no time to stop." Peredur looked around.

No one was prepared for the sight when they finally came upon the final battlefield of Cam's Landing. The ground was covered with dead men and dead horses. The grass was stained a dull rust color, and the churned-up mud on the riverbanks looked like red clay.

There seemed to be no life anywhere; then, in the distance, Gwenhwyfar spotted a small group, huddled on the ground. She detected movement. "There! Let's try to reach them!"

Carefully they picked their way through the maze of corpses, looking, but not hoping to find any of their friends. As they drew closer, she recognized Lancelot, then Bedwyr and Nimue. She began to shout, waving her arm.

Lancelot ran to them and Gwenhwyfar nearly fell into his arms as he half dragged her from the horse and held her close.

"I've never seen such annihilation, Lance. Where is Arthur?"

For a minute longer, he held her tightly; then he moved back, his hands still on her arms. "Arthur is dying."

Gwenhwyfar sagged, but he held her up. "He can't be," she whispered. "Arthur always survives."

"He's lost a lot of blood, Gwen."

She remembered then. "The scabbard! Peredur had it all this time!" Hastily she unbuckled it from the saddle and handed it to him.

"By Mithras!" Lancelot gave a cursory glance at Peredur. "I will deal with you later. Come." He reached for her hand and they ran back to the still figure on the ground.

Arthur was lying quietly, his eyes closed, his face chalky. Blood was seeping through the tight bandage across his chest. Gwenhwyfar dropped to her knees beside him as Nimue took the scabbard, laid it on Arthur, and began a new chant.

Arthur struggled to open his eyes. "Gwenhwyfar," he said weakly, "is it really you or am I in the Otherworld and dreaming?"

"I am here," she said, taking his hand. "Stay with us. We have the scabbard. Nimue will work the magic."

He smiled and closed his eyes again.

"He will live, won't he?" she asked.

"The scabbard will prevent more blood loss," Nimue answered, "but there is only one place he may be healed. Avalon."

"Avalon? The place between the worlds where Myrddin went?"

Nimue nodded. "The solarium on Avalon is a house of glass used for healing. But first we must get him to the Isle. The only portal that I can use is there." She turned to Lancelot. "Arrange a litter."

"Can he be moved now?"

"If we cannot reach the Isle," Nimue answered, "he will be dead by morning."

\* \* \*

They walked steadily throughout the night. Gwenhwyfar tiredly noticed the first red darts of dawn lighting the horizon when they reached the edge of the Lake. The barge lay waiting, the hooded poleman in place.

"Bedwyr? Find Medraut." Arthur gestured feebly from the litter. "I appoint Custennin my successor. You must help him keep Camelot alive."

"I will try, Arthur."

"Not try. Do. Send Galahad . . . and Peredur . . . for the Grail. It will hold . . ."

"Hush, Arthur. Save your strength." Nimue brushed his hair back.

Arthur beckoned Lancelot and Gwenhwyfar to come to him. Bending low, they could hardly hear his whisper.

"She is yours now, Lance. Take care of her."

Lancelot covered Arthur's hand with his. "Always, Arthur. We will raise Elen."

"The child she always wanted." Arthur tried to smile, and Gwenhwyfar could no longer hold back the tears.

He turned his head to look at her. "You cry . . . do you love me then?"

"I've never stopped loving you," she sobbed uncontrollably. "My curse has always been to love both you and Lancelot." She saw Galahad's eyes widen as he looked at his father. *So now he knows. But I must try to save Arthur.*

"Can I go with you, Nimue? I can help—"

Nimue laid a small hand on Gwenhwyfar's arm. "You would not be able to return. The choice I told you once that you would have to make is already done. When you returned to Camelot from Joyous Garde, you saved Arthur. You've done your duty; now follow your heart."

Lancelot drew Gwenhwyfar close to him as he looked at Nimue.

"Arthur can be healed on Avalon, but will you be able to bring him back?"

"I don't know," Nimue answered. "No human has ever passed through the portal twice. As you know, those of us who have fey blood can merge with the Land of Faerie for a short time and return. But Arthur's birth was wrought with Myrddin's wiles; he should be able to pass him through."

"Myrddin?" Gwenhwyfar asked, confused now. "He's dead."

"Not dead. Entranced on Avalon by the queen of Faerie." Nimue turned and gestured to the hooded figure on the barge. "See for yourself."

Slowly, Gwenhwyfar looked toward the barge. Even before the man threw back the hood to reveal the tawny hair, she could feel his golden eyes trained on her. Then, as she watched, a shimmer of light floated beside him, taking form and substance and finally materializing in full human-size form. The woman floated alongside the water, her green gossamer gown and long brown hair fluttering about her, the effervescence of faerie light shimmering in the air.

"I am Morgan le Fey, queen of Faerie," she said in a seductively husky voice, "and it is through my lands that Arthur must pass." Then she tweaked Myrddin's ear.

Gwenhwyfar felt herself getting hysterical. *So that's why Myrddin had swatted the air so often.*

The faerie gestured for Arthur to be moved to the barge. "Oh, you are a handsome one," she crooned as she cradled his head in her lap. "You must not die."

Gwenhwyfar watched as Nimue stepped onto the barge and sat down beside Arthur. He smiled at her and lifted her hand to his lips, a peaceful expression on his face. *He loves her. He always has.*

What sad and cruel irony Fate had bestowed on all of them. Arthur's heart belonged to Nimue just as hers belonged to Lancelot. If Nimue had not been a priestess, would Arthur have married her? And if Gwenhwyfar had been free to love Lancelot . . . Medraut would have had nothing to discover and the fellowship of the Round Table would still be intact. Cam's Landing would not have happened and they would not be standing here now, watching a dying Arthur being slowly poled away from shore.

The ever-present fog unfurled its tentacles, encircling the barge with its damp breath. Only once, before they were lost to the mists, did Arthur attempt to sit up and look back. He gave a final salute before the barge disappeared.

"I think," Lancelot said as they watched the now-empty water, "that we have years of time to make up for. But first, we'll get married."

Gwenhwyfar smiled up at him and nodded. "Let's go home."

From across the still water came the low tinkling of faerie laughter.

# About the Author

An avid reader of anything medieval, Cynthia Breeding has taught the traditional Arthurian legends in high school for fifteen years and owns more than three hundred books on the subject.

She lives on the bay in Corpus Christi, Texas, with her Bichon Frise, Nicki, and enjoys sailing and horseback riding on the beach.

Readers can reach her through snail-mail at 3636 S. Alameda, B116, Corpus Christi, Texas 78411, or visit her website www.cynthiabreeding.com.